WELCOME STRANGERS

*By the same Author*

VISITORS TO THE CRESCENT
THE WINTER CITY
THE SPARROW
THE YOUNG SPANIARD
ASK NO QUESTION
A TIME OF WAR
CHECKMATE
THE HOPEFUL TRAVELLER
THE CLIMBING FRAME
FAMILY CIRCLE
DANIEL COME TO JUDGEMENT
THE BRIGHT DAY
THE MIND HAS MOUNTAINS
LOOK, STRANGER
HE WHO PLAYS THE KING
MARCH HOUSE
GOOD DAUGHTERS
INDIFFERENT HEROES

# WELCOME STRANGERS

Mary Hocking

Chatto & Windus
LONDON

TO PAM AND GEOFF

Published in 1986 by
Chatto and Windus Ltd
40 William IV Street
London WC2N 4DF



British Library Cataloguing in Publication Data
Hocking, Mary
Welcome strangers.
I. Title
823'.914[F] PR6058.026

ISBN 0-7011-2919-0



Photoset by Rowland Phototypesetting Ltd
Bury St Edmunds, Suffolk
Printed in Great Britain by
Redwood Burn Ltd
Trowbridge, Wiltshire

# 1

On a grey January afternoon in 1946 there were more police than usual in Parliament Square and the roads leading off it. Their attention, however, was not focused on the Houses of Parliament, or on Westminster Abbey, but on the Central Hall where the first meeting of the General Assembly of the United Nations was being held.

'Do you think that is Mr Molotov?' Alice Fairley asked, looking down from the window of a tall, straight-faced building just off Parliament Square. She pointed to a man hustling to a waiting car, head bent to avoid photographers.

'I don't even know if he attended.' Alice's companion made it clear that Mr Molotov's movements were a matter of little consequence when compared with this latest evidence of Miss Fairley's distractibility. 'It will go the way of the League of Nations, you'll see. Changing names doesn't bring about miracles.'

'You mean multilateral is the same as grammar school, under the skin?'

Mr Hadow pursed his lips. He had first come to work in the offices of the West London Education Authority in 1911, and did not approve of sauciness in newcomers. He looked furtively at Alice. This was the first time, in his long service as committee clerk, that he had had to share a room with a woman. He noted with disapproval that during a recent absence, supposedly to collect a stencil, she had taken the opportunity to prepare for the evening. Her long, sandy hair had been freshly combed and drawn back from her face in a thick swathe at the nape of the neck. There was something old-fashioned about the face which was not entirely attributable to the hair style. He was reminded of portraits of women he had seen on visits to elderly aunts, women with composed faces and still hands, yet not serene. Something unsatisfied had smouldered behind those eyes. A more imaginative man might have thought that the women would have liked to break out of their frames. Mr Hadow, a bachelor, thought that all women were acquisitive and predatory by nature, and that no man was safe from them until he rested in his grave.

Big Ben chimed the quarter hour. A cloud seemed to lift and expectancy brightened Miss Fairley's face. Mr Hadow was just about to ask her if she had any filing to do (which was unlikely, since he had devised a secret system known only to himself) when the telephone rang and he was summoned to attend on the Assistant Education Officer for Secondary Education. He departed, leaving behind him a sour smell of old, if not actually dirty, clothing.

Alice picked up her handbag, got out a hand mirror and touched up her lipstick. Then she realised that girls in an office in the adjacent wing of the building were looking at her. A trickle of despair ran down her spine. Would she ever be able to adapt herself to this curious world with its mysterious concerns? She had been demobilised from the Women's Royal Naval Service only a few months ago, but already the war years seemed like a period out of time. Life flowed around them, leaving them isolated, a strange territory unconnected with the mainland. She didn't like the mainland very much, and she did not understand what was happening on it.

The activity outside the Central Hall seemed to have died down. Men were running here and there amid the rubble of a bombed site, but presumably these were plain-clothes policemen, since they were allowed to scramble about unchallenged. A small group of men and women were huddled beneath a street lamp near the entrance to Great Smith Street. Earlier in the day they had provided the only drama, booing in a dispirited way on the arrival of the man whom Alice had taken to be Mr Molotov. Passers-by showed little interest in them, or in the comings and goings at the Central Hall.

It was twenty past five. Alice looked round the room, wondering how she was to occupy herself for the remaining ten minutes. Mr Hadow had given her no work to do, and she guessed this was a strategy aimed at getting her removed as soon as possible. 'She spends all her time looking out of the window,' he would say. The girls in the adjacent wing were probably saying it already. She reached to a side-table and took up a report which she had already read several times. She read it again. It had a fascination for her.

The war was over and the battlefront had shifted. The Labour Party, which had come into power with a huge majority, was fired by a crusading zeal to eradicate the inequalities of English society. Education was seen as a major factor in achieving this aim. This was the gestation period of the secondary school revolution, the time when, here, in the offices of the West London Education Authority, and in other offices up and down the land, a development plan was being prepared which would eventually put an end to the iniquities of secondary selection and bring about the age of equality of opportunity. As is the way of revolutions, all that had preceded it was deemed not merely bad, but positively evil. Alice, who had had a keen sense of purpose when the war broke out, was baffled by this peacetime conflict in which, in some extraordinary way she could not understand, she seemed to have got herself on the wrong side. She, a Fairley, so concerned to fight the good fight!

She was the daughter of an elementary school head teacher who was also a Methodist lay preacher. Mr Fairley's salary had been modest. This was a matter of pride rather than regret. He could have done much better for himself, but God had called him to work among the less privileged children. Luxury was not for the Fairleys. A car would have been considered an unwarrantable indulgence, and for most of Alice's childhood communications were conducted without the aid of the telephone. Boarding house accommodation sufficed the Fairleys on holiday, and if any comment was made about private hotels, the parents would say, 'You wouldn't enjoy staying there, now would you?' and the children would concede that it would be very 'stuffy' to stay in such places. Of course, there was no real hardship. The family was always well-clothed and never hungry, although Alice was frequently cold in the draughty semi-detached house in Shepherd's Bush. She and her sisters had been aware that they were fortunate. The Methodist chapel in which the family worshipped was in the poorer part of Acton where the deprivations of unemployment were grimly evident. The Fairleys mixed with and cared about the unemployed. Alice had always been proud that her parents were so much more public-spirited and compassionate than most of her friends' parents. How then had it come about that she now found herself regarded as the representative of an elite?

The answer, it seemed, lay in her education. Her parents had wanted their children to have the benefit of a good education and they had made sacrifices (which were never represented as such) to send their daughters to the Winifred Clough Day School for Girls. They had believed that this was a good and wise thing to do.

But yesterday's good was tomorrow's wrong doing. Alice, on returning from the war, found that in her absence she had become a member of a privileged class by virtue of the fact that she had attended an independent school. What her father would have made of this, she had no means of knowing. He had been killed by a bomb early on in the war. Her mother had married again and would not welcome a discussion on the class system – her new husband had attended a public school, was a graduate of Durham University and a senior partner in a rather superior publishing firm.

Alice read with dismay a description of the conditions prevailing in senior elementary schools which seemed to owe more to Dickens than her recollection of her father's devoted treatment of his boys. It was a relief when the telephone rang. A junior in the general office said crisply that if Alice did not bring her post along straight away it would not go out today. Juniors in general offices, Alice had learnt, carry honorary rank. She hurried towards the big room with the windows facing on to the corridor, enabling its occupants to observe the comings and goings of staff, particularly those entering the Director's and Deputy Director's offices opposite.

'I never can remember this,' she said apologetically as she presented the post folder.

'You people think you can just dump stuff in here on your way out,' she was told sharply. 'We have to get home, too, you know.'

Another thing which Alice had learnt was that however hard other people may work, it has to be acknowledged that general office staff are more stretched and put upon than any. Perhaps there was justice in this claim. Not so long ago, letters for signature had been laid before the Assistant Education Officers neatly contained in leather-bound books, each letter placed between pages of blotting paper. Any book large enough to contain the present volume of post would have needed a small crane to hoist it on to an Assistant Education Officer's desk, and post now arrived at the general office in a series of bulging buff folders. Alice had come too late to understand the impact of these changes on people who had hitherto enjoyed an ordered, leisurely existence. There was little sympathy between her and the general office staff.

It was with a feeling of intense relief that she left the office. 'It gets worse, not better,' she told her friend Irene Kimberley when they were seated in a café in Tothill Street. 'Each morning I feel I have woken up in a strange place. I don't know where I am – or even who I am.'

Irene made rather a business of studying the menu. She was finding it difficult to tolerate the recital of Alice's grievances. They had been close friends since schooldays, but had not seen much of each other during the war. Irene valued Alice as a cheerful person who tried to make the best of things, and she was dismayed by this change in her friend. 'You'll soon settle down,' she said. She had had none of Alice's problems. During the war she had studied at London University, and when she graduated she had entered the civil service. All this time, she had continued to live at home. There had been few dislocations in Irene's life.

'But do I want to settle down?' Alice asked dejectedly. 'I'm not sure that local government is the right thing for me.'

'What else could you do?'

There was nothing else Alice could do. A series of prospective employers had made it only too apparent that she lacked the only skills in which they were interested, namely shorthand and typewriting. It was uncharitable of Irene to draw attention to this, she who had a first class honours degree and now worked in the Cabinet Office. To Alice it seemed that everything Irene touched turned to gold. She had the alert look of a person who finds her employment both congenial and stimulating. Across the table from Alice, her brightness was dazzling. She was inventive with scarves so that they had the effect of making quite ordinary clothes look stylish; once knotted, they did not come undone. Alice wore her scarf as if she had a sore throat.

'There's a woman in the office called Mildred,' Alice said, prodding a spam fritter. 'She dresses like the staff at school, a shapeless sack with a girdle round the middle and shoes like bedroom slippers. She flipflops about looking old enough to be my grandmother. She doesn't have a proper home, just a bedsitter in Kilburn. The only thing that matters to her is that she has a job with a pension.'

'For goodness sake, Alice! *That's* never going to happen to you!'

'Why not? I never imagined myself working for West London Education Committee, but I'm doing it.' Her doleful expression suggested she was only one step from woolly sacks and bedroom slippers.

Irene, suppressing a desire to laugh, said, 'You always were up in the clouds or down in the dumps. You need to find a middle way.'

'But that's the whole point! Can't you see? I *have* found a middle way.' She was quite pale now.

Irene supposed it must be hard, coming back from service life with its constant excitements and changes of scene, men and parties, sleeping while other people were working and going on watch as they went to bed, mixing with people with whom one had no shared values or expectations. There had been times during the war when Irene had been afraid she might be missing something. She could remember being quite disturbed about it at one time, even obscurely frightened.

'Use your gift,' she said. 'Now, if ever, is the time, surely? Write it down.'

'Miserable reading that would make!'

'Not necessarily, if you made it funny.'

Tears came into Alice's eyes. Irene reminded herself that employment was probably the least of Alice's problems. Her home had been bombed, her father was dead, and her mother was now living in Sussex with her new husband. Both her sisters were married and the younger, Claire, was expecting her first child. The family, which had once been so close, was now scattered. Alice, a lodger in the home of her older sister, Louise, must miss that sense of belonging which she had taken for granted in her childhood. Irene, an only child, was particularly attached to her parents and could not imagine what her life would be without them. She made an effort to master her irritation.

'What is it that is so particularly awful?' she asked.

Alice gazed at her. If she could have communicated with Irene in a series of animal howls, she might have managed to convey the extent of her desolation. Instead, she looked out of the window. It was raining steadily, but not spectacularly. Even the wind seemed wearied, sighing as it skirted corners, spasmodic in its assaults on umbrellas and the tarpaulin over a newsvendor's stall. She thought of Alexandria, the colour and warmth, the feeling that everything one did and said was of tremendous importance, that it was all leading to that moment when the curtain would at last go up on life and it would all begin. Instead of which, it had petered out into this. So grey and drab.

They ate in silence, Alice wondering how to change the conversation. It was no use asking Irene about *her* work because she could not talk about it. In spite of this, she gave the impression of knowing everything, so that conversation about national affairs usually left Alice feeling that her opinions were ill-informed and partial as opposed to Irene's silent, all-inclusive wisdom. It was rather like talking to God. Irene would not discuss Mr Attlee, but one sensed that she knew all there was to know about him. While Mr Aneurin Bevan would bring a guarded look into her eyes, the mention of Mr Ernest Bevin produced an affectionate smile. Alice recalled that there was always Ellen Wilkinson.

'Have you met our Minister?' she asked, and without waiting for a reply, went on, 'I must admit I have a soft spot for her, after reading *South Riding*.'

'*South Riding*?'

'The headmistress, you remember, was supposed to be a portrait of Ellen Wilkinson.'

'Really? I had forgotten. Not an exact portrait, I would have said.'

So much for Winifred Holtby.

Irene looked at her watch. 'Are we going to this rehearsal?'

Alice brightened. 'Do you know, I had forgotten!'

'You'll make a splendid prompt!'

'They don't need me at present. I haven't been to a rehearsal yet. You would like to come, wouldn't you?'

Irene said yes, although in fact she did not want to go. Apart from Alice's sister, Louise, she did not know any members of the dramatic society. She gathered that most of the men had recently come out of the services and she did not think she would be at ease in their company. She was reluctant to let Alice see how difficult she found it to mix informally with men.

'Tell me something about this company,' she said when the bus was on its way down the Bayswater Road.

'They have their own theatre in Notting Hill. It was a small factory, but the society converted it some time in the Thirties.'

'They *are* amateurs, aren't they?'

'Yes, but they are very good. They couldn't do much during the war, of course; but now that people are coming back they are planning to do four plays a year.'

'Isn't *Asmodée* a bit ambitious?'

'Oh no! They don't do *popular* plays – Terence Rattigan and all that stuff.'

'Rattigan probably needs professionals anyway,' Irene said, to show that she, too, knew about theatre. 'The lighter the work, the defter the touch. Witness the Lunts.'

'There's nothing light about Mauriac.'

There was not much light in the theatre and it was very cold. Everyone except the producer was muffled in heavy clothing. Louise was wearing a borrowed duffel coat and the men sported service overcoats and scarves; one man was wearing a Mae West. Two girls who were not on-stage were sharing a blanket. Irene and Alice seated themselves at the back of the auditorium. Not one head turned in their direction.

The producer was wearing a pin-striped suit. The theatre was his life and everyone knew it; he had no need of affectation. His was a cold passion, but he had formidable energy which, presumably, kept him warm. He addressed one of the characters on stage in a quiet, dry voice. 'You're not disturbed by any of this, but you are not *impervious*, either. You see? There *is* a difference.'

The man in the Mae West blew on his fingers and said that he did see.

The producer went on, 'I suppose one answer would be to play this scene as if the other characters were some distance away from you – try to put a distance between yourself and them.'

'Not easy on this stage.'

'Theatre is always a matter of illusion,' the producer said austerely, '*You* create the illusion of space and the audience will accept it.'

The Mae West said restively, 'Shall we go through it again?'

'I feel you might find it easier if you didn't look as if you were floating on your back.' The producer threw this line away into the dark auditorium in a manner worthy of Alfred Lunt.

They continued with the rehearsal until they came to the part where the Mae West was saying, 'I often had to pass through France on my way back to school. I loved looking out of the window of the train at night. I used to wish I could be the Devil Asmodée. Do you remember him? The one that lifts the roofs off houses. Nothing in the world has ever seemed to me quite so mysterious as one of those old country houses . . .'

The producer said, 'This particular house is in a remote, *hot* part of the country. These people are stifled, imprisoned by the heat. None of you has so far given that impression. It is hot and sultry, and you must reflect that in every movement.'

The Mae West said something about wondering whether they were putting the play on at the right time of the year. The producer said that the theatre had nothing to do with the everyday, and the season *was* summer. The Mae West, cowed, said, 'Yes, of course.'

'We'll go back to Marcelle's entrance.'

Most of the players were reading from books. It was surprising that in spite of this, and the inappropriate climate, on the second reading one began to sense the inadmissible passion rigidly suppressed. Alice visualised the remote house in south-west France in high summer, the sun streaming through the windows; and then, at the end, in autumn, life turning inwards as Marcelle and Blaise Lebel are left to keep each other company.

Is it all in the play? Irene wondered, or is it partly these people? Are they, now that they have left the war world, having to cut themselves down to the size acceptable in civilian life, to fit themselves into jobs they don't like? Is this where they escape to so that they can let their hobbled passions out in this dark little hall? Or is it just that they can't face the real world? Do they become someone else when they come here, pick up another personality at the door? Or do they find in their adopted character the unimaginable things they dare not permit to surface in their daytime lives? Where is reality for them, inside or outside? But what is Louise doing among them, apart from the fact that she is a good actress?

Louise, of all people, seemed to have no need of a mask behind which to hide, she who had shocked them all not so much by becoming pregnant in her teens, as by her lack of repentance. And there had been at least one man during the war, or so Irene had always suspected. Now, while the others felt warily for emotion, Louise seemed to have no need to dredge deep into herself, the feelings were all there, bubbling close to the surface.

As though her thoughts had been conveyed to him, the producer said, 'This is all coming to you too easily, Louise. Much too extrovert. This woman is a complex character. Try to imagine you have a sore place in your mouth which makes it painful to talk to Blaise. Then, when you are with Harry, we shall notice the change in you.'

The Mae West gave a wolf whistle, and then slapped his hand and said, 'Down, Fido!' The producer looked at him as if he had taken leave of his senses.

'Is Guy coming?' Irene whispered to Alice.

'He stays at home. I offered to look after the children, but he doesn't seem interested in the theatre any more.'

There was a gas ring in the prop room and later the stage manager made tea while Alice and Irene put out cups. The stage manager was a woman. She wore naval bellbottoms tucked into Wellington boots and a shapeless fisherman's jersey with holes at the elbows and splashes of engine oil across the chest. A cigarette hung from her lower lip and one smoke-blinded eye was half-closed. Her conversation tended to the monosyllabic. When the producer spoke to her she said, 'Yup' or 'Roger'. She was the only person to whom he deferred, and when on one occasion she said gruffly, 'No can do,' he answered, 'I'll leave it to you to work something else out.'

'Did you come across her in the Wrens?' Irene asked Alice.

'No. She was an air mechanic. Fleet Air Arm. They ate nails for breakfast.'

The players sat on the edge of the stage drinking tea, while the producer tapped his fingers impatiently as he read through his notes.

Louise said to Alice, 'We shall need you soon.'

The men were telling service jokes, including the stage manager in their company as if she were a man. Alice inclined her head in the direction of the Mae West. 'Do you think he is right for the part?'

'He has a marvellous presence on stage,' Louise said. 'As soon as he comes on, I feel confident that it's going to be all right.'

'He seems a bit lightweight.'

'But he's the only character who stands outside all this. He comes, and he goes, untouched by it – except of course that he takes Emmy away. Don't you understand that?'

'I can see that he's good as a catalyst,' Alice said, still doubtful. 'But Asmodée tears the roofs off houses before he goes.'

Louise shrugged her shoulders, but the producer who was standing near them, turned to look thoughtfully at Alice.

'What an uncomfortable play,' Irene said as they walked away from the theatre, leaving the cast to run through the final act again. 'Thank goodness for four strong walls around me, and no one likely to come tearing off the roof.'

# 2

At the beginning of February, Angus Drummond met Guy Immingham as they left All Saints, Langham Place, after attending a memorial service. Guy's modesty necessitated his disclaiming personal knowledge of so eminent a man as the deceased.

'I didn't know him,' he said, as they walked down Portland Place. 'I came to represent my firm.'

'He was in banking, I seem to remember?' Angus had known the man in the Resistance. The war had forged links between unlikely people. 'Sad to have come through so much, only to walk into a bus.'

At a time when most young men, including Guy, were wearing demob suits, Angus was expensively tailored. Guy, unsure of himself in spite of his good looks, was acutely embarrassed by the package he was carrying – bananas wrapped in newspaper. He felt he must look like an office boy. 'I'm not going back to the office – I've had enough for one day. And, in any case, I shouldn't get back much before six.' He checked himself, remembering he did not have to justify his absence to Angus. 'So I'm bearing my trophies with me. I don't suppose the children can remember what a banana tastes like.'

Angus said, 'Ah yes, atrocious weather in the North Sea, whaling fleets in trouble, wheat crops failing worldwide; but on the credit side, the banana makes a comeback. Well, if you are not going back to the office – and I certainly am not – come and have tea with me. Or something stronger, if you prefer. I live near here.' As he said this, he stopped as if about to cross the road, but really in order to see what the man carrying the tool bag would do. The man turned into a side street. Which is what I would do at this point if I was shadowing someone, Angus thought. He walked on and did not look round again. This was not occupied France, but England, where no one had good reason to be suspicious of him.

Guy was pleased to accept Angus's invitation. They had been talking about the Drummond family at home the other night. Angus was friendly with Irene Kimberley and there had been speculation as to whether they would marry. Irene would do very well if Angus lived in this district. This is what *I* would like for Louise, Guy thought as they walked past a terrace of Georgian houses. Angus said, 'Here we are!' inserting a key in a door marked Flat 1. He picked up letters from the mat and, gesturing Guy into a room off the narrow hall, said, 'If you'll excuse me a moment.'

The room in which Guy found himself was unnervingly quiet. In his own home, the sitting-room showed so much evidence of activity that on the rare occasions when he was alone in it he had the comfortable feeling of life still going on around him. Even in his immaculate childhood home, there had been a sense of his mother's busyness – gleaming ornaments, waxed table, polished hearth. Here there was cool, disinterested elegance which had no need of people. The only sign of occupation was a copy of *The Times* lying on the settee. Guy picked it up. It had been folded with the foreign page uppermost. Anti-Jewish feeling in Poland was reported to have created an attitude of panic. It had been suggested that the Jews had in mind a second exodus which would take them from Europe to Palestine; a sinister co-ordinating organisation had been hinted at. Always trouble with the Jews, Guy thought wryly. Louise's sister, Alice, had been very upset by the Belsen films because her friend, Katia Vaseyelin, had disappeared in Germany in the Thirties. Guy, with memories he could not put out of his mind, had sympathised with her, but Louise had said that grieving over what could not be changed was a form of self-indulgence. It would not have been possible to explain to her that once something has happened, it cannot be undone; that the incineration of Jews, and the aftermath of atrocity which Guy had witnessed, were now a part of the fabric of life and must somehow be accommodated. How lonely one was sometimes! Louise was so different from him. She seemed to need a hidden place that was all her own; whereas he was terrified of finding himself alone. 'Everything I have I want to share with you,' he would insist. 'I want you to know everything that has ever happened to me.' He had always needed others to validate his experiences. His hands trembled on the paper. He had to fight down an impulse to rush out and find Angus. But this did not seem the sort of establishment where one could barge into the kitchen and offer to carry something. His fear of intrusion won a narrow victory over his fear of isolation.

Angus came into the room carrying a tray of drinks. He could see perfectly well what Guy had been reading, but he said, 'The Americans have made their first contact with the moon. A radar signal has been beamed on it, and the moon, it seems, has sent back an echo. Was that wise, one asks oneself?'

'I don't suppose the moon will do us much harm.'

'God knows what the Americans may do to it, though. Probably put a man up there, on the principle that if you can see it, you've got to own it. Not that one should grumble about them; they can be generous.' He picked up a bottle. 'Bourbon, believe it or not! Say when.'

'I'm not much of a drinker,' Guy said hastily.

Angus diluted the bourbon with what he considered a generous splash of soda. He handed the glass to Guy and strolled to the window. There was a car parked further down the street. It had been there on previous evenings; but surely they wouldn't be foolish enough to use the same car all the time? Unless, of course, they wanted him to know that they were keeping him under supervision. It was hard to understand their motives – they were a deeply suspicious people. Perhaps they would never really trust him.

Guy, looking at Angus, envied him the thick hair which showed no sign of receding at the temples, and was as glossily dark as when he was a boy. In his fifties, he would probably look much as he did now: a spare, handsome man. Guy's observations went no further. He did not notice that while the top half of the domed head was donnish – broad, high forehead, thoughtful eyes – the face tapered to a pointed chin which was disconcertingly girlish, giving an impression that his Maker had been divided in his purpose when he fashioned these bones.

'You're at the Foreign Office, aren't you?' Guy asked.

'In and around, you know.' Angus was secretive by habit. He had spent so long impersonating other characters he found it difficult to decide what it was appropriate for him to say.

'Well, I'm definitely *in* Busby and Overton,' Guy said ruefully.

'The firm hasn't changed?'

'That was what I dreaded. But, in fact, it hasn't turned out that way. Old Overton died last year, and his son is one of the partners now. Back from the Commandos and wanting to make up for lost time.' Guy looked into his glass. 'I suppose you might call him dynamic.'

'Exhausting.'

'You can't rush everything. Some of my clients are quite old. I have to spend a bit of time with them, even if their accounts aren't worth all that much to the firm.' He was good with old people.

Angus studied Guy, automatically registering that this was a man he would never be able to impersonate. Innocence is a quality you cannot assume if you don't happen to have it. He recalled Guy in the days when he was first in love with Louise, so baffled by her beauty, so openly vulnerable. Even then, although they were much the same age, Angus had felt infinitely older. In spite of his shyness, Guy had expressed his pleasures with a naïve unsophistication which had amused Angus and which he now found rather touching. Touching, of course, because that naïveté was now flawed. Guy had been a handsome young man in the quiet, self-effacing English manner. He was still very presentable, but his were the looks which owe much to good nature, and do not wear well once the bloom goes off life. Already puzzlement dimmed the trusting brightness of the eyes and there was a trace of petulance in the line of the mouth – nothing important as yet, merely the irritation of the man unable to solve a key clue in a crossword puzzle. But the face was still innocent, in the way that some women will always seem innocent however often they may have been betrayed.

'How *is* Louise?' he asked, as if they had been talking about her.

'Fine.'

'And the children?' Not that he would have recalled them, but for the bananas.

Guy looked out of the window. 'They've sprouted up quite a bit while I've been away. Takes time to get accustomed to it.'

'You were away for long?'

'From Dunkirk onwards. The desert, the Italian campaign.' Angus had expected that, like many rather inadequate men, he might want to take refuge in his wartime experiences, but he responded by turning the conversation away from himself. 'You're still doing the same sort of thing, I suppose?'

'More or less.' He picked up Guy's glass. 'Same again?'

Guy looked at his watch. 'I must be getting home soon.' As Angus was already pouring bourbon, he said, 'Oh well. One for the road. With more soda, please.'

When Angus had refilled his own glass, Guy said, 'What do you make of the United Nations business? You must see more than most of us. It looks as if the Russians are all set to make trouble from the outset.'

'I expect they thought we were making a bit of trouble when we made it clear that atomic energy was one secret we had no intention of sharing with our Allies.'

'But how could we share it?' Guy looked astonished. 'We have to make sure it is one weapon which is never used.'

'And so it is safest in the hands of the only people to have used it?'

He usually monitored his speech carefully, but he was growing increasingly reckless in the expression of his views about Russia. One part of him was obsessively vigilant, the other thought that nothing mattered; it was becoming quite difficult to reconcile the two. Fortunately, Guy had not noticed. He was saying, 'That's how Claire talks. Her husband is very much to the Left, you know – reads the *New Statesman* and that sort of thing.'

'And Claire accepts it as if it was holy writ, I suppose?'

'Oh yes, she says we should be perfecting life here and now.'

'I don't know about that.' Angus had suddenly become languid; even to Guy's not very penetrating eyes it was apparent that vitality had drained from him. 'But that's my trouble. I don't really know what I think about anything.' He did not seem to be addressing himself to Guy.

He wants me to go, Guy thought; I shouldn't have accepted that second drink. He got up, flushed with embarrassment and would have forgotten the bananas had Angus not called after him.

The treat, as with so many of his enterprises, was not greatly appreciated. Louise had tried to suggest to him that it would not help him to settle down with the children if he was constantly making emotional demands on them. James was ten, and Catherine eight, and neither had learnt to dissemble. Louise herself had little use for pretence. Her face registered irritation when he produced his gift. If they ate the wretched things they would have indigestion all night, and if they didn't Guy would be hurt. She left them to resolve this dilemma in their own way.

Catherine said 'Ugh!' when she tasted the banana.

'She's always been faddy,' Louise told Guy. The constant need to explain the children to him emphasised his isolation.

James ate half his banana to please his father, and gave the other half to the dog, who licked it suspiciously and left it on the rug where Guy subsequently trod on it.

Louise gave vent to her annoyance and she and James had one of the arguments which Guy found so distressing. Louise never felt guilty about anger and so she was never shrewish. She had been looking rather heavy about the face, but now, with heightened colour and combative eyes, she was quite handsome. As a girl she had been beautiful; Guy had seen her as a light that glowed at his approach, a flower that opened to his touch. But she had grown into a woman who scoffed at such notions; and although she was more vibrant now than when she was a girl, she was often too forceful for him.

'When you grow up you will leave home and you can do just as you like,' she was saying to James. 'But while you are here, you will have to clear up after yourself.'

'It's not fair!' he protested.

'Oh, nothing in life is *fair*,' she mocked.

'Aunt Claire says that it is wrong to thwart children,' he said when he had cleaned the carpet. 'She says that whatever you do, you must never say "no" to a child.'

'I'm sorry for you two, then,' Louise retorted. 'Think how I must have crippled you!'

'We're glad you are thinking about it,' Catherine said.

'But you've left it too late,' James said.

'Aunt Alice will put you in a book,' Catherine said.

'All about a mother who ill-treats her children, and so they run away . . .'

'And live in a forest, like Hansel and Gretel . . .'

Guy said uneasily, 'What nonsense you children do talk!'

'You can take the dog out now,' Louise said to James.

'What about Catherine?'

'She has to do her practice. As far as the double oak, please, and no further.'

'You're bossy.'

'Someone has to be in charge here, and it so happens it's me.' This kind of exchange had been going on for so long between them that she forgot about Guy. 'Right? His lead is hanging up behind the kitchen door.'

It was not right, but James knew it was no use arguing. And, since she did not make emotional appeals to his better nature, it did not really matter all that much. It did not diminish him to obey her; he did it as a gesture to her, because she was his mother. She made no enquiry as to his motives. Their relationship was something outside the realms of reason. It was quite beyond Guy's understanding.

'You are rather hard on him sometimes,' he said when the children had both gone.

But her authority had limits. When Guy was shocked by James's behaviour he had long, severe chats aimed at bringing the boy round to his own way of thinking. James sulked. Under Louise's regime, it was a matter of rough justice, quickly meted out and as soon forgotten. When they were young and had quarrelled with each other, she had said, 'I haven't got time to sort out who did what to whom, you both go upstairs until you can behave properly.' She made no demands on their minds. It was unimportant to her whether they accepted her opinions or laughed at them. 'You think I'm a silly old cow,' she had once said. Later, when James called her a cow, she slapped his face. In half an hour they had both forgotten about it. Claire said you should never raise a hand in anger to a child; Louise thought it was the only time when it was permissible.

'You're not going to rehearsal?' Guy asked, noting that Louise was in no hurry to get supper.

'The play has been put off until the end of the year. Our producer has had to go abroad for his firm.'

'Will they do something else?'

'Oh yes. *Man and Superman*. But I shan't be in that. I like the part in *Asmodée*. Did you read the play?'

'A bit intense, I thought.'

'You should talk to Alice about it. She loves all that claustrophobic, simmering passion.'

'Is Alice in? If she could stay with the children, we might go to the pictures.'

'I've been to so many rehearsals. I don't like to go out and leave them when there's no need.'

He flinched from crying out his own need, and said pettishly, 'They have you every day when they come out of school.'

'They used to have me to themselves all the time, Guy. They can't understand why they are pushed out of the way so often now.' She saw that he was hurt, and went on, 'I want us to be on our own, too. But it would help if you took them out more often. You would get to know them better without me there to take over. James is right about that! I am bossy.'

'I took them for a walk on Hampstead Heath. James went rushing off with the dog, and Catherine got a blister.'

'When that happens you let James go, and sit down on a seat with Catherine. It doesn't matter about being together all the time. You're not a sheepdog, Guy. The object isn't to get us all into a pen and close the gate.' She rumpled his hair gently, but he was not appeased.

'The pleasure is in being together, surely?'

'But we *are* together. Catherine is playing her scales and James is loitering round the double oak. That's together enough for me.'

'I accept that. But when I give up a Saturday afternoon to take them out, I do expect to have their company. I lost James for an hour and I had to carry Catherine.'

Louise got up. 'Well, I'm going to get supper.'

Guy followed her into the kitchen. 'I don't seem able to make my point . . .'

She whirled on him shouting, a fist emphasising each word. 'If there could be *one* evening when this doesn't happen! Just one, that's all I ask.'

He backed out of the room. A quarter of an hour later, Louise went into Alice's room at the top of the house. 'What are you doing lying on your bed?' she asked irritably.

Alice, who was lying flat on her stomach with her head resting on her arms, replied, 'Lying on my bed, of course.'

Louise said, 'Is there anyone in this house who isn't miserable?'

Alice raised herself on one elbow and screwed her head round to look at her sister.

Louise sat in a wicker chair and began to cry. 'I'm not very happy myself, but I do try!' She drummed her hands on her knees. 'I do try! No one seems to believe it, but I do!'

Alice pulled back the eiderdown and rolled off the bed. She went to Louise and knelt beside her. Louise said, 'What do I do wrong, Alice? Tell me what I do wrong.'

Alice contemplated the linoleum in dismay. It would have been easier to reply had she not had an answer so ready to hand. Louise said, 'Well, go on!'

'Was it a good thing to be in the play, so soon after he came back?'

'I thought he would come, too.'

'He wants you to himself, I expect, don't you?'

Louise sat looking ahead of her. After a moment, she said quietly, 'He wants to come in in the evening and make love to me. I don't mind that, but it's difficult with the children. After all, it's the only time they see him. Then, when at last we've got them to bed – and it's not easy to get children to bed when they know they are being pushed out of the way – he wants to tell me everything that has happened to him at his office; and then he wants to know what I have been doing all day. Or, he might like to go to the pictures, and hold my hand, whisper to me, so that I don't lose myself in the film. He doesn't enjoy music, so we don't often listen to it. If we do, he fidgets and jokes with the dog. When I go out to prepare supper, he follows me into the kitchen. At the end of the evening, I feel . . . as if he had been trying to eat me alive!'

Louise had had six years of freedom. The room seemed to vibrate with her anger. Alice wondered if Guy knew what he was doing when he tried to harness the force in Louise for his own purposes. 'I can see that you *have* to belong to the dramatic society,' she said.

Louise stood up and straightened her skirt. 'I feel better now. So what's your little problem? Is it the cold up here? You can always come down with us whenever you want to.'

'Oh, Louise!' Alice laughed. She had said it so spontaneously and could not even see how funny it was. There would always be room for people to come and go in Louise's life. No wonder she and Guy were having difficulties.

'My problem is that everything is so dull and grey and I'm afraid it's going on forever. And I expect that is how Guy feels, too. Do you remember those books about the 1920s, all the war heroes coming back after giving their youth for their country? *Seven men came back*. They were all so full of misery and self-pity! Well, no more self-pity from me, I promise!'

Louise put an arm round her shoulders and hugged her. 'That's my girl! Now, what about sitting in for us after supper? Guy wants to go to the pictures.'

# 3

In the spring Alice was to spend a weekend with her mother and stepfather in Sussex. She had been invited for Christmas, but had made the excuse that she thought one of the family should be with the grandparents in Falmouth. The visit to her mother's new home could not be delayed any longer; it could, however, be curtailed and she said it would not be possible for her to arrive before the Saturday morning. This was accepted without much argument.

'Austin won't try to behave like a stepfather,' Louise assured her.

This did not alter the fact of his being one.

Louise and Claire had already stayed at the house. For different reasons, they were muted in their reactions. Claire, who had wanted a substitute father, had found Austin Marriott too detached. Louise had found him too attractive. Had he been a new member of the dramatic society, she would have hailed him as a find; but she could not forgive her mother for marrying a man who overshadowed Guy. That he should be more intellectually able did not trouble Louise; but she had not been prepared for so powerful a physical presence. This not only disturbed her, it made her conscious of her mother's sexuality. Austin had not been unaware of her response to him and had treated her with a caution which suggested the experience was not new to him. When their eyes met at the dinner table, or as they sat by the wood fire in the evening, she could see that he was laughing. She was not used to being laughed at.

'You'll get along with him very well,' she said to Alice. 'You'll be able to talk books.'

'That will be like talking politics to Irene,' Alice said. 'He will know everything and everyone.'

Judith had said, 'One of us will meet you at Lewes station.' Alice anticipated the worst: if one did that, one could only be pleasantly surprised. So, as she walked towards the ticket barrier she was rehearsing her conversational gambit – a statement she had read recently to the effect that it would take the publishing industry about seven years to make good wartime losses and restore publishers' catalogues to prewar standards. After that, he would talk about his firm's catalogue and this would probably see them through the journey to the village where her mother now lived.

A surprise indeed awaited her. It was her Cornish relative, Ben Sherman, who was standing just beyond the barrier.

'Austin let me have the car,' he said, taking her case. The car was an old, treasured Rover, and this had represented an act of faith on Austin's part. Four years as a Japanese prisoner-of-war had left Ben with a legacy of unpredictable reactions and poor co-ordination.

Alice, who did not realise how important this small act of charity was to Ben, thought it odd that he should explain about the car rather than his own unexpected presence.

'Are you staying for the weekend?'

'Yes, I came down by the earlier train.'

'Mummy didn't tell me. We could have travelled together.'

'Judith doesn't make that sort of connection.'

So it's 'Judith' now, Alice thought; I *am* going to be one on my own this weekend!

Ben drove the car as though it was a truck, hauling on the wheel, one window wide open so that he could lean out when he turned a corner. It seemed to Alice that he was more concerned with what might be behind him than with the road ahead. As she was thrown against the windscreen, she thought how typical it was of Ben that if he had problems he should manhandle them! She was relieved when they arrived unscathed in the village.

'Stop here a moment,' she said when they came to the church. She made the daffodils an excuse for getting out.

'There are heaps of daffs in your mother's garden.'

'But these I can enjoy!'

There was a bench in the graveyard and they sat side by side, each agitated by exposure to the keen spring sunlight. Wild flowers had thrust up all over the old graves and on a cottage wall near by the white montana was thick as a quilt.

'It was in the spring that Daddy was killed,' Alice said to Ben, who did not need reminding.

'Later than this,' she said, recalling the cherry trees at their most abundant. Not one of them had been touched when the bomb exploded. That was five years ago and the sharpness of grief had gone now, leaving only a dull pain which Alice was beginning to realise would never be completely eased. Lately, however, the good times she had shared with her father had come spontaneously to mind, as though his shattered image was gradually being refashioned. There would be joy as well as sorrow to take through life. If only her mother had not remarried!

'I've been dreading this weekend,' she told Ben. 'I'm so glad you are here.'

'He is really a very decent sort.' Ben spoke warmly.

'I've met him once or twice. I know he's all right. It's Mummy. She doesn't want to talk about Daddy. I suppose that is understandable – Austin might not like it. But it only leaves the present to talk about, and that's something one does with strangers.' It was as though her mother had drawn a hard line across her daughters' lives, cutting them off from their past and denying them a necessary continuity.

'Do you talk about your father a lot with Louise and Claire?'

'No, I suppose not. But we know we can if we want to. We don't have to think, we just say what comes into our minds. That's the great thing with being a family. That, and the taking for granted.'

'You had to be quite careful how you behaved with your father,' Ben reminded her. 'He was a fairly explosive character.'

But Stanley Fairley had passed beyond criticism now and Alice took no notice of this remark. 'What have you been doing with yourself?' she asked. 'I haven't seen you since before Christmas. How *was* Christmas?'

He had spent Christmas with a family in Herefordshire. Their son, Geoffrey, had died in the prison camp in Siam where Ben had spent much of his war service. Last autumn, Ben had set out on a disastrous walk along Offa's Dyke and had had to give up on the second day because he was in such poor condition. It had been apparent that these expeditions to the Welsh Marches were something in the nature of a pilgrimage.

'It was all right,' he said gruffly. He had not been well since his return from captivity and had had to give up his career at the Bar. He had no one to help him ease his way back into civilian life. He had gone to Herefordshire expecting a miracle. The parents had welcomed him eagerly as Geoffrey's friend. But he had looked for more than that. He had wanted a firm place in the family and had had some notion of falling in love with one of Geoffrey's sisters, or with the girl to whom his friend had been engaged. This would set the seal on his friendship with Geoffrey. There was a rightness about the solution, a simple economy which he found as satisfying as an algebraic equation. In the event, he had thought the girls superficial and suspected that they had found him angular and difficult to communicate with. He had learnt that algebra is not subject to the will, that there are certain things which no amount of yearning can ever bring into being. Other people, too, dream their dreams, separate from one's own.

'We'd better get on,' he said. 'Sitting here admiring the daffodils isn't going to solve anything.'

As they returned to the car, he said, 'Austin has been looking at Geoffrey's drawings, to see whether they can be reproduced in a book.' He was still talking about the drawings when they arrived at the house. He had difficulty in opening the gate because he was hampered by Alice's suitcase. It would have taken a matter of seconds to have put down the case and then unlatched the gate.

'Let me . . .' Alice said.

'I did the captions – it was supposed to be a joint venture. And I kept a diary after Geoffrey died. But the drawings are the important thing . . .' Alice could see he would soon pull the gate off its hinges, so he wouldn't have to worry about the latch. Really, what a way to behave, just when she needed to be calm! She leant across him and undid the latch.

'Why ever didn't you put the case down?'

'I was thinking,' he said impatiently. 'I can't be bothered with all that.'

'You're in much more of a bother now.'

But to have put down the case would have involved a movement which interfered with his train of thought. He isn't going to change, Alice thought; he is Ben, of whom I am very fond – only just at this moment I could strike him!

They arrived flushed and disconcerted at the front door to be greeted by Judith, flushed from a calamity in the kitchen.

'Come and have tea,' Judith said after she had embraced her daughter. She led Alice towards the back of the house. Austin appeared in the doorway to the sitting-room and raised one hand in salute, then he picked up Alice's case and disappeared up the stairs with Ben. His restraint, though well-meant, was accounted discourtesy by Alice who was not used to restrained men. A clumsily over-enthusiastic greeting would have won her heart. This brief appearance only served to emphasise that Austin Marriott was master of this house. He was a man who filled any spaces there might be around him, not, as her father had done, by expenditure of a ferocious energy, but simply by virtue of being big. He had the benign manner of one who can look down on others from a comfortable height. As he was not concerned with winning hearts, only with keeping the peace, he did not join Judith and Alice in the kitchen, but said to Ben, 'We'll leave the women to themselves. Come into my study.'

'Pour yourself a cup of tea,' Judith said to Alice. 'I'll clear this up. Austin says I wouldn't hold down a housekeeper's job for a week.' She bent to collect the pieces of broken crockery heaped on the tiled floor. 'They'll do nicely in flower pots.' She was never one to cry over breakages.

Alice, looking down at her mother, could see that there was a powdering of grey over the thick brown hair. This apart, Judith looked young for her fifty years. Her skin was dark and her face wedge-shaped. 'You're never going to be a beauty,' her mother had told her. 'So you'd best make yourself useful.' But a pair of bold dark eyes and a general air of forcefulness can do wonders for a face, and many would account her a handsome woman.

'I wonder any of us can use our hands at all!' Alice said. 'Daddy was always breaking things, too.'

'Your father had two left hands,' Judith said. 'I only break things when I'm in a hurry.'

'But you always *are* in a hurry.'

'Not nearly so much now that I have a country garden again.' Alice was glad that Austin was not credited with this slackening of pace. She preferred an unquiet mother to one tempered by her stepfather.

When Alice had finished her tea, Judith took her on a tour of the house, excluding the study. It was a rambling fifteenth-century house, smelling of old, dry plaster and creaking with age. The rooms, although low-ceilinged and giving the impression of being small, were, in fact, quite long and the furniture was arranged to give a sense of space. People did not need to live huddled on top of one another here. The furniture, Alice noted, was mostly Austin's; it was worn and fitted its surroundings comfortably. The house, however, had the appearance of having recently been polished, scrubbed and generally freshened throughout. There were books and flowers everywhere. Alice said, 'It's very nice,' feeling a stranger in her mother's home. Doors and windows were open and in the sitting-room a grey cat paused in its ablutions long enough to salute Alice with a languid paw.

'And this is your room, darling,' Judith said, after they had clambered up narrow stairs to the second floor. In her own home, Alice had been rebuked for being possessive when she first demanded a room of her own. Here, where the relationships were so much more fragile, the room must be conceded without argument. It was small, with a tiny casement window, irregular walls and sloping floor. Alice guessed it really was her own room, since the other stepchildren were married and would require a larger room.

'It's just the sort of place I love,' she said, and was touched to see how much this pleased her mother, who had not hitherto been very dependent on appreciation.

'We've squeezed a desk in there so that you can write your books.'

*That* will put paid to my writing a single line, Alice thought, her throat aching for the relief of tears.

Fortunately, the telephone rang and Judith hurried away to answer it. A few minutes later, when she came on to the landing to go to the bathroom, Alice heard Austin saying, 'What! All my pretty chickens . . . At one fell swoop?' Judith replied, 'Don't be silly,' in a tone Alice remembered from childhood.

There seemed to be no one about when she came downstairs. Here was a house where one felt one could stroll out at any time without giving offence to one's hosts. This made whatever tensions there might be bearable; but it also imposed no obligation to come to terms with problems. No doubt Austin subscribed to the comfortable masculine belief that, left long enough, problems will sort themselves out. He rescued Alice from the hall and led her into his study. 'It's warmer in here, and we haven't enough fuel for fires at this time of the year.'

Judith told her that Claire had telephoned. She and Terence were coming for the day tomorrow, and Louise would probably come with them. They had a glass of sherry, then Judith went to prepare lunch which, it seemed, had replaced dinner as the midday meal. Alice was relieved when Austin led them into the dining-room. At least they would not be expected to eat with food balanced on their knees, a procedure which had been equated with ungodliness in the Fairley household. This proved the only concession to God. No grace was said. Alice had frequently grumbled about these rituals, but nevertheless expected her mother to be the guardian of tradition. The conversation at table was general, which suited Austin who could talk with ease on a range of subjects. Conversationally, he had perfect pitch. Alice felt it was important to strike the right note. She would be very embarrassed were she to say anything which jarred on the ear. He would think her disharmonies charming because of her youth, but this would not prevent his commenting on them in an amused manner after she had gone. Austin would have been surprised had he realised how exactly she judged the situation.

In other ways, her assessment was less accurate. Because he seemed to her to be so urbane, she could not imagine him to have feelings. She thought him cold, a man with many layers between himself and reality. She noticed that her mother was subdued, eyeing her husband thoughtfully as if testing his mood. It did not occur to Alice that this was a natural consequence of introducing a step-daughter to the house.

As her contribution to table-talk, Alice described rehearsals for *Asmodée*. Austin did not know the play, but said it sounded like *The House of Bernarda Alba*, which Alice did not know. Judith said to Austin, 'You must take me to the theatre. This is something I have missed.' Alice wondered how she could be so disloyal.

'I always feel rather sorry for playwrights,' Austin said, although in fact this had not much occupied his thoughts. 'The novelist can speak directly to the reader, but the playwright has to rely on interpretation.'

'I think the actor who plays *Asmodée* isn't suited to the part,' Alice said. This was one statement she could make with assurance, since Austin did not know either play or player.

'Not sufficient of a devil?' He knew about *that*.

'I think Jacov might do it very well,' Alice said to her mother.

There was a pause while Judith explained Jacov Vaseyelin to Austin. 'He was our next-door neighbour. It was his mother who was killed with Stanley when the bomb came down.' She went on quickly, 'I can't see Jacov playing the devil with anyone. He isn't nearly forceful enough.'

'But can you imagine ever being in a room and not noticing that Jacov was there? I think the actor who plays the part must convey a certain depth . . .'

'And Jacov has depth?' Austin asked.

'Like a well has depth.'

'Alice,' Judith said to Austin, 'is the thinker of my children.'

Austin raised his eyebrows. Alice thought he was querying the statement, as well he might; but, in fact, he thought the remark ill-judged.

Conversation petered out. It was Ben who unwittingly came to the rescue. He saw no need to match Austin's urbanity. As the meal progressed he administered a series of sharp jolts to the precarious calm, taking upon himself the role of scapegoat, becoming the outward expression of the anxieties and frustrations of those around him. He was by turns vehement and taciturn, as awkward in his change of temper as he had been in changing gear. Austin, watching this performance with a wincing compassion, accommodated himself to the unpredictable swings of Ben's mood. His behaviour towards Ben puzzled Alice until she noticed the photographs on the sideboard and remembered that Austin had had a son who was killed at Dunkirk. Her mother had told her that, after his wife died, he had brought the children up himself, hindered rather than aided by a series of amorous housekeepers. He had refused to send them away to boarding school. 'Because they had lost their mother, seemed to me no reason why they should then lose their father.' The death of the son whom he had so cherished must have come very hard.

After lunch, Judith took Alice into the garden while, surprisingly, Austin and Ben washed up. Judith was entranced by her garden and led Alice round the borders introducing her to every shrub, clipping, weeding, adjusting stakes as she went along.

'Do you remember the garden in our Sussex home?' she asked.

'Of course I remember,' Alice said indignantly. 'I was eight when we moved to London.'

'So you were! You and Claire made up a game about a house in Sussex, didn't you?'

Alice remembered the dream house they had constructed to console themselves amid the dreariness of Shepherd's Bush. It had been similar to this house. How strange they would have thought it had they known it was their mother who would inherit their dream!

Alice had longed to have a close emotional talk with her mother, but instead she became engrossed in weeding and tending the plants. By the end of the afternoon she was surprised to realise how much she had enjoyed herself.

'We'll make tea,' Judith said. 'I expect the men are talking about those drawings. Austin says they won't make money, but he is staggered by them.'

'So he won't publish?'

'Oh yes. He says there are some losses a firm must be prepared to bear if it really cares about books.'

'Bully for him!' Alice said grudgingly.

'Those drawings mean a lot to Ben. And I can understand why now that I have seen them.'

'I don't want to see them.' Alice had made herself watch the films of the Belsen concentration camp, and this was horror enough for the present. As she watched, she had soon given up any hope of discovering Katia. Even had she survived, there would have been no possibility of recognising the busty schoolgirl among the moving heaps of bone. Afterwards, Alice had known that life would never be quite the same again because the knowledge that people could do this to one another would always be there.

In the study, Ben was saying, 'About the captions. I can see that, particularly in the early drawings, they don't always fit Geoffrey's conception . . .'

Austin shook his head. 'No alterations! The difference enhances the drawings. One is aware of two people who are very unalike at the beginning. And one of the rewards is tracing how they gradually come together . . .'

'I was the one who came.'

'No. There is more bite in those drawings towards the end. Hadn't you noticed? Let me show you . . .'

Later, when they had finished looking at the drawings, Austin said, 'You've never thought of writing professionally?'

'Not seriously. Should I?'

Austin sat hunched over the table, arms crossed, head down as he thought about this. His son had done some quite respectable engravings. Austin had worried as to whether he was talented enough to earn a comfortable living. Now, when the knowledge was irrelevant, he knew that the realisation of even the smallest gift is more important than comfort, provided a man is able to accept his limitations. He did not know whether Ben had sufficient humility for that.

'You can turn a phrase effectively. It might be worth having a try. Don't dismiss it out of hand because it isn't profitable.'

'I'm in local government at the moment – with London County Council. I need all the money I can get if I'm going to escape from *that.*'

Austin looked across the book-lined room to the window with its view over cool green lawn to the Downs now swathed in blue muslin. 'I must seem to live rather well to you, so probably this advice will come amiss. But, believe me, money doesn't buy much that is worthwhile. It only makes mediocrity more bearable.'

Ben, physically weakened and lacking belief in himself, was not in a state to contemplate risk-taking. Who knew but that the mediocrity might not reside in himself rather than his situation?

Judith called that tea was ready and they went into the kitchen which was pleasantly warmed by the heat of the oven. The rest of the day passed quietly. Alice discovered that one of the advantages of having dinner was that its preparation and consumption filled that time in the evening when darkness draws people indoors to seek one another's company. When the meal was over, she insisted on washing up and Ben, who looked very tired, went to bed. Austin retired to his study. Judith, judging by the banging of doors and creaking of boards, had tasks to perform in various parts of the house. Alice, valuing this time of solitude, thought it just possible she might come to enjoy visits here, although, of course, she would never regard it as home.

Later, in her bedroom, she opened the little window and leant out to breathe in the night air. She could see the light of solitary cottages here and there – a good sight, after so many years of darkened windows. It was a moonless night, and she could only just make out the line of shrubs at the end of the garden. Beyond, although she could not see them now, were open fields and she imagined the breeze brought the earthy smell of them into the room. She hoped that one day she might live in the country again. Her mother and sisters were getting on with their lives. If only hers would begin!

The next day she went with her mother to chapel, and then to the station to meet the new arrivals. Claire hove into sight like a galleon, the loose clothes billowing before her, while Terence bobbed protectively around her, the sun flashing signals from his hornrimmed glasses. Louise was not with them.

'When is the baby due?' Alice asked her mother.

'Not until July.'

'Goodness!'

After she had been eased into the car, Terence told them how astonishingly well Claire was, and Claire said what a pity it was that most women had forgotten that childbearing was natural. Her red hair was more fiery than ever, and her usually pale face glowed with health and contentment.

'I wondered if I should call on Uncle Harry – after all, they live quite near,' she said.

Judith thought it ominous that she refrained from mentioning her Aunt Meg. Claire had a habit of eliminating those people who had offended her. One might have thought Meg to have the greater cause for offence, since Harry had been unduly fond of Claire.

'You can telephone Aunt Meg and see if it is convenient for you to go. I have no idea what she will say. She hasn't been in touch with me since I came down here.'

Claire looked bewildered, as if the mention of Aunt Meg was an irrelevance. She said, 'I'm sure Harry would like to see me.'

'If Aunt Meg agrees, you can certainly go. But you won't be able to do anything else,' Judith told her. 'We only have a limited amount of petrol, and Austin was planning to take you up on the Downs after lunch.'

Claire, who hated being presented with choices, appealed to Terence. 'What do you think I should do?' But Terence had no wish to solve this particular problem for her. As far as he was concerned, he had enough to cope with in the way of family without the introduction of Uncle Harry, who, he gathered, had been Claire's guide and mentor. Terence was disposed to dislike Uncle Harry.

'How does Austin manage to get petrol?' he asked Judith. He found the Rover offensive enough, without black market implications.

'We've been saving it up for this weekend. Usually, Austin cycles to the station. He's rather proud of how fit it makes him feel! And I think he enjoys the incongruity of the briefcase strapped to the handlebars. At first, he insisted on carrying manuscripts in a canvas bag – but after one was almost ruined in a hail storm he had to give that up.'

They had left the town behind. Terence looked towards the green flanks of the Downs, smooth as if a sculptor's hand had stroked them into being. 'I came here on a scout camp once,' he said. 'There was a little winding path that led up and over, somewhere beyond the Bo Peep farm.' He had been wet and cold and miserable, but now saw the experience in a more heroic light.

'There are several ways up,' Judith said. 'Austin was planning to take you to Firle Beacon. It will mean a bit of a walk, but Claire could stay in the car . . .'

'No, I can walk, provided we take it slowly.'

'You must have your rest,' Terence admonished.

'It won't hurt to miss it once in a way.' She would take deep breaths of pure hill air and store them in her lungs against her return to murky Hammersmith.

Terence was silent, afraid that if he argued she would revert to her intention of visiting Uncle Harry. Alice, who had the same fear and very much wanted to go to Firle Beacon, changed the subject. 'How are things at school?' Terence was teaching. As his subject was economics he had had to go into a grammar school where he taught social and economic history at sixth-form level. 'The children are all right – very dutiful and middle-class, of course, like so many peas in a pod. But the staff are intolerable. They spend more time arguing about the effects of the 1944 Education Act than anything else. They are terrified of finding themselves in a school where they really have to *teach*.'

Claire made the explanation she always deemed necessary when Terence's school work was mentioned. 'He's only going to do it for a little while, until he has made his name in journalism.' How this was to come about was never clear, since he did not seem to be doing much in the way of writing. He appeared, however, to have the answer to most of the problems facing the country, so there was no doubting his vocation.

Ben was in the garden clipping the hedge when they arrived. 'You look as if you'll give birth to a double bass!' he greeted Claire affectionately.

'Triplets,' Terence asserted with pride.

Over lunch Terence asked Austin what was going on in the publishing world, and then told him what he should be concentrating on. He then asked Alice about her work, which led to his giving a lecture on the need to abolish all private education. He had in fact been to a county grammar school himself, but he spoke as one of the severely under-privileged.

'I agree with you, of course,' Austin said mildly. 'I only hope we shan't be in too much of a hurry. If we are planning to do away with all forms of selection, I would have thought we would need to think very carefully about how we are going to provide such subjects as Latin and Greek . . .'

'How many schools in fact teach Greek?' Terence leant forward as he asked this question, stabbing the table with his fork. 'And to how many pupils, answer me that?'

'Terence is so passionate in his beliefs,' Claire whispered to Alice.

Ben, who was not much impressed by Terence's passion, said, 'What I find incomprehensible is all this nonsense about secondary modern schools.'

'An interim stage.' Terence flicked aside Ben's remark, irritated at being interrupted.

'Interim nothing. These are the old elementary schools given a different name – same buildings, same staff . . .'

'You can't work miracles overnight.'

'Isn't that just the point Austin was making?'

'He was talking about Greek . . .'

'And if they think they can work miracles just by raising the school leaving age and calling old, out-of-date schools "modern". . . .'

The argument continued throughout the meal.

'Ben is very opinionated, isn't he?' Claire said to Alice when they had a few moments alone while they were clearing the table. 'I suppose one has to make allowances, after all he has been through.'

Ben's raised voice could be heard in the garden. Alice was acutely conscious of Ben, who seemed to rub on her nerves like emery paper. Yet although he provoked and disturbed her, she was quick to answer any criticism of him, and became angry if he was belittled. The Cornish being a clannish folk, Alice had a lot of distant relatives whose kinship would scarcely be acknowledged elsewhere. She had not been aware of her third cousin, Ben Sherman, until she was twelve and had been allowed to go alone to stay with Granny and Grandpa Tippet in Falmouth. Ben, who had recently lost his mother, had also been staying with the Tippets. He had been her discovery and she had been possessive about him ever since. Over the years he had been the recipient of her confidences, and although not always a sympathetic listener, he had usually taken her seriously. She repaid his interest with her loyalty.

She said to Claire, 'Terence had plenty to say for himself.'

'Terence is a teacher. He does know what he is talking about.'

'Ben had a much harder childhood, with no father to provide for him. His mother had to scrimp and save to make sure he had a good education. You know how proud he is of what she did for him.'

'Terence feels *passionately* about that sort of thing! He thinks it is wicked that some people should have to sacrifice so much to give their children what should be theirs by right. If only Ben would let him speak, Terence could explain that to him.'

'Ben admired his mother as she was. He doesn't want Terence to explain her labours away!'

A scratching at the door interrupted them. Claire opened it to admit the cat. She scooped up the animal and sat with it on her lap. 'Don't let's argue. It's so lovely to be together. I do wish Lou could have come. We haven't had a day out – the three of us – for so long.'

"'Why didn't she come?'

'Apparently Guy had planned some expedition for them all that he had forgotten to mention. Terence would *never* do that. We talk everything over together.'

While they were drinking tea they talked over the seating arrangements in the car. Judith was not coming and Austin would be driving; the Rover would seat two in the front and three in the back. It took them quite a time to reach a solution which had been obvious to everyone else from the start: Claire, in view of her condition, must sit in front where there would be more room.

They made a later start than intended because Claire insisted that she must inspect the herb garden; but at last they were on their way and could see trees, fields, hills climbing up into the sky like a Cézanne landscape. At some point along the Eastbourne road Terence suddenly announced that he had seen the path leading to the place where he had camped on the Downs.

'You mentioned the Bo Peep farm,' Austin said. 'That turning is further on.'

But Terence was insistent, and, since this was their day, Austin obligingly turned the Rover on to the narrow lane. There were houses ahead in between trees. It was possible. He was always telling visitors with enthusiasm that there was no end to the discoveries to be made in this area. In spite of his apparent sophistication he was a romantic at heart.

'I hope you are sure?' Claire was aware that the air of quiet certainty adopted by Terence was a sign that he wanted something to be true and should not be mistaken for knowledge.

By this time they had gone some way down the lane and Austin could not, in any case, have turned the car. The lane was narrow with high hedgerows on either side, so the only course was to go on. This delighted Alice who did not like journeys to proceed in a well-ordered fashion from departure to destination. She sat back between Terence and Ben, happy to renounce the pleasures of Firle Beacon in favour of the possibility of getting lost in the darker regions of upland Sussex. Ben, who was already feeling cramped and short of breath, wished they had made for Firle Beacon.

Through gaps in hedgerows they had glimpses of cottages which Alice invariably greeted with 'How remote!' and 'I wonder how they manage in winter.' She invested so much wonder into these remarks one might well have supposed her to be speaking of Tibet. They passed a gateway with empty milks churns awaiting collection. 'At least the milk van makes this path!' Ben said.

Twigs scraped the side of the car, which annoyed Austin; but when he drove to the right the bonnet was smacked by the broken branch of an ash tree. They came to two cottages close to the path and debated whether to ask if there was a way through – each interpreting 'through' in his own fashion, but Terence said he was sure the path went 'on and over' so on they went.

This is the place where the boundary doesn't run, Alice thought, where beyond is now and out of time. She had been there once and had forgotten about it; but since she returned from the war she had begun to search for it again.

The path twisted along the side of the valley, the hills rising steadily in front. There were sheep and cattle grazing. 'A good herd,'

Terence told them, although his vision was so limited he would have been hard-pressed to tell a sheep from a calf at this distance.

Austin considered stopping at a long, timbered house, its russet chimney glowing in the sunlight, and then, seeing broken windows and nettles high in the porch, realised it was empty. 'I hope that's not going to be allowed to rot,' he said, and fell to wondering which of his authors might be entrusted with its restoration. In an unguarded moment, it came to him how much his son would have enjoyed doing this. Further on they passed a telephone box and Claire said, 'Hooray for civilisation!' and laughed nervously. A mud-streaked dog erupted from the back of a farm cottage and dared them to descend from their vehicle and stand paw to paw. The lane, which had widened a little, now became narrower and began to climb.

'I thought it would take us over the top,' Terence said, with the slightest hint of relief in his voice. Ben gripped the edge of the seat.

Some three long bends later, Claire said, 'Anyway, it's been a beautiful drive. And a bit of an adventure.' Her tone made it plain that as far as she and the baby were concerned, this was adventure enough.

Terence had stopped saying much by this time. There was a large farm ahead, separated from the lane by outhouses. The overhanging hill was now so high it had assumed the proportions of a mountain. A path that might have been scored by a thumbnail twisted up it. Alice said, 'I don't think that can be our way, do you?'

'A jeep might do it,' Austin said. 'Certainly not the Rover.'

He was contemplating backing the car all the way to the Eastbourne road when he realised that the lane ended here in a wide, rough area of mud and rubble, a rudimentary turning space. They all laughed with relief, and Austin said it had been worth doing anyway. He had begun to turn the car when Ben asked him to stop for a moment. He got out and walked to the side of one of the outhouses where he leant against the wall, steadying himself by taking long deep breaths. When he came back, he said to Austin, 'I'll guide you round.' It was not necessary, but Austin did not argue.

As they set off again, Terence said he could not think how he came to make such a mistake.

'It *is* a very long time since you were here,' Claire said. 'And you're not a country person.'

Terence, wounded by this reminder of a childhood spent in Isleworth, took off his glasses and began to punish them vigorously with a handkerchief.

Alice said, 'It is nice to know these places still exist, so remote . . .'

Ben said, 'What *is* all this about places being remote? You make it sound like a virtue instead of an inconvenience.'

'It's good to know some places are still unspoilt . . .'

'Unspoilt by what?' He jerked his head in the direction of the farm. 'For all you know, the farmer beats his wife and children regularly every morning before breakfast.'

'Should we have asked the way at the farm?' Claire said anxiously.

It was some distance away now, hidden behind outhouses.

Austin said, 'They could only tell us to go back.'

The sun was dipping behind the hills and the lane was in shadow. After they had been travelling for a few minutes in uneasy silence, Alice said, 'You get a better view this way. The hedges don't seem so high.'

'It's the tilt of the land,' Terence told her.

'I wouldn't have thought that would have made any difference.' She had been bruised by Ben and now asserted herself. 'And anyway, it didn't tilt when we came.'

'You may not have thought that it did, but it did,' he said angrily. 'There was a distinct tilt.'

They bumped on in silence until Claire said, 'We haven't come to that telephone box yet, have we?'

'That was miles back,' Terence snapped.

'*I* didn't see it. And I don't remember the path being so rough, either.' She laid her hand on her stomach.

They went a few hundred yards further, then Austin said quietly, 'This isn't the same path.'

Ben said, 'It *must* be,' but he was not arguing, only puzzled. They all knew that they had not passed the telephone box.

'You couldn't have guided Austin down the wrong path,' Alice said to him. '*You* are so practical.' She had forgotten about stepping out of time and was beginning to realise they were going to be late back for tea.

Austin said, 'Well, we shall have to go on, we can't turn here.' The path began to rise steeply. Soon, they could see the roof of the farmhouse some distance below.

'This *is* the path over the top,' Terence said triumphantly. 'I knew there was one.'

'We're going in the wrong direction,' Alice said.

'As long as we get over the top, it doesn't matter which direction we go in . . .'

'And what do you imagine there will be over the top?' Ben demanded. 'Apart from more of this.'

'We can't go up there, can we?' Claire looked up apprehensively.

'It's not Everest,' Terence snapped. 'It's not even Snowdon. In fact, the highest hill in this area is only about 400 feet.' He had looked *that* up on the ordnance survey map before setting out.

The path twisted and climbed. The air was sharp. They stopped talking. When they were two-thirds of the way up the hill, the path came to an abrupt end. There was a low stone wall ahead of them and hedges on either side. It was quite impossible to go on, or to turn the car.

Austin wound down the window, letting in the fresh evening air. They all sat staring ahead, reluctant to believe in the wall.

Terence said, 'There must be a gate.'

Ben opened the door and got out. He walked to the wall and leant his elbows on it. Although the wall continued in a low semicircle as far as he could see, no broken stones indicated habitation, however ancient. Whatever had been here, the earth had long since covered it, so that there was only green turf clipped close by sheep. In Siam, where nature worked faster, the jungle cemetery where Geoffrey was buried would be a tangle of bright green vine leaves and young trees with long tasselled blossoms.

In the car, Terence said, 'Perhaps someone meant to build up here and then decided not to.' Practical explanations were important to him.

Claire said, 'I think we'll go back now.'

Austin switched on the engine and looked at the petrol guage. 'I'm afraid we're very low on petrol.'

'But we have enough to get us home,' Claire assured him tightly.

'And even if we haven't, the people at the farm will be sure to have some,' Terence supplemented firmly.

Alice, feeling the tension mounting with each utterance, said, 'Ben and I will walk down there.' She opened the door and stumbled in her haste to get out. 'It won't take us long. You just sit here and enjoy the peace.'

Austin called after her, 'There's a can in the boot. I'll get it for you.'

Claire looked out of the window, eyes wide with alarm. 'Alice, don't go!'

'I'm not going anywhere – only down to the farm.'

'You can come and sit in the back with me,' Terence said sharply to Claire.

But she continued to look at Alice, her eyes pleading for comforts long past.

Austin came from the back of the car and handed the petrol can to

Alice. She said, feeling suddenly conspiratorial, 'It will be a long time before you take all of us out for a trip again!'

'It will be a long time before I'm trusted to,' he said wryly, thinking of Judith waiting at home.

Alice walked away, betrayal sitting like a hump on her shoulders. It was the same feeling she had had on the morning when they first went through the gates of the Winifred Clough Day School for Girls, and she had said to Claire, 'You'll have to look after yourself now, and it's no use crying because I shan't take any notice.' At the little school in Sussex, Alice had been held responsible for her sister. But in this large school for over six hundred pupils, where Claire would be in the kindergarten, far removed from the classrooms inhabited by the juniors, Alice had imagined herself free of her sister's dependence. Now Claire was married and shortly to become a mother, but her eyes still spoke their need of her dearest companion.

'We're going down to the farm for petrol,' Alice told Ben defiantly.

'*Why* do we want petrol?' He had become like a child lost in a maze, refusing all advice, wilfully determined to find his own way out. In this instance, finding his own way meant making his own assessment of the petrol situation. Alice, aware that he must not be hustled even though she did not understand why, waited patiently while he went back to the car.

A bird glided overhead, its wings making big, slow-moving shadows on the grass. She began to draw together the threads of a story about a chance-found place in the hills where strange gods had once been worshipped – or, perhaps, a god which was her god seen through other eyes. The unknown god, long forgotten, but still present . . .

Ben was coming towards her. 'Are you happy now?' she asked.

He stood, meditating this, while she waited, legs apart, at ease with herself. She was wearing a honeyed tweed skirt with a sweater in the same pale colour, and her face was lightly ambered by the sun. The sandy hair, drawn back, disappeared into shadow behind her ears. He saw her as carved all in one piece – an impression she strove for but seldom imagined herself to achieve. It was the eyes which held the whole together, serious, considering, and – perhaps an effect of the level light – seeming to reflect, as unwavering water reflects the changing cloud patterns of the sky without itself becoming ruffled. It came to him as he stood looking at her, that this was the person in whose embrace he would both find and lose himself. Hereafter, she would thrust up, rooted as a tree from the soil of his imagination. He would always retain this image of her wholeness, even when it bore little resemblance to the fragmented person he encountered every day. His Alice was like the woman painted by a great artist, standing with upraised arms in an orchard, forever held in dappled light, or half-turned in welcome from a gate, the swing of the shoulders, the wind-combed hair, fixed for all time – or, at least, for all the time he had. Whether she could ever fulfil the promise that he saw of peace and refreshment, of mystery and fruition, it would have been hard to say, and perhaps irrelevant, since it represented his truth and that was what mattered.

'All right,' he said. 'We'll go down to the farm for petrol.'

He was stunned by the revelation he had had, and could scarcely reply intelligently to anything she said. And Alice, who dreamt of finding someone who would put all the bits and pieces of her together and present the finished work to her, sharp and clear as crystal, walked beside him, unaware, as she would always be, of his vision of her.

'This is beautiful, isn't it? I'm glad we came.' She swung the petrol can unconcernedly in the direction of the hills. 'I wish I could paint it.'

'Do you paint?'

'No. But I'm going to classes on art appreciation.' The lecturer had opened up a new vision of the world, and in her gratitude she had fallen in love with him along with the shifts of light and shade to which he drew her attention. 'The classes are held at the City Lit.,' she said. 'They get people who really know their subjects – Nicholas Medd and people like that.' Her heart gave a little flutter as she spoke his name.

To the west, the sun enflamed a huge cornucopia of cumulus, but to the east the thinning blue of the sky was hazed, composing fields and woods in the calm of evening. A solitary cow, dejected, rubbed its flank against a tree. 'I expect it has something wrong with it, poor thing – so it's in the isolation wing,' Alice said. The cow looked mournfully to the next field where its companions munched contentedly.

Now, the woods came close to the path; they had hardly noticed how close on their way up because their eyes had been drawn to the hills. The trees were pricked with green but underfoot there was a russet carpet of last years' leaves. A beaten track twisted towards a glimmer of slate-grey water. 'I suppose we haven't got time to explore,' Alice said regretfully.

'No.'

They walked on, leaving the hidden pool undisturbed.

Near the farm, Ben stopped. 'They probably won't give us petrol. Why should they?' The thought of approaching strangers was bad enough, without having to ask a favour.

'I'll go,' Alice said. 'I don't mind.'

'Certainly not.' He was offended. 'You wait here.' He took the can from her and strode across the yard. A collie rushed out and circled him, barking hysterically. Ben disappeared round the side of an outhouse and the collie came back to vent its considerable spleen on Alice, its yellow eyes calculating how far it might go. She stood her ground, suspecting that any move would be regarded as licence to bite. After what seemed a very long time, Ben reappeared accompanied by a lumbering, brick-faced man who called off the dog and shut it in one of the sheds.

It was apparent that the farmer and Ben were not on the best of terms, but Alice could tell from the way Ben held the can that it was now heavier.

'We are very grateful to you,' she said, in case Ben had failed to make this apparent.

'You've got to get down before you'll have any call to be grateful.' He was not appeased. 'And how you're going to manage that, I don't know. I've heard of some fool things in my time, but . . .' His voice rumbled into incoherence. His dog, snarling from the window of the shed, assured them that were he free he would have their guts for garters.

'Good for you!' Alice said to Ben as they made their way up the lane.

When they had moved out of sight of the farm, Ben said, 'I'll have to sit down for a moment.'

'Yes, all right.'

He sat with his legs drawn up, his head resting on his knees, his body clenched tight as a sheathed knife.

'I'll take the can up to Austin while you wait here,' she said, thinking that Claire would be getting in a state by now.

'*You* can't carry it up there.' He looked at her, outraged eyes making it plain that what was beyond him was out of bounds for her, too.

Alice stiffened. 'No, I'll be all right.'

'It's a steep climb. You can't possibly manage it. That can is quite heavy now.' Outrage had given way to that special kind of pleading which works on the premise that if a statement is made with sufficient assurance the other person will not have the insensitivity to challenge it.

Alice picked up the can and began to walk up the lane. After a few minutes, she was aware that he was following her; she walked faster, her heart pounding not so much with exertion as anger. 'I suppose he expects me to go at his pace,' she thought. 'But there are limits to how much one humours him!'

In the woods, night rose from the ground in holes of darkness, while above the tops of the trees smoke twisted briefly and was lost in the greying sky.

Claire, looking beyond the wall where Alice would set her story, said, 'What an awful place.'

The unknown attracted Alice, who was not primarily eager for answers – she had been presented with plenty of answers in her childhood and had not found them nourishing. Mystery drew her, not always comfortably, beyond the edge of vision. Edges gave Claire vertigo.

Terence patted her shoulder comfortingly. He wished that they could at least have turned the car so that they looked down towards the farm. He regarded Nature, when uncultivated by man, as essentially hostile. 'I wonder they don't build up here,' he said resentfully. 'With so many people needing homes, we can't afford this kind of waste.'

'Where would they get work?' Austin asked, tapping his fingers on the wheel.

'I'll have to get out,' Claire said. 'It's awfully bad for me to be shut in here all this time.'

'You'll catch cold,' Terence warned.

But she insisted on getting out, and stood with her back to the wall, from where she could see that all too soon the lane dissolved in shadow. The air was cool and seemed to have travelled a long way across nothingness.

Austin watched Terence's efforts to soothe her with wry sympathy, but he made no attempt to help. Terence would have to shield Claire for the rest of his life, so the sooner he learnt how to set about it, the better. Austin's first wife had been an anxious creature, approaching childbirth with fear as though there was something in life itself which might destroy the new life within her. Many people had said that the son was like her, but Austin had thought that though the boy was sensitive, his was a more robust spirit. Whether he had been right, he would never know now. Why, he asked himself, why? He had not thought enough about this loss, had put it away for safe-keeping, something to be attended to another time because one must not fuss. These deaths are something that happen in wartime, to be expected . . . And this acceptance was taken for mute courage. But *what* was it that had happened? A young man, gentle, rather dreamy, who might – or might not – have made a living as an engraver had been blown to pieces on a beach, leaving behind him a few poems illustrated with scenes of summer hedgerows and birds in spare, winter trees. In the name of God, *why* should it happen?

'What will we do if they don't get petrol?' Claire asked.

'I'm sure they will.' Terence was more resolute than he felt. 'I don't see anyone refusing Alice!'

'Oh?' Claire was not comforted by this. Praise given to someone else diminished her; she felt it physically as if something had been extracted from her own body to feed another's. 'Well, you don't know Alice. She isn't a bit reliable. For one thing, she doesn't have a sense of direction. And for another, she gets distracted very easily. Just now, she is probably mooning over the view instead of getting back here as quickly as she can.'

At this moment, Alice came into view, walking very smartly as if to disprove any tendency to distraction.

'All's well!' she announced triumphantly.

An optimistic asssumption. Until this moment, they had seemed to be walking on eggshells; now that they found themselves on firm ground, resentment could no longer be held in check. Claire was furious with Austin for not getting out of the car immediately he saw Alice. Being somewhat in awe of her stepfather, she addressed her irritation to Terence. 'Well, don't just stand there! The petrol has got to be put in. That was the whole point of the exercise.'

Terence, who was not sure whether the Rover received petrol in the back, front, or side, turned back to the car. Austin got out leisurely and took the can from Alice.

'Where is Ben?'

'He'll be here any minute. I got worried about Claire so I hurried a bit.' Her gleaming pink face was evidence of this.

While Austin fed in the petrol, Terence stood beside him, one hand stroking the bonnet, rather as if the car might take fright and stampede.

Ben came slowly towards them, exhaustion and humiliation making his appearance spectral in the waning light. 'I've been examining the path,' he said. 'It's not going to be easy to back her down.'

'I shall guide him,' Terence said.

'You don't know anything about cars,' Claire called anxiously.

'My father had a car.' He went on less truthfully, 'And I often navigated for him.'

Alice tried to make her peace with Ben. 'We'll sit inside. I think we've earned a rest, don't you?'

'I told you I had been examining the path. I shall help Terence to guide Austin.'

Austin got in and started the engine. 'It's just possible I shall be able to manage without assistance.'

But as neither Terence nor Ben was prepared to join their women-folk, the journey began with Ben to the left of the path and Terence to the right, each giving instructions. Alice thought it was like one of those strenuous male duets in opera where the tenor and the baritone contend for dominance. At some stage, the contention reached a crescendo during which Terence became particularly excited and, shouting to Austin that he was to take directions from him, leapt to the right to illustrate what was required and tripped over a boulder. In the moment before he disappeared from sight, he seemed to have as many thrashing arms as a starfish. Austin stopped the car, muttering under his breath, 'For the first time I have an unimpeded view.' Alice was convulsed with laughter.

Terence reappeared, crawling, his glasses hanging from one ear. Ben went and stood over him, as though examining an unfamiliar species of fauna.

'What *are* they playing at?' Claire was mystified.

Alice went into further paroxysms. Austin got out of the car and joined Ben. They both knelt beside Terence.

'He's hurt himself,' Claire said soberly. 'My poor love! It was my fault for being so beastly to him.' She got out of the car and went to Terence, leaving Alice to compose herself.

Terence had broken his ankle. For the remainder of the journey, Ben sat in front with Austin while Claire, who had become surprisingly matronly, soothed Terence. Alice made herself small and inconspicuous, as befitted one who had behaved like an over-tired child.

That night, Claire nursed Terence while Ben had nightmares as he tried to drive a truck through glutinous jungle mud, all the time belaboured by a guard shouting 'Speedo! Speedo!' Judith and Austin indulged in mutual recrimination – she accusing him of behaving irresponsibly and he insisting that her children were impossible. Alice, with the writer's horrid gift of detachment, had shuffled off the cares of the day, and was sitting at the desk she had sworn she would never be able to use.

It had just this minute occurred to her that her story must be told with clarity and simplicity because it was for children. She had not realised until now that she must write for children, who were the true inhabitants of the world of the imagination. At the beginning of the story the children came upon a cave up in the hills where a group of people, quite unlike the people of their own time, lived under the symbol of the fish. Subsequently, the children would search for the cave but never find it again; although, in the end, after many adventures, they would find the symbol quite by accident on an old stone unearthed in the garden of their own home. She had the beginning and the end, and was discovering that the real test is how one deals with the gap in between.

# 4

On a bright May day, the Drummond family had one of its rare reunions. To celebrate this – or, as Angus Drummond put it, to heighten the bizarre nature of the event – Mrs Drummond arranged a trip to Kew Gardens. 'Bunny does so love to get out,' she explained. During the course of an inactive service in the Royal Naval Volunteer Reserve, Drummond had only once been to sea. Unfortunately, on this occasion the ship was torpedoed and he had sustained an injury which paralysed him from the waist down. He had been a good-looking man, bestriding his hearth in the manner of a rakish country squire rather than a London banker; but now his body was heavy as lard, his face purpled with rage and strong drink. Mrs Drummond, who had been a meek, genteel woman, always ailing, had gained new zest for life each day of his illness.

Angus had invited Irene Kimberley to join him on this expedition. 'Though I warn you it will be fraught with danger.'

'It's difficult to imagine what ill could befall anyone at Kew in lilac time!'

'Let me tell you that on our only childhood trip there, my father threatened to drown Cecily in one of the ponds, and then insisted on spending a long time in the hothouses where I was sick and my mother fainted. The only survivor, as usual, was my sister Daphne.'

Irene knew more about the Drummond family than Angus realised. She and Alice had been friendly with Daphne at school. Although invitations to Daphne's home had been rare, there had been one occasion when they had gone there to play tennis and had witnessed a particularly unpleasant scene between Mr Drummond and the unfortunate Cecily. Irene had no difficulty in visualising his behaviour in the hothouses.

Angus did not usually talk much about his parents. So when he wryly suggested he would welcome her support on this occasion, she was delighted, imagining it to represent a new stage in their relationship. She paid particular attention to her appearance, eventually deciding on a lime-green linen dress which looked both cool and refreshing, and would no doubt have the same therapeutic effect as an application of eau de Cologne. Eau de Cologne was impeccably feminine, and she was aware that at times Angus winced from the keen edge of her mind.

They were to meet on Kew Green. When Angus and Irene arrived, Daphne and Peter Kelleher were already waiting.

'Mother not here yet?' Angus asked Daphne, who smiled in reply. He turned to Irene. 'My mother, as you no doubt recall, tends to be late.'

'She has a good sense of timing,' Daphne said, 'Never arrive before your audience.'

She made the statement quietly and without bitterness. Facts unpalatable to most people seemed to give her little trouble. A small, compact young woman, she still retained something of that schoolgirl mischievousness which makes every day seem glowing. Yet Irene thought that since she married she had become rather formidable. Or was it that as one gets older one realises that the 'funny ways' of one's companions are not superficial accretions, like a boil on the chin, but an integral part of the personality? Had they been right to laugh because Daphne supported Mosley and imagine she would shed such notions along with her lacrosse stick? If they had been mistaken in her, so had the school staff, whose only reservation had been that she failed to make the exertion necessary to outshine her companions. She had been accepted as a good all-rounder, equally able in the classroom as on the games field, but with a tendency to laziness. She had seldom bothered to rebel. Yet one had sometimes been aware that rebellion was not necessary for her because she did not take the school seriously. Certainly, she had found nothing there of sufficient importance to compromise her.

'There!' Daphne said. 'Perfect timing!'

Her mother had arrived, sitting well back in the driving seat of the car and holding the wheel as if it was a bowl of flowers which she had yet to decide where to place. Unfortunately, her judgement was faulty and she bumped the curb. Her husband shouted, 'That's the only bloody tyre you haven't ruined!'

Cecily darted from the car like a frightened rabbit, and was immediately seized with a fit of sneezing which rendered her incapable of helping in the business of transferring her father into his wheelchair. She lived at home in order to assist her mother, but Nature, recognising her inadequacy, had presented her with a series of minor ailments which effectively protected her from exploitation.

'Family only!' Mrs Drummond sang out gaily as the others moved forward to assist. 'Angus and Daphne are so good at this.' Neither, in fact, had found the time or the opportunity to acquire this particular skill.

Peter Kelleher stood to one side without protest. Irene, who had only met him briefly, studied him with interest. There was little chance of his resenting scrutiny since he seemed unaware of her presence. Really, she thought, he is just how an explorer should be, rough hewn in stone – or perhaps too pinkish for that – rough hewn in terracotta. The kind of sculpture one might expect to come across in a wild, alien region, with eyes focused on some feature of the landscape a vast distance away; in this case, the gasworks on the far side of the river. Irene did not think he was deliberately rude. When she spoke to him he answered her with courtesy, peering at her as though wondering what life could be like down there. She supposed that birds came into his line of vision more often than people.

'You are living in Norfolk now,' she said, in the absurd way in which one tells a person something which cannot have escaped his notice.

He admitted gravely that this was so, and went on to tell her about the house which they had bought near King's Lynn. He had almost exhausted its possibilities by the time Commander Drummond was settled in his wheelchair.

As they walked into the Gardens, Daphne said to her husband, 'My father is so unspeakably awful now. I suppose in some ways, he always was, but he had a certain grandeur. Why did he let this happen to him? Why didn't he kill himself?'

'You have the morality of an ancient Greek,' he told her, not joking. He was a man who made few jokes.

The Drummond family had been linked to the practices of the ancients by more than morality. Daphne said, 'Thank you for coming with me. I couldn't have come alone.'

He had no intention of allowing her to do this, or anything else for that matter, alone.

At first, all went well. The lilacs were at their best and Mrs Drummond quoted the poem in a high, fluting voice. Commander Drummond said the smell made him puke. Cecily began to sneeze and he shouted to her to get out of the way if she couldn't control her disgusting habits. She sat on a seat and wept.

'Should we stay with her?' Irene asked Angus.

'I think it's mainly the sneezing. She's a rather moist person altogether.'

Irene, who was constantly being told how much she missed as an only child, counted her blessings.

Peter and Daphne, who had fallen behind, now caught up with them. Mrs Drummond refused help with the wheelchair. 'You go on,' she said. 'Don't wait for us.' They took her at her word, glad to have the opportunity to talk among themselves.

Daphne told Irene about her new home while Peter and Angus talked about their wartime experiences. Kelleher had spent some time in Yugoslavia, a lonely and often dangerous mission for which he had volunteered because it offered the solitude he needed. Angus, with no illusions of being master of his fate, had gone where he had been sent. Even now that the war was over, habit made them careful of what they said. Angus mentioned a few of the people he had known, but Kelleher, whose most memorable experiences involved places and animals, did not respond.

They walked up the broad avenue towards the pagoda. Behind them, they could hear Commander Drummond complaining, 'What is the point of the thing if you can't go inside it.'

'It provides a focal point.'

'What do you mean, focal point?'

Mrs Drummond, who was not sure what she meant, said, 'Now, you mustn't tire yourself, Bunny.'

Daphne said to Irene, 'I want to have Alice to stay.'

'She would like that. You and she were so friendly. She misses you.'

Commander Drummond said, 'Well, don't say things you don't understand. Even if you are a fool, there is no point, focal or otherwise, in advertising it.'

'What became of that fellow Alice was so fond of out in Alexandria?' Daphne asked.

'Gordon was killed.' Irene did not add that Alice had found out, after his death, that he was married.

'I'm sorry about that. I always thought Alice would marry before any of us. What about you? Anyone of interest?'

'There's no one in particular at the moment.' Irene hoped she conveyed that there was no shortage of unparticular men.

Angus said, 'I still find I have nightmares because I repeat an item of news and then can't remember where I picked it up; whether it was just a newspaper story or top secret. My mind worries away over this kind of thing all day.'

'So long as you don't get involved with my brother,' Daphne said. 'He's a nice enough old thing, and I'm fond of him; but he's not the sort of man who is any good for a woman.'

'I've never given it a thought. We both like music.' Irene put up a hand to admire a rhododendron bloom and yellow pollen dusted her bare arm.

Cecily appeared, running down a path through the shrubbery, pink-faced and panting. She joined her mother and father, attempted to help push the chair, and was repulsed.

'I wish she would go off and live somewhere on her own,' Daphne said. 'They don't need her. My parents have never been so involved with each other as they are now!'

Irene, not knowing how to reply to this, looked at her watch. 'Half-past three. Would tea be an idea?'

'Yes, indeed. Let's wait another quarter of an hour before we suggest it. Then, with any luck, we shall be able to go home. And after a dutiful half hour or so, it will all be over.'

'You're not staying overnight?'

'Yes, but in town. With a friend of Peter's – Ivor Ritchie. Did you ever meet him?'

'The man who was with you and Peter and Louise when that café was bombed? Wasn't he badly injured on D-Day?'

'Yes, he had to have a leg amputated. But he's one of those people who, the more you take from them, the more they put into life. Unlike my father.'

'That's hardly a fair comparison.'

'I don't try to make fair comparisons.'

Kelleher said in reply to Angus, 'I'm a fairly solitary individual, so I don't talk much with anyone other than Daphne – certainly not about the war.'

'The war is still going on in my mind, I'm afraid.'

Daphne, who had glanced back at her parents, said, 'Where *are* we going now? My mother is looking uncommonly purposeful.'

The answer soon became apparent. Mrs Drummond was heading for the hothouses.

'Bunny feels the cold so now,' she called cheerfully over her shoulder. 'And this is one way of keeping warm.'

She proceeded to bump the wheelchair backwards up steps towards the house where the larger tropical plants and trees could be seen through a blur of steam. Cecily tried to come to her aid, but she refused help. 'I have to do this on my own most of the time, so I mustn't rely on anyone else.' Commander Drummond bellowed navigational instructions as if he imagined himself on the bridge of a ship, as well he might as he pitched and tossed. 'One more heave and we're there! Hang on tight, Bunny,' Mrs Drummond cried. 'We don't want you overboard.'

'I abhor hothouses,' Kelleher said to Daphne. 'When we travel I shall show you all this in its natural setting.' He called to Angus, 'We'll wait here for you.' He and Daphne sat on a seat, and Irene, who found humidity tiring and felt it would ruin her dress, joined them. Cecily said she had a headache and went to look at the pond.

Angus, following his mother and father into the hothouse, wondered why hell was not depicted like this, instead of with flames so Pentecostally bright.

His mother read all the labels on the plants, as if his father had lost his sight as well as the use of his legs. She was as impervious to abuse as to protest. Yet, throughout his childhood, she had suffered from migraines which could be brought on at the first sign of her husband's displeasure. Angus could remember hurrying home from prep school, terrified of what might have happened to her in his absence. As far as he knew, his father had never attacked her physically. But he had often hit Cecily, and had devised tests of Daphne's spirit which were usually carried out in the privacy of her bedroom. Throughout all this, Angus had tried to comfort and protect his mother, who constantly proclaimed her dependence on him. Now, she behaved as though he had ceased to exist. She was totally absorbed in her husband. 'She has been waiting all this time to be needed,' Cecily had explained to him. 'It has all been dammed up inside her, and now it just pours out over him.' Angus, watching his mother pushing his sweating father further into the jungle plants, felt she had become infected by his father's malignity.

On the pretext of examining a rapacious creeper, Angus let his mother go ahead. By the time he caught up with her, she had succeeded, with remarkable dexterity, in ramming the wheelchair between a palm tree and a plant of hideous fecundity.

'I don't know how you managed this, ma'am,' an attendant remarked, with what Angus thought was considerable forbearance.

'She does it because she is a fool,' Commander Drummond told him, 'And my son is too useless to lift a finger.'

'We'll soon have you free, sir,' the attendant said, pulling ineffectively. 'What goes in must come out.'

'As Antony said to Cleopatra.'

'Oh Bunny, don't be fractious.'

Angus said to his mother, 'How could you do this?' Sweat was pouring down his body, he felt he was made of wax which someone was mercilessly melting.

'I think I probably pulled a little too hard to starboard – or is it port,

I never can remember.' She had always prided herself on her vagueness; practicality was something shown by servants.

The attendant's efforts had only served to push the wheelchair further into the plant, so that the leaves now folded themselves about Commander Drummond's chest.

'This plant has prickles the size of a marlin spike,' Commander Drummond roared.

Peter Kelleher had come in to see what was happening. 'The simplest thing would be to shift you,' he said to Drummond. 'Then we can tilt the chair and get it out.'

'He's a dead weight, I'm afraid.' Mrs Drummond seemed resentful at having the problem so quickly resolved.

'I'm not going to be handled about like a parcel,' Drummond grumbled.

'Just for a moment, you are.' Kelleher parted the leaves of the plant in which Drummond was embedded and put his hands under Drummond's armpits. He said to Angus, 'You take his feet.'

Angus was sickened by the prospect of touching his father's flabby, helpless flesh. But by now a small, interested crowd had collected. He bent forward and lifted. It was Kelleher who bore the greatest weight, but Angus was shaking all over when they put his father back in the wheelchair.

When they had wheeled Drummond into the open, Daphne forced herself to come to her father. 'Are you all right?'

He looked at her. 'Are *you* all right?'

'Yes.'

'And that's all that matters? No pity to spare for me?' She met his eyes steadily. 'There isn't a grain of hypocrisy in you, is there? Not a single, snivelling, sentimental impulse. Well, you can thank me for that, at least.'

Back at the Drummonds' house in Shepherd's Bush, they talked politics while Cecily prepared tea. Cook had gone during the war, and the one elderly servant who did the household cleaning had been forbidden to prepare food since the day that Commander Drummond threw her offering across the room.

'Blow them all up,' Drummond advised Irene, on being informed that she worked in the Cabinet Office. 'Or lock 'em up and set fire to the place. Let 'em roast slowly.'

Commander Drummond was a man who had a particularly strong need to express his feelings physically. His confinement had resulted in a concentrated verbal ferocity which was not always a true representation of his views. When he spoke of shooting all the members of the Cabinet, or bombing the Lefties out of their lairs, he was concerned more with his own problems of execution than with actual shootings and bombings.

'And half of them are perverts,' he said, renewing his attack on the Cabinet. 'Any man who isn't whole, put him up against a wall and shoot him.' He glared, daring them to make the connection.

Angus made other connections. At the Nuremberg trials a grim description had been given of the destruction of the Warsaw Ghetto. Every block had been set on fire and when the Jews emerged from their hiding places and dug-outs they were shot. Those who preferred to stay in the burning buildings until heat made them desperate had jumped from upper storeys into the street, where, their bones broken, they had tried to crawl into blocks of buildings which were only partly in flames . . . As Commander Drummond spoke, Angus remembered that Stroop, the SS Commander in Warsaw, had praised his officers as people who excelled by their dashing spirit. He imagined his father would approve of Stroop.

'But in a confident, positive society, there wouldn't be any need for that, surely,' Irene was saying. She was a tiny creature, and looked, as she sat opposing Drummond, a miniature of grace and elegance. But any illusion of fragility was shattered by the enormous eyes which seemed to fizz with intelligence. 'It's only in a sick society that such people would ever gain a hold over the nation. Don't you agree?'

Drummond, who did not favour young women popping off like tonic water on his hearth, said, 'Go out into the garden, my dear. You'll see how quickly a weed chokes healthy growth if it isn't plucked out.'

Irene appeared to reflect on this objectively, while seething inwardly at the contemptuous manner in which he had called her 'my dear'. 'I suppose it all depends on what one regards as a weed,' she conceded. 'Mostly, it's something that *we* didn't plant, so it spoils the neat little patterns we make. I think every good gardener should be able to tolerate a few weeds. One doesn't want to become obsessive.'

Kelleher, who did not regard the extermination of weeds as symbolic of other ills, said, 'Our obsession for interfering with nature will eventually destroy our universe.'

'I thought the atom bomb was going to do that, according to some of our Leftist friends,' Drummond sneered.

'General Marshall said atomic energy could be man's greatest benefit or it could destroy him,' Irene said. 'You can hardly call a United States general a Leftist.'

Kelleher shook his head. 'Man has no need of the bomb to destroy himself. He can do it with his own hands if he has a mind to.'

Mrs Drummond said, 'Really, what talk for the drawing-room!' She looked sadly out of the french windows, regretting a world now past, which she had not, in fact, found halcyon.

After this, they sat in silence, listening hopefully for the rattle of crockery which would herald Cecily's arrival with tea. Kelleher had introduced a theme which none of them wished to pursue.

'What an afternoon!' Irene exclaimed to Angus as they walked towards Holland Park afterwards. 'Poor you, if you have to put up with that very often.'

'We all live on the edge of chaos,' he said.

The trees were in tender leaf in the broad avenue and Irene found it impossible to be unhopeful. 'I suppose we always have,' she said cheerfully. 'Perhaps we need to be reminded of it from time to time?'

'I can't accept confusion.' He looked without any lifting of the spirit at a laburnum spilling like scrambled egg over a brick wall. 'I need things to be capable of solution – that's what attracted me to cypher.'

'And to communism?'

'It has an appeal, I must admit.' He sounded as if he was idly considering its possibilities. 'A definite, clearly defined ideal – whereas all we have is half-truths.'

'You're lucky to have so much as a half-truth. Cherish it!'

But this involved an acceptance of the incompleteness of life which he could not contemplate.

They came to Norland Square where she lived. 'Thank you for coming,' he said, and paused, as if he would say something more. He had, at this moment, a look which always turned her heart. At one time, it had seemed to be the look of the deprived, staring at all the bright objects in shop windows which they know they can never own; now, momentarily, it was the look of the damned.

'Angus . . .' She shook his sleeve. 'You know, don't you?' Her eyes told him, without equivocation, that she would give him anything he wanted. But it was too big a thing for her to make the offer lightly; and he was daunted by the timidity he must overcome if he was to possess her.

'I'm a hopeless creature,' he said. 'You'd be better off without me.'

'Is that what you want?' she challenged.

'Of course not. I'd be devastated.' He bent and kissed her. There was no excitement in his embrace, that would come later when, in recollection, her own body would stimulate emotions he had not aroused but which she would gratefully attribute to him.

He stood at the corner of the street, watching as she went up the steps to her front door. He looked more sad and deprived than ever, but in fact walked quite briskly along the street once she had gone into the house.

By the time he reached home, it was of his father that he was thinking. His father and Stroop had now become one and the same person, a person who represented the corruption of the Western world.

# 5

Heather Mason was in London on leave. Although Londoners might think that life was not easy, Heather was impressed by the absence of any sign of real hardship. She was working for the United Nations Relief and Rehabilitation Administration and had recently been at a camp for displaced persons in Austria. Yes, she thought, looking around Leicester Square, dingy and gap-toothed with bomb craters, but with cinemas still open and people sitting over tea in cafés, Londoners were not doing so badly.

She made her way to the public telephone box where she consulted the directory and then dialled a number. 'Is that Louise? Remember me? Heather Mason, Claire's friend.' It was surprising how the hurt of that friendship came back now that she was speaking to Claire's sister.

Louise, generous as ever, said that Heather must come to supper. 'Come now. We'd love to see you.'

'I only got back from Austria yesterday, so I've got one or two things I must do. But I'd love to see you all later. The reason I telephoned is that I want to get in touch with Jacov Vaseyelin. Nothing personal, just that I have a . . . well, a message . . . for him. He isn't in the 'phone book and I wondered whether you would know where I can reach him.'

'He's not easy to get on the 'phone. But he's directing a play that is due to open at the Players next week. So you might find him at the theatre.'

The pips went and Heather shouted that she would get in touch again – she was not used to the telephone and always shouted in the hope of confounding the pips.

She looked up the Players Theatre in the directory. It was quite near, just off the Embankment. She had an idea that actors only rehearsed in the mornings, but perhaps, so near the opening night . . . ? She hesitated, willing to be convinced that it would be a wasted journey. I have to do this sometime or other, she told herself. Action did not usually daunt Heather. Her whirlwind entry into the Winifred Clough Day School for Girls typified her approach to problems; she regarded them as hurdles to be jumped. Tall, gangling, gawky, she had long legs and what she described as vaulting ambition. She was one of the few scholars from a working-class family who took full advantage of what the school had to offer while making only those minor modifications in her own personality which can be expected of most growing girls. More recently, in UNRRA she had worked in camps where other resources than high spirits and Cockney grit were required – and found. So why should she feel so daunted by the prospect of this encounter with Jacov Vaseyelin?

She turned in the direction of the Embankment. It was after five when she reached the theatre, but they were still rehearsing. In reply to her enquiry as to whether she could go into the auditorium, a harassed electrician said sourly, 'Do what you like. You can get up on stage and join in the mumbo-jumbo for all I care.'

They were coming to the end of the rehearsal and the cast showed signs of wilting. Not so the director. A frenzied puppet, mass of dark curly hair bobbing over forehead, Jacov waggled his head this way and that, imitating, mocking, eyes bright with derision. As he contrived to inject life into a play which struck Heather as a rather static affair, he coaxed, wheedled, was sarcastic, and briefly delighted. On several occasions he leapt with balletic grace onto the stage to demonstrate how he wanted an emotion expressed, a movement executed, shoulders hunched, a hand stretched out, fingers widespread. 'Remember,' he exhorted, 'This has nothing to do with real life. You are here to act, act, *act*.' Someone named Stanislavski and Jacov said, 'Very boring!' And to illustrate his boredom, he leant back in his seat, staring up at the ceiling as though his attention had become transfixed by something much more interesting which was happening in that shadowy area. The actors drooped until, refreshed by his vision, he condescended to give them his attention once more, hands clasped at nape of neck, rocking gently to and fro.

When it was over, he sent them on their way with an artful mixture of praise '. . . taking shape splendidly now . . .' and threat '. . . can't afford to slacken . . .'

The last member of the cast departed. Jacov remained sitting in the fifth row, bending over his notes. Heather walked up the aisle and sat beside him. He looked at her without surprise, perhaps thinking she was a member of the backstage staff.

She said, 'I'm Heather Mason. You probably don't remember me, but I was a friend of the Fairleys.'

He said, 'Ah yes, yes!' She could imagine him saying this to small-part actresses, the same false light of recognition in his eyes.

To spare them both further embarrassment, she said more directly than she had intended. 'I'm sorry to barge in on you like this, but I couldn't find your 'phone number. I work with UNRRA, and I'm just back from Austria.' She stopped. Perhaps it was because of his restless activity that, while directing, he had given the illusion of a big man, filling the rumpled pullover with ample flesh. Now, he had become a thin creature which had crawled inside it for shelter. Heather had the sense of this creature crouched somewhere in its woolly depths, only the eyes giving its live presence away. Its terror was unmistakable.

'Katia?' he said.

'Nothing definite,' she said quickly.

There was a dim blue light in the wings, and somewhere out of sight the stage carpenter was at work, monotonously banging nails. Empty cups and overflowing ash trays had been left on the edge of the stage, presumably for the cleaner to attend to. A hollow rumbling like an approaching tumbril echoed round the auditorium. The tiny theatre was under a railway arch. Heather imagined the train carrying people home to Shepherd's Bush and wished she was one of them.

She knew now why she had felt so daunted at the prospect of this encounter. She needed challenges and there was no challenge to answer here. Jacov Vaseyelin threw down no gauntlet. He is frightened of me, she marvelled; and it is not only because he fears what I may tell him. A fear that was centuries old looked out from Jacov's eyes. It was no use to say, 'I am Heather Mason. I've had an uphill fight, too. You have no reason to fear me.' Reason had no place in this. She was guilty because she bore no brand.

One of us has to begin, she thought, and said, 'Tell me what news you have had of Katia.'

At first it seemed he would not go even this far with her. Then he said tonelessly, 'I have found out that in 1941 she was at Buchenwald.'

Heather cursed her impulsiveness. She had little to add to what he already knew. Buchenwald . . . Once again she was struck by the absurdity of the conjunction of Buchenwald and the Winifred Clough Day School for Girls. To conceive of the same person having a role to play in both was a cosmic casting error. Katia had been four years her senior, and had the Vaseyelins not been Claire Fairley's next-door neighbours, Heather would have known little about her.

In those days, Claire had shared everything with her dearest friend. So Heather had learnt that when Katia visited her Jewish grandparents in Germany, she had secret meetings with a German boy whose father was a friend of Hermann Goering. Heather had looked at Katia with new respect. But all she had seen was a big, bosomy girl with a thorny tangle of dark gold hair, and pronounced sweat marks under the arms, who moved with a slow surging of the body as though she was constantly breasting new crests of emotion. Heather, who had been given elocution lessons in an attempt to tune her speech to the well-modulated pipings of her fellows, could see that only a cosmetic exercise on the Hollywood scale could have shaped Katia into the accepted mould.

She said, 'It's only an incident, I'm afraid. But I thought you ought to know . . .'

A train approaching the station blew its whistle. Jacov said, 'Give me a moment.'

The scream of the train whistle continued in his head. He remembered Katia on the last occasion he had seen her. She had been leaning out of the carriage window. . . . 'We're off!' she had said triumphantly, but it was the train on the next platform which began to move. She looked at it angrily, as though it was stealing time from her, and spat on the platform. Jacov was aware of a change in her. Hitherto, her precocious physical behaviour had invited experiences for which she was not ready. Now, as she turned her large protruding eyes on the people hustling to board the train, he was aware that her raw eagerness had been infused by a certain amusement. Her clothes were the same ill-fitting jumble of style and colour she had worn for the past three years; but now, her personality, presiding imperiously over this rag-bag, compelled it into her service as though it was her own distinctive livery. He warned her of the need to be careful. On no account was she to become involved with Germans, particularly German men. She listened without the resentment which was her customary response to all advice, her eyes continuing to appraise the people who would be her companions on the journey. 'You don't have to be so solemn about it,' she said. 'It's all a bit of a laugh. As long as you know that, you can handle anything.' She craned her neck, impatient for the whistle which would send the train on its way, carrying her beyond all strictures. When it started, she remained at the window, her head turned in the direction in which she was going. She had always rebelled against the passive despair of her parents. For her, things were going to be different.

He said to Heather, 'Tell me.'

'I see a lot of refugees in my work. When I get an opportunity, I ask about Katia. The other week, I talked to a woman who said she remembered her. She said they had been together on the train which took them to their first camp. That must have been a long time ago. I didn't know whether to believe her. I was even more doubtful when she said she remembered Katia particularly because she boasted about her father being a great concert violinist who played all over the world. Katia told her, "When they know that they will let me go." '

Jacov had become very still, but she was not aware of this. If she had ever heard that there was a Mr Vaseyelin who played the violin outside tube stations, she had forgotten about it. Heather went on, 'She said that at first Katia kept saying "As soon as they find I'm from England they will let me go." She said they had no idea how long they travelled. The windows were boarded up and they could not tell day from night. She said that, several years later, she saw Katia again at Buchenwald.'

'What else happened?'

'That was all she could tell me.'

'Oh, but there must be more. You needn't be afraid to tell me. My aunt was burnt to death by a mob in St Petersburg. They jeered and laughed as she died. I heard my parents talking about it. For months I couldn't sleep for thinking of it. Now I never think of it. It is better to know. There is nothing worse than not knowing.'

'But, Jacov, she didn't say any more about what happened to Katia. I don't think she knew. And, in any case, she was only concerned with her own story. She told me this bit about Katia because she thought it would interest me in *her*.'

'Then it may not have been Katia. There must have been other girls whose fathers played the violin.'

'No. It *was* Katia. She asked me whether Katia had a sister, because sometimes, in the railway truck, Katia called out "Alice!" '

He put his head in his hands. For a moment, a dark curtain had been twitched aside, but to reveal so little it would have been better to have seen nothing.

Heather said, 'Do you think I should tell Alice?'

'No. You mustn't tell her.'

And I shouldn't have told you, she thought wretchedly. He began to shake. Heather put her arms around his shoulders, and, since he seemed unable to do so, she cried. 'What can it have been like?' It was this stage of the journey that had a horrible fascination for her, not what came afterwards which was unimaginable – *this* time while you were still *you*, not a number, dehumanised, but a person who had gone to bed with plans for the next day. What could it have been like to find yourself herded into a truck in the middle of the night? Perhaps it was just cold and uncomfortable, and you worried about draughts, and whether you would have pneumonia by the time it had all been sorted out and you were free again? Did you take it stage by stage, this journey into oblivion? She could not believe you could step immediately from light into darkness. Jacov, his fingers gripping the seat in front, had no such difficulty; and perhaps what he imagined for Katia during that stage of her journey was worse than it had actually been. Or is hope an extra burden to carry?

He had been shaking so violently that it had become hard to snatch breath and he had a terrible pain in his chest. As the sharpness of his awareness of Katia diminished, so his alarm for himself increased. 'I think I am having a heart attack,' he said to Heather.

Heather, on surer grounds with hypochondria, said firmly, 'No, you've just worked yourself into a panic. Sit back quietly and take a few deep breaths. You'll be all right.'

Each concentrated fiercely on his indisposition. It is such a short time one can give wholly to another's tragedy. He gave a wretched sob. Heather said, 'That's better.'

The clipboard with his notes on it was on the seat beside him. He fumbled for it. Heather said, 'Won't the janitor, or whoever it is, want to lock up?'

'I have the keys.' He hunched down into the seat.

'You can't stay here on your own.'

He looked around him, surprised. If there was one place where he would be all right, it was here. 'I've spent the night in a theatre before now.'

'Well, you're not going to do it tonight,' she said sharply. 'You need to eat. Is there anywhere we could go?'

She was by no means confident of her prescription, but to her surprise it seemed that food was the one comfort he could accept. They took a taxi to a restaurant in Soho where he was obviously well-known. Apparently restaurants were akin to theatre for him. He made ordering seem part of a holy ritual, each act of which must be performed with due ceremony. The waiter played his part faithfully. Between them they created an illusion of plenty while studying a menu severely restricted by the regulations laid down by the Ministry of Food. When the food came, he gave it his undivided attention. One might have thought he had cause for celebration. But later, when they came out into the street, he shrank back in the doorway. 'Will you come to my flat with me?' As she hesitated, he said, 'For coffee, perhaps . . .'

'Only for coffee, no perhaps.'

She wanted to walk, but he insisted on taking a taxi. He did not like walking in a city at night, and had never learnt how to find his way from one place to another without difficulty.

In the taxi, he said, 'Why only coffee?' He made a practised gesture with his hands and did something rueful with eyebrow and mouth.

'I've got a beau of my own in Germany.'

'So far away?'

'No, right here, next my heart.' She produced a snapshot.

The flat was in Westminster, well appointed. He explained, 'I share it with a friend. He is away playing in America. We are seldom here together, fortunately.'

Heather looked round the room. Not only were the photographs all theatrical, but most were of people in costume, ranging from Regency buck to *Playboy* Irish. She could remember playing Bottom in the school production of *A Midsummer Night's Dream*. Even she, uninhibited as she seemed in comparison with her school fellows, had experienced a surprising sense of release when she put on the ass's head. Apart from the photographs, the room would have served as the setting for innumerable Thirties light comedies. At least she was seeing it in close up – normally her view would be from the gallery.

Jacov, who had absented himself to prepare coffee, returned draped in a long silk dressing-gown.

'Oh, very Chu Chin Chow of China!' she commented. He pursed his lips. On closer scrutiny, she saw that the dressing gown was old and in such a state of dilapidation that it would probably be unwise to wash it. Either he had pinched it from a theatre wardrobe, or it had been handed down through generations of Vaseyelins. 'I keep forgetting you're a Russian aristocrat.' She bobbed her head and steepled her hands in a mock gesture of peace.

He said, 'I remember you now. You were Claire's friend.'

It was her turn to take offence. 'I told you that when I introduced myself.'

'But it meant nothing to me then.'

'I was the common one the Fairleys were so kind to,' she said, and hated herself for it, because they had been genuinely kind. 'Do you see them often?' She longed for news of Claire, but it was Alice whom he had seen recently.

'And Louise? We all thought she was terrific.'

Jacov, who had made love to Louise a month ago, during the interval between a matinée and an evening performance, screwed up his eyes as though recollecting her in a more distant past, and agreed that she was terrific.

'I couldn't understand their mum marrying again. Isn't that odd? I used to rag Claire because they had such a special idea of themselves as a family, but it came as a right old shock to me. English people are all puritans under the skin. Is that the way we strike you?'

'I don't know about English people. Only the Fairleys.'

His monkey face screwed up in an expression of grief so raw it had nothing of the theatrical about it. Grief on stage must be recognisably grief, however bizarrely expressed it must not make you look as though you had peeled an onion which was stinging your eyes fit to blind them. 'Mr Fairley was my first English friend.' It was what he always said to explain this rending grief whose origin he did not himself understand.

If I'm not careful I'm going to stay here comforting him, Heather thought. And I bet there's only one kind of comfort he understands – *and* I don't suppose he has to exert himself overmuch to get it. She gulped down her coffee and got up. 'What you need is a strong drink and a couple of aspirins before you go to bed.'

*That* was monstrously inadequate advice considering the circumstances, she thought as she strode along Victoria Street. But, considering the circumstances, what was there to say?

Ten minutes later, Jacov was sitting in a taxi. The theatre was empty when he got there and he could not find the light switch. He fumbled his way to the auditorium and thence to the lighting box. But when he touched the switch, no lights came on. The main switch had been turned off. He had now become quite disorientated. There was no crack of light. However long he remained here his eyes would not make out so much as a wrinkle in this enveloping blackness, certainly there would be no outline of seat or exit door or proscenium arch. He started to shuffle, hoping to make his way to the stage door, but after a time he realised he was in fact going down one of the aisles. He sat on the floor which he soon realised was a mistake because now that he was still he was aware of the thunderous pounding of his heart. He was also aware that he was quite alone, as isolated as an explorer in the middle of an empty continent. No, that was fanciful; this continent had no contours and he had no form. He held up his hand, but saw nothing. If comparisons must be made, he was a man who had fallen down a well. If he was not to die here and now of a heart attack, he must remain absolutely still. He tried to remember the opening lines of the play. No words came. He pressed his face against the side of a seat and terrorised himself into oblivion. The cleaner discovered him the next morning. The doctor at the hospital told him severely, 'You worked yourself into a state of hysteria. Didn't you realise you had a lighter in your pocket?' He recommended a week's rest, which was the last thing Jacov needed.

Heather telephoned Alice at her office the next day. 'Louise gave me your number. She said it was all right to ring you. I wondered if we could have lunch.'

'I can't leave here until one,' Alice said, eyeing Mr Hadow who was snuffling disapproval. 'But I'd like to see you.'

'One o'clock then. I'll meet you outside. It will give me time to sunbathe in St James's Park.'

It was a bright day and all of Heather's exposed parts, face and neck, arms and legs, were scalded salmon pink by the time Alice came out of the office, looking very composed with her hair parted in the middle and drawn back, and wearing a brown linen dress which did not suit her colouring. They greeted each other a little awkwardly. Heather had been Claire's friend and not, therefore, a person to be taken seriously, certainly not a companion for oneself. It is difficult, however, to maintain an older sister attitude walking beside someone so much taller than oneself, and by the time they reached the café in Great Smith Street Alice had become less dignified.

'I thought you were going to university,' she said, when they had squeezed into a corner table. 'Then, the next I heard, you were driving ambulances.'

'I was going to Bristol. But it didn't seem right, somehow, with a war on. Then, when the war was over, it seemed too late. It's upset my dad. He was so proud of my scholastic achievements he thought I'd become a vice-chancellor! There's going to be no stopping our lass, he told our neighbours.'

'How is your dad?'

'He's a local councillor now. We all tease him he'll become the mayor if he doesn't watch out. He says if he does they'll have to get a smaller car. He's not going to be driven round in a hearse! What do you make of local government?'

'It's so dull, Heather! We had the most awful fuss this morning because someone had done a lot of letters for secondary heads using pink paper for the copies when it should have been yellow. Pink is for primary schools.'

'And that matters?'

'The general office is in a state of dementia!'

The waitress came bearing vegetable hotpot for Alice and spam fritters for Heather. When she had gone, Heather said, 'There were lots of men clambering up poles and lamp-posts in Whitehall. What's happening?'

'They are preparing for the Victory Parade. I meant to go away. I've seen enough of people in uniform to last me a lifetime. But the Wren friend I was going with has changed her mind at the last minute. Now she wants me to stay with her, because she has found an unattached male and dare not let him out of her sight for as much as a day. I stayed in her house once before and nothing would persuade me to do it again.' Alice shuddered at the memory of her visit to the home of Felicity Naismith.

'I'd like to get away,' Heather said. 'Could I come with you instead?'

She thought Alice might consider this presumptuous, but in the WRNS Alice had become used to going on forty-eight-hour leave with anyone who happened to be off duty, so she agreed readily.

When Alice returned to the office Mr Hadow was at a committee meeting. She had had a bigger lunch than usual and felt sleepy. She was also depressed. This was probably because her period was due, but the fact remained there was quite a lot to be depressed about. She wished she had thought of trying to get into UNRRA. She read through the minutes she was to stick in the Secondary Education Sub-Committee minute book. Attached to the minutes was a report on secondary education, listing the sins of the grammar schools, not least among which was the emphasis placed on character building. Multilateral, or comprehensive, schools were not going to need to do this; apparently simply by *being* they would effect a fundamental change in the human condition. The language was very persuasive and it was difficult to resist the conclusion that her own schooling, with its emphasis on standards and values, had been harmful; and that the ideal of service to others had been a form of atonement, something to be undertaken in order to justify being more fortunate than other people.

She looked out of the window and was aware once more of being watched by girls in a room in the adjacent wing. She waved and they turned their heads away and began to busy themselves with bits of paper; one of them reached for a telephone. 'Well, that's got them moving!' Alice thought, reaching for the glue.

She was not good at sticking in minutes and was glad when a girl from the general purposes section came in. 'I always make them corrugated however hard I try,' she said sadly.

'You need to press down from the centre and then ease the page outwards.'

It was too late for the first two pages, but the advice worked wonders for the remainder. Her companion watched her. Peggy Trotton had been a Waaf, and she and Alice had become friendly and often exchanged reminiscences of their war service.

'The first warm day,' Peggy said, 'and they are all grumbling about the heat! Mr Stubbings came in and told them they should have been in India. When he had gone, they all began to tell their bomb stories, just to make it clear who suffered most.' She picked up a piece of blotting paper. 'I should put that between the pages if I were you. You've been a bit heavy-handed with the glue.'

They looked out of the window. Thanks to the adjacent wing, the room was always in the shade, but they could see sunlight on the roof of Westminster Abbey.

The telephone rang. 'Have you got Miss Trotton with you?' a woman's voice asked accusingly.

'Yes, she's been helping me with the minutes.'

'My dear girl, if you have any difficulties you must ask Mr Hadow about them. I need those figures urgently.' The receiver was put down.

'What figures does she want?' Alice asked.

'The number of lettings of secondary school halls in the three years prior to the war – because the wartime figures won't be representative. It means looking up the minute books for those years, and it will take all the afternoon. You can tell her that if she rings up again.'

'Why does she want to know?'

'The caretakers are on about it. And in order to prove they are being unreasonable we have to go back to 1936.'

Alice hunched over her desk. 'My soul will shrivel up if I stay here. I can feel it happening already.'

'It's not your soul you have to worry about. Do you realise all the kids here think there is something odd about us? We have had the greatest opportunities known to womankind and we *still* haven't found a husband.'

Alice had this thought in her mind as she entered the City Literary Institute that evening. The seating pattern in the room where her course was held had been established in the autumn and was rigorously adhered to. The seats at the front were occupied by those who wished to impress the lecturer with their keenness, and the ones at the back by those who sought to demonstrate their nonconformity. The seats under the window had been taken, not because of the view (the window sills were too high to allow of any view) but because the radiators were situated here. There remained the seats in the middle and by the door. Alice sat in the middle, a position in life to which she was accustomed.

'I don't like Raphael,' the American woman in front of Alice confided. 'But I just know he's going to win me over. He's so positive, isn't he?'

'At least he will tell us what we should look out for.' Alice agreed with the judgement passed on the lecturer, but was not prepared to commit herself to Raphael, whom she imagined to belong to the parted lips, rolling eyes school of religious art. In a few minutes, she was marvelling at the gentleness in the face of the madonna, the differentiation between the unformed body of the child and the body of the woman. The lecturer had a mop of dusty, lemon-coloured hair and a little pointed face which also had a lemon hue. He had very pale eyes and grey teeth. He looked as though he had never been in a strong light. But he had such enthusiasm one could only imagine he daily drained himself of vitality to give to others. 'Be grateful!' he squeaked excitedly, pointing to the picture on the screen. 'Here is a human hand – a thing of flesh and bone! Four hundred years later you will see paintings by much-admired artists where the hands are like blocks of wood! Here is drapery which is not only different in texture from the flesh, but different in kind from other drapery. It is silk, not wool, or lace . . .' Even so, he admitted when he had finished for that evening, 'Raphael is not entirely to my taste.'

'But you did him justice, that is what I admire so much!' Alice told him later when they had coffee in a dingy café near by.

'One must never encourage people to sneer at a great artist. To sneer is easy. People love to find flaws, it makes them feel clever – and safe. They stand in front of a Rubens and are affronted because the women are huge, and then pass on to complain that Botticelli's colours are cold. But ask them what is good, and most of them are dumb.'

They sat talking about art for nearly an hour. He was interested in her way of looking at paintings, while she assumed him to be interested in her.

The weekend with Heather was quite successful in spite of the fact that it rained most of the time. They stayed in a small inn on the edge of marshland and spent the days wading through mud. Heather was a good companion, able to laugh at misadventure – quite a clown, in fact, singing the Great War songs and making them comic, yet sad. In their more serious moments they talked about their wartime experiences and the difficulty of settling down.

'After all,' Alice said, 'it's not as if we had settled before we went away. We hadn't made a start. The war postponed it.'

Heather, who was going back to Austria in a week's time, said, 'I can't imagine starting anything over here. There is so much to be done in Europe.'

Alice could feel dampness seeping through the seams of her jacket. 'I hope there's something hot for supper,' she said.

The inn was named The Welcome Stranger. This is what we are, Alice thought, as they trudged towards it in driving, misty rain, Heather singing 'Laddie in Khaki'. We are strangers to be given a welcome on arrival, who will the next day set out on our journey, strangers still.

This thought rather appealed to her. Perhaps she could make a book out of it, set in a marshy, undefined landscape – a Hermann Hesse sort of thing. One would have to find endless variations on the theme of misty marshland, of course, if it was not to become monotonous. It would be quite a challenge.

There was little time for such a challenge in the months which followed. At the beginning of July Claire gave birth to twin girls and her family was called into immediate service. Quite apart from the help needed with the babies, there was the question of finding more suitable living accommodation. Even in the first days of their marriage, the room at the top of a Victorian house in a seedy part of Hammersmith had seemed unacceptable to Claire and Terence. Now it was quite intolerable, and much against their will, they had to accept the hospitality of Claire's Aunt May, who lived not far from Louise in Notting Hill.

Alice entered into the house-hunting with zeal, often going off on her own at weekends to report on accommodation in Richmond, Ealing, Twickenham, Kew, and all the other places which Claire and Terence had previously said were quite unthinkably suburban, and which now seemed so eminently desirable. While she made sensible reports on her investigations, she nevertheless found herself more often asking, 'Could I live here?' than considering the needs of Claire and Terence. She endowed each small house with a personality of its own, and she wrote a series of short stories, some amusing, some disturbing, all on the theme of the house choosing its partner. The stories flew from her pen, something she felt any seriously-intentioned writer should frown upon. Nevertheless, they read well, and one evening when she felt particularly reckless, she put them in a large envelope and sent them to a publisher. Within a month they had been accepted. Alice was astonished that anything conceived so light-heartedly should be accepted with apparently equal lack of reflection. She sat in the book-lined room of the fiction editor and studied the woman for any sign of mental instability.

'What are you writing now?' There was no doubting the alert professional interest.

'I'm half-way through a children's book.'

This was received without a great deal of enthusiasm. 'You hadn't thought of a novel?'

Alice, thinking with shame of the Hermann Hesse novel still waiting in her drawer, said she hadn't yet 'got down' to it.

'There's one story here that I thought had the makings of a novel.' She thumbed through the typescript. 'The one about the rather silly girl, whom you make so amusing, who is always planning new lives for herself and never gets beyond the first chapter. One can see her life as a series of first chapters.'

Alice, already a third of the way through her own life, said she would think about it, although she was determined that this was one theme she would not pursue.

'I think you could make it very funny.'

Irene had suggested she might write about local government because she could make it funny. No one took her seriously except herself.

# 6

In September, Joseph Tippet died, sitting in the armchair by the window where for far too long he had been imprisoned by arthritis. He had never complained. 'I'm used to living in cramped spaces,' he had said. His eyes had grown so weak that it was doubtful whether he could see beyond the roofs of Falmouth to the blue waters of the Carrick Roads. But his memory was not impaired, and as he stared out of the window he saw as if it was yesterday the grain ships loading in the harbour. 'I'm going to sail in a clipper when I grow up,' he had told one of the old seamen. 'Then you'll have to look lively, lad,' the old man had said sadly. And, indeed, Joseph had spent most of his life in steam ships.

'He never really understood life on shore,' Ellen Tippet said to Ben, who had come to Falmouth to stay with her. 'I miss him – though goodness knows, he was seldom here in body, let alone soul. I miss having someone to meddle with, I suppose that's the truth.'

Ben's maternal Grandfather had been Joseph's cousin. It was not a near relationship, but Ben had few close relatives. His American father had gone down on the *Lusitania*, and Ben knew little of the American side of the family. His mother, an only child, had been orphaned in her teens. Ben had cherished the Tippets.

'You've got all your children and grandchildren,' he said. To him this seemed riches enough. Three of the grandchildren could be heard quarrelling outside the window where they had been put to work weeding the flower border.

'I'm a burden to my children.' Sitting by the window in Joseph's armchair, she might have been engraved in the glass, there was so little of her and that so brittle. 'They'd like to put me in a home. Except for Judith. She and that new husband of hers came to the funeral. She thought I could manage – but then I'm no problem to her; she's so far away it won't be her has to come in each day to make sure I haven't had a fall.'

Ben said furiously, 'Don't you let them put you away! Shutting you up in a home, saying it's for your own good, when all they want is to get on with their lives without having you on their conscience!

You've lived a long time and you've earned the right to die in your own way. If you burn yourself alive, or fall down the stairs and break your neck, so what? If you're happier living on here and taking the risk, that's your decision.'

The blue eyes considered him as if he was a very distant object, rather than a distant relation. 'That sounds more like you. I was beginning to be afraid you had lost all your fire.' Ben groaned and put his face in his hands, a gesture only half-mocking. He had come to stay with Ellen Tippet in her time of trouble because he had had some idea of repaying her for her goodness to him after his mother's death. It had been a mistake to think of giving comfort: what he should have remembered was Ellen's ability to discomfort. She had the gift of seeing the future. Only the other day Ben had pointed with approval to work being carried out by a young couple on a cottage near by. Ellen had shaken her head and said, 'There will be too many tears in that house.' He had spent the first few days of his stay avoiding personal discussions as much as possible. Now, it seemed, he had given her the opening she needed.

'War gave you a bit of a jolt, didn't it?' She dismissed the years in prison camp as if they had been an isolated incident. 'You thought you had the world in the palm of your hand before you went to be a soldier.'

'Be that as it may, I know that I can't go back to the Bar.'

'I could have told you you wouldn't make your living at the Bar.'

'As I recall you did tell me, more than once.'

'Well, you've been brought to the truth of it now.' She made it sound as if the whole Malayan campaign had been fought for no other purpose.

'A hard way to learn,' he said wryly.

'But you're one will only learn the hard way.'

'And you would like to smooth my path by telling me where it is leading?'

She settled back in her chair, face calm, eyes remote as they always were when she was exercising her gift. 'No one will ever smooth your path for you. But I'll tell you what I see, though you won't accept it now. They told you at school you had the makings of an advocate, didn't they? So you thought you were going to be the Attorney General. But that won't be the way of it. It won't be court appearances and rich rewards for you. I see you working for other people.'

'I'm doing that now.'

'No, I don't mean being employed by other people. I mean working for people who need you, not people who can pay you. I see them. But not very clearly.' She closed her eyes, not in order to see the more clearly, but because she was tired.

'In another age, you'd have been burnt as a witch,' he told her fondly.

'I'd have had a fine time first, though. People paid more attention in those days.'

'You would have enjoyed stirring up trouble?'

'Not trouble, so much. But people need stirring up. Look at what happens to most of them. Men particularly. Dead wood by the time they're forty.'

'Joseph wasn't. He had a good life while he was at sea. He said to me once, the sea was unpredictable, it never let you feel you had mastered it, so you must always be on the alert.'

'I don't know about that.' Joseph had been too much a part of her life's history for her to be able to see him as clearly as she saw others; and, in any case, he had had two lives, about one of which she knew nothing. Perhaps as a protest against this limitation of her powers, she made one of those lightning raids into other people's territory which had earned her more respect than liking. 'But I do know it's not like you to give up something you've set your heart on just because you've had a few tumbles. You're the sort to pick yourself up and fight harder than ever. So there's some good reason why you aren't going back to the Bar.'

'I've had more than a few *tumbles*. They only bruise the body.'

She shook her head. 'I know your nerves are all to pieces, and you're very sorry for yourself. But you're the kind who pulls through. Provided you want to pull through. So why don't you want to?'

'Success was what I wanted.' He resigned himself to her. Why else had he come, knowing her as he did? It must have been some need of her strange wisdom which had brought him back here. 'I owed it to my mother. She worked all the hours God gave to give me a chance.'

She nodded. 'She had your life planned for you, and no mistake.'

He reacted angrily to the implied criticism. 'She wanted me to have a better life than she had. That's what most parents want for their children.'

'Oh, she had nothing to be ashamed of,' Ellen said peaceably. She hadn't liked Lizzie much, but no one could doubt either her good intentions or her indomitable courage. 'So why aren't you fighting, since you owe her so much?'

'It doesn't seem worth the effort. I said I wanted success, but it wasn't that. The really important thing was beating everyone else. I wouldn't have been a success in my own eyes if I had not been acknowledged as the greatest advocate of my time. And when *that* happened, I'd have felt cheated because the great advocates of the past were safely dead and couldn't compete with me. The dead have an unfair advantage. Does that sound a good way of life to you?'

She shook her head.

'When I left the camp in Siam, I was one of the lucky ones. And as the train took us away and we watched the jungle receding, believe me, I knew just how lucky I was. And I knew that life was a gift. It doesn't any longer seem a good idea to spend the rest of it running, looking over my shoulder from time to time to make sure no one is catching up with me.'

He got up and went to the window. The house was perched high with steep steps leading from the front door to the street. The grandchildren were jumping from them instead of weeding the garden as they had been instructed. One of them, a red-headed boy with long legs, was jumping from the third step. Ben said, 'Years ago when I came here, Guy challenged me at swimming – and he won. I spent the rest of that holiday working out why he won so that I would be able to beat him. But I think the thing which angered me most was that he did it so effortlessly. He was a natural swimmer, you see, he just gave himself to the water. Everything I did demanded effort.

'I suppose you could say that at the moment, I am giving myself to the water. Not because I want to, but because I haven't any choice. I have no energy, no ambition, I don't know where I am going or what is to become of me, and it doesn't seem to matter.'

Ellen nodded her head in satisfaction, as though in some obscure way he had vindicated everything she had said. 'You'll find your path when you stop thinking so much of yourself.'

The boy leapt now from the fourth step, seeming for a moment to give himself to the air before landing as surely as a cat on the pavement.

'You need to get married.' The visionary had departed and it was an old woman who spoke. 'Once you had a family to provide for, you'd soon sort yourself out.'

'Oh, I shall marry!' He spoke of it as an accomplished fact. 'But the sorting out comes first.'

'That's the way of it, is it?' She was alert again. 'So long as you haven't a particular girl in mind, me 'ansome! Men have this idea – always have had – that the girl will be there waiting while they do whatever business seems more important to them than marrying her, whether it's going soldiering, or sailing the China seas, or just sorting themselves out. Then, when they've proved whatever they needed to prove, they say she's fickle because she's found someone else in the meantime. Someone who put her first!'

'But the girl is always first!' he exclaimed. 'She is a part of whatever a man does. You were always a part of Joseph's life however far away he was.'

'And do you imagine that Joseph was always a part of my life when I was trying to see the children through school and worrying about the slates coming off the roof! Do you think Joseph was with me when I lay in bed alone night after night and year after year? If you do, then I'm sorry for any girl who marries you!'

'You're just like a woman. You make every conversation so personal.'

'Everything *is* personal. You didn't pluck all your ideas out of the air. They came to you because your father went down on the *Lusitania*, and your mother had to rear you on her own and made up her mind you weren't going to suffer for it. Hasn't everything you've been saying added up to that?'

He thought about this and then said, 'You've left out the jungle.'

'I don't know about the jungle.' She was suddenly tired and concerned only with herself and the past. After a few minutes, she said, 'I wouldn't want you to think I've had a bad life. Joseph was a good man. I could have done much worse.'

A thin wail rising to a rending howl indicated that one jumper had not been as sure on her feet as the red-headed boy. Ben went to bring in the wounded.

The weather was fine and he walked each day, pacing himself carefully, not overtaxing his strength. Sometimes the children came with him. He enjoyed their company, but was anxious when they roamed out of his sight or began to clamber over the rocks. When they went in different directions he worried at them like an old sheepdog whose powers are failing. After these outings he was close to tears when he returned, fearing he would never recover.

One evening, he told Ellen about the book which Austin's firm was bringing out in the following spring.

'Well,' she said, 'I daresay you'll feel glad when that's behind you.'

It was not at all what he felt and his face showed it.

'He sounds an interesting person, this friend of yours,' she went on. 'I can visualise him when you talk about him. I see him growing older, slow and thick-set, the sort who seems rather a dull fellow. Then one day when you look into his face and see that smile behind the eyes that you always thought so kindly, you realise there's something quite wickedly amused in it. He's laughing at all the people who are so self-important, rushing here and there at other people's bidding, while he's taking things easily, doing exactly what he wants with his life.'

'It was doing what he wanted that killed him. Drinking when he was thirsty and the stream looked inviting.'

She watched as the tears came into his eyes. She was too old for tears. 'You can't die someone else's death. And you can't live their life, either. You've done what you had to do for him now, and that's an end to it. He wouldn't have done any more for you. So let him be.'

'He was my friend.'

'Don't make a millstone of him, then.' He turned his face away and she sighed. 'I'm old. Once I knew so much about what the future held for people. Now, I can only see what they shouldn't do. I'm not much help to you. You'll have to find your own way.'

She could never leave well alone, though; and before he left, she said to him, 'Look, I've been reading in the paper about this man who is in prison in South America. You took up arms against the Japanese, but all he has done is speak his mind! Why don't you write to him? Who could do it better than someone who has been a prisoner himself?'

'Do you imagine that the kind of people who imprisoned him would allow him to receive letters?' he asked impatiently.

'You could find out. You're a barrister. You must know something about the law in other countries.'

'It would be a waste of time.'

'You said when you left prison camp, you knew that life was a gift. He's still in prison.'

Ben did not think of this conversation for several weeks. Then, when he met Angus Drummond for a drink in Whitehall, he remembered it.

'There's something I've had on my mind,' he said casually, after he had bought beer for himself and a double whisky for Angus. 'And you're probably just the person to give me the answer.'

'Don't rely on it.' It was not in Angus's nature to give answers readily and the nature of his work confirmed him in this reluctance.

Ben took the newspaper cutting which Ellen had given him out of his wallet. He passed it to Angus. 'Someone I know thought of writing to him. Not a bad idea, I suppose. Letters mean a lot to prisoners. But is it feasible?'

Angus read the paragraph, fingers of one hand pressed lightly against his left temple, shielding the eyelid which had lately developed a slight twitch. His mouth turned down fastidiously. 'I wonder why well-intentioned people get themselves so worked up over what is happening in places half-way across the world! I suppose it's because distance simplifies issues, puts everything into neat black and white categories. I don't imagine your friend has ever considered writing to Nunn May, for example.'

'Nunn May!' Ben looked at him in surprise. 'He wasn't put in prison for speaking his mind!'

'No, only for handing over information to the Russians that should be used for the benefit of mankind as a whole, not just kept in the hands of one country which will undoubtedly use it for military purposes.'

'Which the Russians wouldn't? He was a traitor.'

'No, a scientist.'

On this occasion, Ben was too concerned with his own objective to wonder at the inconsistencies in Angus's behaviour. He said, 'Nunn May had a fair trial. This man hasn't been brought to trial. And I expect a lot of people write to Nunn May. You're not telling me *he's* not allowed to receive letters, I take it.'

Angus, quite pleasantly surprised by his own recklessness, decided he had gone far enough.

'Can you conceive what it must be like for this man?' Ben asked angrily. He had not given it much thought until Angus's indifference, as he applied himself to his whisky, graphically illustrated the plight of the unknown man. 'I was a prisoner with thousands of other men. Our government knew roughly where we were held. We had a chance. And, in any case, we were soldiers. If the war went against us, we would lose our lives. This is the fate of soldiers. But this man has just dropped out of sight. He has ceased to be. This piece of paper may represent the last thing that is ever heard of him.'

Angus drained his glass. A defence mechanism in his brain had switched off the sound of Ben's voice as soon as he began to talk about people dropping out of sight. He said, 'The South American peoples are so volatile. It's no use expecting them to behave like us.'

'We may be the last people who will ever mention his name!' Ben might not have reached Angus, but he had succeeded in disturbing himself.

Angus handed back the cutting. 'I have no idea under what conditions this man is held.'

'Well, I mean to find out.'

Even when he had calmed down, he still thought it a good idea. The exercise would see him through a difficult period, and would pass the time more profitably than concentrating on his own miseries.

# 7

It was in Louise's home that the Fairleys gathered at Christmas. Judith and Austin came up for the day. It had not seemed practicable for Claire to travel to Sussex with the twins, and Aunt May, who always spent Christmas with them, had said she was too old to go far on Christmas Day, although she was only seven years older than Judith. The arrangement suited most of them; for various reasons, they had not wanted to spend Christmas in Sussex. Judith reconciled herself to their decision by reflecting that if she had had her children to stay, she must also have invited Austin's daughter and family. Austin told himself it was only one day, and with any luck there would be plenty to drink and it would all pass in a haze of bonhomie. At this stage, he was blessedly unaware that charades and a sing-song were an inescapable part of a Fairley Christmas.

After chapel, Alice went to a pre-lunch party given by a Wren friend who was staying in London. She had too much to drink and had to lie down in the afternoon, well aware that she had disgraced herself in the eyes of her family, to say nothing of having spoilt her Christmas dinner. The sleep made her feel worse than ever, and when Louise brought her a cup of tea, she said, 'You had better go to the bathroom before you are sick.' Alice hurried to the bathroom and was very sick; after which she had a quick wash and felt much better.

Claire was feeding one of the twins while Judith nursed the other. 'Breast feeding is very important,' she informed her mother.

Judith, who had found great pleasure in feeding her babies, thought Claire was too tense for the infant's comfort. She wondered why Claire found it so important to establish the fact that she was a splendid mother. Was it just part of her anxious personality, or had the children come before she was ready for them? Certainly, sitting here, red hair bushed about thin shoulders, she looked like a young girl playing at families rather than the mother of two demanding babies.

'You *are* getting as much rest as you can?' she asked.

'Rest! With these two!'

'If you and Terence want to get away for a weekend at any time, I'd be happy to have them.'

'Would Austin mind?'

'I don't think so.' Judith modified this statement by adding, 'The house is large enough for him to shut himself off if he needs to.'

Claire thought how different it would have been if her own dear father were still with them. She longed to say to her mother, 'Isn't it awful Daddy can't see them?' How deceived she had been in life! She had been given something that seemed eternally secure, a home, parents, unchanging love; then, suddenly, it was all whisked away as though it had been an illusion. She felt she had had two mothers; and the present mother could not be related to the mother who bent over her at night to kiss her, and was always on hand when she felt sick. She wanted a mother preserved in isolation from life, someone to whom she could return when she felt the need, but who barely existed when she had no need of her. She felt resentful and obscurely cheated. Her mother had adopted a role, played a part for a given time. She saw her father now as the one who was whole, complete, utterly sincere – also, dead, and so not answerable for any deviations from her idealised picture of him.

'I was surprised at Alice,' she said, still concerned with deception. 'Do you think getting her book accepted has gone to her head?'

'It was gin which went to her head.' Judith had been surprised, too. 'Goodness knows what she got up to when she was in the Wrens. I expect she will steady down now she's home again.'

Jacov, Ben and Irene were joining the party in the evening. Alice prepared herself leisurely. She had a pretty, champagne-coloured dress which she had worn a lot when she was in Egypt. Here, it looked rather colourless, and she was delighted when she remembered the shawl which Jacov had given her so long ago. As she took it from her drawer, she recalled that moment when he had displayed it for their inspection. Something for the dressing-up trunk, he had told them, looking round for a suitable guardian. They had wondered to whom he would entrust this glistening thing – to Claire, so young and eager, to Louise, so beautiful? How surprised they had been when he had chosen Alice! And how strangely it had disturbed her. She must have been particularly full of self-dislike at that time, because when he put it round her shoulders it seemed like a brilliant butterfly alighting on a cabbage leaf. But now, feeling its soft silkiness against her skin, she was no longer the plump, pigtailed Alice, but the young woman waiting eagerly for Gordon to call for her at her quarters in Alexandria. The heat, the smell of drains and flowers carried on the first breeze of evening, the sky brilliant as the shawl, shot with sequin stars – all this splendour no longer seemed alien, but a part of herself. She wished Gordon could have been here, sharing this day with her. He had been so *much more* interesting than Terence! The stab of jealousy reminded her how ashamed she was of her single status. But the shawl was a promise that wonder is woven into the fabric of life; and as she took it up and spread it around her shoulders, it seemed to have magic properties and she felt she was gradually growing into it.

Irene was preparing to leave home. She would be the best-dressed among the women, in a close-fitting wine gown with a gold brooch at the throat. She would be noticed, as a well-composed picture stands out among those in which the artists have been unable to resist the temptation to fill in all the spaces. A man, looking at her, might see she had no need of other adornment than the simple brooch; but he might also feel that she was complete in herself. She was twenty-five and already gave the impression that marriage was of no interest to her. She would not be the subject of pity.

She went to the door of the drawing-room, and seeing her parents sitting comfortably reading, she wondered if she really wanted to go out. What security in the depths of the familiar armchair and the steadiness of their undemanding love! 'Don't wait up for me,' she said. 'One of the men will be sure to walk home with me.'

Her mother said, as though it was a matter which must be decided among them before Irene left, 'What do you think Sir Stafford Cripps will have in store for us now that he is President of the Board of Trade?'

Her husband, a senior civil servant, said, 'Naught for our comfort, you may be sure.'

'I think he has integrity,' Irene said. 'He won't ask anything of other people he isn't prepared to sacrifice himself.'

'I'm sure he sleeps on a bed of nails every night,' her father agreed.

Her mother said, 'You had better make the most of this evening, my dear.' Their own Christmas fare had been rather stringent, not with the intention of self-sacrifice, but because Mrs Kimberley did not like cooking.

As she left, Irene could hear them discussing Sir Stafford Cripps, whom her father thought would have been much happier as a medieval monk. Her mother thought he might not have liked being indistinguishable from his companions of the cloister. Irene, who loved her home, thought the noisy Fairley party would be a poor exchange. As she walked along Holland Park Avenue she enjoyed briefly that moment of being between two worlds. But when, ten minutes later, she came in sight of Louise's home, saw lights glowing and heard laughter, she experienced a dread so intense it took all her will-power to keep her on course. She did not understand parties, with their fragmented conversation, spontaneous bursts of unprovoked laughter and equally bewildering displays of ill temper, children's hysterical excitement, and, worst of all, the sudden silences. She, who at home with her parents would sit for hours without speaking, found these moments of silence at a party full of menace. It seemed to her that at family gatherings one could be made more aware of the dangers of human intercourse than on any other occasion. And it was all so haphazard, she thought unhappily, like a mystery coach outing without a driver.

When the front door was opened by Guy, there was no hint of uneasiness in Irene's manner. She was perfectly capable of dealing with social occasions, provided they did not get out of hand. The presence of Austin and Judith, to say nothing of Aunt May, would ensure a degree of sobriety and good sense. She went to pay her respects to Judith and Austin. Austin seemed to her the most presentable of all the men in the room. She had a liking for older men because they had learnt so much about life; Austin certainly gave this impression. He responded to her sparkle, but could have wished for greater warmth. He was a man who valued warmth above all things.

Guy sat talking quietly to Aunt May, who might otherwise have been neglected. Alice, Louise and Jacov were discussing *Asmodée* which was in rehearsal again. Jacov, who would not have hesitated to produce it had he had the chance when he was with the St Bartholomew's Players, now maintained that it was too difficult for amateurs to attempt. Terence was playing a card game with James, both intent on winning. Catherine, Ben and Claire were playing a guessing game which frequently involved them in laughter which seemed to be at the expense of other people in the room. The dog was asleep on the hearth. This Irene correctly judged to be the early evening lull before the storm.

Soon it was announced that James had devised a variation of the murder game in which a detective would question each guest and must then name the murderer. Austin was voted detective and was asked to leave the room while a murderer was elected. He departed with alacrity to the dining-room, where he stretched out in the one armchair and closed his eyes. James wanted Ben to be the murderer, but Judith said, 'Austin will expect you to choose a man. Why don't you have Aunt May? He won't think of her. And Jacov can be a red herring.'

Well, really, I don't know . . .' Aunt May was not sure what was going on.

'You just have to answer questions and mislead him,' James told her, adding to her confusion.

She need not have worried. Austin rather fancied himself in his role, and there were several suspects who took the opportunity to give a solo turn. Long before Aunt May was due to be questioned, Louise said, 'We can't do this all the evening. Catherine wants to play charades.'

'Who was it who did it, dear?' Aunt May whispered to James.

'It was you, Auntie. Didn't you *hear*?'

'I thought I had been murdered.'

'No, that was Aunt Alice. You *can't* have missed that awful death scene.'

'Alice hasn't been herself today, I'm afraid.'

He plumped down beside her on the rug and stroked the dog's ear. 'I don't want to play charades. It's silly.'

Claire said she must look at the twins and took Irene with her to pay her dues of admiration. Guy poured drinks. Catherine and Alice went to find clothes for dressing up. Louise said to James, 'Catherine played your game, so you must play hers.'

'We didn't finish my game.'

'You should have worked it out more carefully beforehand.'

'How was I to know people were going to be so silly? Aunt Alice took so long dying we were late starting with the detection.'

'You should have known what would happen, they are your relatives.' She was in her element, glowing with good humour. If she had had her way, the house would have been full of people every day.

Later in the evening, as they gathered round the piano for the inevitable sing-song, she was proud to have brought so many of her family together. Even Guy's parents had come in briefly for tea, leaving soon afterwards because Mrs Immingham could not stand the din. She had sat most of the time staring in offence at Austin, whom she thought a man of the world – a term synonymous with the evil which filled the space beyond the confines of her own home.

Austin, who had heartily disliked making a fool of himself at charades, wearing a straw hat with the brim turned up to make him resemble Bud Flanagan, was surprised at how much he enjoyed this old-fashioned singing. He had a fine tenor voice and Ben a good, strong baritone. They did a spirited rendering of 'Oh my darling

Clementine' and followed it with 'Shenandoah' as an encore. Terence, who had been unexpectedly good at charades, did not enjoy the singing. He was separated from Claire by Jacov, who was making much of her, saying she was still his little girl. 'It can't be true what they tell me? You married, with twins? Never! You are still in your gym slip'. Terence was sorry to note that Claire seemed to find this nonsense very pleasing.

Alice said to Catherine, who was sitting beside her on the stool turning the pages of the music, 'What about you playing, love?'

'I shall make mistakes.'

'We all make mistakes, Catherine,' Guy said.

Ben said, 'Come on, Kate! It will be a change from your Aunt Alice playing everything in the wrong key.'

She responded better to Ben than to her father and tentatively began to play, soon gaining confidence. Alice sat beside her, turning the pages.

James was trying to make the dog howl to the music. Guy, about to tell him to stop, changed his mind. 'Shall we take him for his walk?' The dog's response was so immediate that James had no time to turn the suggestion over in his mind. 'We won't be long,' Guy said from the door. No one was listening.

It was cold. They walked in silence, shy with each other. The dog darted delightedly from tree to tree, occasionally pausing to wait for them, head tilted, tail thumping. The street was silent, and there was no sound of traffic from the distant main road. There were lights in all the houses, and where curtains had not been drawn they could see brightly coloured glass globes hanging from the branches of Christmas trees. But the sound of voices and laughter was muffled. On this day, life turned inwards, contained in numerous individual boxes, a discontinuous event. Guy and James walked like exiles in this mysterious vacuum. Or adventurers? The idea came to each simultaneously, without words. They felt daring, drawn together in a kind of conspiracy.

James said, 'Who do you think Austin would have chosen?'

'I rather think he had his eye on you.'

'I wouldn't mind being a detective.' They walked on for a few paces, then he said, 'Did you always mean to be an accountant?'

'I think I thought of being an actor at one time.'

They crossed the road and turned in the direction of the park. James said, 'I never know when Jacov is acting and when he's himself.'

'You don't remember the St Bartholomew's Dramatic Society, of course; it was before you were born,' Guy said. 'But I played quite a few parts with them.'

'What did you play?'

'Well, there was the artist fellow in *Dear Brutus* . . .' The dog had squeezed through the park railings and was barking to them to join him. Guy tried to remember the other parts, but all he could think of was schoolboy, soldier, accountant . . . As he stood looking into the park with his son beside him, he had the feeling of being someone else; someone he rather liked, but very shy, a person he doubted he could persuade to return to the house with him.

'We'd better go back or we'll be in hot water.' As they walked slowly homeward, he said, 'I don't see you as a detective, somehow. But I tell you what. If there is anything you find you *really* want to be . . . well, you must do it . . . or be it, I suppose I should say.'

'Yes, I will,' James assured him easily.

When they came to the house, the dog ran round to the back garden and Guy, who was reluctant to go inside, said to James, 'I'll get him.' He let James in by the front door and then walked round the side of the house.

Light spilled onto the lawn from the kitchen window. He looked up and saw Louise at the table preparing food. Jacov was standing beside her. They were not talking. Guy stood, waiting for them to begin a conversation, but they did not speak. Louise took sandwiches from their wrapping in a tin and placed them slowly, one by one, on a plate, while Jacov watched, so dark and close he might have been her shadow. When she had finished with the sandwiches, he put up a hand and pulled gently at her ear, and for a moment she turned her head so that her cheek rested against his hand. Nothing else happened. Yet there was such luxury in this leisureliness! The sureness of people who have no need to snatch at each other.

After they had left the kitchen and the light had been switched off, Guy stood in the garden, scarcely breathing in the effort to prevent thought forming which might fragment this image which would then pass like broken glass into his system. Slowly, he let the image down into that well within himself which he never disturbed; slowly, so slowly it went that not a ripple disturbed the darkness of its passage, and in the end it disappeared without leaving a trace.

The dog came up and sniffed his hand, then gently licked it. Guy patted the rough, wiry head. 'Come along, old chap. It's cold out here, isn't it?'

After Austin and Judith had left, taking Aunt May with them, and the children were in bed, Guy poured more drinks and he and Alice tried to recapture the febrile gaiety of wartime companionship; while Jacov told unlikely stories of his tours with ENSA and Ben remembered concert parties on board the ship which had carried him and Geoffrey to Singapore. Louise listened, tolerantly amused. Claire and Terence were obviously ill at ease. Irene joined them and encouraged them to talk about their plans for the twins, which were surprisingly detailed considering the age of the infants.

'It was good of you to look after Claire and Terence,' Alice said, when she bade Irene farewell.

They had, in fact, been her protection, but Irene said, 'I thought they looked a bit lost, poor things. They seem only babes themselves.'

Jacov walked home with her, adapting himself easily to her sobriety.

# 8

Early in the New Year, Terence and Claire moved to a small house in Kew; a move which was accomplished with the utmost difficulty. There had been a heavy fall of snow which prevented the removal van getting near the house; and such furniture as Terence and Claire possessed had to be manhandled some distance. Claire stood most of the day by the front door, waiting to identify each separate item and give directions as to its destination – downstairs with Terence, or upstairs with Louise, who had come to help. There were great dollops of snow on the laurel bushes and a more delicate filigree on the holly tree. Footsteps made no sound and the struggles of the removal men seemed to be taking place in the world of the silent cinema. Occasionally, she heard the rattle of defeated engines as a slope proved too much for a car or van. Few people passed by; only those who had need had ventured out. The sky looked soiled above the glaring white of the snow.

During one particularly hazardous journey one of the removal men fell, breaking a long mirror and cutting his hand. 'It's lucky we are not superstitious,' Claire said to Terence, looking queezily at the blood stains in the snow. Even so, this could hardly be regarded as an auspicious beginning.

Once the perils of moving were behind them, and the essential services had been restored to some form of order, Claire and Terence addressed themselves to the decorations. Both were too fastidious to consider living within walls which looked as if they had been papered by long-dead occupants. 'Anyone would think you had been brought up in the East End and expected to find bugs behind the wallpaper,' Alice laughed.

It was reluctantly decided that the greater part of the paintwork would have to await better weather, but that the bathroom must be tackled. Terence's father offered his services, which surprised Claire, Mr Straker having shown little interest in his son and still less in his son's wife. 'He does it in order to get away from my mother,' Terence told Claire. But Claire thought that Mr Straker, a rotund, highly-polished man with button eyes embedded in a pearly face, was quite capable of finding more congenial ways of doing this. Unlikely as it might seem, she had the impression that he was performing the necessary function of seeing the young on their way. He carried out his task with detachment, something written into the genetic code rather than a matter of the affections.

Occasionally Mrs Straker accompanied him, driven more by loneliness than any desire to be with her daughter-in-law, let alone the twins, whom she ogled without making any truly motherly gestures. She smelt strongly of perfume and was heavily made up, not in the hope of attracting her husband, but because this was her understanding of putting a brave face on life. She had little in common with Claire; indeed, it was difficult to imagine what Mrs Straker might have to contribute to any relationship. She was so nervous that the most mundane statement could evoke a spasm of giggles.

'I do so hate the smell of paint, don't you?' she said to Claire.

'I'm too grateful to Mr Straker to let it worry me,' Claire replied, although she had only recently complained to Terence of having a raging headache.

'He'll have his own reasons for doing it.' His family seemed reluctant to impute good will to Mr Straker. 'When you've been married longer you'll know all about that.'

'I've been married for eighteen months,' Claire said loftily. 'And Terence couldn't be more considerate.'

'You wait until it's ten years.' Mrs Straker spoke without malice, resigned to her lot. 'Men get tired of being with the same woman.'

'You'll be coming to the christening, won't you?' Claire changed the subject.

'You've left it rather late, haven't you?'

'Yes, I'm afraid we have.'

'I thought perhaps you weren't going to have them christened. I know young people don't worry so much about that sort of thing nowadays.' She might have been speaking of the creosoting of a fence or the lagging of pipes.

'We felt, after consideration, that it would not be fair to allow Vanessa and Hilary to suffer for our beliefs,' Claire said.

Mrs Straker, anxious not to be thought critical, said, 'If they were Baptists they wouldn't have to be christened. My sister's daughter . . .'

'But we are not Baptists. We are not, in fact, believers.'

'No?' Mrs Straker was baffled by this, never having given thought to either belief or unbelief.

'No, indeed. But compromises are sometimes advisable in a society which still holds to certain old-fashioned practices. Then, there is the question of ritual. While we don't believe, we think the ritual itself may be important. We should not wish to deprive our children of ritual.'

Mrs Straker, nervous at being exposed to this earnest explanation, twisted an orange curl around her forefinger and giggled. 'It doesn't worry me one way or the other, dear,' she assured Claire. 'If you want me to come to the christening, I expect I will.'

'And then, I believe there may be some legal complications. So, for the children's sake . . .'

'Are you going to have godparents and all?'

'That, of course, is another factor. We wouldn't want to deprive them of, not just the material benefits, but the moral care which a proper godparent – though I like to think of them as guardians – would feel it their duty . . . Anyway, it's going to be Alice and Louise and my friend Heather.' She was glad she had been in touch with Heather again. At least one of the godparents would understand her role.

Mrs Straker said, 'Do you mind if I smoke, dear?'

'No, of course not. And I'll make tea. I expect Mr Straker is ready for refreshment! While I'm getting it, you might like to see Terence's article.' She picked up a weekly journal and handed it to Mrs Straker. When she returned with the tea tray, Mrs Straker, who had been gazing out of the window, gave a guilty start and stared intently at the journal, which Claire could see at a glance was upside down. Poor Terence! He had told her that his father's comment had been, 'I don't want to read all this socialist clap-trap.' Even *that* showed a degree of understanding beyond Mrs Straker's.

'You must be very proud of Terence,' Claire said, scarcely able to control her rage.

Mrs Straker, looking frightened, giggled. 'I'm sure I don't know where he gets it from.'

'He takes after his grandfather,' Claire told her. Terence spoke constantly of his working-class grandfather who had been one of Nature's scholars.

'That must have been Grandfather Straker.' Mrs Straker disclaimed responsibility. 'He never knew my father. I didn't think he would have remembered Grandfather Straker – he died when Terence was five.'

Mr Straker came in, dapper in white overall. Claire thought that even in the nude he would look the commercial traveller he was. He ignored his wife and said to Claire, 'You had better come and make your inspection. The bathroom is completed, subject to the approval of the clerk of works!'

'This is very good of you,' Claire said, as they went up the stairs.

'It's not easy for young people setting up a home.' They stood in the entrance to the bathroom. 'Will it do?'

'It's marvellous! The brushwork is so smooth. No professional painter would ever have made it look so good.'

'Ah well . . .' While they were standing there, Terence passed along the landing, carrying Vanessa, bottom resting in the crook of his arm. The baby gazed over Terence's shoulder, eyes seriously considering the small space that was her world. The two moved like horse and rider in easy accord. Once, their heads momentarily facing, they exchanged a grave look. There were no chortles and no baby talk, but the trust and love were unmistakable. There was regret in Mr Straker's little button eyes. 'I hope you make a better go of it than I did.' He gave a dry laugh. 'Can hardly wish you less, m'dear.'

Claire, embarrassed, repeated her praise of Mr Straker's brush-work.

Over tea, Mrs Straker prattled restlessly, her eyes seldom leaving her husband's face. He ignored her.

Later in the evening, Claire said to Terence, 'Don't they ever have anything to do with each other?'

'What do you mean?'

'He behaves as if she wasn't there.'

Terence, who had grown up in this situation, said, 'I hadn't noticed.'

Ben came to visit them and did a bit of carpentry. Although he was fond of Claire, he had motives of his own. His lodgings were bitterly cold and he had to devise ways of keeping warm when he was not at the office. The carpentry helped. At other times, he wandered round the hothouses at Kew, sometimes spending whole afternoons there at weekends until he became quite an expert on tropical plants. Most often, however, he sat in the library at the British Museum. He was slowly amassing information about the conditions under which people were held without trial in countries around the world. As he worked, England, with its strikes, food rationing, its discontent and class hatred, seemed to become irrelevant. It was not that he hated his country, rather that he did not seem to belong in it. It was no longer the country he had fought to save – perhaps that country had not existed except in his own imagination. Whatever the answer, he must create a place where he *did* belong and start from there.

In February, when *Asmodée* was put on, the conditions were atrocious. Power supplies to industry had been cut off and it was reported that power station stocks were running low. Each performance they expected the lighting to be cut off. People came carrying rugs and hot-water bottles, wearing boiler suits, flying jackets and fur hats. 'Not very cheerful, is it?' one woman complained during the interval. 'They might have given us something to laugh about.' On the whole, the audience was respectful, being largely composed of people who prided themselves on their intellectual grasp. Alice, hunched on a stool in the wings, was perhaps more moved by it than was proper in a prompt. She was finding life very dull and could have wished for an *Asmodée* to tear off a few roofs.

A week after the run of the play ended, further snowstorms swept the country, isolating towns and villages and blocking main railway lines. There were ice floes in the North Sea, the Channel, and off the Thames Estuary. British and Polish troops and German prisoners-of-war were engaged in clearing vital roads.

On her way to work, Alice passed an abandoned car, its windows snowed up save for little slits at the top, like a yashmak. Flower pots and tubs foamed and garden lawns were heaped sugar. Sprigs of fir pushing out from a stunted tree resembled the sides of an engraved vase, delicately enfolding swathes of snow. In the high street a bus that had made an effort and failed was evidence that nothing could be expected in the way of road transport. Alice struggled to the tube station. There was the silence of death on the crowded platform. She arrived at work two hours late. Mr Hadow, who had probably spent the night in the office, seemed surprised that she should have encountered any difficulty. 'When I first started work,' he told her, 'if there was any trouble with the weather, I got up at five o'clock and walked to the office.'

Miss Bruce, the head of the teachers' section, who lived within walking distance, was concerned with other matters.

'Scandalous!' she said, throwing the report of the staff sub-committee down on Alice's desk. 'Scandalous to suggest that people who deal with *caretakers' wages* should be considered on the same level as those who deal with *teachers' salaries*.'

The Asistant Education Officer, who had been unwise enough to choose this moment to come to see Mr Hadow, made a wry face behind her back. 'It's a damned sight more difficult to deal with a school caretaker than a headmaster. Old Norris at Bedford Park Grammar School is working for the day when our blood flows in the gutters. The most the headmaster will ever do about us is to make a complaint to his governors.'

'Are you really telling me that you think that young person in general purposes section should be paid as much as my Miss Adlam?'

'Well . . .' The Assistant Education Officer backed towards the door. 'I *can* see an argument for it.'

'Let us hope that none of the members of the staff sub-committee can,' Miss Bruce said to Mr Hadow.

The Education Committee had larger issues to meditate upon. At this unpropitious time, London County Council had released details of its scheme for the reorganisation of secondary education, which involved the establishment of County High Schools for up to 2,000 pupils. This created quite a flurry of invective in the offices of the West London Authority, where it was considered that schools for 2,000 were much too large. The Ministry of Education, however, favoured the London County Council in this, as in many other matters.

Alice, reading proofs of her book under cover of the draft Development Plan, wondered if any of this mattered now that the new ice age had come. Although pleased about her book, it was people who she anticipated would bring her happiness; and people seemed to be eluding her, when not actually moving away from her. She had imagined that having a book published would involve her in a social whirl of parties and had visualised herself dining with the famous in Hampstead. But so far she had not had so much as a sherry and a dry biscuit. True, she was going to stay with Daphne and Peter Kelleher in Norfolk in March, so her social life was not without pleasure. But, while she looked forward to this, she was aware that it was a diversion. She could not spend her life on the fringes of other people's marriages. But *how* was she to spend it?

The relationship with Nicholas Medd, her art teacher was not developing. She joined the Overseas Club, and enrolled at the City Lit. for a class in French. The answer might well be that she must travel; and in order to get a job abroad, it would be useful to be proficient in at least one foreign language. When she had improved her French, she might take up Spanish. She read the situations vacant columns as she would study a menu to see what tempted her. She was not called for interview; which was hardly surprising, as she was not measuring herself up to the employers' requirements, but rather examining them to see what they offered in the way of opportunities for travel, excitement (newspaper offices rated high in this category), and the chance of meeting interesting people (anything at the BBC). Her situation seemed desperate.

She struggled through snow to theatres; in the lunchtime, she trudged determinedly to exhibitions at the Tate or to the National Gallery, arriving exhausted and with only time to look at one or two pictures; she re-read a novel by Hermann Hesse, who had been awarded the 1946 Nobel Prize for Literature. But nothing could ameliorate the misery of an eight-hour day in the Education Department; she was wishing her life away at an alarming rate.

She wondered whether Guy felt the same. He was always very tired when he returned home and Louise was the one who had to deal with all the household problems. He grumbled that she 'never sat down for five minutes' and 'never kept her mind on any one thing'. On the rare occasions when he was called upon to do two things at the same time he became confused and aggrieved. There was a particularly trying episode one evening when his mother telephoned while he was clearing snow from the entrance to the coal shed.

'She says they are frozen at the main,' James told him.

'What am I supposed to do about it?' he asked angrily.

'She wants to know if you can go round there this evening.'

'I can't leave this to speak to her.'

'You could tell me,' James suggested.

'But how do I know whether I can go round there until I've finished here?' he stormed. 'How *do* I know?'

James retired and soon afterwards Louise came into the yard. 'I've told your mother you will come if you have time.'

'I'm not going to *have* time if I'm not left alone to do this, am I?'

'It's a pity he hasn't got a more interesting job,' Alice said to Louise when they were washing up later in the evening, and Guy had departed for his parents' house, shouting over his shoulder, 'I've brought work home from the office. I shall probably be up half the night after this!'

'You may not think his work interesting, but Guy probably does,' Louise was quick to defend him from what she saw as implied criticism.

'I don't see how anyone can be interested in figures.'

'It's no use doing what other people think of as exciting, if you don't find it exciting yourself. Cooking can be more rewarding than climbing a mountain – or writing a book – if it's cookery that moves you. And I daresay the same applies to figures. No one is meant to be a failure.' Louise looked challengingly at Alice, who had been thinking in terms of her own failure, not Guy's. She went to the larder to collect scraps of fat and bread for the birds.

Alice accepted this criticism. She had been brought up to believe that whatever you do, you must do well and cheerfully. At the Winifred Clough Day School for Girls great emphasis had been laid on this, and on the value of service to others. She was one of the school's failures. Unable to make the best of the small change of office life, and with no desire to serve the community, she was, it seemed, selfish, dissatisfied, pleasure-seeking; a person who considered herself set apart from the ordinary run of people, yet with nothing to show in the way of worth, let alone outstanding talent.

Louise, coming back from the snowy garden where she had filled the birds' tray, said, 'Not everyone is made for the heights, you know.' She was troubled about Guy, who spent a lot of time with clients who were elderly and impecunious. She guessed that the firm had given him its lame ducks because no one else had the patience to deal with them. But how long would it be before they began to complain that his financial contribution did not justify the amount of time he spent on these clients? He would take it very hard if that happened. She realised, none better, that the tools with which Guy tackled life were fragile.

Alice went slowly up to her room, a leaden weight in her stomach. Louise was right, of course. A great many people spent their days doing work they found boring and uninspiring. But she had never thought she would be one of them.

Icicles hung from the inside of her window sill, but in the bowl on the dressing table, hyacinths thrust up pink and unconcerned from their green shield. Outside, the lights from street lamps splashed on the snow; a wind was blowing and the canopies of snow breathed and rippled as though something was living within them. Night gave magic to the scene, hiding the sick sky.

She would not conform; she would not believe that boredom was to be her lot. So, she must resist. She would not buy a season ticket, and from now on she would vary her route to the office, even if the journey sometimes took longer. At all costs, she would not establish a routine.

One other change she effected about this time. On Sundays, instead of going to the Methodist chapel, she attended an Anglican church in Notting Hill. The vicar was reserved and a little aloof; not a cold man, but one who held certain matters to be his own and no one else's business. Time-wasting callers at the vicarage were not always made to feel welcome. Although he was capable of deep feeling, this was not constantly on display and he was considered to be unfriendly. He could be candid, but not in the gauche way which enables people to say affectionately, 'he has put his foot in it again!' His bursts of candour, sudden and unpredictable, frequently broke through a man's guard. These characteristics had earned him the reputation of a man not entirely to be trusted. He was an important influence in Alice's life because he stood at the point at which she had arrived, a signpost in a time of need.

'However dark things may seem,' he said one week in his sermon, 'little rays of light and understanding will break through. Perhaps this is all there will ever be, all we have a right to expect. But so long as we are open to receive them, that is all that matters. Whatever happens, we must never shrug our shoulders and say, "Well, I had such dreams and nothing came of them; but things haven't been so bad, I've got along somehow." You must never do that to yourself. Delve into your despair and rage against it, rather than that. But never subscribe to the doctrine of the littleness of life.'

Alice delved into her despair: daily, quietly, persistently, she raged against the littleness of life in the West London Education Authority. And she kept herself in a state of readiness. The worst thing which could happen would be that she might accept her situation, so that when the chance came to break free, she could no longer take it.

# 9

Towards the end of March there was a slow thaw. Life would become more bearable and it would be easier to travel. 'So,' Daphne said to Peter, 'Alice will be coming. And I have asked Angus and Irene and Ivor as well. That will solve our outstanding hospitality commitments.'

'Are we committed to Irene?'

'She is my friend.'

'I thought Alice was your friend.'

'Alice is my particular friend.'

'I had no idea there were these grades of friendship.'

'Does it matter? If there are several people they will spread themselves about and you won't find it so irritating.'

In the event, there was less time for irritation than one might have foreseen.

To her disappointment, Alice had to work on the Saturday morning and so could not accept Angus's offer to take her by car. Car journeys were a rarity and she would greatly have enjoyed the opportunity of exploring unfamiliar territory. Railways bisected land unnaturally, whereas roads wound their way through the heart of the countryside. Alice was much taken with getting to the heart of things.

The train, on this occasion, provided plenty of opportunity to study the countryside, stopping for long periods at isolated level crossings while the wind moaned in the telegraph wires and drove misty sprays of snow against the windows. The snow was melting and the fields were ribbed with dark mud. Here and there a cluster of houses and a church had that look which, seen from a distance, buildings so often have in a flat countryside of being dumped arbitrarily without regard to their surroundings. A long ditch kept the railway line company. It was almost full of water and Alice wondered idly what would happen when all the snow had melted. It seemed likely that this section of the line would be flooded. The thought that Nature might provide her with a few extra days' holiday was not unpleasing.

As the line came close to the coast she had a glimpse of the sea, a bubbling mercury beneath a violet sky. It was late afternoon by the time King's Lynn was reached. Alice was able to recognise Peter Kelleher from the snapshot which Daphne had sent to her. He was standing by the ticket barrier greeting a man who must have travelled by the same train. She waved and walked towards the two men.

'Ah, Alice!' Peter Kelleher said, taking her suitcase to give himself time to remember her surname. His memory still failing him, he indicated the other man and said, 'This is Ivor.' The man thus addressed was too amused by his friend's predicament to attempt a more formal introduction. Nevertheless, there was no doubting his interest as he looked at Alice. Seldom, she felt, had she made such an immediate impression on anyone. She was not sure, however, that this was a cause for self-congratulation. The eyes which examined her might be making notes for a portrait which would not necessarily be flattering, or even recording a description of her to be circulated later. She wondered if he was a policeman, but decided that he was more likely to be involved in the overthrow of law and order than its maintenance. As they walked to the car she realised he was lame.

She hesitated by the car, waiting to be told where to sit, and wondering whether the back or the front would be easier for him. In the event, she sat in the front while Ivor stretched out sideways in the back. She guessed he had not suffered some temporary injury, since no explanations were given. Men were usually only too willing to tell you if they had broken an ankle at rugger. A cloven hoof, perhaps? She felt uncomfortably aware of those eyes behind her.

'I don't know whether you have been here before?' Peter Kelleher asked courteously as they drove out of the town.

'I've been to Sheringham.'

'You know something of East Anglia, then. But you will notice some differences in our part of Norfolk.' He began to talk about the Viking raids in the Dark Ages. Alice thought he was not unlike a Viking himself. One could imagine an axe being used in the hewing of those features. She was cold and hungry after the train journey and perhaps this accounted for the discomfort she felt in the company of these two men who seemed to her in some inexplicable way to be violent. She could not think how to respond to Kelleher, but as he seemed content to continue his exposition without any encouragement from her, she fell to staring out of the window at the landscape which was unbelievably watery. Kelleher pulled into a hedge to allow a farm lorry to pass; a spume of spray in its wake covered the car windows. Later, when the windows were clear again, and Kelleher was talking about the wool trade in the Middle Ages, she saw that the snow was still banked high along the hedgerows, but to the south there were trees with their roots in slag-grey water. They came to a lane which was completely waterlogged and Kelleher had some difficulty turning the car. He was obviously used to overcoming difficulties, and soon they were on a road which the slush had not yet turned into a river.

'I shouldn't think these fields could absorb much more water,' Ivor said.

'We'll have to hope there is no more rain. The Ouse is very high.'

Although it was getting dark there was a strange green light which wavered and rippled across the fields. Kelleher had completed his brief survey of the general historical background of East Anglia, and was about to deal with Norfolk in particular, when they came to another lane which was waterlogged. This time they had to turn back. After several miles, Kelleher found a lane which he considered passable. Soon, however, the car wheels stuck fast in thick mud. Kelleher, glancing down at Alice's shoes, said, 'You had better stay here.' She felt she had failed a test. He and Ivor got out and gathered twigs and branches from the hedgerows which they made into a kind of cradle embedded in the mud. Eventually, after some spade work, the wheels moved again.

It seemed a long time later that, at the end of a very long lane, Alice saw a dim light shining from the window of what she took to be an isolated farm. Kelleher said, 'Daphne has opened the gate. Good!' Daphne was waiting in the porch, wearing trousers and muddied Wellingtons. Kelleher drove the car up to the porch so that Alice should not spoil her shoes. In some respects, he would be a meticulous host.

'I've obviously worn the wrong clothes,' Alice said apologetically.

Daphne embraced her. 'You mean to tell me you didn't bring your swimming costume? You're here at last, that's the important thing.' To Alice's surprise, the room into which the front door opened was lit by an oil lamp. Daphne picked up her case and made for the stairs. Another lamp somewhere above cast a pallid light on the treads.

The stairs creaked alarmingly and some of the boards were spongy beneath Alice's heel. She gained the impression the house was not only old, but decrepit. At the end of a dark, low-ceilinged passage Daphne opened a door into what, at first sight, seemed to be a large closet lit by yet another lamp. 'We shall have spent more on lamps than the house soon,' she said. 'But it has been fun collecting them. This one is particularly pretty.' Alice edged into the room. There was barely space for the two of them. 'It's a bit poky, I'm afraid. We haven't really got room to house so many people. Angus and Ivor are bedding in the sitting-room. There's not much in the way of washing facilities, either.' She indicated a ewer and basin on a small table wedged beneath the tiny window. 'We don't have running water, let alone a bathroom. As you can see, we have no electric light.'

'And the lavatory?'

'Outside the kitchen. There's a po under the bed. Should I have told you all this before I asked you to stay?'

'Of course not!' Alice contrived to sound undismayed. In normal times, she would have been entranced; but in this weather she had looked for all the comforts of home at the end of her journey. She said, 'Irene and I could share if that would help.'

'Her room isn't much bigger than this.' Daphne laughed. 'The house is tiny. This is what comes of marrying a man who would be perfectly happy to spend his life in a tent.' She had the look of a woman who has found the companion of a lifetime.

'I want to hear all about it,' Alice said, more eager than envious, because if this could happen to Daphne, there was hope for her.

'Yes, but not now. The dinner has suffered one or two setbacks as a result of the time it took Peter to get you here. And if there is one thing we *are* fussy about, it's our food! So we'll talk later. The weather being what it is, we shall have hours and hours to exchange news while the men go floundering about in the mud.'

'I haven't brought trousers, I'm afraid.'

'Oh, I shall change for dinner. We are nothing if not inconsistent. I must go. I've left Irene slaving in the kitchen and she may have done something dreadful by now. She has no idea about cooking, did you know? She is barely to be trusted with boiling an egg.'

She went out. Alice looked round the room. There was no dressing-table and no place to hang clothes, but she was used to living out of a suitcase. What did trouble her was the appalling smell of damp plaster. She went to the bed, drew back the covers, and sniffed. The smell was here, too, only with the difference that the main ingredient was damp flock. I slept in the desert, she thought, so I suppose I can manage here without coming to any harm, as long as I wrap up well. She had brought a raincoat with her; if the worst came to the worst, she could put that on top of the mattress.

She decided to go to the lavatory without more ado. The ground floor consisted of one room, the kitchen area being confined to the short stroke of an L. Irene greeted her with a roll of the eyes. A pewter-coloured cat with white paws was in possession of the lavatory seat. The wind rattled the latch and screamed through the cracks around the door.

'I've disturbed your cat,' she said to Daphne on her return.

'She spends hours in there. We've christened her Scatology – Scat, for short.'

'Well, she's not there now. She went off in a great huff.'

'Drinks will be served shortly. You had better change.'

Changing presented little problem. She had brought her one and only warm dress which was suitable for social occasions, a cherry wool with a close-fitting bodice and a skirt with the fullness gathered to one side. Alice thought it very feminine, but Louise, who had accompanied her when she bought it, had said, 'All the interest in that dress is in the skirt and it won't show when you sit down.' Alice thought philosophically that this would not matter here, since they would probably not see one another very well top or bottom.

She paused at the head of the stairs, looking down. Somewhere out of sight she could hear Irene and Daphne talking. Angus was standing by the chest on which the lamp was burning, gazing into the bowl as if he had gone into a trance. The wan light thumbed shadows which gave his face the sinister inscrutability of an oriental mask with blackness where the eyes should be. Ivor was tending a wood fire in the hearth, watched hopefully by a springer spaniel who, judging from his condition, had had an eventful outing in the fields and now asked for nothing more than an evening of rest and warmth. The front door opened and a surge of wind sent the lamp flickering wildly. Smoke gusted from the chimney and Ivor swore. Kelleher closed the door. 'It's raining again,' he said. He crossed the room, holding out a bottle to the unseen Daphne. 'This will do, I think.'

Daphne said, without it seemed having had time to study the bottle, 'No. This is a celebration. There's no "will do" about it. *And* we shall need two bottles.'

He came into sight again, looking down at the bottle in immense surprise, and made his way out into the night. The wind surged in even more fiercely and Ivor threw down the log he had in his hand. Angus said briskly, 'My turn. I used to be quite good at this when I was a backwoodsman.'

Fancy Angus ever being a backwoodsman! Alice thought as she made her entrance. Unfortunately, her slow descent of the stairs coincided with Kelleher's return, and yet another gust of wind sent her skirt up around her waist. Ivor, the only one to notice, said, 'Very fetching. Could we have that again?'

Alice laughed. 'I did buy it for the skirt.'

He said with mock gallantry, 'Surely because it matches the colour in your cheeks?'

In the kitchen area, Daphne said, 'That's more like it.'

Alice said to Ivor, 'Any colour in my cheeks is going to disappear rapidly if that fire doesn't get going.'

'No, you have your own supply of warmth.' He was not serious, yet he was not flirting – at least, not as Alice understood it. Later on, when they were all sitting in front of the fire drinking sherry, he was the one who kept the talk going. He talked fast, his mind darting from one subject to another, just as the flames now leapt from log to log as the fire established its hold. His was not the incessant barrage of words behind which others can take their ease; it demanded a response. It was apparent that other people interested him, less certain whether liking played any part in this curiosity. He was a restless, stabbing person, with hands that, never still, threw grotesque shadows on the wall which reminded Alice of Christmas party mimes. His eyes, as he looked from one to another, were bright and uninvolved as the flames licking the wood. Although he was probably much the same age as the other men, he looked older; his pale skin was chapped, and there was a gossamer web of lines beneath the eyes and a withered dryness to the mouth. Alice, who had by now realised that he had lost a leg, presumably in the war, wondered whether he had put too much energy into making a recovery. She was reminded briefly of Ben, who was also a casualty of war and frequently drew too heavily on his reserves of energy.

The fire was roaring in the chimney – or was it the wind? Certainly the flames were throwing out a lot of heat and the dog was asleep, stretched on one side, front paws gently crossed. Alice said, 'How blissful!'

'No.' Daphne shook her head. 'It's cats who know all about bliss.'

Ivor said, 'Really? A few short, sharp encounters and the rest of the day spent nose to tail – is that bliss?'

'It's the way they move their limbs.' She demonstrated, arms upstretched, wrists arching. She must surely have been aware that, in the black dress with its low, draped neckline, it would be the movement of her breasts which would command their attention, evoking desire rather than bliss. Kelleher looked almost stupefied with lust – a sight which seemed to afford Ivor mischievous delight. Irene fingered the brooch at her throat to see if the catch was still secure, and this did not escape his eyes. He is quite different from Ben, Alice thought; he has no morality. He is like something from a fairy story; one of those creatures neither good nor bad. A probe! She had scarcely noticed any of the others since they had gathered round the fire.

Now, above the crackle of the fire and the roar in the chimney, they could hear the rain pounding on the roof, cascading into a water butt, coming down so fast that even the most thirsty land could surely not absorb it. 'Can plants choke?' Irene wondered.

'It is overdoing things a bit,' Daphne said. 'The cat won't like it.' She went to the front door and called, 'Scat, Scat . . .' The wind sent her voice tearing back into the room. She closed the door with difficulty. 'It's a solid sheet of water. The poor little thing probably dare not move.' She looked at the dog, who had raised his head. 'If you were a gentleman, you would go and fetch her.' The dog thumped his tail.

'This will bring down the last of the snow from the roof,' Kelleher said. 'Let's hope the tiles don't come with it.'

Daphne said, 'I think we might as well eat now.'

They moved into the kitchen area, where a big, blackened pot was bubbling on a range of some antiquity. Occasionally something unrecognisable, which might well have been a toad, broke surface. Daphne never did tell them the ingredients; it was sufficient that it tasted delicious. Angus praised the wine.

The men dominated the conversation. They were all rather knowledgeable and talked about world affairs as if they were playing chess with political leaders as their pawns. There was scarcely a situation they could not have improved upon. Alice thought this merely boring until they got onto the subject of Empire. They talked about the recent 'disturbances' in India and Egypt with cool disapprobation. This was a subject on which Alice's father would have had much to say. But how differently he would have expressed himself! While these men talked of errors and misjudgements in which they did not see themselves as involved, he would have grieved passionately over his country's guilt. He would have prayed for forgiveness, not only for those in power, but for himself since this was his country and he was as much a part of its failures as its glories. To him, his country was his larger family – a notion these men would have laughed at. As she listened to their talk, so knowing yet so detached, she wondered at what altars such men worshipped. They seemed to her like travellers coming from the darkness to a strange house, staring in at some desperate scene framed in a lighted window, observing the pathetic contortions, the fumbling ineptitude of the participants, silent witnesses in no way involved.

She thought of Gordon, who had found himself inadequate to deal with racial hatred in Alexandria and had been diminished and humiliated by the experience. 'Don't you feel ashamed?' she asked. They looked at her, Peter surprised that she should interrupt male conversation, Ivor applauding not the sentiment but the audacity. Only Angus responded. 'I feel ashamed so much of the time it has become the condition in which I live.'

Daphne said, 'Oh, don't talk such nonsense, Angus! What have we got to be ashamed of? If the Hindus and the Moslems tear each other apart, it won't be our fault.'

'But we do seem anxious to get out quickly so that we won't be involved,' Irene said.

'Very wise of us.'

Kelleher said, 'Oh dear, oh dear!' and poured more wine.

After the meal they returned to the fire. Peter poured brandy which Alice recklessly accepted. Irene refused. The fire hissed and spat as if green wood had been put on it. The smell of wetness pervaded the room – not the good smell of grateful earth, but something much less pleasant. The brandy had undoubted healing properties. Alice thought what luxury it was to sit here by the fire, safe from the storm. Irene was curled neatly on the hearthrug, stroking the dog's head. Angus was on a stool behind her, but she did not lean against him, nor did his hand rest on her shoulder. It pained Alice to see them wasting the firelight like this.

Daphne had seated herself on the arm of Peter's chair. Her dress fell away to reveal firm, rosy breasts whenever she leant forward, which she did rather often, as though about to pour herself over him like a libation. Her face was flushed by the flames. His hand was on the small of her back. They were intoxicated with each other.

Irene and Angus began a conversation about Mozart. Alice could think of nothing to say; her senses were drowned in brandy and rain and some other element which made the blood heavy in her veins. She looked up and saw that Ivor's eyes were on her. He laughed, as if he understood how she felt better than she did herself. And perhaps he did have special powers. He was a force, not a person. With the coming of this thought, he was beside her on the settee as if she had summoned him. 'Why are they so frightened?' he whispered, closer than was necessary since Irene and Angus certainly would not hear him. Irene was talking about Mozart's mastery of tone colours. 'And do they think Mozart, of all people, will drive out this particular demon?'

'It *is* a bit overwhelming, isn't it?' Alice said.

He looked at Daphne. 'She's a witch. A real, live witch.'

'I had been thinking it was an evening for fairy stories.'

'Oh? Why so?'

'I. . . .' She was in confusion, what with the rain and the brandy and the firelight; and now, in spite of the warmth, she was shivering.

He said, 'I see.' His fingers traced the little crease which circled her throat. The touch, very light, generated such agitation at her source that a rising corkscrew of pain and pleasure sent spasms throughout her body. She gasped and as her lips parted he bent over her, his tongue flicking out. The room was filled with a strange, greenish light. Irene and Angus had gone to the window, drawing back the curtains. The streaming windows threw a reflection on to the walls so that they, too, appeared to be running with water. The last of the snow came away as though it was taking a section of the roof with it. Alice felt something inside her shifting. One might imagine the whole house to be gradually dissolving.

Ivor whispered urgently, 'Come upstairs.'

And then it was Peter who was saying come upstairs, and Ivor had turned away from her. 'What is it?'

Daphne said, 'The cat is out.'

'Never mind. Upstairs. We'll get what food we can.'

Alice found herself half way up the stairs, gripping the banisters. 'I don't understand,' she gasped, and looking down she saw that one of the floorboards was coming up, and then another, and another. And still she did not understand.

The men were splashing through water, handing up food, kettle, bottles. The dog pushed past her and padded up the stairs, complaining deep in his throat. Daphne was crying, actually crying about the cat! And there was the most awful smell.

Kelleher thrust a loaded tray into Alice's hands and said, 'Take it into our room – the door is straight ahead.'

Most of the available space was taken up by an enormous bed covered with a rug which Kelleher had been given by a Kurdistan tribesman. How could anyone who wanted to live in the open air so confine his movements in his own home? Alice felt a rising panic at the thought of being trapped in this cramped little house. She put the tray down on the bed and went to the window. It was black dark and the rain was a wall of water pressing against the panes, streaming through the leads. The sill was awash and water ran down the plaster. As a cleaner it was not effective, leaving streaks in the grime which it would be hard to remove. But that would be the least of the Kellehers' problems. Irene and Daphne came in burdened with a ladder and soon the men followed, soaked to the waist. The dog put his head back and began a profound lament.

'I expect he wants to go out,' Daphne said. 'What *are* we to do?'

'We'll designate Alice's bedroom for that, if she doesn't mind,' Kelleher said. 'Does everyone know the geography?'

Irene, Angus and Ivor did not, and departed with him to investigate. Daphne called after them, 'You had better put this in there' and handed Irene a chamber pot.

'What is the dog's name?' Alice asked Daphne.

'Towser.'

Alice put her arm round his neck. 'Oh poor, poor Towser! He is so terrified.' Towser, falling readily into his role of scapegoat, shook from nose to tail.

'There's nothing much we can do about this at present, so we might as well get some sleep,' Kelleher said when he returned. 'Angus and Ivor and I will mount watch in turns.'

'I'm quite capable of doing a watch,' Alice said.

'We shall need you refreshed and inventive by breakfast time.' There was no point in arguing, she realised. No doubt years spent with primitive tribes had given him a mud-hut mentality.

'I shall make myself comfortable before I sleep, then.' There were advantages in being first. It was only when she stood on the landing, looking down, that she began to take in what had happened and she was still some way from full realisation. Water lapped beneath her, reeking from its passage across the fields and coated with the remnants of their dinner and less readily identifiable matter. The logs had floated to the surface together with the hearth brush and a biscuit barrel. None of the furniture was visible. Had the flood reached its highest point, or would the water continue to rise?

She guessed the men were debating this when she returned. Kelleher was saying, 'The next high tide will be about nine o'clock tomorrow morning.'

By dawn they were all awake. The rain had stopped but there was no radiance, only a slow thinning of the darkness, revealing a world that looked like one huge, grey watery eye.

Daphne said, 'Breakfast? We had planned to give you a rather splendid breakfast. What a shame!'

They had cheese sandwiches and orange squash with a dash of whisky for warmth. Ivor and Kelleher had made sketches during the night of constructions which would float; much favoured was a wicker-work and canvas contraption to be made from the one bedroom chair and the mattress cover. Irene said, '*You* may go in it, but I shall wait to be rescued by one of those splendid old fishermen one is always seeing sitting on the shingle mending nets.' The idea of waiting did not appeal to either man and Kelleher explained that this was an adaptation of a very ancient type of boat. Irene said, 'We have no statistics of how many people drowned in them, though.' Alice felt confident that his enthusiasm was academic and that neither he nor Ivor would embark on a thoroughly foolhardy enterprise.

Angus said, 'I suppose we should investigate the roof – just in case.' He was leaning out of the window looking upward. 'Is there any way we can get there from inside?'

'No,' Kelleher answered. 'I had a good look during the night.'

'In that case, I think I might manage. . . .' He swung himself out on to the sill. 'If I could get up by the chimney, we could fix that ladder of yours by a rope, just in case . . .'

He accomplished the climb without difficulty. It was the rope which presented the problem. After an exhaustive search, during which the cat was discovered asleep in a cupboard, they had to admit defeat. Eventually, Angus secured the ladder with strips torn from the canvas mattress cover which was to have formed part of the wicker boat. He tested the apparatus on his descent and it held him. The entire manoeuvre had been executed quite elegantly and without any sign of fear.

Daphne was sitting on the bed, rocking to and fro, holding the cat against her face. Kelleher watched her broodingly. 'What it wants is milk,' he said.

'It wants love, poor little thing. She thought we had deserted her.'

Kelleher poured rather more milk than he would normally have considered wise, granted their situation, and the wretched animal immediately wrenched free and drank its fill, pink tongue flicking over the rim of the saucer, greedy for the painted flowers. Kelleher watched it with satisfaction. 'Unsentimental creatures, cats – motivated by an unusually high degree of self-preservation.'

Irene said to Angus, 'I was terrified you were going to fall.'

'The brickwork provided plenty of holds,' he said drily. 'The only danger was it was so loose! I wonder how much they gave for this place?'

Kelleher and Ivor were studying a map of the area. Alice appointed herself watchman. Now that it was fully light there was still very little to see save water. She thought that far in the distance she could make out what might be the upper storeys of another house, but there was nothing to give form or substance to the landscape. Nothing, indeed, to suggest it had ever been a *land*scape. She watched a barrel float by and wondered what it had contained. There followed a dustbin and an easy chair, lying on its back, revealing an underside of canvas webbing through which the stuffing was seeping. After a period when there was nothing much to be seen, she noticed a big, whalelike object moving slowly in the direction of the house, and as it got nearer she saw that it was a dead cow. She screamed and put her hands over her face, convinced it must smash into the house.

Ivor came to her.

'I can't bear it if we are going to have lots of dead things in here!'

'It's gone now.'

'It's probably stuck somewhere just beneath us. We shall *smell* it.'

Seeing that she was really disturbed by this, he leant out of the window. 'All gone,' he assured her. 'Come and satisfy yourself.'

She looked out warily, ashamed of being the first person to show signs of panic.

Daphne was saying, 'The poor dog is probably bursting. He's so well-trained.'

'He is perfectly all right,' Kelleher assured her. 'And has left evidence to prove it, haven't you, old chap?'

'He must be so bewildered, though,' Irene said. 'All his values turned upside down in this way and he can't ask any questions about it.' She comforted him and he licked her face. Later on, she said, 'How long will we be here. It's Mummy and Daddy I'm thinking of. They will be so dreadfully worried.'

'The police launches will be around soon – and anything else that can float,' Ivor said. 'The spirit of Dunkirk again!'

'People do know you live here?' Alice asked Daphne. The house could hardly be said to be a landmark, and she did not imagine the Kellehers would have made much effort to make themselves known to their nearest neighbours – wherever they might be.

Kelleher said, 'They will be bound to take note of any building which is sticking up above the water – this house is probably more noticeable now than ever before.'

'And, in any case,' Ivor said, 'as soon as we see a boat we shall make our presence known.'

'How?' Alice asked.

After some discussion, they agreed they should fly something from the chimney. A sheet would be no good, it would be lost in the greyness. A red flannel blanket was unearthed and this time it was Daphne who made the ascent. 'If things get worse the idea is that we all use this ladder, isn't it?' she challenged the men. 'So the sooner we make sure we can do it, the better.' She negotiated the ladder with commendable athleticism. Irene and Alice exchanged wry glances.

'I think the level of the water must be going down a little,' Daphne said when she returned. 'I could see the top of Angus's car.'

'I wonder if it is possible to salvage anything from it,' Angus said.

'Hardly worth the effort, surely?' Ivor looked surprised. 'Unless you have left anything of particular value in it?'

'A few papers – in my briefcase.'

'But not of national importance, presumably.' Kelleher was not asking a question so much as making a statement.

Ivor, however, was interested. 'One hopes not. Since they will be irretrievably damaged.'

Angus said, 'I should have kept it with me. What a bore!'

No more was said of salvaging the briefcase.

As the morning dragged on and it became apparent that they were not in any immediate danger, the main problem was how to occupy themselves. The Kellehers announced their intention of taking a couple of hours' rest and departed for the small room which had initially been allocated to Irene.

'A couple of hours!' Ivor commented. 'Rather excessive, one would have thought.' He strolled to the window. 'If anyone else feels the need of rest, I should be quite happy to sit on the landing.'

Alice's stomach lurched. How mortifying that dismay should so soon replace desire! Irene and Angus were vociferous in their assurances that they were not in the habit of resting in the daytime, and Irene went so far as to condemn such practices as valetudinarian. Neither she nor Angus offered to sit on the landing.

When eventually Peter and Daphne returned, Ivor said without preamble, 'Alice and I would like a rest now.'

Alice said, 'No, Alice would not!' but she followed him out of the room to Irene's dismay.

Ivor, as soon as they came into the bedroom, knew his mistake. She had that maddening air of innocence which some women can assume in the most doubtful situations, and which often confounds a man's worst intentions. He played for time.

'What is wrong with your friend Irene? Is she afraid of what would happen, or that nothing would happen?'

'Both, I expect, like me.'

'You are certainly very tense. You weren't like this last night.'

'Last night we had a lot to drink, and the fire was warm, and now I'm cold and frightened and I haven't had enough to eat. . . .'

He drew her down beside him on the bed, where she sat bolt upright. 'I can't promise you hot soup, but I can very soon stoke those fires again . . .' She gasped convulsively as his hands touched her stomach and moved between her thighs; but her body was hard and knotted as wire.

'What is it?' he asked angrily.

'I really don't know you very well. And I can't come to this cold.'

He sighed, 'All right, all right! We'll talk, shall we? Tell me about yourself. Unless *you* prefer to talk about Mozart, too.'

'There's not much to tell.'

'Relax!' He eased her down on the pillow, gentle and persuasive now. 'You must live somewhere. In a wood, perhaps, with your grandmother close by . . .'

She tried to answer in the manner of the fairy story, 'I live with my sister, Louise, and her husband, Guy, in a house in Holland Park, and . . .'

He sat up, propped on one elbow. 'You are *Alice*!' He had changed completely.

'Well, yes . . .' she faltered, bewildered.

'I'm sorry.' In the watery light his face was green with rage. 'They are so full of themselves, those two, they don't bother to introduce people properly.'

'Does it matter?' She felt suddenly full of tenderness, now that he was no longer bringing any pressure to bear on her, and she stroked his face. 'Stop looking like an outraged merman! They *did* introduce us, after a fashion – they said that you were Ivor and . . .'

'But not that I was with them when that bomb came down.' She could not think what he was talking about, until he said, 'Louise never mentioned me?'

'No, I don't think so . . .' All the breath had gone out of her and she felt flat as an empty sack.

'She wouldn't, of course.' She would not forget the bitterness in his voice, or the way he went on, speaking as of an unimportant person mentioned in passing, 'But she told me she had a sister, Alice, who was out in Alex.'

She watched him sitting hunched on the edge of the bed, winded as a fighter who has taken a kidney punch. After a time, when he made no movement, she got up and began to tidy her clothes. He said, 'I'm sorry. I wasn't prepared for this.'

She stood staring at the door, then suddenly drummed her feet on the floor. 'I can't go back in that room! I can't! And I can't stay here! Oh, this dreadful flood! Why can't we all just die?'

'There's no need for that.'

She turned on him. 'You . . . you and *my* sister!'

'It wasn't . . .' He paused. Kelleher's voice rang out, 'Come on, you two! Ship ahoy!'

As they came into the room Angus, Daphne and Kelleher were leaning out of the window, waving and shouting. There were answering shouts in the distance. Irene was standing to one side as though she had little interest in what was happening. She looked at Alice, eyes enormous with grief.

Below a man was shouting, 'If you can readjust that ladder, you can climb down to us quite easily.'

This time it was Kelleher who climbed up. Angus and Ivor took the ladder from him and secured it to the bedpost. Daphne made the first descent carrying the cat. 'Towser won't be able to make it,' she called up. They made a cradle of sheets and lowered the dog. Their haven was a good-sized motor cruiser. 'Quite a commodious ark!' Daphne exulted. As they settled themselves, talking to their rescuers, a police launch came by. The water level was lower and Irene said to Angus, '*They* might be able to get your briefcase.'

'The police have more important things to do.'

'It's worth a try.' She did not note the sharpness of his tone; now that the need for control had passed, she felt as if something in her mind had snapped. 'He's got diplomatic papers in his bag,' she explained to the policemen. It did not seem important. She simply had to put words together and these were the first which came to mind. As the engine started up, she found more words, the one tumbling over the other. Angus was unexpectedly stirred by this ill-considered intervention; it moved him as her tact and reticence had never done, and gave her a new value. He put his arm round her shoulders and drew her close. Alice, painfully alone, thought, 'How stupid! He is sheltering her now, when there is no need!' Over her shoulder as the boat moved away, she could see the police launch circling Angus's car.

Their rescuers took them to a hostel where they spent the night. It was not until the next morning that they were asked to go to the police station.

'We managed to salvage a few of your things,' the policeman explained. He looked at them with interest, which was surprising as he must have spent weary hours dealing with people in the same plight, and some far worse off. He was a plainclothes officer. The harassed sergeant who had greeted them on their arrival had called out to colleagues, 'Where's Cotter? This is the party he wanted to see.' Cotter, thus summoned, had ushered them into this small room at the back of the building. The yard beneath the window was occupied by a large number of unclaimed and incompatible animals, each complaining in its own fashion. Raising his voice above the clamour, the policeman said, 'Just a matter of identification.' He walked to a table pushed against the wall, talking all the time. 'You'd be surprised how awkward some folk can be, especially at a time like this. You save a few of their possessions and they accuse you of pinching the rest.' He paused by the table. 'Just the two cars, were there?' As though another car might be one of the items the police could be accused of pinching. They told him there were two cars. He read out registration numbers and Kelleher and Angus produced the necessary proofs of ownership.

'Well, that settles that.' He looked at Kelleher. 'Not much in your car, sir, I'm afraid.'

Kelleher said rather crossly, 'I don't keep much in my car.'

'Very wise, sir. But you might like to take a look at these few items.'

Kelleher looked without favour at a mound of tools and directories for which he would have little further use. It seemed scarcely credible that this was the way the police were spending their time during this emergency.

The policeman indicated a rather larger pile. Daphne said, 'My brother was staying with us. As he was away from home, he would naturally have more in his car.' Why at this stage she should choose to be so defensive was not clear, even to her, unless it was the bottle of whisky which troubled her.

The policeman said, 'Quite so' which, as Daphne said afterwards, was probably the Force's equivalent of 'rhubarb, rhubarb'. 'Nothing of much value, I would think, except this.' He pushed the bottle of whisky to one side and opened the briefcase. His interest seemed to centre on a small object which Alice saw only briefly before Angus, moving closer, blocked her view. It might have been a small book, or a tin of talcum powder. She was never sure afterwards what her first impression had been – as in a dream, the sequence once lost was never re-established. The policeman laid the object on the table. 'Yours?'

Angus said, 'Yes.'

'Neat little contraption.'

'Yes.'

'You usually carry it about with you, do you, sir?'

'No. It needed repair. I was going to take it in on Monday.' Angus turned it over with one finger. 'It doesn't look as if there will be much point.'

The policeman nodded. 'Beyond repair, I should think. A pity.' He, too, turned it over. 'Didn't know we made this sort of job.'

'We don't.'

There was a pause while the policeman frowned down at the object. 'You work at the Foreign Office?'

'Yes.'

While all this was happening, Kelleher had moved away and was now leaning against the window, looking down at the animals as though he found their plight of more concern than anything which was happening here. Ivor was rummaging through the items on the table which had been taken from Kelleher's car. 'I hope we're not expected to take this lot away with us,' he said to no one in particular. 'The police must have dustbins of their own, surely?' Alice and Irene unconsciously took their cue from the two men and dissociated themselves from what was taking place. Daphne was sitting on a chair, seemingly about to go to sleep.

Angus appeared quite undisturbed. He answered questions laconically, never volunteering more information than was required; yet not giving the impression that there was anything which he wished to conceal. One might have supposed from his manner that, whatever equipment was in question, it was common practice for every Foreign Office official to carry it in his briefcase. The policeman never managed to take charge of the interview. He was very tired and had no real wish to become involved with the affairs of the Foreign Office and bring the wrath of the Special Branch down on his head. Eventually, he said, 'If you'll wait here, I'll just get one of my men to bring a form for you to sign.' He looked malevolently at Ivor. 'And we shall expect you to remove *all* this stuff.' Having established some measure of ascendancy he withdrew and was soon replaced by a big, fresh-faced sergeant, a man of endless patience and experience against whom Kelleher's irritated protests washed as harmlessly as rain on a turnip.

'And now this neat little job, zurr.' For the first time he looked at Angus. One was aware of a stillness in the man as the small, light eyes focused on this new subject then, like the flash of a camera, the eyes brightened. 'Why, it's Major Drummond!'

Angus said, 'Mr Drummond.' Then to demonstrate that he, too, commanded a good memory, 'Sergeant Fletcher?'

'Yes, indeed, zurr. As you see, I've come back to the country. It suits me better. I was never one for town life.' The platitudes came out amiably enough, but he was not an amiable man and had no wish to be thought one. Angus, looking at him, had an odd feeling of cherishing this man, not for himself, but for the role he was undoubtedly to play. He was sad, however, when the small eyes fixed on Irene. 'Why, it's Miss Kimberley. It is still Miss Kimberley, I take it?' As Irene made no reply, he went on, quite unabashed, 'And how would Mrs Immingham be?'

Irene said, 'Very well.'

'The children would be growing up, I expect.'

Irene agreed that this was so.

'Well, now, I hope you'll give them my very good wishes and tell them I often thinks of my time with them.' He pushed the object towards Angus who put it in the briefcase. Surely, Alice thought, catching a glimpse of it out of the corner of an eye, it *was* a book? 'Perhaps we shall meet again, zurr.'

'At Philippi, no doubt.'

On the way out, Kelleher stopped at the desk to ask the constable on duty what was to become of the animals. The constable said, 'We've got lost children.' He seemed to think this a sufficient answer. Kelleher appeared to regard it as prevarication. The others left them arguing.

As soon as they were in the street, Alice said to Irene, '*Who* is Sergeant Fletcher?'

'He was Louise's lodger during the war. You would have been abroad at the time, I think.'

'You mean the man who had the rooms I'm in now? Why didn't you introduce us?'

'It was hardly a social occasion. Besides, I can't stand the man.' She was more upset than Alice had ever seen her.

Angus took her arm. 'Don't worry.' He was quite unconcerned, one might even have thought him elated. Irene looked up at him, her eyes full of apprehension which Alice could not understand. But as her main worry at this time was whether she would continue to see Ivor, she soon put the matter to the back of her mind.

# 10

Ivor Ritchie worked at the War Office, not far from the building where Alice worked. It was not surprising, therefore – particularly as Alice's plans seemed suddenly to necessitate a daily walk down Whitehall – that they should meet a few days after their return to London. They talked for some minutes and then, after a moment's hesitation, during which he seemed to toss a mental coin, Ivor suggested that they should have a drink. Had she been less interested in him, Alice might have interpreted that hesitation as a sign of reluctance, if not actual disinclination. As matters stood, she preferred to believe that he had paused because he recognised that this was no casual encounter. His subsequent behaviour fitted this reading well enough. A few days later he asked her out to lunch. Soon, scarcely a day passed when they did not see each other, either for lunch, or for a drink at the end of the day. Sometimes, but not often, they would walk in St James's Park together. It was all very chaste. Alice sensed that this amused Ivor.

She was sure that this was not the way in which he usually conducted his encounters with women. She had met men like him during the war, adventurers all; and had admired the women who knew how to handle them, while realising that such men were not for her. Had it not been for that revelation about Louise, she would probably have had the sense to dismiss Ivor from her mind once she returned to London. But his involvement with her sister had transformed him from a marauding stranger into a particular, yet more mysterious person. How far had his affair with Louise gone? She remembered that, in speaking of Louise, he had begun a sentence . . . 'It wasn't . . .' which Kelleher had interrupted. At that time, Alice had been too upset to follow this up. Now that unfinished sentence haunted her. What had he meant to say? 'It wasn't serious,' perhaps? That made matters worse. It meant that either he had played with Louise, or that Louise had betrayed Guy casually. But Ivor did not behave as though his affair with Louise had been casual. The strength of feeling he had betrayed gave a new and interesting dimension to his character. She could see him as a tormentor, but was it possible that he in his turn could be tormented? She persuaded herself that these doubts necessitated her seeing him again in order to give herself peace of mind. When she was with him, the physical attraction was so strong that peace of mind was the last thing she worried about. Then, when they had parted, it became the reason why she must see him again. The solution, of course, would have been to ask him outright. But that was impossible. If she spoke to anyone, it should be Louise. And in any case, a direct answer might well not be forthcoming – or it might bring to an end this tantalising relationship before a more substantial bond had been formed.

In June Ben dined with Austin and Judith at a restaurant in St Martin's Lane. The occasion was the publication of the book of Geoffrey's drawings. It was not the kind of book to merit a launching party; and, in any case, Austin's firm did not consider that providing large quantities of bad wine for literary critics and journalists did much in the way of increasing the sale of books. Ben, who had no wish for publicity, was well-content to have the opportunity of being with the two of them. By the time the main course arrived, they had exhausted the subject of the book.

Beyond the window a placard outside a newsagents announced 'Soviets say No.' On this occasion, it was the Marshall Plan to assist in European Rehabilitation to which they were saying no, on the grounds that US aid would constitute an infringement of national sovereignty. Their detractors, of whom there were many even among ardent socialists, said it was in their interests for Europe to remain weak.

'Destruction, not rehabilitation, is what they thrive on,' Judith said.

'It's more complex than that,' Austin, himself a mild socialist, protested.

'I sometimes think there are just two kinds of people,' Judith said. 'Those who want to break us down; and those who want to build us up. The Russians are the breakers down.' Most of her judgements related to people, only a few minor adjustments being required when considering the behaviour of nations. That morning Austin had dismissed her comments on the work of one of his authors in a particularly cavalier manner.

Austin shrugged his shoulders in mock despair, but Ben said, 'In which category would you place your mother?'

'A builder-up,' Judith replied promptly. 'She wants to help people to find themselves, which isn't to say that she always succeeds.

Whereas *some people* are only concerned with putting others down.'

'In order to build someone up, you have to be strong yourself.' Austin had never learnt that a woman's asides are more important than the main theme. 'The Russians, at the moment, are weakened, and they are fundamentally insecure.'

Judith, tiring of the subject, said, 'Well, I wouldn't mind a bit of Marshall Aid, anyway. I'm sick to death of queueing for things that other people get on the black market. Do you know that Alice gets up at six in the morning to queue for nylon stockings – nylon, mind you, not silk! – at some scruffy little place at the Elephant and Castle!'

'How is Alice?' Ben asked. 'I took her out to lunch when her book came out, but she didn't seem very excited about it.'

'She got one or two good notices,' Austin said. 'She may have hoped for more.'

'But there hadn't been time for any notices when I saw her. It can't have been that. She didn't eat much, either – which isn't like Alice.'

'She's not a happy girl just now,' Judith agreed. 'We have been quite worried about her, haven't we?'

'She's in love.' Austin refused to admit worrying about his stepdaughter.

'Oh, that's your answer to all women's troubles! Find the man! I think something upset her during that dreadful time she had in Norfolk.'

'Then it was a man, not flood water. She's in love, I tell you. It's plain as a pikestaff!' And then, looking at Ben, he thought, oh my goodness, I shouldn't have said that!

Judith said grudgingly, 'I think you may be right this time. She's thinner than I've ever seen her. I would have thought she would have talked to Louise about it, but she doesn't seem to have done.'

'Did you like her book?' Ben asked Austin rather loudly.

Austin accepted the change of subject readily. 'I thought it very competent. Not a one-off, either. She knows how to spin a web with words.'

'Yes,' Ben nodded. He used words as if he was waving flags. As he read Alice's stories, he had realised that he would never become a writer: he was not going to compete on unequal terms with Alice.

'You think she will be a success?' Judith asked, not for the first time; she could not hear Austin's praise of Alice too often.

'I think she will have a following, not large, but faithful.'

Judith looked away, thinking of Stanley and how proud he would have been, telling all his friends, pretending to talk objectively and getting far more angry than anyone else over every adverse criticism. For a moment, she thought, what am I doing sitting here?

Austin was saying, 'I think we might have a liqueur with our ground acorns, or whatever passes for coffee – to celebrate all this literary activity.'

Judith said curtly, 'Not for me, I can't take all this drink.'

Austin looked at her in surprise. *Now*, what have I done? he wondered. Is it because I have said that Alice is in love, which she undoubtedly is; or is it that I have not been fulsome enough in praise of her book? He had little idea of the extent to which Judith's way of life had changed since she married him, and could not conceive that almost everything she did, except the gardening, required some adjustment on her part.

While Austin was dealing with the bill, Judith said abruptly to Ben, 'You have always got on rather well with Alice. Couldn't you help her now? See a bit more of her? You could probably help her to sort herself out better than I could, being the same generation.'

'I *do* see her.'

'Casually, yes. But if you made a bit of an effort? I suppose that's asking rather a lot . . .'

They parted outside the restaurant. Austin said to Judith as they walked away, 'What did you say to Ben to make him look so thunderous?'

Ben had a burning pain in his chest which continued well into the afternoon; it was only later in the day, when the pain still had not eased, that he was prepared to admit that it might have another source than indigestion.

The opportunity to make enquiries about Alice presented itself sooner than he had expected.

The following day Guy was working late when one of the partners came to see him. He was a large, Teutonic young man whose blue eyes had the surprised glare of the thwarted child. As he put a folder down on Guy's desk he looked as if he might be about to launch into one of Siegfried's more petulant outbursts. Guy read the name on the folder – Lady Browne. The man said, 'You shouldn't be spending so much time on this old duck.'

Guy's eyes were cold and angry; his mouth set obstinately. 'Her affairs are in a muddle. And she has been with this firm a long time and depends on us for help.'

'Eggsactly!' The eyes popped open even wider. 'That, old man, is just what I am getting at. She has indeed been with us a very long time, from the Crimean War onwards, I would think!' He found this very funny and brayed amusment. Guy looked pained. 'You may be interested to see this breakdown of the time spent on her and the amount of money which it has brought in. I've done a similar exercise on two or three of your other clients.' He laid a double-width sheet covered with figures on top of the file.

'She can't afford to pay much.'

'And we can't afford clients who can't afford to pay for our services.'

Guy looked at him uncomprehendingly and he gave a crowing laugh which ended in a little snort of contempt. He seemed to have quite a repertoire of farmyard noises. 'What I am saying is that you will have to advise her to find another accountant. Perhaps you might say that she doesn't need our sort of specialist service – that there must be someone locally who would be much better suited to her needs.' He yawned and scratched his midriff, already bored with the subject. 'You will know how to put it. You are so good with these people.'

'I couldn't do that!' Guy was appalled.

'I'm afraid you will have to – and that goes for the others.' He was offhand rather than authoritative – Guy did not merit a show of strength. 'See to it, will you, old man.' He strolled out of the room and could be heard in the corridor joking rather coarsely with one of the cleaners.

Guy sat gazing in front of him for some time. Then he pulled a sheet of paper towards him and began to compose a long memorandum explaining why it would be wrong to take the action proposed by the partners. He was not happy with the result, and when he got home he telephoned Ben to ask him to meet him for a drink the next day.

They met in the evening at The Two Chairmen in Westminster.

'I don't like to trouble you with this.' His sensitive skin was flushed and his eyes sought the spaces in the crowded bar. 'But you are trained in this sort of thing . . . I thought you might care to take a look at what I've written.' He gave a nervous laugh. 'Pick holes in it . . . and that kind of thing.'

Ben studied the memorandum with misgivings.

Guy said anxiously, 'Is it any good? I mean, please suggest any alterations . . .'

'It's money they are worried about, I take it?'

'All the time.'

'Then however good this is, you won't shift them, will you? You haven't even mentioned the financial aspect.'

'But I've explained about the circumstances of the clients involved . . .'

'Who are poor. Which the partners already know and don't like.' Ben tapped the memorandum. 'These arguments won't hold any water with them. If they saw a blinding light on the Damascus road they would think it was warning them of a bad investment!'

At a near-by table an architect was airing his grievances. 'All they cared about was the cost of the service road! The whole bloody building has got to be squashed up in a corner of the site so that they can save money on the service road.'

Ben said, 'You see? It's the world we live in.'

'I'm not worried about aesthetic considerations!' Guy would have had no qualms about squashing a building up in the corner of a site. 'It's people I deal with, not bricks and mortar.'

'Wouldn't the old lady be better off with a firm that is a little less sharp?'

'*What* firm?' Guy asked. 'In the past most accountants have carried a few lame ducks, but it doesn't mean they are prepared to take the other firms' cast-offs.' He folded the papers and put them away in his briefcase. 'I suppose I could do it privately. That's the answer. Louise won't like me bringing more work home, though.'

'Why don't you get out?'

'How?' Guy smiled faintly. 'It's a very thrusting profession now, and I'm not a thrusting person.' He said this, Ben noted, with a certain satisfaction. No doubt his colleagues had some grounds for finding him difficult to work with. Even so . . . 'They can't all be sods. Start looking. What about a country town?'

Guy brightened, seeing an immediate picture of homely old buildings clustered round a sleepy market square. 'Now, that *is* worth considering.'

'And how is Alice?' Ben asked.

'Alice?' Guy thought about Alice, who was the least of his problems. 'I don't really know. She's out rather a lot.'

'I saw her mother the other day. She said Alice was getting thin.'

'She's not eating potatoes,' Guy recalled. 'She and Louise had a row about it on Sunday.' He took a long draught of beer. 'Shaftesbury, now. I've always thought that was an attractive little town. What's the name of that hill – Golden something?'

'I'm going down to Herefordshire again in the autumn. I thought

I'd have another crack at Offa's Dyke. She might like to come. It would be a change of scene. We might make up a party?'

'Yes,' Guy said. 'And then, there's Ludlow . . .' His face had become drawn. 'I really must do something – time goes by so quickly . . .'

After he had left Ben he walked home through the parks, looking at the old houses lining the busy roads. They had an air of having preserved within their walls the spaciousness and peace of another age. He thought, 'I mustn't let life just slip away like this.' The palms of his hands were sweating. He did not want to become one of those elderly men one saw sitting on park benches, or in club rooms, with that puzzled look on their faces as though wondering where it had all gone wrong. One saw films, read books, heard older people talk about men who lived contented lives, passing their days quietly, respected in their community, doing a reasonable job, a certain amount of good. It must be possible still, somewhere, mustn't it?

At the weekend, Alice and Louise sat in deck chairs in the garden. Louise was sunbathing. 'I must get rid of these strap marks, or I can't wear that dress tonight,' she said. Alice turned a page. Louise said, 'What are you reading so intently?'

'*Asmodée*.'

'That's yesterday's news!' Louise laughed. 'We are going to do Tennessee Williams's *Summer and Smoke* in the autumn. It's a beautiful play. Not nearly so hysterical as some of his stuff. I can't undertand why it isn't done more often. Perhaps because people are so impatient. They can't get any pleasure from long, slow days, or long, slow plays.' She rocked her deckchair gently, looking lazily up at the sky, confident of pleasure.

'What do you think it means when Emmy and Harry are out in the garden and Marcelle says to Blaise "I hate this night which has closed in on them. This betrothal night which they will remember even after their love is dead . . ."?'

'She is jealous of her daughter, of course.'

'Yes, but it isn't jealousy which makes her say that their love will die – that is something she seems to take for granted, as though it's a rule of life.'

'The early rapture certainly dies.' Louise looked at Guy who was spraying the roses with a soapy concoction of his own devising. 'I am sure he should be doing that in the evening, not now while the sun is so hot.'

'Why does it have to be at night? "I hate this *night* which has closed in on them." And then one talks of a dark night of the soul. Always darkness where passion is concerned. I remember Miss Lindsay at school saying that Romeo and Juliet end up in the tomb, as do Aida and Radames . . .'

'She would, she had a warped mind.'

'But it's true! Look at Cleopatra, and Othello, and . . .'

Louise called to Guy, 'There are two ladies here who need your ministrations much more than those roses.'

Guy put down the watering can and went into the kitchen where they could hear him filling a kettle. Louise closed her eyes contentedly. 'A nice cup of tea is just what I need. Much better than holding an asp to one's bosom.'

Alice closed the book. Louise said, 'Don't take it so hard; whoever it is, he can't be worth it.'

Tears came into Alice's eyes. Louise said, 'I'm sure I was never so solemn about my love affairs.' For her, one golden day would always wipe out the memory of a month of storms.

Guy came and put out a deck chair for himself; then he fetched a small table, placing it carefully on a smooth patch of grass. He did all this with meticulous attention to detail. Then he came over to Louise and inspected her back. 'There is still the faintest of strap marks.' He ran his fingers lightly over her back.

Perhaps his hands were cold. Louise gave a little shiver. Alice, turning to look at her, saw that her head was tilted back, her eyes half-closed. Her face had that unfocused, almost imbecile appearance which pleasure can present to a person coming cold upon a love scene. As Guy walked unconcernedly away, Louise whispered, 'My artful little monkey!'

She is thinking of Ivor! Alice experienced a wrench of pain so bitter it startled her into saying, 'Daphne introduced me to someone who knew you – Ivor Ritchie.'

Louise, who might have given the guilty start Alice anticipated had Jacov been mentioned at this moment, replied at once, 'The love of my life! How did he seem?'

'What do you mean, the love of your life?' Alice asked, disconcerted by Louise's manner.

Louise spoke more soberly. 'There was a time when I thought I would never get over giving him up.'

'*You* gave *him* up?'

'Of course.' Louise looked coldly at Alice, offended that anyone might imagine that a man would give her up. 'And there's no need to look so old-fashioned. We weren't lovers . . . at least, not in the way you are thinking.'

'Is there another way?' There was certainly another way for her, but she had not imagined it to be so for Louise.

'There must be. I have never felt like that about any other man.'

'Then, why, how . . .' Alice asked, thinking of the force that was in Ivor and the strength that must have been required to withstand it.

'I wouldn't be sitting here if I had become his mistress. There would have been no going back.' Louise looked at Guy who had come out of the kitchen carrying a tea tray as though it contained sacred vessels. He had donned an old straw hat to protect his sensitive skin from the sun. 'He will have used the best china, and covered that tray with a lace cloth. He is so much more gracious than I shall ever be! How could I have left him?' She spoke with a wry tenderness so different from that moment earlier when Guy had rubbed his fingers across her back that Alice was more puzzled than ever.

'You must be very much in love with Guy,' she said doubtfully.

'He needs me. He needs me much more than Ivor needed me.'

Alice, remembering Ivor's white face and the rage which had consumed him at the memory of Louise, thought that perhaps Ivor had needed Louise more than she realised.

'Don't mention his name in front of Guy,' Louise said, watching Guy setting the china on the table. She asked no questions about Alice's meeting with Ivor. It would never have occurred to her that Ivor would betray anything other than a casual interest in Alice.

Alice, aware of this, said snappishly, 'Oh, I shall rush up to him the minute he has finished laying the table and say, "Did you know that Louise had an affair with a man called Ivor Ritchie during the war?" '

Louise smiled and stretched out an arm to Guy. 'My darling, how good you are to us.'

He came over to her and again inspected her back. 'Shall I rub oil on for you?'

'After tea, my sweet.'

Alice picked up the copy of *Asmodée* and began to read again. Louise went to the table and poured tea. Guy eased himself into a deck chair. 'Ben had some idea we might all go on a walking holiday together. What do you think? I expect your mother would look after the children.'

The holiday resolved itself into a long weekend to be taken in October, as Guy and Louise were committed to a summer holiday with the children in August. Alice agreed to the proposal because she could not envisage a future which stretched as far as October. They were to walk in the Chilterns. Too much time would be wasted in travelling were they to go to Offa's Dyke. 'Leave that for another year,' Louise said. 'When we have more time.' Alice marvelled that they could take the circumstances of their lives so much for granted. Why, in October, let alone another year . . . She was still seeing Ivor more often than she had dared to hope.

He would never know how attractive he would have found her had Louise cast no shadow. There were moments when she seemed to emerge and stand on her own; and, since on these occasions he experienced a certain unease, he guessed that there might have been something he would have sought in her. But these glimpses came too rarely for him ever to forget that she was Louise's sister. He was fascinated by the variety of emotions which could be roused simply by being in her company – pain, pleasure, the desire for revenge and a deep, secret merriment. There seemed infinite possibilities to choose from at the end of every stroll in the park or along the banks of the river, or as the last notes of a concert died away. The important thing was not to settle for any one of them. Their affair would then become like any other and he was not short of that kind of satisfaction. He had already told her he had two mistresses.

One mistress would have been a matter for concern. There being two, she could only assume that neither contented him. Indeed, he must be very discontented since, in spite of having two mistresses, he sought her company so often. But it troubled her that there was no suggestion of their becoming lovers. Gordon had not become her lover because he was married. Was she always to be involved with men who, for one reason or another, did not seek to have their way with her?

'Don't you find me attractive?' she teased him.

'You know that I do.'

'Is it because of Louise? I don't mind that. I'm used to being second to Louise.'

'I could never be sure of my motives, Alice. Believe me, I'm not usually so scrupulous. But I don't think I have ever made love to anyone as an act of revenge.'

'That sounds very lofty – not a bit like you.'

He laughed. She was never sure how serious he was about anything. But however he had answered, it would have made little difference, since she would have used it as grounds for hope. Had he told her that he hated her, she would have thought: now, that is a good sign because it shows real feeling; and the fact that he had to tell me is even better; we are drawn together by this hate.

But although he never told her that he hated her, he did occasionally display an anger which seemed to surprise himself as much as her. Once, when she had been talking about Claire, whom he had never met, he said savagely, 'The Fairley sisters are the three sirens. You lure men with false promises while you ensnare them in your moral net.' He spoke as though there was something inherently wrong in morality.

'You think your way of life is the only way, don't you?' he said. 'It's not true. Each person is a kind of exploration, the discovery of an alien culture.'

Sometimes he frightened her; but was it possible that he, too, could be frightened? 'Are you afraid of making love to me, is that it? Do you think I would change you into a frog?'

'No, a husband.'

She made no reply, and he said impatiently, 'You are too honest for your own good, Alice. You should protest more.'

'I wouldn't insist on marriage if you didn't want it.'

'Oh no! But you would look at me with those grave, steady eyes offering freedom – "leave me when you will . . ." I can't imagine a more potent weapon.'

'I never think of myself as having weapons.'

'No? Yet you are very expert with those eyes.'

'What nonsense you do talk! But I can't argue with you, I'm not incisive like you. You have no difficulty keeping company with your ideas; while I'm always pursuing mine; just when I think I've grasped one, I see it from another angle. And so it goes on.'

'That is most endearing and will see you through life very well.'

He was on the defensive: she had turned him into a mortal! 'There now,' she said, 'and I thought you were a separate creation; while it turns out you're just a person with a strong sense of self-preservation.'

'That was rather good for someone who has to fumble after her thoughts.'

When she was not with him, she went over and over such conversations, elaborating them while she prepared minutes or filed reports; they echoed in her mind when she went to the cinema so that she could not talk sensibly about whatever film she had seen. There was no one in the world but Ivor. He was round every street corner, on the end of the telephone whenever it rang at home or at the office; above all, he was in her dreams.

She dreamt one night of a house which stood by a lake whose waters mirrored it without a single ripple breaking the image. The next day she experienced such pain and longing that she could not remain still and was constantly finding an excuse to leave her office to walk in the corridor, or to run down the front stairs and up the back stairs, anything to release the tension which built up whenever her limbs were inactive. In the evening, she walked through the streets into Holland Park. That night, she wrote a poem about the dream and by containing her experience within a framework of rhyme and rhythm, a pattern of formal phrases, the pain became more manageable.

So long the house has stood secure
Insensitive to storm and fire
The still lake water, crystal pure,
Mirrors a peace beyond desire;
Amid the dusty, twilit trees
The nightingale no longer sings
And strain and stress and long unease
Have years since fled on cobweb wings.

But now, across the cloistered lawn,
A wind comes thrusting from the sea,
As barbed and bitter as the thorn
That draws the blood of agony;
The bay tree bends compliant back
Before the invader's dancing lash;
The house, new-twisted on the rack,
Awakens as the cymbals clash.

The flames of dawn consume the night
And chaos strides within the gate,
The house in terror turns to fight,
In anguish knows it is too late;
And knowing, smiles, and hears once more
The tender, final agony,
Through broken glass and splintered door,
The nightingale's sweet litany.

Later, looking at the poem, she saw that it told her much about the intensity of her need for love, but very little about Ivor. It could have been inspired by another man, and seemed to foreshadow a time when there would be no Ivor.

'He *will* take me,' she thought. 'He *must*. And I will have had something Louise didn't have.' Until now, she had always thought of herself as being without a shred of jealousy of Louise.

It was more than Ivor which was at stake. It was her chance of happiness. And happiness? Happiness was the secret of Kashmir, of that world beyond the dim curtain of the present, a world brilliant with all the colours of the spectrum whose citizens lived in an eternal now. She saw Ivor as her pass to cross this frontier; through him she would leave behind the sepia world of absence and unanswered need.

The only person in whom she confided during this time was Irene, who had problems of her own. Irene listened, wincing, to Alice's account of her latest encounter with Ivor.

'I admire you for actually *saying* these things to him.'

'You mean you wouldn't have done?' Alice was quick to sense disapproval.

'I think it's more that I couldn't bring myself to let him see my feelings.'

'You think I have cheapened myself?'

'Honestly, I really do admire you.'

'You make me feel I have done something awful.'

'I think you are very brave.'

'I don't want to be brave. I want love.'

'Oh, really!' Irene pressed her fingers against her lips. Her face looked pinched. 'I'm sorry, Alice. I'm afraid I'm not being much help to you.'

Alice saw Ben on several occasions. He had taken to calling in on Louise and Guy in the evening, and when Alice was out in the garden, hoping for a few minutes alone, he would join her. He seemed to understand that she was deeply unhappy. But his behaviour was more unpredictable than ever. At one moment he would surprise her by his sensitivity, the next he would be abrasive or irritatingly obtuse. He could accept her ill-humour with wry tolerance, and then become unexpectedly hurt by some casual comment she had not intended to be taken seriously.

'I can't cope with you being so touchy,' she told him one evening.

'What else can't you cope with, Alice?'

He was standing beside her, and now he placed his hands lightly on her shoulders. She cried out, scarcely knowing for what.

'Alice, tell me. . . .'

But she pulled away from him and ran into the house.

The day before, Ivor had failed to meet her in the evening. She had waited for an hour outside the café where they were to have had supper, then she had found a telephone box and dialled his home number. The line had been engaged. She had dialled several times with the same result.

Days went by, then he telephoned her at the office and asked her to lunch with him. When they met, she was immediately aware of a difference in him. He looked at her as though it was much longer ago that they had last met and he spoke in the light insulting manner in which an acquaintanceship can sometimes be disclaimed, without regard for conviction. In the café, he said casually, 'I'm sorry about the other evening. But I had to work late.'

'You could have telephoned.'

'Yes.' He smiled, creating an opening for her. 'So?'

She made no reply, unwilling to be forced into a move of his choosing. But later, when they were walking in St James's Park, she said, 'I don't suppose there is any point in going on, is there?'

'Probably not.' He was deliberately cheerful; but she noticed that he was limping badly. It was a hot day. Perhaps the heat had upset him.

'I wouldn't know what to do without you,' she said gently.

They stood on the bridge where he had once taken Louise's hand. He said, 'You will manage well enough. Underneath all that uncertainty, there is a very strong-willed person. You will get what you want from life, Alice.'

'I don't recognise myself when you talk about me.'

'That is because you like to think of yourself as gentle and malleable.'

'I think you are the most hurtful person I have ever known.'

'When it comes to hurting, I can't hold a candle to a Fairley.'

So, it was Louise to whom he was talking! And it was Louise, no doubt, who had fuelled what fire there had been in their relationship.

'Now what have I said?' he asked, studying her face.

She turned away. 'It doesn't matter.'

'That's a stupid remark, when obviously something matters very much.'

'But not *me*!' she shouted. People turned from feeding the ducks to look at them. 'It's not *me* that matters, is it?'

For a moment, he was touched and made a movement towards her. Then he checked himself. If he tried to make amends, another situation, more potentially harmful, would soon arise and he was beginning to lose his way in this labyrinth into which he had allowed himself to be lured. He said, 'I don't think I am very good at these farewells that go on and on like the last chords of a Beethoven symphony.'

She pushed past him roughly, so that he overbalanced and had to cling to the railings of the bridge to support himself. A woman standing near by said to her companion, 'What a way to behave – and to a cripple!'

Alice, walking beneath the arch of plane trees, was already playing the game so dear to women of constructing an ending which she could have borne. If only we could have talked it over like civilised people and decided between us that it would not have worked; if only we could both have come out of it feeling enriched; if only we could have remained friends; if only, if only. . . . But what bearable ending was there when two people were free and still did not choose each other? He would probably go back to his flat and listen to music that evening, taking deep breaths of relief that it was all over. Or perhaps it didn't even matter that much? He would listen to music and think of Louise. While she, Alice, would compose letters to him which she would never send. And would walk through the leaden streets, or stare from the office window, wondering despairingly if this was all, *all* there was ever going to be.

# 11

Jacov came back from an all-night party and sat reading the paper. It was August and the room was hot and stuffy. He found this unpleasant, but it did not occur to him to open a window. There was a report on a speech by Herbert Morrison about the latest economic crisis. Although Mr Morrison contrived to sound quite jaunty about it all, it was doubtful whether his comments would give much joy to anyone. 'Even the little homely things matter,' Jacov read. 'Get more than ever out of your garden and allotments. Bottle and preserve all you can. If you can, raise poultry. Step up salvage, save paper, save pig food, save . . .' Jacov turned to another page. India and Pakistan had come into being at midnight on August 14th – or should it be the 15th? How confusing for the Indians. While all the celebrations were going on, Moslems and Hindus were engaged in killing one another. He turned to the book page where there was a muted appreciation of *The Judge's Story* by Charles Morgan; on the opposite page there was a less than respectful review of a play which he had produced at the Lyric Theatre in Hammersmith. He was pleased to note that most of the blame had been laid where it belonged, on the ample shoulders of the leading lady. He put the paper down and went to the radiogram, found a record of Scheherazade and poured himself a brandy. The music was just beginning to work its magic when there was a banging on the front door. The woman with the gauze scarf tied over hair curlers contrived a certain Byzantine elegance and when she spoke it was without any hint of aggression. 'Do you know what time it is?' Her eyes dwelt wearily on the brandy glass. 'Obviously you don't. Then I must tell you that it is just after six.' Jacov could not decide whether she thought it was early or late for brandy; but it was clear to him that she did not like Rimsky Korsakov.

'No, Mr Vaseline,' she said slowly, as though speaking to the very hard of hearing. 'It is *music* I don't like. I am tone deaf. It is a misfortune, but then none of us is perfect. And at six o'clock in the morning, as well as being tone deaf, I am not very tolerant.'

'I will turn it off.'

'Thank you. I hoped you would.'

They bowed to each other and she departed.

Jacov finished the brandy, standing by the window looking down at a postman who had paused while emptying a pillar-box to talk to a road sweeper. He envied them this brief companionship. Usually, he slept most of the morning; but six o'clock was too late to begin sleeping. He had no idea what else could be done with the morning hours, since music was not allowed. He decided to breakfast at Lyons all-night café near Westminster Bridge.

As he walked along Victoria Street, he realised that one of the reasons he had felt he must get out was that she had called him Mr Vaseline. The people in Pratts Farm Road, Shepherd's Bush, where he had lived when he was a schoolboy, had spoken of 'the Vaseline family'. It was already beginning to get warm and would develop into one of those long, enervating summer days: days on which Alice and her friend Daphne would practise tennis shots in the Fairleys' garden and Katia would sulk because she had not been asked to join them. His mother would say, 'You do not want to run about red as a lobster like a peasant'; while the twins would play the gramophone as loud as they pleased and the Fairleys would not complain. The twins were alive and in Canada; he must write to them. And Alice. Alice worked just off Parliament Square. He must ask her to lunch with him – sometime when he could be sure he would be up by lunchtime. He would take her to The Ivy, she would enjoy that. Did she know that he and Louise were lovers? He suspected not. 'No one must ever know about this,' Louise constantly insisted. 'I don't want people to gossip and make fun of Guy.'

Once, when he had not seen her for a long time and was angry, he had said, 'It might be simplest to give them nothing to gossip about.'

She had answered almost as though it were a matter in which he was not involved, 'I couldn't go on . . . I just couldn't go on without this.'

'You could leave Guy and marry me.'

'And what should we do with the hours when we weren't in bed, Jacov?'

'I should be at the theatre.'

'You are very selfish. What a good thing it's Guy whom I love!'

He came to Parliament Square, which looked quite provincial at this time in the morning, and crossed Whitehall without any assistance from the policeman on traffic duty.

He went into the Lyons opposite the Houses of Parliament where he was immediately rammed by a trolley of dirty crockery pushed by a large, moist woman in an overall. 'It's 'elp yourself, luv,' she said, when he sat down. She abandoned the trolley momentarily to smear a grey cloth over the surface of the table. Jacov took a tray and inspected the dishes on offer, rejected congealed poached eggs in favour of baked beans on toast.

Business was becoming brisk and several of the tables were occupied. There were sober-suited men who might be civil servants or policemen, a brick-faced, rakish individual who was Jacov's idea of a journalist, an ambulance driver, two girls surrounded by suitcases festooned with foreign sticker labels, and a particularly malodorous tramp. Jacov sat at an empty table near the two girls.

One of the girls was saying, 'There's going to be a ban on foreign travel, did you see? It's lucky we didn't wait any longer.'

Her companion said, 'I wonder what Mario and Guiseppe are doing now.'

'Same routine with two other girls, I expect.'

'I don't think Mario was like that.'

'My brother says you can never trust an Italian. He was quite shocked we went. He said they were worse than the Germans. You knew where you were with the Germans.'

'I don't think Mario and Guiseppe would ever do anything . . . you know, really nasty . . . do you?'

'You never know, do you? What about those English fellows at Amalfi? Talk about letting yourself go when you get on foreign soil!'

The baked beans were tasty and Jacov was considering a further helping when a shadow fell across his table.

'Jacov Vaseyelin, isn't it?'

Jacov looked at the dark, distinguished man whom he certainly should not have forgotten. 'I saw you recently at the Criterion. Otherwise I might not have remembered you, either. I'm Angus Drummond.'

'How extraordinary!' Jacov, delighted to have company, cleared a space on the table. 'I was thinking of your sister only this morning.'

'Daphne, I assume.'

The girls at the next table were making plans for future summer holidays. 'It's ever so cheap in Austria. A friend of mine stayed in a hotel where King Farouk stays, and it only cost her a few pounds a week.'

'But they are all blubbery and pink. I don't like pink men.'

'They're not pink – not nearly as pink as Englishmen!'

'Well, there you are, then. I go abroad to get away from Englishmen.'

Angus said to Jacov, 'Do you ever think of going back?'

Jacov looked perplexed. 'How could I? The house was bombed. And, anyway, I don't like Shepherd's Bush.'

'I meant to Russia.'

'Russia!' Jacov responded to this theatrically and several people turned to look at him. 'I was only four when I left Russia. All I can remember of it is snow coming down outside a window. I remember more than that about Lithuania.' His voice had dwindled as he spoke but one person at a table near by continued to take an interest in the conversation.

'You don't think it's important to go back to your roots?'

'I haven't got roots in Russia or Lithuania.'

'So, I suppose you would say, you've put down roots here. That's interesting.'

'No, I don't think I would say that.' Jacov, used to speaking other people's lines, was uncharacteristically disobliging on this occasion. 'I don't really know what people mean when they talk about putting down roots.' He pointed to a glass of water on the ambulance man's table. 'You know there are some plants which will grow, just in water? Well, I suppose I'm like that.' The idea pleased him. 'A lotus, perhaps.'

The ambulance man peered suspiciously into the glass.

'But you *have* made a life for yourself here, roots or no roots. I admire people who can fit into a new country, adopt a different culture . . .'

'Did you enjoy the play? I thought it was rather gloomy myself.'

'The play? Oh, yes. I thought you were very good, especially in the last act.'

'Oh, that last act!' Jacov clutched his temples, attracting general attention once again. 'One of the critics wrote "Mr Vaseyelin is a superb communicator. He plays the final scene as if it is a matter of life and death that we should understand the motives of this tormented man." And I had no idea, not a glimmering, of what it was all about!'

'So, how do you manage?'

'You must tell yourself before you go on stage – this is so, because *I* say it is so. You must will it. What you do must be unquestionable, because *you* are doing it. If you really believe that, most of the audience will believe it, too. At least while they are in their seats!'

Angus sat, elbows on table, cupped hands folded like protective leaves around his face. 'Yes,' he said, 'I can understand that.'

'I really am very hungry this morning. Can I get you something? I'm going to have more baked beans.'

'I think I might manage another round of toast.'

Angus watched Jacov walk to the service counter. In spite of what seemed a remarkably good appetite, he was thin as a modern sculpture – no more than a coil of vibrating wire topped by a tangled mop. The face eluded the kind of delineation the camera excels at. One could understand why he had not made more films. His would always be the face which gave memory the slip; one would search the cast list and say 'of course!' and then forget. And yet, this indeterminate man who could not be associated with any one place, or identified with a particular culture, this irrational, imprecise man, incapable of exact definition, could, by a sheer act of will, become conqueror in his own kingdom. Surely a proof that once the will is engaged, circumstances can be made to work for it.

When Jacov returned, Angus said, 'It was a happy chance our meeting. I may have to go abroad for a little while – one of those confidential trips.' He could see that Jacov was not really taking this in; he had been right to think that he would show little curiosity. 'It will be Irene's birthday while I'm out of the country – Irene Kimberley, you remember her?'

Jacov, busy cutting the toasted beans into neat squares, nodded his head. 'She and Alice came to see me when I was playing at the Q Theatre. Very perceptive, I thought. She . . .'

Angus intervened quickly, 'I have a small present for her. Something I don't want to trust to the post. Would it be too much to ask you to deliver it to her on the appointed day? I could give it to Alice, of course; but women are such talkers, and this is to be a surprise.'

'I should be delighted.'

'It's not until October. I'll let you have it before I go.'

Jacov said, 'I will put a ring round the day on the calendar.' It was to be hoped he studied the calendar.

'I don't know when I shall be going. It could be quite soon.' It was surprising, the need to talk to someone, not for advice, of course, but because the excitement demanded a voice. 'It all depends on how quickly a man who gained certain information will be able to market it. It is the assessment of his character and ability which will be the telling factor, rather than the information itself. And he gives the appearance of being rather stupid – and a busybody. An unfortunate combination. Few people have patience with the stupid and fewer still can tolerate the busybody, especially if he is telling them something they should have discovered for themselves.'

'What is he trying to market?'

The question startled Angus. Jacov Vaseyelin was not stupid and although he had at first not been particularly interested in what Angus was saying, his brain had had no difficulty in deciding what was crucial to this issue. Angus said, 'A few facts and quite a lot of theory. Nothing important.'

'But important enough to be the deciding factor in your leaving the country.'

Angus realised in dismay that he had played this game with the wrong man. Jacov Vaseyelin, with his background, was probably instinctively suspicious. He would know that during the war Angus had been involved with the Resistance movement; from this he might well deduce continued involvement with the intelligence service. To find himself cast for a part, however peripheral, in a transaction with such a man, and at a time when that man was talking of leaving the country, might well throw Jacov into a blind panic.

Angus said, 'You mustn't take me seriously. I am given to making cryptic remarks. My sister Daphne says I enjoy devising puzzles because I can't tolerate the commonplace.'

But it was too late. Jacov had pushed his plate to one side; his appetite for food had gone, and also, it seemed, for company, since he was obviously preparing to leave. He said to Angus, 'I think your best course would be to deliver your present to Irene when you return. I am sure she would accept your apologies for any delay.'

And yet, Angus thought, I have said so little! But enough, I suppose, to touch a chord in someone who most of his life has been morbidly afraid of spies. As he watched Jacov's precipitate exit, he thought grimly that if anyone *had* been observing this ridiculously over-dramatised exchange, they might have found stronger grounds for suspicion than any Sergeant Fletcher could provide.

Angus finished his toast and had another cup of coffee; he did not think he was being watched, but the pretence of appearing unruffled was instinctive. In fact, he was very ruffled indeed. It was true that he enjoyed being cryptic; and when he had made oblique references to Sergeant Fletcher as a man with information which he might, or might not, be able to market, he had not given much weight to what he was saying. But Jacov had deciphered these coded messages with which Angus hoped to fool himself as well as others. He had said with commendable clarity, 'But important enough to be the deciding factor in your leaving the country.' The situation had been more real to Jacov, the hazards more clearly perceived, than to Angus Drummond, the person actually involved.

Angus had always known that a point must be reached where there was no going back. What he had not realised was that this point could be reached and passed without his ever noticing. Now, he saw that it was a long time past. A very senior man in his branch of the intelligence service had connived in Angus's exploits; but this man would not continue to do this once there was a risk that suspicion might fall on him. Angus had had a lot of luck, more than he could have expected, certainly more than he deserved. But that, too, was in the past. He was near the end now.

'You can't sit here all morning. You'll have to shift yourself when we get really busy,' the woman with the trolley said to the tramp.

'I shall have one more coffee.' The tramp spoke in a hoarse but not uneducated voice. He delved into his rags and produced a few coins, counting them to make sure he could make good his promise.

'Well, make it quick,' she said, good-natured but firm. 'It's getting hot in here and you're more savoury than the baked beans.'

It occurred to Angus, looking at the tramp, that he found the man quite as distasteful as his father would have done. Not that his father was squeamish, but he could not tolerate failure. The tramp was the epitome of failure – always assuming that the aim in life is to be acceptable in one's own society, and that the tramp was aware of this and had tried conscientiously but found he could not measure up to the requirements. But supposing he had made a deliberate decision? One day, looking at himself in the mirror, he had not liked what he saw and had simply walked away from it. In that case, it was the tramp who denounced the failure of society, disassociating himself from its values, rejecting its received truths. Why couldn't *I* have done that? Angus thought. Then, from time to time, I would meet my father and, stealing up behind him, look over his shoulder – like Lear's fool! How strange, that I can contemplate what I suppose people will call a betrayal of my inheritance, yet find this rejection too difficult, too wholesale. The tramp is strong enough to stand alone, while I can only change sides.

He went out into the street. It was a morning that seemed to hold a lot of promise. There had been other such mornings in his life. I can't always stand on the edge of the day, he thought: thresholds are for crossing.

Ben sat on the tow-path, making notes. It was just before seven in the morning and a mist came up from the river, which was low, the tide still going out. The river smell mingled with that of the Brentford gas works. All this Ben noted. He had been having a bad time lately. The doctor had suggested he should see a psychiatrist. 'But I'm not ill,' Ben had pointed out. 'I just don't feel well.' When it became apparent that he was not to be shifted from this diagnosis, the doctor had made one or two suggestions. Chief among them was that Ben should make a practice of going for a walk each day and note in detail exactly what he saw. As a therapy it seemed to work rather well, concentrating his mind on his particular surroundings instead of the abstract terrors with which it preferred to concern itself. 'The river moves sluggishly carrying a tin of Spam down to the sea,' Ben wrote. 'Mud, wrinkled and whorled like melting toffee . . .' Or toffee in the making? No, no, no! This was just what he was not supposed to do. He scribbled hastily, 'piece of paper fluttering from half-closed dustbin, one woollen glove on end of post – hopefully waiting to be claimed?' Now, how did I *know* that? Well, it wouldn't have put itself on the end of the post, would it? 'Willows, all present and correct, lined up on parade, just as yesterday.' No, not true. Misty today, blurred with moisture, all the leaves running into one another.

One good thing about this little exercise was that it disposed of the notion of the sameness of days. Each day had its individual fingerprint. Each day was a gift. He had made a vow to remember that when he left the jungle behind. Mustn't think about the jungle, or Geoffrey and the others . . . Water is still now. That Spam tin isn't going to make Barnes bridge, let alone the sea! And that church across the bank is quite definitely made of stone, not cotton wool; the mist is beginning to clear. Nothing lasts forever, not even the monsoon rains . . . A police launch coming up from Hammersmith, very neat and trim. I wave, but they don't respond. I am odd, but not odd enough to merit their taking an interest. A woman coming along the tow-path wearing something long and shapeless in faded cotton. Her straw hat has seen as much service as the one I wore in the jungle. She carries an easel and has a satchel hitched over one shoulder. She is also bare-footed, but from choice, not necessity – her feet press into the soil like roots as she studies the river and its banks as though they had been arranged for her purpose. Now, I must go. The woman has disturbed me. I can see Geoffrey hunched under a tree, drawing that other river . . .

More traffic about now. When I reach the road the windows of the pub are open and someone is playing a radio as they clean out the bar. The sun is breaking through and I am sweating already; it is going to be a scorcher. I shan't go back to my lodgings. If I go back, I shall be unable to get myself out again. It isn't staying away from the office that I mind, it is going back and facing that look they will give me which says that there is nothing physically wrong with me. How odd, that after all that has happened, the thing that really puts me in a lather is going into the office after I have had a day away sick. So, I will catch the train at Chiswick Park, and get something to eat at that stall outside Waterloo station. And my landlady, Mrs Milbrook, will get in a panic because I haven't returned and she will tell the police and . . . The doctor is quite right. As soon as I allow my mind any sort of freedom it constructs some minor disaster! And anyway, Mrs Milbrook enjoys calamity.

Not a bad train journey, too early for the crowds. And at the stall outside the station no one takes much notice of me. All sorts of strange people here, nothing excites the stallholder. When I stand here, eating a cheese roll, I have a sense of real freedom and I think I may manage after all. A positive thought! Follow it quickly with another. There is something remarkably satisfying about a cheese roll. It will carry me through the morning very well.

Alice played tennis in the park with a friend from her office. The girl wanted to join a tennis club which had a high standard, because her boy friend was a member. 'I need a lot of practice before I play myself in there,' she said to Alice. 'Otherwise, I shall play myself out!' So Alice practised with her daily. When the weather was fine, they played early in the morning before going to the office. This was the time which Alice liked best. When the day was pearly and fresh, and the town was only just coming to life, she had the feeling she had had on night duty of being in a territory of her own, as though time was also place. It was surprising how few people had yet discovered the existence of seven o'clock in the park, this place of escape, where other people had not yet thought of you, let alone had hopes for you or formulated demands. Fellow explorers, walking dogs or feeding squirrels, passed by absolved of any need to make acknowledgements, safe in their solitude.

It was over two months since she had seen Ivor. As she hit the ball hard and flat across the net, Alice felt it was conceivable that she might get over his loss; and when she angled her smash deep into the corner, there was such exhilaration that it could not be disputed that other excitements might one day present themselves. The friend collected balls, and stood thinking about her service. Alice, well within the baseline, thought where she was going to put her return. The service was weak and the server stayed back; Alice popped the ball gently over the net. They changed ends. In a café opposite the park a man pulled down a faded green awning and then began to arrange a few chairs around a table. For the first time in many weeks, Alice realised that she was not merely hungry, but ravenous.

When the game was over, she put on a dirndl skirt and slipped off her tennis shorts; then she changed into white sandals and was dressed for the office. She was not returning to Holland Park, nor was she eating with her office friend. She was doing something much more interesting.

At a small hotel in Pimlico she breakfasted with Jeannie Clinton Hobbs. They had last met in Alexandria, when Alice was a coder and Jeannie the Commander's writer. Alice had wondered whether Jeannie could possibly be so radiant under more temperate skies. In fact, there being less in the way of competition, the effect was even more overwhelming. Her presence seemed to fill the small dining-room, and not only because she talked rather loudly. Later, Alice wrote that Jeannie's hair tumbled like a golden cataract about her shoulders; then she crossed out the word 'tumbled'; Nature had had too much assistance from artifice for there to be any suggestion that even one curl did not know its place. Eyes and eyebrows owed their definition to the discreet use of mascara. A fellow coder, Madeleine Flint, who had not liked Jeannie, had once pointed out that she was a very *sandy* person who practised alchemy. In the morning light, Jeannie's face glowed from its immersion in cold water followed by a few brisk slaps on the cheeks. She wore a low-necked dress in buttercup yellow and the man sitting at the table opposite was bent on discovering to what regions the golden tan extended.

'Of course, he is quite distraught,' Jeannie told Alice and the other occupants of the room. 'And I feel devastatingly sorry for him, poor lamb. But it would be quite wrong for me to turn down this wonderful opportunity of going to Kenya. And now that I've given up my flat, there is nothing to prevent me staying there for quite a while if I like it. So it wouldn't be right for us to be tied by an engagement. I think I did manage to make him see that.'

Alice felt her hard-won control slipping. 'He'll probably find someone else,' she said.

'I should like to think so.' But plainly this was not an idea which could be entertained seriously.

'And, anyway, you can't have loved him much or you wouldn't have given Kenya a second's thought.'

Jeannie trained her radiance like a searchlight on Alice. 'And what have *you* been doing with yourself?'

'Playing tennis.'

'As long as it's tennis and not another man. The last time I saw you so thin was during the Gordon affair. You're like me, of course, you are so *warm*. Though I never lose weight. In fact, I thrive on emotional ferment. I would rather have an *unhappy* love affair than be uninvolved.' Her manner made it clear that unhappy love affairs existed only in the realm of speculation: Jeannie never entered the field unless she was assured of success.

When she talked about her various men friends, however, her conversation related more to the places to which they had escorted her than to the warmth of feeling they had aroused. The externals of Jeannie's life were going to be interesting. She would dine at fashionable restaurants, visit exciting places, have useful contacts all over the world. Perhaps in her forties one might begin to suspect that nothing much was happening inside her. But by that time there would be a new way to travel excitingly, the fashionable restaurants would be different, and the useful contacts of another type. To this extent, Jeannie would always be adaptable. She was also eminently practical and would never stretch beyond her reach.

Perhaps I accept defeat too easily, Alice thought, dazzled by Jeannie's confidence. I should have telephoned Ivor. He might have expected it. I could still do it. If I can get away from Jeannie soon, I might even . . .

'What time do you have to get to work?' Jeannie asked, seeing Alice studying her wrist watch.

'Half-past nine. On two days we start at nine, and on three at half-past. But there's talk of our starting at nine each day in exchange for having all Saturday mornings off.'

'I don't know how you stand it! This darling specialist I worked for was so marvellous about time off. I could go and get my hair done – or slip out to the shops. And, of course, it is quite the nicest part of London.'

'I like being near St James's Park.'

'But, my dear, *I* was just off Wigmore Street! Anyone who is anyone shops in Wigmore Street at some time or another. Not that I'm a bit of a snob. Quite the contrary, in fact. There was a dear old road sweeper with whom I became great chums. I liked those old characters much more than some of the dowager duchesses who came and wasted dear Jamie's time.'

Alice, remembering that Jeannie had referred to the Commodore as Roddy, wondered if she had really called her employer Jamie.

A woman crossed the street to the gardens in the centre of the square, walking with that mixture of care and inattention peculiar to the very old to whom the business of putting one foot before the other is of more concern than oncoming traffic. She unlocked the gate, after some little trouble, and went into the gardens. 'She goes there every morning and just *sits*,' Jeannie said. 'Sometimes she reads a book and sometimes she doesn't even do that.'

Whereas I have played tennis, am breakfasting with a friend, and shall soon be on my way to the office, Alice thought. Jeannie will go shopping and buy a frock, then she will lunch in this new restaurant a friend has told her about, and in the evening she will come with me to the Open Air Theatre. Although the frock may not be quite what is needed for Kenya and my office will definitely be boring, the restaurant may be a disappointment, and the seats at the theatre too hard, we shall have had something to show for our day. Yet the woman sitting in the shade of the plane trees looked as contented as the Buddha.

'And she can't be hard up because she has lived in the square *all* her life; and she has seven children and umpteen grandchildren all of whom seem to be doing very well for themselves,' Jeannie said. 'I had a chat with her one day. Her family is spread out all over the world; but she has hardly travelled at all! Can you *imagine* it! She could have gone anywhere and done anything!'

'I think having seven children and umpteen grandchildren counts for quite a lot! In fact, when you are old, I should think it counts for more than anything else.'

'But it is so *important* to take one's opportunities. That's why I'm going to Kenya, although it means breaking with Dougal.' Jeannie liked to have a moral justification readily to hand for her actions.

Alice, unimpressed, said, 'Wasn't Dougal an opportunity?'

'There will be plenty of men in Kenya.' She looked at the woman whom she seemed to regard as some sort of challenge. 'At least you would think she could hobble as far as Harrods!'

'She probably feels she has earned her rest.'

'She may have done, Alice, I don't deny that. But one should never give in. Plenty of women of her age go on cruises. They do everything for you. From the moment you arrive at Victoria *everything* is taken care of, and you don't see your luggage again until you go to your cabin.'

'A girl at our office went by sea to southern Italy this year. They took her luggage at Victoria and she didn't ever see it again.'

'Some cheap little travel firm, I expect. Not the P & O Line.'

'Any sort of travel would seem luxury after a troopship, wouldn't it?'

'To say nothing of that awful journey to the desert!' Jeannie looked down at her freckled, golden arms. 'I used to think there were some little creases and crevices in my body that would harbour grains of sand for ever more.'

'Do you have any news of Madeleine or Gwenda?'

'Gwenda married a Wog. Didn't you know? I can't think what her life can be like now that the Egyptians have turned so nasty.'

'I wouldn't have missed Egypt, though, would you?'

'It was the best time of my life!' Jeannie, taken aback by her own spontaneity, added, 'But one must never look back. That is why I am so keen to go to Kenya.' A thought struck her. 'Why don't you come? It's a marvellous climate and women have a wonderful time out there.'

'I hadn't thought of it.'

'But you should. England is pretty drear, isn't it? We've gone back centuries. I never wanted for necessities when I was a child, and I don't suppose you did, either. But now the only people who can live comfortably are the ones who trade on the black market. And as long as we've got this socialist government, things won't get any better.'

If I don't see Ivor again, I shall never get any better, Alice thought. She made her excuses and hurried out in search of a telephone box. When she found one, she realised she had no idea what she was going to say. She walked on. Ivor lived in this area. Several times in the past weeks she had walked by his flat, hoping for a glimpse of him. She had looked up at the windows, willing them to reveal something of the life within. Gradually, she had realised how little she knew about him. She had very little to feed on; and misery needs fuelling as much as ardour. Lately, misery had begun to lose its edge. But this meeting with Jeannie had agitated the pain.

As she walked down Victoria Street the pace of the city was quickening. In Strutton Ground, the market holders had already set up their stalls, and one man was taking stockings out of a suitcase while his companion drew the attention of passers-by to rolls of parachute silk. Nearby a policeman stood with his hands behind his back, neither looking for nor anticipating trouble. A crawling bus disgorged passengers while the conductor repelled boarders. It was very hot and petrol fumes hung on the still air. People with anxious faces darted amid the surging traffic, hurrying, hurrying, driven by the need to be driven. And there, at the entrance to Strutton Ground, blocking the narrow pavement while people pushed to get past them, were Ivor and a woman. They were quarrelling. Short and dark, her ample bosom plumped up with rage, she stood with feet slightly apart, fists clenched. The fighting pose suited her so well it must surely be habitual. And the little chopping gestures of his hands as he dismissed whatever she was saying seemed as well practised. They were as careless of censure as of any inconvenience they might cause others. There was a kind of rapacity in the way they prolonged their quarrel, as though they could not have enough of it. One sensed, in the fervour with which they attacked each other, that greed was an essential element in this relationship. A climax was reached, and suddenly it was all over. They looked with amused contempt at the passers-by, and then made their way to a stall where they joined forces in provoking the vendor of parachute silk.

So that is that! Alice thought as she walked slowly up Victoria Street. Light sparked on glass; steps rang hard on pavements. Near Caxton Hall demolition men were at work and bricks fell in showers of dust and grit. She clenched her hands, hating this jagged city.

'You are late,' Mr Hadow informed her with satisfaction.

'I got involved in an argument. One that was none of my business.'

Claire finished washing the breakfast dishes, looking at Heather through the window. Heather, an exemplary godmother, was playing with the children in the garden. It was Claire's belief that children should never be *made* to do anything. She could not help but observe, however, that Heather was allowing them more freedom than she herself would have done. Of course, she would never have issued a direct instruction; but she would have *explained* why sitting on the grass at this time of the morning was not advisable. Advice, when given by Claire, was meant to be followed. She had always been an anxious, unadaptable child who turned counsel into an absolute rule of conduct. Only recently her mother had laughingly reminded her how once, when they were visiting their aunt's house, Alice had closed a window because the rain was coming in, and Claire had cried out, 'They have to be open because that's how we found them!'

In a few minutes, a neighbour would call to take Vanessa and Hilary to spend the day with her own children, so that Claire and Heather could have a few hours to themselves. Claire, who had been looking forward to this, was chilled by the fleeting nature of time. She had always needed to possess her joys, and since they, too, tended to be transitory, the only way she could do this was to satisfy herself of their endless repetition. As a child, she must be assured that another party invitation was sitting on the mantelpiece; that before the last chorus rang out across the sand, plans had been made for another Crusader camp; that the next meeting had been arranged before she parted from a girl friend . . . But now, all that she could be sure of was a morning and an afternoon which would pass all too soon: the following morning, Heather would leave. She had been home for three weeks and had only managed to spend four days with Claire and Terence. UNRRA had closed down in June; but next week Heather would start work with another relief organisation in Germany. 'I wouldn't ever come back to England for good now,' she had said.

Once, Claire would have taken her trouble to God, praying fervently – and loudly – in their bedroom at the top of the house in Pratts Farm Road, while Alice tried to distract her by humming noisily or banging dressing-table drawers. On one such occasion, when rebuked, Alice had said, 'I can't stand all this "Well, here we are again, God, what are we going to make of today's load of rubbish . . ." '

'Don't you believe God answers prayer?'

'I don't know what I believe.'

This was not good enough for Claire, who needed a strong framework in which to live. For a time, religion had provided that framework, and then the Force which moved in the great void in which her little structure was erected had ceased to tolerate it. The icy winds of loss and doubt had crushed it to matchsticks. The business of reconstruction was painful, the enterprise too hazardous, the risk of another failure beyond bearing. While Alice would live in that necessary tension between belief and unbelief, Claire must search for a structure which was so strong that no Power could threaten it. The best remedy, of course, was to cease to believe in the Power. But the void was still there. As she meticulously scoured the kitchen sink, she felt small, fragile, absurd.

The neighbour came round the side of the house and greeted Heather. 'Perhaps if you came down to the front gate with me they would go more calmly,' she suggested, as they put the children in the pushchair which Terence had constructed, and which Heather privately thought resembled a miniature tumbril. 'They don't separate very well.' But, in Heather's cheerful presence, the children suffered themselves to be trundled away without protest. Heather returned to the kitchen and found Claire tearful.

'It's only for a few hours,' she said, imagining it to be the children's departure which had occasioned this grief. No wonder the poor little mites couldn't separate!

'I wish you weren't going.' Claire strove to sound as if this was something less than complete tragedy, while despair opened up a well in the pit of her stomach. Heather was good with the twins and helpful about the house, but this was not what had made Claire feel so much less burdened over the last few days: it was the absence of effort. She tried all the time with Terence and the children; from the moment she got up until she dropped exhausted into bed, she slaved at being a good wife and mother. Whereas with Heather she had been so happily at ease that the tasks she had had to perform had seemed to be done by magic, so unaware had she been of busy hands and brisk feet. She said, 'I don't have any other women to . . . not *any*!'

'You've got Alice. You and she were always so close.'

'Not any more. Alice gets on better with Louise, now.'

'Well, you've got Terence. He may not be another woman, but he must count for something.' Heather had been jealous when Claire married, and there was still a need for vengeance of which she was immediately ashamed.

'You don't understand about marriage.' Claire spoke in the superior manner she adopted only too readily, as though referring to a state experienced by only a few. 'Marriages have to be *made*. It's the making that is tiring.'

'Thanks for the warning.' Heather was to be married in November. 'Any other useful tips while you're about it?'

Claire had been affronted when Heather told her that she was getting married. '*You*, married!' she had said. If Heather was so faithless, who would keep the memory of their past affection green? Now, she studied her friend thoughtfully. Heather's madcap mischievousness had been all very well at school, but she seemed to have grown into her angularities rather than out of them. It was possible, no doubt, for tall, ungainly women to make good marriages, but the odds must surely be against it.

Claire said, 'I hope you know what you're doing.'

'We'll manage. We've been living together for quite a while. I'm not fussed about getting married; but we both love children and we don't want ours to have to grow up explaining how enlightened their parents are!'

Claire seemed to see her friend across a great chasm. Intellectually, she applauded Heather's matter-of-fact attitude to morality, yet at the same time she was rent with grief and desolation. The tears which she had been holding back erupted like lava from the subterranean depths of her despair. Heather, realising this was no ordinary weepiness occasioned by the demands of motherhood and the strains of housekeeping, rushed to put her arms round her; and not for the first time Claire flinched from her friend's impetuosity. But the involuntary stiffening passed without notice amid the frenzy of her sobs, so Heather continued to hold her until at last Claire relaxed against her shoulder. 'Now, what is this all about?' she asked gently.

'I miss Daddy so much . . .' Claire needed to identify a single cause as explanation for all her troubles; and the death of her father had long served this purpose.

Heather accepted this, though she put a rather different construction on it than Claire. 'It happened at the wrong time for you,' she said. It had been apparent at school that Claire did not find the growing up process easy; and on her father's death she had been robbed of the time needed to work through her adolescence. She seemed to have moved into the adult world while remaining in many ways a child.

'And after your father died, there was Uncle Harry of blessed memory, wasn't there?' Heather recalled. 'We fell out over him. I still think he was a bad influence on you, quite apart from his being a bit lecherous. You were always saying he taught you to try to live more like him, and see what you could do *without*. Maybe you discarded too much? I know I'm a fine one to talk, being a natural heathen, but your religion used to mean a lot to you, and if it helped you . . .'

'He's the God of the Gaps, I've learnt that now. And what gaps science hasn't filled, Marx has.'

'All right, so God's gone away. But what about those games you and Alice used to play? Will you make up stories like that for your children?'

'It was wrong, all that imagining. Uncle Harry taught me that. I'm not going to have *my* children growing up in a dream world. And you know what Freud says about fairy stories!'

'Lordy, lordy. There must be something between the Epistle to the Ephesians and *Das Kapital* you can give them for a bedtime story!'

This produced a fresh outburst of weeping. 'Everyone's so changed and I'm so lonely.' Heather, holding her close, wondered how she could make Claire see that it was she who had changed the most. Or perhaps she hadn't? Perhaps she was still behaving as she had when she was a child and someone at school (probably me!) had said something to disturb her. Only then, the adult world had had answers which comforted her. Now, she was one of the adults.

When Claire had recovered, they went to Kew Gardens and sat on the grass looking down the long avenue towards the Pagoda. Heather noticed how physically undeveloped Claire was, still thin as a hazel stick, the little freckled face peering tentatively from the bush of frizzy red hair. In spite of her own robust nature and gawky strength, Heather had always felt herself subject to Claire, who effectively manipulated people by a series of emotional rewards and punishments. Herself more mature now, Heather realised that what she had often taken for cruelty was really Claire's only weapon: there was no other way that she could hold her own. Oh, lovey, she thought, if only I had known this sooner!

'The Pagoda is closed because someone once jumped off it,' Claire said. 'At least, that's what we were told when we were young.'

'Don't be so morbid!'

'I'm not morbid. I was informing you.'

'Then I'll inform you. It's very lonely for you, imprisoned all day with the kids. You need to join something.'

'I did go to a Quaker meeting. But it wasn't any good. Rather like a Methodist prayer meeting, except that those who were moved to speak had a more extended vocabulary. And *what* moves them? I don't want to listen to the predictable rumblings of other people's subconscious. And if it's supposed to be the Holy Spirit, that just takes me back where I started going wrong. Also, it was not all that *silent*.' This was what had really irked her. Silence, in her view, had to be absolute. 'People came in late and left early. And in the period in the middle there was a large dog who kept shifting his position and sighing. I found myself watching him. Every so often he lifted his head and rolled his eyes hopefully at his master. When it was all over, his joy was quite bounding!'

'You don't seem to have got into the spirit of it, if I may say so.'

'I can't concentrate if people fidget. And anyway, I like to know what I'm supposed to be concentrating on.'

She was talking more easily now. After a few minutes, she said, 'I suppose I could join a choir.'

'And fret because you weren't chosen as soloist?'

Claire laughed and admitted, 'I expect I would. What do *you* suggest?'

'Something where you've got a definite task allotted to you. Singing might be the answer. A smaller group than a choir, though – and you the only soprano!'

'I'm not as bad as all that!' But Claire did not mind Heather's candour; there was a personal quality about teasing which she had always found gratifying.

They stretched out on the grass in companionable silence until it was time to eat their packed lunch. As they ate, they talked of mutual friends. Heather told Claire about her meeting with Jacov – 'only you mustn't tell Alice about Katia, because it would upset her.' Claire, who did not like to be told what she must, and must not, say to her sister, made a mental note that this was something Alice *ought* to know. Fancy Heather presuming to advise on a matter where only the Fairleys were involved!

In the afternoon, they walked along the tow-path and Claire sang Greensleeves as they looked across the river at Syon House, stately amid serene green lawns. Claire said, 'I think I'd like to have lived then.'

'And been seduced by the lord of the manor? We'd *both* have been skivvies then, you know. No middle class in those days.'

Claire, for once, did not rise to the bait. 'Can you imagine us, both working in the kitchens? Carrying those enormous stew pots into the Great Hall?'

'Stirring in a few turds because we hated their guts and having a laugh about it!'

They walked on and when they came to where The London Apprentice was hidden by trees they made up a thriller, all Dickensian mists and unseen oars stroking dark water. As Richmond Bridge came in sight and the afternoon shadows lengthened, laughter dwindled in regret. If we had been braver, what would we have made of our life? Heather wondered. Claire, unable to ask herself this, built up her defences as they left the river behind.

# 12

'October!' Alice exclaimed. 'And hardly a yellowed leaf to show for it.'

'Those are evergreens,' Ben said.

'Not all of them. I know an evergreen when I see one.'

Louise and Guy, sitting behind them in the coach, hoped they weren't going to bicker all the time.

They passed through a village with a Green Man public house, its sign depicting a truculent Robin Hood, one hand on hip, the other holding his bow like a staff. Then they were out in the country again, fields on one side, beech woods on the other. It was a clear autumn day with a blustery wind and a lot of cumulus clouds chasing one another across the sky. Ahead the Chilterns banked steeply and Alice, who had only stayed at Jordans, and then briefly, was delighted by countryside that was new to her and could not forbear from extolling its particular qualities. The hills, she felt, were more blue than Sussex hills; there was, in fact, a blue tendency to the landscape as a whole.

'It's autumn,' Ben pointed out.

'Not only *that*. The sky is enormous. There's a quite different feel. It's landlocked – I have no sense of the sea over the next hill.'

'Landlocked is the middle of a continent,' he said.

Alice said that, to her, Buckinghamshire was landlocked.

The hills dived down into villages of great charm. Buckinghamshire buildings, they all noted, merged admirably into the landscape, so that, seen contained in the window frame, one could scarcely have said whether they were designed for the hills or the hills as a backcloth for them. 'No wonder there are film studios here!' Louise exclaimed.

'We're long past Denham,' Ben said.

She leant forward and tapped him on the shoulder. 'Stop *pouncing* on everything we say. You're not in court.'

'Even so, it would be nice to hear one accurate statement.' He was good-natured in his chaff and put an arm round Alice's shoulder. 'It's your literary career I'm worried about. You're not going to write one of those reminiscences of a country childhood, are you – "As I came over the brow of the hill . . ." Or *gurt* hill, I suppose it would be.'

Alice did not respond. She was gazing with satisfaction at a sturdy flint farmhouse, forming with its long, low barns a compact unit, the lines clean and neat. The little complex was plain and grey and abiding, as befitted a county which had reared men as staunch as John Hampden. John Hampden was one of Alice's heroes.

They came to a village with wide grass verges, a few yellow beech leaves scattered on the deep greensward. '*See*,' Ben said. 'Goldengrove unleaving.' Just beyond the village the coach driver stopped and they got out. A sign above an overgrown track pointed the way to the youth hostel.

'I'm glad to see *you* travel light,' Ben said to Alice as she hitched her haversack over her shoulders.

'Years of experience.'

'I wish you'd tell your sister how to do it.' Guy was hampered by a heavy suitcase. 'We're going to look ridiculous.' He had never been to a youth hostel before and only now, as they set out down the lane, did he realise that it would be quite different from the small guest houses in which he had spent his youthful holidays.

There was only the warden at the youth hostel, and he was too agitated to take note of their luggage. 'There are no other people staying here,' he said. 'I've got rather an emergency – my mother has been taken ill. But you are all responsible people. You can take care of yourselves, can't you? I mean, you don't need me to supervise you.' He gave a nervous neigh of laughter. 'I'll just show you round and leave a key with you.' He led them on a tour of the building, which did not take long as it was small with limited amenities, and he was in a considerable hurry. He seemed peculiarly excited by his mother's illness.

'It's rather like a log cabin in New England,' Alice said to Louise as they made the beds. 'Do you remember how we loved *The Country of the Pointed Firs*?' She went to the window and gazed out at the wood, still green, with here and there the trunks of young birches, spindly as undernourished children. Further away in the lane, the sunlight was pale on an elm, softening its elephant grey ridges to corduroy. 'I wouldn't mind *living* here.'

'I wouldn't mind some tea. Let's investigate the cooking facilities. I've a feeling they are more or less non-existent from the way he glossed over them.'

Ben and Guy had already investigated. Guy had found a kettle and

Ben was lighting a primus stove. Ben said, over his shoulder, 'I don't think his old mother is ill, do you?'

'He *was* in a hurry to leave,' Guy said.

'It wasn't *that* kind of impatience, though. I bet he's got a girl friend tucked away in one of the villages.'

'Perhaps he had her here – when there were no youth hostellers,' Alice said, thinking what a secret place it was; but Louise said, 'Too overlooked. All those trees.' They were so close she felt they might invade the room if one was not vigilant.

After they had had their tea, they walked down to the village, now nestling in the shadow of a bare, blunt hill. It was early evening, a touch of primrose in the sky. The berries were bright in the hedgerows and on the mountain ash, and rosy apples were hanging from boughs. In the cottage gardens there were big yellow daisies, dahlias and peonies. 'All the robust flowers,' Louise said approvingly.

'Mummy would be out spraying those dahlias!' Alice said.

There was a great beech tree in the centre of the village with a bench beneath it on which Louise and Guy sat while Guy took out his ordnance survey map. 'We haven't got long,' he said. 'So we mustn't waste any time. Where shall we walk tomorrow?'

'You work out a route.' Louise leant back against the trunk of the tree and gazed at the small pond with the church just beyond, which was the most there seemed to be of open space in this narrow village. She had felt very oppressed in the youth hostel and was only now regaining her zest for this holiday to which she had looked forward so much.

'How far do you think you could walk?' Guy asked Ben, who had only recently recovered from a bout of malaria.

'As far as anyone else,' Ben answered snappishly. 'You have no idea how many miles I walked in Siam.'

'Break us in gently.' Alice came to his rescue, although she felt she could walk for miles and miles in this crisp, acrid air. She was already beginning to regret not having put on a sweater beneath her raincoat.

Guy was wearing a v-necked pullover and an open shirt. Casual clothes did not suit him and his pale, surprised neck looked unprepared for exposure. Alice noted with interest that on Ben the effect was quite different; the unbuttoned collar became an adornment out of which the neck thrust like a strong stem supporting the bold flower of the head. She then noticed that, despite his recent illness, he was distinctly more mettlesome than Guy – though that was probably because all the nerve ends were exposed. A little tremor went through her, as though she had actually touched him. At that moment he looked at her, and she saw her own shock mirrored in his eyes. The air between them quivered. Yet Louise was speaking as though nothing unusual was happening.

'No one is to talk about their war experiences on this holiday. If I hear one word from any of you about the desert or the jungle, I shall go home.'

Guy said, 'When I was at Mersa Matruh . . .' and she punched his shoulder. 'Get down to your maps, sirrah! You have yet to prove you can lead a country walk.'

And Alice was standing there, surely as conspicuous as a beacon flaring a signal!

Louise and Guy dwindled over the ordnance survey map. The sun was going down, the darkening hills growing more massive. All the small everyday comforts receded with the dying of the light. And man and woman confronted each other.

'Supper,' Louise said, as Guy folded the map and put it in his pocket.

The water in the pond was only faintly touched with colour, a memory of the primrose in the sky. As they turned into the shadow of the lane leading to the hostel, and saw that the trees had closed their ranks, Louise whispered to Alice, 'Honestly, do you like this place?'

The air smelt of woodsmoke, just as though the setting sun had really set the damp trees alight. Louise said, 'I'm not very keen on our loping off into the wood like this; and I don't like that miserable little hut.'

Guy said, 'Primitive man would think it was a palace.'

'We're not primitive, are we?'

Ben and Alice were silent. Louise hoped they were not going to be out of temper all the time.

When they reached the hut, Alice remained outside, taking deep breaths and gazing at what she could see of the sky through the tangle of branches. 'I must learn to be sensible,' she told herself. Since that glimpse of Ivor with the woman she had thought little of him and had imagined herself quite recovered. But obviously this was not so. She must still be in a very unstable condition and quite unable to command appropriate responses to situations. Otherwise how could it be that at the very moment when all her senses should have warned her against impetuosity, she should experience this irresistible spiral of joy? She had had that feeling before, and what had come of it? A voice that was not unwise insisted that this was different. She said, 'It's like enough,' took three more deep breaths, and entered the hut. Here the everyday world seemed to have established firm control. This was mainly due to the fact that Louise had forgotten to bring a tin opener and several substitutes were being tried. Ben, who claimed that he was used to opening tins with a bayonet, proved less successful with a penknife and a hunt for the first aid kit ensued. 'At least we shall have used all the facilities,' Louise said, when eventually it was found. 'Now, keep still! It's only a small cut. There's no need to be in such a dance about it.'

It was half-past seven by the time they sat down to eat. 'Baked beans with a dash of blood,' Louise said. 'Quite like old times for you troopers.'

After the meal, Louise said it was too cold to sit about and she and Guy went to bed, leaving Alice and Ben to wash up. Alice, slowly drying the dishes, wondered what they would do when they had finished. She had been alone with Ben on many occasions; by the sea, in Gunnersbury Park, in the cinema, they had laughed, argued, walked and swum, without giving a thought to the matter of their being alone.

In the little room where they had eaten, the trees came right up to the window and she could see the light from the oil lamp hoisted like a child's toy among the dark branches. Ben opened the outer door and appeared to stare intently at something in the darkness. Alice could feel the cold air pushing past him into the room, smelling of leaf mould.

He said, without turning round, 'Let's go for a walk, shall we? It's too cold to sit about in here.' There was a pile of logs to the side of the grate, but neither considered the possibility of getting a fire going.

They walked along a track at the edge of the wood. Moisture dropped from leaves and brambles clawed their limbs. Alice's tongue was tight as a spring against the roof of her mouth. After a few minutes, Ben said, 'I'm sorry if I was bad-tempered earlier on.'

'You weren't particularly.'

He held branches aside for her to pass. The path was leading them out of the wood and they could smell wet stubble. 'You mean I'm usually bad-tempered?'

'No, I meant you were a bit scratchy once or twice, but not bad-tempered.'

They walked on until they came to the top of a gentle incline and the valley lay before them, huge and milky in moonlight. Alice, freed from constriction, held her arms wide. 'The country is so enduring!'

'You only want it to be enduring. In fact, it's changing rapidly. These won't be working villages soon. They already have quite a few people living in them who work in the towns.'

'Perhaps they settle here because they feel the country *is* enduring, because they want to put down roots in a saner life.'

'Which they hope to achieve by importing their way of life into the country? Newly painted houses with spruce little gardens and no pot holes in the roads!'

She remembered how often, in his absence, she had cited him as the one person who would feel as she felt. And just as often, when they were together, he had been argumentative and contrary. Yet the feeling that, at some deep level, they were in accord had always persisted.

'But it *is* saner, Ben,' she said gently. 'The scale is right, for one thing. It's one in which human beings can operate.'

'No doubt it's better for individual people to have room in which to breathe,' he acknowledged. 'But the villagers will suffer when all the little cottages have been snapped up by city gents.'

'How hard you are on my dreams!'

'Oh, Alice!' he cried out. '*I*, too, have dreams, believe me! I have spent years of my life thinking that things could *be* just because I willed them so. But there are some things which no amount of yearning and longing can ever make so.'

'You mustn't talk like that!' She was shaken by the intensity of his feeling. 'I have always thought of you as the sort of person who could make anything happen if he set his mind to it.'

'I'm not as confident as I once was.'

Mist was forming in the fields and they could see hedgerow trees rising up from nowhere, like floating bunches of broccoli.

Alice said quietly, 'What is it that you want so much, and aren't sure of, Ben?' She waited for his answer, her breath coming light and shallow.

He began to talk passionately about some project he had been working on to do with people who were imprisoned without trial in countries of which Alice knew little and cared less. 'I feel it matters more than anything else while I am working on it. And then, when I am doing other things . . .' (Like standing here with me, Alice thought) 'I think how stupid it is to imagine that anything worth-while could ever come of it. Then I remember how much letters meant when I was a prisoner, how we went wild with joy when the first letters came. I tell myself, then, that I should be more humble. Be content with small beginnings . . .'

A great swathe of mist had banded across the distant hills so that only their tips appeared now, lightly stencilled on the sky.

Alice said with all the enthusiasm she could muster, which was not much, 'If you feel as strongly as that about it, I am sure you should carry on.'

He, too, stared at the misty hills. After a few moments, during which Alice felt droplets forming on her eyelashes, he said, 'I have been wanting to tell you about it for so long.'

Her interest kindled quite miraculously. 'I should like to know much more about it. I hope you will show me . . . well, whatever it is . . . letters, or reports, or . . .'

They continued their walk. Ben said urgently, 'You can understand now why I get so fed up with people who want to come and bury themselves in places like this. The sort of people who go through life afraid of change; protecting a cherished view – of society, family life, whatever matters to them – screening it from the wind, shoring it up against settlement. Petrifying themselves in their own past.' He made a dismissive gesture in the direction of the valley.

'But I don't think they *are* like that,' Alice protested. 'They want the country to be enduring, a place where they can find peace and contentment. And I can understand that. I don't know that I would want to live in it myself – at least, not until I was old. But I want it to be there when I need it.'

'But is that how we find peace and contentment?' He stopped abruptly. 'I would have thought we find it in ourselves – or in one other person.'

After a pause, they began to walk again. Alice, treading warily, said, 'That's putting quite a weight on another person.'

'It would have to be a special person.'

She said breathlessly, 'It *is* very beautiful, you must admit that. So strange in the mist. Do you think that perhaps if I was a painter I wouldn't project my hopes and longings on the landscape? That I would see it as it is?'

'Artists select the angle that suits their particular vision.'

Somewhere across the fields a barn owl hooted and Alice said, 'I wonder what *he* sees?'

'A hedgerow full of shrews, I expect.'

'You're unromantic.'

'No. I was hoping you were going to ask me what I saw.'

It was quite a few moments before she did ask him.

'I see you. In everything. All the time.'

As he put his arms around her, Alice had a feeling of enormous relief that something that seemed to have been so long in rehearsal had at last come right.

Guy and Louise, who usually slept heavily after making love, were wakeful, each absorbed in their own thoughts. Guy, imagining them to be in sympathy, said, 'It's very peaceful, isn't it? I would rather like to live somewhere like this. On the outskirts of a country town, perhaps, in an old house with a decent-sized garden.'

'And who would do the gardening?'

'I expect I could turn my hand to it.'

'You mean you would turn the earth over now and again.'

'We could have a wild garden – that's acceptable in the country. And the children would love it.'

'You can't have a wild garden on top of a wilderness, sooner or later you don't see the dividing line.'

'I wasn't talking about wilderness,' he said irritably.

'You said you would like to live somewhere like this, and *this* is wilderness.' She gestured towards the window. 'All those trees, just waiting to take possession of this clearing.'

'Oh, I see.' He had thought of living near Tunbridge Wells, somewhere in the Ashdown Forest. But he had regarded the trees as picturesque fixtures; he had no wish to throw down challenges to the forest.

Louise not only knew his methods of approaching a difficult subject, she could read the signs of the oncoming depression which was beginning to cloud his nature. She said, 'What's this all about, anyway, this talk of old houses and country towns?'

'Oh, nothing.'

He went to cover like a frightened animal, and she lay beside him, hardly less frightened. He had been heartrendingly attractive when he was a boy, possessed of that particular freshness and tentative charm which does not travel well in adult life and tends to leave a person insubstantial as an unfinished portrait, a speculation never followed up by the artist. She had ignored all the warnings of older people and had given herself to him. Now she was not disposed to blame him. It was not so much that he was weak, as that he seemed not to have been provided with very adequate means of self-defence. In which case, the impulse to run away was wisdom of a kind. But she had not foreseen that he would arrive so soon at this point. Her own crises came like great tides; she felt their surging within her body and was ready for them. She was not ready for this. She felt as if the roots of one of the trees had descended on her like a giant hand, pushing her down into that mound of dead leaves whose smell seemed to fill the room. However hard she wrestled and twisted she would never break free; and even if, pinioned though she was, she won a breathing space, she would never gain complete release.

Long after Guy was asleep, she heard Alice and Ben come back and wondered what they had been up to. She did not think Alice would go too far. Although she did not repent of, or regret, her own sexual escapades, she tended to take a severe view of the lapses of others. There was nothing hypocritical about this, only a failure to understand that she did not have a monopoly of emotional integrity. She was very fond of her sister, but still saw her as she had been at school, a nice, solid pudding of a child, untutored in the ways of the world. After a time, she got up and went to investigate the sleeping arrangements. She found Alice already asleep in the other room, while Ben had bedded down in the dining area.

She went to the outer door and listened to the unfamiliar sounds in the wood, the scurrying in the undergrowth, the sharp cry of terror.

In the first morning light she got up and dressed; and went out to where the wood dwindled into pasture land. As she walked she did not analyse her feeings or try to construct avenues of escape. Although she was no stranger to her impulses, she had little facility for stringing her thoughts together. It was the functioning of her leaden body which occupied her as she struggled with the intense difficulty of co-ordinating limbs and pumping air in and out of lungs. That rooted hand still pressed on her head and shoulders when she returned.

Alice and Ben had prepared breakfast by this time. Guy said sulkily, 'You won't want to walk now.'

'Yes, I shall. I've got up my appetite for eating *and* walking.'

Alice was spilling happiness over the porridge she was stirring and Ben had a spurious air of being interested in everything and everyone while really paying no attention to anything that was said. They were both well content to do the washing-up again.

As they prepared for the walk, Guy said to Louise, 'We mustn't leave too much to them.'

'They won't mind. Hadn't you noticed?'

'Noticed?' He was intent on watching her put up her hair. She had adopted this style some time ago and it suited her. But he had preferred the loose, soft waves which had half-concealed her face and given her an air of mystery – a style which had also made her look more girlish. Now that the hair was swept up and back, one was made aware of the features: the tip-tilted nose delighted, the brilliant, forthright eyes challenged attention, but hers was not the fine bone structure which defies the years, and one also noticed the heaviness of the jaw and the thickening of the neckline. There was no doubting that this was the face of a woman. The beautiful girl had gone and would not linger to be glimpsed sometimes on the edge of vision. Guy preferred to think of his wife as a girl.

'At least you can let your hair down on holiday!' he protested.

'I'm over thirty now. I don't put in for ingenue parts in the theatre, so I'm certainly not going to play them in real life.'

'Always the theatre.'

'*You* used to love it. You wanted to be an actor.'

But he had not loved it since he had realised that he was not good enough to act professionally.

'Jacov was saying only the other day that you never come to see him,' she said, pinning the last coil in place.

Was there an element of challenge in this reference to Jacov? If so, he came nearer to answering it than usual. 'I didn't know you had seen Jacov recently.'

She waited. She would not volunteer information, but she would answer honestly anything which he chose to ask. Guy said jokingly, 'I'm not sure I approve of that.'

'I have known Jacov longer than you. It was through him that we met.'

And more than that. They had made love that first time in the basement of the Vaseyelins' house. Mr Fairley had always blamed Jacov for Louise's seduction. Guy, confused by conflicting emotions, could not bring himself to say any more. But he comforted himself with the reflection that Jacov belonged in the theatre and that whatever passed between him and Louise was probably as unreal as the charades the Fairleys had always loved. He was coming to see, even if he did not quite understand, that Louise must be allowed her charades because there was more danger for him in interference than acceptance. But later, when they were walking in the Chilterns, and Alice and Ben had fallen behind, he said, 'You won't play an ingenue any longer because you are not young enough; yet you played Marcelle in *Asmodée*, and she was older than you.'

'Ah, that's different. Plenty of meat in older women!'

He screwed up his mouth fastidiously.

Behind them, Alice and Ben were marvelling at the way life worked itself out – a mixture of fairy tale and detective story, the threads of magic industriously woven into their separate lives so that, to the eyes of an outside observer, the outcome must always have been apparent, their eventual coming together inevitable. A fairy godmother, or chief inspector, might have seen that once the importance of all the clues had been assessed and placed in position, there was only the one solution. Why, even at birth they had been related – but not too closely – so that they shared a common heritage. They eulogised Cornwall and the sea, and spoke with affection of Joseph and Ellen Tippet. Alice thought, but did not say, that she could see how Gordon and Ivor had been a part of the pattern; while Ben silently accepted the need for his unhappy love affair with Daphne Drummond.

'I told Geoffrey all about you,' he said. And it was true that he had spoken of her once or twice.

'When I was in Cairo I thought how wonderful it would have been to share it with you.' She had had him particularly in mind because Jacov, who was out there with a touring company, had been unable to summon sufficient energy to take her to the Pyramids.

They had not then thought of each other in terms of love and marriage; but this they now perceived had always been their intention, though veiled from them until they should become ready for each other.

They were climbing a plateau overlooking the Vale of Aylesbury. Ben was beginning to find it necessary to stop quite often to admire the view; and Alice readily accommodated herself to his pace.

Guy, a good walker, was enjoying himself. The height, and the wide sweep of the land, lent him power and he became daring. 'It was an odd sort of play, *Asmodée*, didn't you think? There were some things in it I didn't like at all. Do you know the lines that stick in my mind? Blaise saying, "I won't tolerate anyone else having an influence over someone I care for. It's revolting to me. Like dirty fingerprints on a clean sheet of paper." ' He gave a keen thrust to the other man's lines which he could never allow his own deliveries. But there were always dangers in talking theatre to Louise.

'Really? A typical masculine sentiment. Do you remember Valentine in *Love for Love*? "You're a woman – one to whom Heaven gave beauty, when it grafted roses on a briar. You are the reflection of Heaven in a pond, and he that leaps at you is sunk. You are all white, a sheet of lovely spotless paper, when you first are born; but you are to be scrawl'd and blotted by every goose's quill."

'Can you imagine a woman ever saying that to a man? If a woman finds a man has been unfaithful she is supposed to accept it as natural to the species, not maunder on about spoiling white paper. And as for looking in ponds, my impression is that men more usually see their own reflection there.'

They had reached the plateau while they talked, and at this point

Alice and Ben caught up with them. The matter was not discussed again.

Ben was very shaky, and Alice said, 'I think we've both had enough.' It pleased her to sacrifice her own enjoyment in order to protect him; but she was a little irritated when he said, 'If Alice doesn't feel she can go any further, I'll walk back with her.'

It was evening when Louise and Guy came slowly down the blunt hill above the village. He knew that he had little time at his disposal. 'Let's sit down for a moment,' he said. She sat, parting the grass with her fingers, watching the little insects which she had disturbed come boiling to the surface.

'I have been thinking that perhaps we ought to move,' he said. 'A small country town would be a nice place for the children to grow up.'

'What about your job?' She looked at him in the direct way he always found discomposing. 'Is there something wrong?'

He turned away, and she observed the lines of strain in his neck, the nervous movement of his Adam's apple as he swallowed his pride. If she was aware at that moment of his weakness, she saw his need even more clearly.

'I'd prefer to leave before I'm asked to.'

'If they can't appreciate you, you certainly better had!' she cried warmly. 'But do you think it will really come to that?'

'There have been hints lately.'

'It's not fair, when you work so hard. I suppose it's a question of money – you don't bring in enough to satisfy them.' She spoke with contempt for financial acumen.

'I'm afraid I'm a bit slow, too.' He groped for her hand. 'Oh, my darling, I've let you all down very badly.'

'You've tried. No one can do more than that.' For a moment or two she was silent, thinking of the children who would have to leave school and friends, of Jacov who would drift out of her life, and of her husband. 'But if we must, we must.' She had always made her decisions quickly, if sometimes unwisely. 'The question is, where?' She would bargain about this. 'I'm not going to be buried in some dreary little market town.'

'View!' she exclaimed scornfully when he mentioned Shaftesbury. 'We're not moving for the view! I would settle for Primrose Hill if we were.'

'What then?' he asked uneasily.

'*I* need something to do, Guy. The children will be at school all day. And we don't want more children – or do we?'

He hesitated. On his return from the war he had resented the place which the children had established for themselves in her affections and from which he felt himself excluded. He had not wanted more children. She, aware that the coming of a child who would experience no long separation from its father, might further alienate him from Catherine and James, had accepted his decision. But now, still thinking of that isolated house in deep country, he remembered her in the days when she was carrying Catherine and had been at her most dependent, and it seemed to him that another child might mean that for long, luxurious years he could store all his treasures in one safe, secure place. 'I'm not sure . . . A new way of life, and a new life . . . ?'

He looked at her and flinched from what he saw. The eyes are the only window of the being encased in its structure of flesh and bone. Yet one would have thought these to be the least suitable of features to express that inner being – as little capable of signalling a myriad changes of mood as two poached eggs! By what miracle of veins and nerves the eyes responded, Guy did not know. What he did know was that they were the surest heralds of Louise's feeling, impeccably distinguishing the spark of anger from the sparkle of laughter, the drowsy stupor of love from the lethargy of boredom. But the sign he found most disturbing was when he saw no light in them; then they registered a displeasure that went deeper than anger into some profound regret. At such times, he feared she had discovered that secret vice which he suspected in himself without having any idea what it was. He did not perceive that these moments most often coincided with a situation in which he betrayed his need to possess her completely. On such occasions he could always convince himself that he was expressing the full extent of his love which demanded that everything must be shared between them, something for which she must surely be grateful rather than angry. Nor would he ever acknowledge how deeply he resented the very idea that she might have an existence separate from his.

He turned from her gaze and dug the toe of his boot into the stony soil. Another child would not be a solution. Her energies would be diverted at a time when he most needed her. But what would happen if she became involved in a life outside her home? For a moment, the risk of moving seemed too great.

'We're a bit young to find a safe haven, aren't we?' She stood up, brushing at her skirt, and they walked down to the village. 'If it's got to be done, then let's make an adventure of it.'

He took her hand. 'As long as I've got you, I can do anything.'

'Then you don't need to go to Shaftesbury for the view,' she laughed, refusing the sentimental declaration he craved because she had already given enough.

He pursed his lips. 'I did think of Ludlow.'

'But we don't know anyone within hundreds of miles of Ludlow.'

'There's Sussex. But you probably don't want to be so near your mother.'

'I'm fond of my mother. Just because I can't get on in the same house as her, it doesn't mean I don't want to live in the same county. Sussex would be like going home. After all, I was born there.' And didn't Lewes have a Little Theatre? It wasn't just the parts she would play that raised her spirits, but the prospect of the company of men. 'Lewes has nice views,' she said to Guy.

Alice and Ben ate their supper happy in the rightness of their life sentence. That night, Ben slept the sleep of the physically exhausted, while Alice spent the wakeful night of the emotionally over-stimulated.

She woke the next day with a slight headache and a tendency to review her past life and catalogue the benefits of independence. She went into the wood before breakfast to snatch a few moments on her own, in the hope of composing herself, and Ben followed to find out what she was doing. She was not accustomed to accounting for her movements.

It was agreed at breakfast that Louise and Guy should have a day to themselves. Alice and Ben set out on a circular walk which the guidebook assured them included all the glories of the Chilterns area, from grassy uplands and enfolded villages through beech woods to a pleasant market town on the old coach road to the Midlands, said to possess a character of welcoming charm which never palled on the wayfarer. They were just about to enter the beech wood when Ben decided that Alice had had enough of wayfaring.

'I'm good for many more miles,' she assured him.

'But you said you couldn't finish yesterday's walk.'

'This is today.'

'We've walked the same distance. You don't want to push on and then find you can't manage the journey back. I don't suppose there are many buses.'

Looking at the beech wood, it seemed to Alice to be of the utmost importance that she should continue the walk, on her own if need be, but that whatever happened, she should not be hampered by his indisposition. She had made a generous gesture yesterday and he had reacted by assuming its repetition.

During the wakeful hours of the night she had dwelt less on Ben's virtues – his constancy and honour, so lacking in Gordon; his forcefulness, unmarred by Ivor's subtle cruelty – than his possible weaknesses. She had thought of the way in which his war experiences had made him moody and unpredictable. She had recalled men whose personalities had changed disastrously after they had been injured in battle.

She must find out now, before things went any further, whether Ben was so injured by his experiences that he would not be able to tolerate a wife who would sometimes wish to go for a walk on her own.

'If you don't want to go on, would you very much mind if I do?' she asked, trying to make it sound like a question rather than a declaration of intent.

He bent his head, making a business of studying the route while he calculated the mileage still to be covered. It was a purposeless exercise, since he had already come too far. Ahead, sunlight fell through the trees in shafts of autumnal glory. Alice was staring at the wood and he imagined her to be drawn by its beauty; whereas in fact it was of him that she was thinking, hoping for her due of generosity. He traced his finger along the line of the route they must follow. 'I expect I could pick up a bus to this market town he's so sold on. There's bound to be a coaching inn. If you really want to go on, we could meet there for a drink – say about six o'clock?' He made the suggestion without enthusiasm.

'That sounds fine,' she said brightly.

He handed her the guidebook. 'If you're sure you're not nervous? It will be lonely in the wood.'

'Beech woods aren't dense; they are airy.'

'If you turned an ankle . . .'

'I don't turn my ankles.'

He stood watching her as she walked away, looking gloomy if not actually reproachful. She felt guilty and surprised by her own bloodymindedness. It was herself as much as Ben that was being put to the test. She had been so overwhelmed with joy by the discovery that he loved her, and had apparently loved her for some time, that she had reacted precipitately and was now as unsure of herself as of him. A lot of the beech leaves were down and the wind was a dry rustle in the branches. The path she followed was well-defined and she walked steadily, fists bunched in the pockets of her jacket, eyes on the ground. Only occasionally did she raise her head to see the trees and sparse leaves so finely scored against the glancing sunlight that the scene might have been engraved on glass.

It was not a lack in Ben, but in herself which now occupied her thoughts. She did not think he was the kind of man whose loving tentacles would close around his wife so that she had no freedom of movement. But she did fear that because of his experiences he might have to set himself limits and she could not face a life in which she would always be expected to accommodate herself to his pace. She supposed it was possible that she might learn to do this voluntarily as an act of love, but not in answer to his expectations. She did not have sufficient humility for that and it would sour her. She felt sour and tense already.

And yet . . . Alice came out of the wood and walked across a meadow towards a brook where little trees moved gently on slender shanks, casting long, wavering shadows. The grass was aglimmer with shining greenness and a piebald horse posed there, head to one side, in a waiting stance. He longs for a flank to nuzzle against, she thought; and I long for a hand in mine. She began to quicken her pace, walking through her own shadow as the angle of light shifted, fearing that she had something to lose, might already have lost it.

In the market town, she found the coaching inn without difficulty. She was a little late, but then he would not have expected that she could be exact in her timing. She went into the saloon bar. It was not crowded and she saw at once that Ben was not there. 'This is nothing to worry about,' she told herself as she made for the ladies. 'It will give me time to tidy up.' But she did not take much time and her hands were shaking as she combed her hair. He had not arrived when she returned to the bar. No doubt he had come punctually at six and, being an impatient person, had refused to wait; he would have left a message for her and gone for a stroll. She went up to the counter and said to the elderly man who was polishing a glass, 'I was expecting to meet a friend here. Did he leave a message for me?' He held the glass up to the light as if studying a rare jewel. 'No one's left any message.' As she turned away, she heard him say to the men drinking at the far end of the counter, 'Notice the sling bag? Wrens. We used to have a lot of them in here during the war.' His tone implied they had been up to no good.

There was a bench outside the inn and Alice sat on it to compose herself. Obviously, Ben had been taken ill. She should have asked where the nearest hospital was before leaving. There was always the police station. The police would not make nasty comments; they might even take her there in a police car. Her mind refused to work on this theory. Of course! There would be more than one coaching inn in a town this size. All she had to do was to make enquiries . . . But she remained sitting on the bench. He had been so happy yesterday and the very next day she had turned on him and shown him the worst in herself. The feeling that this was the one important love of her life asserted itself with a certainty which brooked no argument. How could she so wilfully have subjected this precious gift to analysis, questioning this, making a condition of that? For whom else had she ever felt such love, respect, trust, tenderness, combined though these delightful reactions might sometimes be with the most extreme exasperation? If only she could have one more chance, she would . . .

And there he was, at the far end of the street, walking leisurely towards the inn! She stood up and he recognised her and waved. As he came closer, she saw that he was carrying a small parcel.

'There's a woodcraft exhibition in a barn just outside the town,' he said. 'I had a long chat to one of the old fellows there who makes chairs. I wouldn't mind turning my hand to that. As a hobby, of course. My grandfather was a carpenter. I didn't have much money on me, but I bought this for you.' He handed her the parcel, which contained a small wooden basket, and turned in the direction of the inn. 'Most of the industry is in High Wycombe now . . .'

'I don't want to go back there,' Alice said. 'The man at the bar behaved as though I was hanging around for a man.'

'Well, you were, weren't you?' But he put his hand under her elbow and steered her towards the market square. 'I passed a little café that was still open. I don't know about you, but I feel more like tea and buttered toast than anything else.'

Over tea, he talked about the life of the woodsman. 'There are still some charcoal burners, you know. Only a few. And the woodcutters still use the kind of woodbreak the Romans would have used . . .' He sketched it for her on the back of the guidebook.

He did not ask her about her walk, so great was his interest in the wood trade. No doubt he had been angry when she had gone off without him, but he had soon put it behind him. The agonies of separation had been all hers. If she was to have a complaint about his behaviour in the future, it was likely to be that once he was absorbed in something which aroused his interest nothing else registered with him.

'I don't think you have given a thought to me walking through that lonely wood,' she said.

'You obviously didn't come to any harm.'

Perhaps a time would come when she thought he depended too little on her company? If so, she knew that this was something she would learn to accept.

When they were sitting in the bus on their way back to the youth hostel, he said, looking out of the window, 'In a month or so I'll be in better shape. We'll do a really long walk then.'

'We'll do Offa's Dyke in the spring,' she said.

In the evening light the hills were damson blue, a long smooth line unbroken by trees; but beneath, in the valley, evergreens massed like dark clouds.

Why did I insist on walking when we might have sat together in that wood? Alice thought. I have lost one glorious day that we could have shared. It must never happen again. Gifts are for the taking.

# 13

They had not unpacked before the telephone rang. It was not Judith with news of the children, as they had anticipated, but Irene. 'There is something I have to tell you,' she said. 'May I come round now.' Louise, who took the call, simply said 'Yes', although she would normally have resented such a brisk demand. Irene's tone had not suggested that the matter could wait until the next day.

It was a dull evening with a hint of fog. Winter had come suddenly. It had touched Irene. When he saw her coming towards him, it had seemed to Angus that her feet barely touched the ground, so light was her step; but now that verve which he had so valued in her had gone. As she walked, head down, chin deep in the high collar of her coat, her features were drawn together as if she were trying to force thoughts into order through a grid of pain. The quiet, ill-lit streets passed by on either side – she was barely aware of her own movements as she tried to compose herself to tell her story lucidly. She would begin with the coming of the two men.

There had been no hint of winter to herald their advent. It was a perfect late autumn evening, the air fresh and smelling of the last grass cuttings, the outlines of trees sharp against a clear sky. She sat by the window marvelling at its serenity. A light breeze stirred the fallen leaves; and, reflected on the window pane, tall white anemones danced on the garden wall. Her parents were at a concert, yet she thought of them as present and sharing this quiet moment; as they perhaps thought of her as they listened to the Elgar piano quintet. Although she was an only child she seldom felt alone, and as yet had had no sense of the absence of love.

She liked reflections on glass. They seemed to impose a pattern – or made one more aware of an actual pattern? She was meditating this, and debating whether to adjust the sash window, so that she could feel the air on her face at the cost of losing the reflection, when there was a knock on the front door.

'Miss Kimberley?' the taller of the two men asked, and smiled, as if to put her at ease before boarding her vessel – there was something about the smile which prompted buccaneering imagery. He had very broad shoulders, but the rest of him tapered away into a dark, well-cut suit; in the evening light his face glowed mahogany, but the eyes had no colour. It occurred to Irene that he was the kind of man her father would not have welcomed at his club. By this time they were all standing in the hall and the tall man had suggested they should go into the drawing-room. She could not remember afterwards at what stage he had told her that he was a policeman making a few enquiries. The other man followed him like a shadow. No doubt he was there to testify that the interview had been conducted according to whatever conventions obtained in this situation – a partial observer.

'I believe you are a friend of Angus Drummond?'

'Angus! Has he had an accident?' It was her one involuntary remark and did more to establish her innocence than anything she said or did subsequently.

'We are trying to get in touch with him, and having some difficulty. We wondered if you had any idea of his whereabouts?'

'You've tried his flat?' she said stupidly.

'It seems he has not been there for several days – judging by the accumulation of milk and daily papers.'

'His office?'

'It is his non-appearance at his office which has given grounds for concern.'

'His family, then – they live near here, in Shepherd's Bush.'

'We have spoken to his parents. It seems they have not seen him for over a month.'

'They weren't very close.' She felt a need to dwell on the more homely details of Angus's life, as though by doing so this matter might be kept on a domestic level. Her hopes, longings, her chance of happiness, all were running out, and yet she sat straight and still, behaving in a manner she imagined to be quiet and reasonable, unaware that her white face and brittle eyes gave the appearance of a person in shock. She said, 'He has a married sister who lives in Norfolk.'

'We are interviewing all his friends and relations. That is why we are here. Do you remember when you last saw him?'

'Just over a week ago. We went to a concert.'

'He seemed all right then?'

She thought about this, aware that Angus was not a person whose state of mind or heart was reflected in his behaviour. There was a gulf between the inner and outer man too wide for boarding enterprises. She said, 'He seemed quite lively. More so than usual, in fact.' Her tendency to deliberate created the impression of her having something to hide.

'You mean he was excited?'

'By the music, yes.'

'You knew him well, I take it?'

No, she thought, I don't think it can be said that I know him at all. Her head jerked up. 'Why do you ask if I *knew* him? What has happened to him?'

'That is what we are trying to find out, Miss Kimberley.'

'You say papers had accumulated at his flat. Did someone go in? He might be ill.' This was urgent. Why were they all sitting here speculating?

'It had occurred to us that he might be ill. Someone did go in to his flat. Everything was in order, and as far as could be seen, nothing was missing – not even toilet effects, such as toothbrush, razor.'

A toothbrush and razor, mundane necessities to give such a turn to the heart! She pictured Angus somewhere beyond her reach, lost and vulnerable, without means of shaving or cleaning his teeth.

The tall man was speaking. 'We have not precluded the possibility that he has had some kind of breakdown involving loss of identity.' His companion was looking round the room. She saw now that his function was to make background notes. Her father was a liberal-minded man who read widely. On the book shelves would be found Marcus Aurelius and Karl Marx; *The Anatomy of Melancholy*, Laski's *Grammar of Politics*, Plutarch's *Lives* and Camus's *L'Etranger*.

The tall man said, 'You mentioned a sister in Norfolk. I believe you stayed there with Mr Drummond some time ago – during the floods?'

'Yes.'

'Then you will recall an incident at the police station when Mr Drummond was asked about the contents of his briefcase?'

'Not very clearly. We were all rather tired.'

'But you knew that . . . certain equipment was discovered?'

'Yes.'

'Did you know what it was?'

'I think I thought perhaps it was a camera – or a wireless transmitter – or that something else was concealed inside some sort of container . . .'

'This didn't strike you as odd?'

She thought about this and about Sergeant Fletcher who had been Louise's lodger. On a night during an air raid on London, he had come into the sitting-room when she and Angus were baby-sitting for

Louise. He had been the second visitor that night. The first had been a man who had brought copy for Angus which he said was urgently required by the printer. 'One of those rather sad little working men's groups,' Angus had said by way of explanation. But Sergeant Fletcher, who had seen the man leaving the house, had said he was a 'proper little Bolshie'. Angus had asked her if she would be able to forget the incident, and she had replied that she would not talk about it. It was not possible to dispose of it: knowledge is irrevocable. And although nothing of any great moment had happened during that encounter, the man had seemed to her to be one of those unfortunates, so riddled with sickness that their very gaze can contaminate. She had had a feeling of corruption from which she had never entirely shaken herself free. The incident had disturbed her much more than the discovery of this equipment which, whatever it meant to these policemen, to her belonged in the comparatively healthy world of John Buchan.

She said, 'I knew Angus had worked with the Resistance during the war.'

'And you thought that would involve carrying such items as wireless transmitters – or cameras – about with him in peacetime?'

'I didn't think one thing or the other.' She was aware of how staccato her voice had become. 'I wanted hot soup and a bath.'

'You never mentioned the incident to him afterwards?'

'No. I never talked to him about his work.'

'And did he talk to you about *your* work? Which is also of a confidential nature?'

'Never!' She was stung by the suggestion that he would have used her and responded more vehemently than might have been thought necessary by people concerned with facts rather than emotions.

'But you talked generally, no doubt, about politics and public figures who might be known to you both?'

Panic was rising up her digestive system in little bubbles which exploded at the back of her throat. She was having to do a lot of swallowing. 'Not really. I try to avoid that. And Angus wasn't given to expressing his opinions.'

'But people give their sympathies away in small things. Most of us have some idea of our friends' political affiliations.'

'We talked about music mostly. It was what we had in common.' She had said this so often, to protect herself from the curiosity of friends who wondered how far things had gone between them. Now, it seemed, it was the simple truth, a brief meeting of the minds, desolate of emotion. Or perhaps not even that. A congenial companion with whom to attend a concert! She would have preferred this rakish policeman to suspect her of being a high-class tart with more intimate matters to relate than tone variations in Mozart.

In all this time, because she knew where the questions must be leading, she had answered them as though it was natural that they should be put to her. This was a mistake. She realised this, but, threatened as she was by the volatility of her digestive processes, she could not trust herself to challenge the policeman.

He said, 'The disappearance of a man engaged in intelligence work is a serious matter, as you will understand, and inevitably gives rise to certain conjectures. What would you say to the idea that Mr Drummond might for some time past have been in the pay of a foreign power?'

'He couldn't have been!' Even as she said it, she knew it sounded more like a wish than a statement of belief. What could one *believe* about Angus? Elusive, self-doubting as he was, he had little prepared his friends to protest his innocence. She said, 'He wasn't positive enough about anything to do that.'

'I find that a rather strange statement, Miss Kimberley. A man who is not positive may be open to conviction, wouldn't you say?'

'I didn't mean positive in the sense of not being certain. I meant that he was rather negative in some ways.'

'So, in your judgement, there would be nothing he would hold to – for want of a better phrase?'

The phrase was in fact so close to what she thought that she was dismayed and could not think how to answer.

'I get the impression, Miss Kimberley, that although you are very upset, you are not surprised.'

'I can't take it in. Secret equipment and people in the pay of foreign powers! How can I be surprised? These things don't happen – not to ordinary people.'

He rubbed his hands together and then held them up in front of him, examining the palms. 'Your father is at the Home Office, I believe?'

'My *father*!' She sat up even straighter, suddenly quite imperious. 'You are surely not suggesting. . . .'

'No, Miss Kimberley, I am not *suggesting* anything.' He noted with amusement the difference in tone when she referred to her father. Here was a person about whom Miss Kimberley entertained no doubts. 'I merely wondered if Mr Drummond often came here and chatted to your father.'

'He didn't, as a matter of fact.'

'Did your father not like him?'

'It had nothing to do with my father. Angus never . . . I think perhaps he didn't want to be involved with my parents.' Imperiousness petered away. 'We weren't engaged. We had certain interests in common . . . music and . . . well, mostly music.' I had so little, she thought, and now I am having to tell them how little I had. She clenched her hands and wished that she was a whore.

They asked a few more questions. When they left, he said, 'We shall have to see you again, Miss Kimberley. In the meantime, if you remember anything which may be of help to us, I would be grateful if you would telephone me. Remember that he may be ill and it is important to find him before he comes to any harm.' He handed her a card with a name and telephone number written on it. 'I appreciate that Mr Drummond may not have seen your parents very often but, nevertheless, we shall wish to talk to them.'

Her mother, when informed of what had taken place, had been incredulous, distressed, and then angry. But it was her father's response that Irene remembered. He had stood stiff and straight as a soldier, so unlike his usual stance; then he had stretched out his arms – he who made so few gestures – and said, 'Oh, my precious child!' When she looked into his face it seemed, even then, that some internal spasm had frozen the features leaving only the eyes to speak his pain and bewilderment. Her mother talked about it, endlessly starting sentences which she never finished, as was her habit. But her father had not given himself time to come gradually to full realisation, he had absorbed it in one instant before the defence mechanism of brain and body could be summoned to his aid.

And the worst thing of all, she thought as she walked towards the Imminghams' house, is that none of us believed in Angus enough to doubt it.

They gathered round her in the sitting-room, Louise, Guy and Alice, and Ben, who was staying the night. She blurted out, 'Angus has disappeared. They think he's on the way to Russia.'

They were incredulous. Louise said, 'I wouldn't have believed he had it in him,' which seemed to suggest that she had rapidly convinced herself.

Ben said, 'We don't *know* that he has done anything of the sort. He may have gone for a walk and fallen down a well, or over a cliff. Or simply had a breakdown. I would think him quite a likely candidate for a breakdown.'

'You must have been with him just before he disappeared,' Louise said. 'How did he seem to you?'

'He *was* a little different.'

'You are probably imagining that,' Ben said.
'No.' She had thought something had kindled in him and had gone home excited and hopeful. 'However major the work, Angus's enjoyment was usually expressed in a minor key. But this time I felt his pleasure, as though the music went through him.' She appealed to Louise. 'You know the way it can?'
'Dance up and down the spine? Yes.'
'Yes. That was it, exactly.'
When she left, Alice walked with her as far as the main road. 'Irene, he didn't say *anything* when he left you?'
'No. But when I turned into the house, he was still standing on the edge of the square, looking at me.'
Alice thought that most fellows would watch their girls safely into the house.
'You think he's gone, don't you, Irene?'
'Yes. He may not get away with it. They may have got on to him too quickly. In which case, I suppose he could still be somewhere in this country, hiding . . .'
'But *why* should he do such a thing?'
'I've been thinking a lot about that in the last few days. Although he was . . . is . . . so reserved, he's not a strong personality. He's not like Ben, who will battle his way through his difficulties. Angus tends to embrace his and sink down deeper and deeper. I believe he had a need of a structure which could hold him. It would have to be something fairly uncompromising. He couldn't cope with complexity. I suppose Russia may have seemed to be the answer – much more tidy than democracy.'
'He *can't* have thought their system was better than ours!'
'From the way he sometimes talked, I think now that he did believe that. The further you are away, the greener the grass, and the less you see the weeds.' She looked down the lighted avenue towards the bright ring of lights where the trolley buses turned round at Shepherd's Bush Green. 'And yet . . . it could simply be that he felt he would break away from his father at last.'
A car stopped outside one of the handsome terraced houses in the main road and several people got out, waving to a man who had appeared on the balcony. They went up the steps, the girls holding up long skirts. One of the men raised a bottle aloft. A light appeared in the hall and then fanned out across the steps as they were admitted, laughing and talking all at once. An old, hunched man paused to watch them and then walked on, chattering to himself like an ageing sparrow.

Irene said, 'Oh, Alice, whatever reason he had for doing it, he's made the most awful mistake! More than anyone I know, Angus needs his anonymity. He's sacrificed that now. He'll be under the microscope for the rest of his life.'

'Would you have gone with him, if he had asked you?'

'And killed my parents?' It was a choice she could not bear to contemplate. He had not asked it of her, but she would ask it of herself until time and other griefs blurred his memory.

Alice was used to demonstrating affection to her family, but not to her friends. Something, however, seemed to be called for now. So she pecked Irene's wan cheek and said, 'I am so terribly upset for you. I shall be thinking of you.'

Irene said, 'Yes, I know you will,' and turned away abruptly.

Alice watched her friend walking away with a feeling of guilt. Not for the first time she was aware of how unprepared the emotions so often seem for the big occasion, how they lag behind the mind. She wanted to experience an immediate and deep sympathy for Irene, but the truth was that at this moment she felt cheated of the opportunity to tell Irene in some detail about the mutual discoveries which she and Ben had made. As for the affair of Angus, she could not rid herself of a sense of importance at being involved, however peripherally, in a matter of national concern; and she was awed by the thought that she actually knew someone capable of such monstrous conduct. But not so awed as to prevent her from imagining how this material might one day be incorporated in a work of fiction. As she walked slowly back to the house, she indulged her curiosity about Angus – his past and future movements. She was, in fact, still very much in the world of John Buchan, and although she could see that Irene was suffering, she thought she would soon get over it and be herself again; and that it would all be for the best, because Angus could not have been good for her.

The others were still occupied with the matter when she joined them. Louise was scornful and said she had never thought much of Angus anyway, describing him as insipid and standoffish. Ben was irritable. Guy was silent.

On one matter they were all agreed; although none cared to voice a reaction so unworthy, they thought it a pity that they had had to find this out now, just when they had returned from a nice autumn break.

'We'll clear up in the morning,' Louise said. 'I can't put my mind to anything.'

Supper was a tired meal with long silences interspersed with spasmodic exclamations of non-belief and speculation. As they were preparing to go to their rooms, Ben said, 'She'll lose her job, poor girl.'

'Lose her job!' Alice exclaimed.

'She works in the Cabinet Office, doesn't she? She can't expect to stay there after becoming involved in this affair. The people at the top may escape punishment, but not those lower down the scale.'

'But she isn't involved.'

'She's involved by association. She was his girl friend – and since guilt of one kind is soon translated into general misbehaviour, a lot of people will believe there was more to the relationship than friendship. Even if they don't believe it, they will have to allow for the possibility.'

'So what?' Louise flared up. 'It's not a crime to sleep together. They would hardly have been whispering national secrets into each other's ears!'

'But they didn't sleep together,' Alice protested. 'I'm sure of that.'

'How can you be sure? And what business is it of their employers?'

'For goodness sake don't go round talking to anyone like that, Louise,' Ben said. 'You won't do Irene any good.'

'I don't need to be told how to behave by you, Ben Sherman.'

'Don't misunderstand me. *I'm* not making a moral issue of this. I don't care how many people Irene has slept with. All I am saying is that it's important Angus wasn't one of them.'

'Irene isn't like that,' Alice said.

'I didn't say . . .'

'On the contrary,' she shouted, 'You've been doing all the saying.'

They made their peace, sitting on the stairs while Louise and Guy did the washing-up. But there was a cold area somewhere inside Alice which the glow of physical pleasure failed to reach. As she made her way up the stairs after she had parted from Ben, she was thinking of Irene. The stairs seemed steeper than she had remembered and the muscles she had ill-used on the Chilterns protested. Irene enjoyed her job, and her parents were so proud of her. She sat on her bed and listened to the noises in the house dwindling into silence, and she remembered that other time when she had sat alone while her parents tried to come to terms with the fact of Louise's pregnancy. Her father, so proud of his daughters, had been broken by this discovery.

It is all going to happen again, she thought incredulously. This terrible breaking-up process, when will it end? Is *nothing* safe and secure? Not, it seemed, as long as one had beliefs of any kind. To believe in anything, or anyone, is to launch oneself onto a dark sea. As for love, that is the ultimate hazard. She lay thinking of Ben. Their love was so new, and, wonderful though that was in itself – the freshness, the never-to-be-recaptured excitement – they could not yet give each other that sustenance which comes after years of joy and troubles shared.

She could not sleep, and at one o'clock decided to make herself a cup of tea. As she went down the stairs she was surprised to see a light beneath the kitchen door. Her heart beat faster, hoping she would find Ben there. But it was Guy who greeted her when she entered the room. 'I couldn't sleep. I have bad nights sometimes. Would you like tea?'

Alice sat at the kitchen table. She looked at Guy in the dressing-gown that Louise had made out of an old travelling rug, the material of which had not been sufficient to contain his long frame. His pyjamas had bunched up in the narrow sleeves so that his bare forearms protruded, freckled and fuzzed with golden hair. His toes insecurely gripped sandals which flip-flopped as he moved. She noted that his state of undress aroused in her no curiosity, only a sense of his defencelessness. She was touched by the care with which he observed the rites of tea-making in which Louise had instructed him, and which she, in turn, had learnt from her Cornish grandparents. She thought of Granny Tippet, alone now in the house in Falmouth looking out over the Carrick Roads.

Guy poured hot milk for himself and tea for Alice; then he, too, sat at the table. Alice said, 'How *could* he? After all the risks he took for his country, how could he have betrayed it?'

Guy frowned down at his cup, waiting for the milk to cool. 'You start fighting for something, knowing exactly where you are and what you believe, and you end up not so clear about things as you were when you started. At least, that's my experience.'

Alice, who had not thought of Guy as having this kind of experience, was surprised. 'I always thought you had a good war.'

The remark had something unintentionally dismissive about it which stung him. He said, 'The war in the desert was fairly straightforward – or so it seemed to me. But the Italian campaign was another matter. Something happened there that I haven't talked to anyone about before.'

Apparently there was to be no end to the revelations of the night. Alice composed herself to listen.

'We had to hold a farmhouse. I was never quite sure why. A handful of us. While we were there two men turned up – Partisans. One of them said he had something he wanted to show us. He took me and two soldiers up into the hills, to a cave. The Germans had rounded up all the people in one of the villages – they were supposed to have harboured the Partisans; they took them up to this cave and shot them all. The bodies were lying there, rotting. Men, women, and children.'

Alice had heard similar stories, but had not met anyone who had actually witnessed such a scene. 'It must have been awful,' she said, although at the moment she could not take in this particular awfulness.

'The odd thing was that I didn't feel what . . . well, what one might expect.'

Alice, who was not sure what was to be expected, stirred her tea and tried to look wise.

'I didn't feel angry so much as . . . a sort of horror at myself for being there. I felt as if I was a part of it. Ever since then, I've had times when I have felt like those people who go to the police and confess to crimes they haven't committed. I suppose none of us can be sure what we might do, given the circumstances . . .'

'Never, Guy! Not you, of all people! Not children!'

'No, it's stupid, I know.' He gave his familiar embarrassed laugh. But after a moment, he went on, 'You can never be sure, though, can you? About yourself. At least, *I* can't. There was that kid who used to come to the house with James. You must remember him – Harry Ince. One of those unpleasant, manipulative children, and a thoroughly bad influence.' He sounded rather priggish as he talked of the child. 'He was the kind of little perisher who goaded one into anger. Louise said she had to keep a strong grip on herself, or she would have clouted him. But, of course, we had the answer to that situation; if we had chosen to exercise our authority we could have refused to have him in the house. Only that seemed to be making rather too much of it . . .' It seemed he might be going to explore the safer question of the rights and wrongs of such forbearance, but he stopped short. For a time he sat looking down at the wrinkled skin forming on the top of the milk. Then he said, 'Those men were soldiers. The Italians had been their allies and then they turned against them. Perhaps some of their comrades had been killed by the Partisans. They were fighting a running battle in Italy, being driven back all the time. It was the end for them. I had heard some of them talk when they were taken prisoner. They didn't regard the Italians as human, they thought they were vermin.'

'You would never . . .'

'No. No, of course not.' The laugh again. But it was three years since it had happened, and he was still plagued by uncertainty. He looked round the room, at the Welsh dresser with the blue and white plates and the big porcelain wash basin in which James had planted orange pips in a brief experiment in rural science; at Catherine's painting of marigolds pasted on the wall, as bright as a Van Gogh if nothing else. His forehead wrinkled. 'I even imagine it happening here. The other week, when you were out, Claire and Terence came round with a friend of ours, Barry. Louise happened to comment on the number of black people one sees in London these days. And Claire took her up on it at once. You know what Claire is like when she gets her teeth into a cause. She got under Barry's skin and he started saying things that he probably didn't mean, just to annoy her. Then Terence began to talk as if he was addressing a political meeting. The upshot was that Barry said if the blacks ever showed up in Holland Park, he would go out with his shotgun. And Louise said, "Make it two shotguns. I'll stand by your side; Wild Bill Hickock and Calamity Jane defending the old frontier." '

'She didn't mean it. Not Louise.'

'She doesn't like them en masse. Come to that, neither do I. At least, I wouldn't mind them in their own country . . .'

'But you wouldn't go out and shoot them in this country!'

'No. I think it was Terence and Claire I felt like shooting for spoiling the evening.' He pushed the cup to one side. Milk slopped about the sides of the cup and a sweet, sickly smell came from it. 'I've read books about the concentration camps. And there were some things I *couldn't* understand. The *aimless* killing – a guard smashing a child's head against a wall because it was eating an apple he wanted. Now that is *quite* outside my comprehension.' He looked at Alice as if he expected her to derive some comfort from this assurance; but saw only his own darkness reflected momentarily in her eyes.

He looked towards the window. The blinds were not drawn – Louise had refused to draw blinds since the war ended. He could see the underbelly of a giant moth against the window; it hung there quite still and one was aware of little white feet. There was something rather obscene about it. He didn't like it peering in at them out of the night.

'When I was small, my mother put one of those texts in my room because she thought I was afraid of the dark – which as it happens I wasn't – "There is not enough darkness in the whole world to put out the light of one small candle." '

They looked at each other uneasily and he laughed as if he had made a joke in poor taste.

Alice said, 'I don't know about that; but I do know *you* will never do anyone any violence.'

'I'd like to be sure.'

'Well, I am sure. You're not a monster, Guy.'

His eyes filled with tears. 'You won't tell Louise about all this, will you? It's just that Louise is always so sure – and I wouldn't want to . . .' Whether it was himself he would not want to put at risk, or Louise, was not clear.

# 14

Louise and Guy went to Sussex to fetch the children and the dog. Louise, who had other matters uppermost in her mind, left Guy to tell Austin and Judith about Angus while she went out with the children.

As Judith and Guy talked about Angus, Austin thought of his son. Austin had prided himself on being of the E. M. Forster persuasion; and would have said that if he had to choose between betraying his country or his friend, he hoped he would betray his country. Admittedly, it had never been possible to identify a particular friend on whose behalf such drastic action might be called for; but so far as his country was concerned, he had considered his due of patriotism had been paid once and for all in the mud of Flanders. Now, he saw that more might be involved than a simple choice. His son had died for something. Certainly not for his country, right or wrong; but for some undefined, inarticulate thing which he had thought worth dying for. Austin would never be able to understand this. But he saw now that he had, by virtue of being alive, a certain responsibility to look carefully into his own heart.

Judith said, 'Well, it's happened and there is nothing we can do to change it, Guy. I hope the girls aren't too upset.' It was her belief that a firm stance and a confident manner will see one through most crises.

Austin looked at her. She was that kind of woman who conveys a reassuring impression that all is right in the world, not by anything she says, but by her very presence. She was capable but cheerful with it, and would shake the cobwebs out of one's mind as briskly as she would plump up a pillow or draw back the blinds. There was a slight air of untidiness which suggested that while she was good at restoring order, she would not demand the highest standards. Getting things done was her priority. She would not be one to grieve over a chipped plate or a watermark on a table. Austin, who had loved her for this very robustness, now found himself wondering what resources she could call upon were her practical remedies ever to fail. He realised he did not know her well enough to answer this question.

Judith, interpreting his silence as indifference, thought that if Stanley had been here he would – for better or for worse – have taken the matter into his own hands. No doubt Austin was wiser, but she was not sure she respected him so much.

Guy said, 'Well, that's the bad news. Now for the good. I don't know whether I am supposed to tell you, but . . .' He told them about Alice and Ben.

Louise, meanwhile had taken the children and the dog up on the Downs. James and the dog enjoyed the walk, but Catherine kept complaining that she had a blister. The wind was cold. Perhaps it had not been an ideal day for this kind of outing, but Louise, always impulsive, must act when inspiration came to her.

'Wouldn't you like to live here?' she said. 'And get away from smelly old London.'

James looked solemnly down at Lewes huddled in autumn mist. He knew his mother better than did Catherine. 'Are we going to live there?' he asked, pointing.

'Probably.'

'I should hate it!' Catherine said fiercely, winding her scarf around her head and ears.

'You might be able to go riding, you'd like that.'

'No, I wouldn't. Amy Potter has a horse at her uncle's farm, and she spends all her time mucking it out when she goes down there.'

'You'd have to take the manure along with the horse.'

'I don't want either.'

'It's no use arguing with her,' James said to Catherine. 'If she's made up her mind, we'll have to live here.'

'But I shan't be happy here,' Catherine said.

'Our unhappy childhood will give us an understanding of all the oppressed people in the world,' James said.

Louise buffeted him on the head and the dog jumped between them, suspecting foul play.

'*Why* do we have to come here?' Catherine asked, kicking at a stone, deliberately scuffing the toe of her shoe.

'Daddy wants to work here.'

'I thought it was Daddy!' Catherine muttered. James got on quite well with his father now, but Catherine had never reconciled herself to him. Catherine saw Guy's weakness, James was kinder.

Louise said, 'If you spoil that shoe you'll have to go barefoot to add to your miseries.'

'Why does he want to work here?' James asked.

'People in London are very ambitious and they only think of money.'

James looked down at Lewes as though expecting to see its goodness sprouting up through the mist.

'Daddy cares about people,' Louise said. 'He wants to help them and be kind to them – even if they can't afford to pay big bills.'

Catherine smiled knowingly. James was more impressed. Louise said, 'We ought to admire him for that, don't you think? And try to help him? Yes?'

'What about my school?' Catherine said. 'I *love* school.'

'That's not what we hear at the beginning of each term.'

'And I've got lots of friends.'

'You'll make friends here soon enough.' Louise put an arm around each of them and drew them to her. 'I'm sorry, my chicks. It's going to be a wrench for all of us. But I think it's something we've got to do. So let's think of all the good things, shall we? Only eight miles from the sea.'

'I won't be able to play with Peggy, Mummy,' Catherine wailed. 'I love Peggy. We share everything.'

'Peggy can come to stay with you.'

Catherine's eyes overflowed. She cried rather too readily. Louise, who knew how hard the last two years had been for her, turned her head away, biting back impatience.

'It's really going to happen, is it?' James asked. She could tell that he was already trying to accommodate himself to it. He was not so selfish as Catherine, and in the long run might suffer for it. Or perhaps not. The ability to make the best of what life hands out cannot be learnt too young.

'I think so. But that doesn't mean we can't have a say in *how* it happens.' They looked at her, and she raised a fist conspiratorially. They turned to walk down the hill, waving their fists and laughing, while the dog danced in front of them.

Alice had decided she needed time on her own. 'Apart from anything else,' she had said when Ben telephoned her during the lunch hour, 'I *must* wash my hair.'

'You can wash it and I'll dry it.'

A delicious idea. 'But we have years ahead of us,' she said firmly.

'Don't rely on my drying your hair when we're a staid married couple.'

'And I've got all my holiday clothes to wash. We've got plans for every other evening this week; it won't hurt us to be apart tonight.'

Ben said he would go to see Claire and Terence. He had promised to help Terence put up some shelving.

That evening Alice sat for some time dreaming over her supper. All day hope had been rising in her like yeast, affecting everything that happened around her. It seemed impossible that there should be such personal joy without a corresponding change in the state of the world, let alone the West London Education Authority. She had smoothed over a disagreement between Mr Hadow and Miss Bruce, the head of the teachers' section, pouring over the ruffled waters the unction of her blessedness. Now, eyes half-closed, feeling steamy warmth on her lids, she meditated over a cup of tea.

Eventually she cleared away the supper things and went into the bathroom to wash her hair. Her body, eased of all tension, seemed to function with fluid effortlessness. By the time she had washed her hair she was beginning to regret that she had not accepted Ben's offer to dry it. When she heard a knock on the door she marvelled at his prescience. She wound a towel round her head and went joyfully to meet him.

In the dim light from the hall lamp she saw a man with unkempt hair and a stubbly beard; his shoulders were hunched as if accustomed to supporting something – a ladder? Of course, the window cleaner! She recalled that Louise had said the man was rather odd. This was embarrassing. Louise never paid without first carefully inspecting the windows.

'I'm afraid Mrs Immingham is away . . .'

He said, 'Can I come in, Alice?' and stepped inside. It was Angus.

'I'm sorry to do this to you. Could we talk somewhere at the back of the house – just in case your neighbours have seen me and are curious. I'm fairly sure I haven't been followed.' He followed her to the dining-room door, but waited in the hall while she drew the curtains. He went on talking. She had never known him so talkative, or so – lighthearted, seemed the only word. 'In fact, I gave them the slip some time ago.'

When she realised who it was, Alice's heart had come into her mouth and she had swallowed it; she felt she really had done for herself. For the next few minutes the business of keeping the bits and pieces of her person in the right place and more or less functioning seemed more important than anything else.

Angus said, 'I decided they were less likely to look for me on their own backdoor step – so I've been sleeping rough on the Embankment. During the day I sat on one of the benches. There were several other people doing the same thing – people who have dropped out of sight. The police don't bother with you. The thing which really helped me was a dog. He adopted me and sat on my lap. A terrier, with those big, mournful eyes. When he got tired of me, I knew I had to move on. Those odd characters aren't easily parted from their dogs. Someone might have noticed.'

Alice sat on a stool, rubbing her hair.

'I dodged about a bit after that. I need to get in touch with Daphne and Peter. I know they are in London, but I haven't been able to get an answer when I've rung Peter's flat. I passed the theatre where Jacov is playing. It occurred to me he might get a message to them. I managed to get into his dressing-room. The stage door keeper was one of those little men with such a huge grievance against members of the theatrical profession he would have let Jack the Ripper in. But Jacov got in a panic and I had to leave in a hurry.'

Alice brushed her hair and switched it back, inserting pins with practised fingers.

'I came this way last night, and I saw you and Irene walking towards the main road. There was a party of people going into one of the houses in the terrace.'

'Why didn't you speak to us?'

'Too many of you. It's always better to approach a person on their own. I saw Guy and Louise leave early this morning carrying a suitcase.'

Alice said in a brisk, businesslike voice which surprised herself more than it impressed Angus, 'I'm afraid I don't feel I can handle this on my own. So I am going out to fetch Ben. Then we'll talk.'

'I'm not sure about that. People with legal minds can be rather tricky customers. Ben might persuade you to go to the police.'

'Ben and I are going to be married,' Alice said, as though this dispensed with the matter of the police.

'I only want to telephone Daphne and Peter. I'm not planning to involve you in any way, other than allowing me the use of the telephone.'

'You can use the telephone while I fetch Ben.'

He considered this, or rather, he considered her. He had undertaken dangerous missions at the bidding of others; now he was acting on his own account. He had no mind to fail. He realised that if Alice Fairley was all that stood in his way, he was prepared to remove her. He was surprised, but not unpleasantly. Day in, day out, year in, year out, he had looked at people and places with the same eyes. Things stale. Now, momentarily, it was all new, a quite different universe. *All* things were possible. Their eyes met and Alice was afraid.

He said, 'And where is Ben?'

'Kew.' Immediately she regretted admitting that he was so far away.

Angus closed his eyes. For some reason he had imagined that Ben was much nearer. Now we all have time for thought, he reflected wearily.

Alice got up. 'I am going to put my raincoat on,' she announced. She made this statement in order to give warning of her intention to move, then paused to see what he made of it, rather as if he was a snake which might strike if she made any abrupt movement.

He said indifferently, 'Away with you, then.'

Alice hurried towards Holland Park Avenue. She felt a mad urge to run, but bridled herself to a brisk pace. She was very frightened, and her fear alerted her to the need to maintain control of her body; if body raced, mind, to say nothing of emotion, would soon outstrip it. The roads were dark, arched by trees; and lamps, far apart, looked through the tangle of branches like pallid faces. In the past, she had found, and rather liked, a certain secretness in this area. Now, it had become a superior sort of warren which afforded too many hiding places. At first, she was convinced that she was being followed. She thought she heard footsteps, not her own; when she turned her head, a shadow danced over a garden hedge. She adjusted her scarf, buttoned up her raincoat, and composed her mind to deal with such matters as whether there was anyone she could telephone who would take a message to the Straker household (the police would hardly be appropriate in this case), and the efficient organisation of her journey. Try to remain calm as she might, there was no question but that the task of transporting herself from Holland Park to Kew seemed a business of more rigour than her wartime journey to Alexandria. There had been a national enemy to fight then, an enemy distinct and out there. Now the enemy was personal, private, and in her own home.

There was no direct route to Kew. Usually, she walked to Shepherd's Bush Green and took a bus to the Odeon, Acton, where she caught another bus to Kew. She did this because she was familiar with the route and liked travelling by bus; that it might be time-consuming had never worried her, since time was available to be consumed. But now that she was applying herself to the matter, calmly and sensibly, she realised that it would be better to take a bus to Stamford Brook station where she could get a District Line train to Kew Gardens. At this hour, the trains would probably be more frequent than the buses.

She came to a telephone box and paused for a moment. The vicar? But Claire and Terence did not go to church, and even vicars, good shepherds though they might be, would not expect to run carefully coded messages round their parishes on behalf of total strangers. And as she did not know the name of the vicar anyway, it was no use wasting time on speculation.

It was just before eight o'clock when she reached Holland Park Avenue. The dead time of the evening. There were two men and one woman waiting at the bus stop. They had the look of people who have been overwhelmed by the non-events of life; should a bus now appear one felt they would treat it with the scepticism with which other unfortunates learn to regard mirages in the desert.

'How long have you been waiting?' Alice asked.

The woman blinked as though coming out of a trance. 'Twenty minutes.' She jerked her head. 'He's been here half an hour, haven't you, dear?'

The man thus addressed turned to Alice and raised a wide-brimmed black hat which suggested some affiliation with highwaymen. To complete the effect, he wore a long, caped overcoat which trailed the ground, sweeping into its folds cigarette ends and discarded bus tickets. Alice recognised him as a friend of Mr Kimberley who wrote poetry and paid to have it published in pamphlet form. 'Every journey is an adventure, is it not? Even we, who travel by the humble bus, must remember that, as we make our pilgrimage to Acton, Hammersmith, or the far reaches of Chiswick . . .' This put him in mind of another poet. ' "For lust of knowing what should not be known . . ." '

'Here they come!' the woman said.

In the distance a moving line of lights had appeared; now visible, now hidden by the branches of trees, now emerging again, slowly, majestically, the buses descended from Notting Hill, taking shape and substance as they drew nearer, their destinations branded on reluctant umber brows. The first to stop was an 88. Mr Kimberley's friend said pleasantly to the conductor, ' "For thee the waggons of the world are drawn!" '

'What's all this?' the conductor asked suspiciously.

'I was hymning the arrival of your caravan, sir.'

The conductor, by no means mollified by what he took to be a variation of the "why do they always travel in convoys?" theme, said sourly, 'Where do you want to go?'

' "Beyond that last blue mountain barred with snow/Across that angry or that glimmering sea . . ." '

'This bus stops at The Askew Arms.'

'Yes, well, that will have to serve for the time being. We will make our journey to those isles where good men rest another time.'

'You want your head seen to, mate, if you think it's restful working on the buses.'

Alice, apprehensive, and confused by this unlikely exchange, ran along the line of buses. There were three 88s, all of which now showed signs – weary sighs from the nose of the beast, leisurely descent of driver to stretch cramped limbs – of having come to a good watering place. The fourth bus was having none of this, and was pulling clear as Alice reached it. Glancing up, she saw the word 'Green' and swung herself aboard with a feeling of enormous relief. Turnham Green would suit her even better than Stamford Brook. No sooner had she sat down, however, than it occurred to her that the destination might well be Shepherd's Bush Green, which would explain the sudden acceleration of speed as it came into the home stretch. She ducked her head, as though by dissociating herself from its unfolding, the situation might miraculously be resolved in her favour. She took out her purse and busied herself counting change. The bus started, stopped, started again and kept going. By the time it could be assumed that it had left Shepherd's Bush Green behind, Alice had another problem. She had only one shilling and three pence in her purse, and an exhaustive examination of the contents of her handbag had yielded only a halfpenny with a hole drilled through the King's nose. A shilling would surely be sufficient for the train journey? The conductor had come down from the top deck and was now leaning against the stairs, moodily indifferent to fares. Perhaps he would assume she had got on at the Green if she handed him the three pence. She closed her handbag, relieved, and looked out of the window. To her surprise, she saw that the bus was approaching a station. It seemed rather soon for Stamford Brook, and she could not think what other station was on this route. She peered intently, heart thumping, and saw the familiar underground rail sign alongside the unfamiliar words: Wood Lane. She leapt up and pressed the bell.

'I thought this went to Turnham Green,' she said to the conductor.

'*Kensal* Green,' he said aggrievedly. 'That'll be three pence.'

'I don't want to go there.' She jumped off the bus while it was still moving in case he insisted. The road was empty of traffic. She stood looking this way and that. Kensal Green. The name filled her with quite disproportionate dismay. She had never been to Kensal Green. Although it was probably only a few miles from places with which she had been familiar all her life, it now seemed to represent something menacing. Had she discovered herself in Tahiti, Fiji, or even Portofino, she would have known she had been transported into the realms of fantasy; but Kensal Green was only that slight degree adrift. It was that moment in the nightmare when the familiar door opens into the wrong room. But she had been saved from that. She had only gone as far as Wood Lane, which was just on the periphery of the known childhood land. Did she remember, as she stood there, that time when Katia, hemmed in by crowds, had been in danger of being carried beyond Shepherd's Bush station? Certainly, as she stood watching the bus trundling away, she was shaken, not so much by her narrow escape from exposure to the outer regions of Willesden, as by that fear of what lies beyond the ordinary.

She turned to face Shepherd's Bush Green. It would be quicker to walk back, rather than wait for another bus. As she made her way, every now and then breaking into a panic-stricken run, then steadying herself, a bus overtook her but refused to stop, although the conductor looked with morbid interest at her receding figure.

At Shepherd's Bush Green she made careful enquiries before boarding a bus which did, in fact, take her to Stamford Brook station. There was a train waiting as she came racing on to the platform. She looked at the indicator board, saw that a Richmond train was signalled, and jumped in as the doors began to close. She landed in a heap on the floor and knew at once that something was wrong. The District Line trains stood tall above the platform; the floor of this train was well below the level of the platform. She was on a Piccadilly Line train, which did not normally stop at intermediate stations between Hammersmith and Acton Town.

'You were lucky,' a man informed her, as he helped her to her feet. 'We'd been stopped here for ten minutes, and he only opened the doors the once. You know how bloody-minded they can be!'

Alice sat back and watched while first Turnham Green, then Chiswick Park stations flashed by. She felt sick with apprehension. Something malign had taken possession of the machinery of everyday life.

At Acton Town too many possibilities presented themselves. She could go back to Turnham Green and wait for another Richmond train. There was a shuttle service which at one time had linked Acton Town to South Acton where she could get a main line train to Kew. Only she wasn't sure if the shuttle still operated. Or she could catch a bus. The bus service was unreliable. So why was it that she found herself outside the station waiting for the bus? It was because the very sight of all those railway lines fanning out from the station disturbed her. It would be no use crossing to the other platform and going back, she still wouldn't come to the place where it had all started to go wrong. The place names would get stranger and stranger, and she would not dare to ask where she was, and she would be carried further and further away from Ben. So, she waited for the bus.

It was cool and quiet by the bus stop. Just beyond the station was a small parade of shops set back from a wide pavement; here were a grocer's, hairdresser's, an off-licence, and a bakery with a small tea shop at the rear where Alice remembered her father taking the family after a visit to Gunnersbury Park. She had had a crusty roll, still warm, and a Devonshire slice. Claire had got jam on her new frock and had cried so unrelentingly that they had had to leave before Alice could eat the cream split she had kept for last. Such were the heartaches of those days. Beyond the shops were small, mock-Tudor houses, and in the distance, enclosed by high walls, was the park itself. At one time there had been a pond outside the gates with a horse trough near by, and often a gypsy caravan encamped; an old man at the Acton chapel could remember seeing Disraeli drive up to the park to be greeted by Baron Rothschild. One had been aware of a rural and, for some, more gracious past which had vanished now. The area still seemed quiet, comfortable, sane.

And she had felt so much a part of it once. Where had it all gone wrong? How had it come about that people who lived within a few miles' radius of this place, whose lives had been contained by streets and houses as trim and sane, had been heirs to such unrest? She and Claire had walked in the park with nothing more to exercise their minds than why Daphne always spat out the pips when she ate a pomegranate, and Katia came to school with egg on her face – 'You'd think just *one* morning she would wash properly!' How unbelievable it would have seemed to them had they known that within a few years their father would have been dismembered by a bomb in the quiet street where they lived, that Ben would become a prisoner on the other side of the world in a land they had barely heard of, that Mr Drummond would be paralysed, and Angus, so disarmingly diffident standing on the Drummond lawn handing round cucumber sandwiches, would have betrayed his country! While Katia, anything but diffident, would have disappeared without trace. Is shipwreck the fate of all those who look for a smooth passage through calm waters? By the light of the street lamps, Alice could see the names above the first three shops; none appeared to have changed hands since the time when she first saw them. It was all a bad dream, they seemed to be saying.

She could hear singing now. The door of a house on the opposite side of the road opened, and a chain of young people emerged; waggling hips and flicking legs, they followed their leader out onto the pavement, chanting, 'I came, I saw, I conga'd . . .' Several of the girls had rolled up their blouses to expose bare midriffs, while the men had grasped whatever colourful item was available to serve as a cummerbund. Their leader sported a handlebar moustache so impressive as to resemble the horns of some magnificent beast attached to his upper lip; on his head he wore a tea cosy with an ostrich feather stuck in it. Someone had a pair of castanets. Delighted to have at least one witness to their performance, they all waved at Alice as they side-kicked their way to the back gate. Alice, who only a few days ago, would have joined in with zest reporting later to friends 'We danced in the street!' – watched them with detachment, feeling about a hundred. They went singing to the rear of the house where their voices dissolved in general hilarity, overtopped by a great bellow, 'I'll have your knickers off for that, you naughty girl!'

A bus was coming. The conductor was Irish. Sure and they were going to Kew, where else? And even if they hadn't been, they would have gone just to please her, if only she could manage a wee smile, now? Within a quarter of an hour, she was saying to Terence, who had opened the front door, 'Ben, I must see Ben!'

Behind Terence, she saw Claire's alarmed face angled round the kitchen door. The ginger cat came and rubbed its head against her legs.

'He's gone,' Terence said. 'A few minutes ago . . .'

'I must see him!' Alice turned and stumbled down the drive, pursued by Terence with whom she wrestled clumsily at the gate, much to the diversion of the next door neighbour who had been about to draw her bedroom curtains under the impression that the day was drawing peacefully to its close.

'You can't go running off like that,' Terence said, lugging Alice up the drive. 'And anyway, you will never catch him. I'll go on my bike.'

Claire was already standing by the front door with a torch in one hand. He went to a shed, removed a padlock from a wheel, and prepared to set off. He had not asked any questions. Claire and Alice, and the next door neighbour, watched as he wheeled the bike on to the road, mounted, and wobbled off, hunched over the handlebars like a gigantic tortoise.

'How kind he is!' Alice said, surprised and ashamed, thinking how often she had made fun of him.

'Terence is like that,' Claire said, 'If anyone is in trouble, he drops everything. You had better come in and tell me what your trouble is.' Her voice held a hint of disapproval.

'It's not what you think, whatever that may be,' Alice said when they were sitting in the kitchen and Claire had squeezed two cups of lukewarm tea from a pot where it had been stewing for some time. She did not consider it wise to say too much. 'I've had bad news . . . about a friend, and I need Ben's advice.'

Claire contemplated this statement, thumbnail inserted between her front teeth. If this was tact, Alice was surprised. In the circumstances, a request for enlightenment would not have been unreasonable, even from someone less aware of their dues than Claire. She sipped her tea. Now that the action had been taken over by Terence, she felt the kind of detachment from what was happening around her which she often experienced just before a bilious attack. Quite apart from any considerations of discretion, she could not have summoned the energy to tell her story twice. All she wanted was to hand the whole matter over to Ben in as few words as possible. Claire said, 'I had been wondering whether to tell you or not.'

'Tell me what?'

'About Katia.'

'Katia?'

'Heather told me.'

'What did Heather tell you?'

'This business about a woman who had been on the train with Katia – the train taking them to the camp – saying that she called out your name . . .'

'Name? I don't understand.'

'She called "Alice". Apparently Jacov told Heather not to tell you. Now I suppose he has. Is *he* in some kind of trouble?'

Claire could not think of anyone else who would give enough trouble to make Alice come pounding over to Kew at half-past nine at night. She associated the Vaseyelins with trouble. Had not her father been killed in Mrs Vaseyelin's house, no doubt answering one of her many calls for help?

The sound of the key turning in the lock saved Alice from the need to make any comment, and the sudden raucous awakening of the twins occupied Claire.

Terence, owl-eyed and short of breath, had not failed to convey a sense of urgency, with the result that Ben was in a highly nervous state. His love for Alice was something salvaged from havoc while there was still the possibility that darkness might prevail. Alice, for her part, was no longer primarily concerned with Angus. She was like a child desperately crying for a nightmare to be dispelled. They clung to each other, seeking reassurance that life was good. It was some time before Ben, perceiving that she was uninjured, said, 'Then *what* is it?'

She shivered, very cold now that he had released her. 'Not here.'

He was mystified when she hustled him out of the house. 'What's *wrong*? You've scared me clean out of my wits.' He peered at her in the dull light of a street lamp, on the verge of anger at finding her apparently more composed than himself.

She told him what was wrong. It did not take many words, and when they were said she felt so relieved at having passed on her burden that she could have sunk down then and there on the pavement and gone fast to sleep. He said, 'Good grief!' After that he did not speak for quite a long time. They trudged past the wall of Kew Gardens and were in sight of the river before he said, 'We shall have to think about this.'

Alice, who had been confident that he would have got it all sorted out by now, said, 'What is there to think about? He's there.'

'You let him in,' he said gravely.

'What else could I have done?' She was stung by what she took to be an accusation. He gave her shoulders a little shake and lapsed into Cornish. 'We've got to talk about it, me lover. People will say much worse things than that by the time we're through.'

They came to the parapet of the bridge and stood looking down at the river. The tide was at the ebb, the water was still, and mud glistened, wrinkled like the discarded skin of a snake sloughed along the banks. The smell of putrefaction mingled with the habitual fumes from the gasworks.

Ben said, 'We'll have to hand him over. The question is, what is the best way to go about it?'

'We couldn't just *hand him over*, could we? Not Angus.'

'If we don't, we become involved. And it's a matter of treason. People don't think well of it.' They watched a barge emerging slowly from beneath the bridge. The pungent smell of smoking fish from the galley was so strong one could almost hear the crisp brown skins rustling in the blackened pot. Ben said rather sharply, 'Do you want him to get away?'

'I don't want him to be caught.'

'But do you want him to get to Russia? Taking whatever information is useful to them with him?'

'We'd have the police round at the house,' she said evasively.

'There'd be pictures in the papers. Louise and Guy would never live it down.'

'There'll be pictures in the papers either way when this comes out – if *that's* what you're worried about.'

'I'm thinking of Louise and Guy,' she said obstinately.

'It would be better not to go back – just to go to the nearest police station and let them deal with it. You know that, don't you?' He spoke in his hectoring, courtroom manner.

'Ben, we couldn't! Not without seeing him again, talking to him. That would be an unforgivable thing to do.'

'You don't think what he has done is unforgivable?'

She felt the ominous vibration of his anger. In the dim light his face seemed composed of ill-assorted knots and cords. This was the man she had feared he might become.

'I know what you are thinking . . .'

'You can't possibly know what I am thinking!' His voice rose a notch. 'You didn't know the men whom I watched dying by inches in that nightmare place, while people like Angus were playing their game . . .' The staleness of the phrases sickened him.

'It wasn't just a game, Ben. Not with Angus. He had a very bad home life . . .'

'A bad home life, indeed!' She winced, knowing his scorn was merited. 'Hundreds and thousands of people have had bad home lives without betraying their fellows. Because *that's* what he has done. Don't make any mistake about that. It's not just a matter of handing a few secrets over in order to annoy the government. These things are paid for in blood.'

'There was something very unhealthy going on in the Drummond household.' Alice was aware of the inadequacy of this description, just as Ben had been aware of the impossibility of conveying the horrors of the prisoner-of-war camp. 'And then spying can't have helped, can it? It must blur the picture – constantly playing a part until you don't know who you are, or what you are supposed to be believing at any given moment . . .'

'What about this chap Kelleher, then? He was in some sort of intelligence outfit, wasn't he? What was his home life like?'

'He was dropped over Yugoslavia. But I remember Daphne saying he wasn't as far into the wood as Angus.'

She stopped, aware of another voice: Louise, saying she could not live so far into the forest, fear in the voice. Louise and fear! How strange that conversation had been.

Ben was silent. Alice thought that he, too, was seeing a path into the wood gradually become so overgrown that the traveller did not seek a way out, because this was another kind of place and once you were in it, there *was* no way out. But it was the mention of Daphne which had brought him up with a jolt. He remembered his affair with Daphne. To say that they had loved each other would have been grossly to misrepresent their bitter, tormented relationship. Each time he penetrated her she had reacted with a ferocity born of some private agony in which he played no part. Now, staring down at the still, dark water in the shadow of the bridge, the rank smell of her pain and disgust was in his nostrils. And yet the beauty of her body had haunted him, and in one of his worst fevers he had seen her naked form grow into a tree in which the blossoms were the faces of the people he had known, good and bad, all hung from the same tree. He said, 'I think you may be right. We can't hand him over just like that.'

'Oh Ben!' Her relief was so enormous she knew it was not Angus's survival which had seemed to hang in the balance as they argued. She leant her head against his shoulder. 'What shall we do?'

'We must persuade him to give himself up. And,' he warned, sensing how easily she relaxed, 'we shall have to be fairly ruthless about it.'

'Yes, yes.'

He saw that she did not realise how serious this was, and he was glad for her. But at the same time her unawareness disturbed him. In his weakened state he imagined her to be more fragile than in fact she was.

'It's not just us, remember,' he said, 'Louise and Guy are going to be involved in this, too, if we're not careful. It's their house. And, one way or the other, he has got to be out of it tonight.'

'There's a bus coming!' she cried, eager now to be on the way.

There was no light showing from the house when they came in sight of it. No shadows moved behind the trees in the road. They went up the few steps to the front door, and Alice thought, as she inserted her key in the lock, that she could not believe in this.

The house was quiet. She put on a light. The telephone was standing on the hall table and a note had been secured on the front of the dial. Ben picked it up and they read, standing close together. It was from Daphne. She said that she and Peter had called and taken the package.

Ben said, looking at Alice, 'Before we talk about this, you are going to have something to eat.'

She was so relieved she felt she could eat hugely, but when they were tackling scrambled eggs on toast in the kitchen, she found difficulty in swallowing.

'I can't get Angus out of my mind. Peter would have been hard on him. He's a very uncompromising man – the John Buchan type, who wouldn't tolerate betrayal. He wouldn't have had any of the scruples we have had about handing Angus over.'

Ben said quietly, 'It's passed out of our hands now. Try not to think too much about it. And for goodness sake, don't tell *anyone*. For their sake, as well as ours. Knowledge is guilt in this situation.'

'Shouldn't I get in touch with Daphne?'

'Leave it to her. She will get in touch with you when she thinks it right.'

Daphne thought it right the next day.

On her way to work the next morning, Alice bought three newspapers. *The Times* had a report on spy fever in America. Following the investigation of Abraham Brothman, President Truman had ordered a check on the loyalty of all government workers. How did one investigate loyalty? Alice wondered. In one of the other papers there was a picture of the woman involved, described as a beautiful spy, looking plump and rather homely.

In England, although Mr Bevin, exasperated by Stalin, had exploded 'Now he's gone too bloody far!' the only real excitement was engendered by preparations for the marriage of Princess Elizabeth and Prince Philip of Greece. Exhaustive reading failed to discover any suggestion that the Foreign Office might be exercised by anything more grave than the reception of six reigning monarchs who would be attending the wedding.

From the office window there was ample evidence of preparation. 'You'll have a splendid view,' the junior said when she came in with the post.

'What about all the coupons, then?' Mr Hadow said, sour in the shiny suit which had acquired a greenish hue as though mould was growing on it.

'*You* don't have to worry about that, Mr Hadow,' the junior said cheekily. 'You're not buying a wedding dress, are you?' She winked at Alice.

Mr Hadow was proof-reading reports for the Further Education Sub-Committee which was concerned with preparations of another kind. The Olympic Games were to be held next year on the borders of West London and the Further Education Sub-Committee could think of little else. Arrangements for the Royal Wedding, which would be over in a couple of hours, were as nothing in comparison with the burdens imposed by this long-running event. And what were the problems of accommodating six reigning monarchs compared to hordes of athletes with infinitely variable temperaments and impossible diets?

'I could tell them the result and save them all that trouble,' the junior said, reading over Mr Hadow's shoulder. 'The Yanks will win everything. It stands to reason. All those steaks they eat. Look at Wimbledon!'

'We'll have to send you along to the next meeting, Mavis,' Mr Hadow said, in unusual good humour.

'Why do they have to have a torch from Greece, then?' she asked, still reading.

It was while they were discussing this that the telephone rang. Daphne said, 'Meet us for dinner at the Strand Palace tonight. Eight o'clock. We can exchange all our news then.'

'The Strand Palace!' Ben exclaimed, when Alice telephoned him during her lunch hour. 'How can we talk there?'

He repeated the question when they met. Peter and Daphne were waiting for them in the foyer. Alice saw Peter's head and shoulders rising like the figurehead of an antique ship above a sea of bobbing heads. Daphne, when they cleaved their way through to her, demonstrated that modernity, too, could be arresting. She wore a New Look dress in Lincoln green, the billowing hemline well below mid-calf. Her head was tilted at that angle which made her seem to be issuing a challenge to an unseen opponent and her face was bright as holly. Alice, who had scarcely slept all night, caught sight of her own face in a mirror, peaked, with owls' eyes. Daphne exchanged a long unsmiling look with Ben before turning to introduce her husband. It was not only for Peter's benefit that she had paid particular attention to her appearance this evening. One owed it to one's self-esteem to let an old lover see how one had flowered in his absence.

In answer to Ben's question, Kelleher said, 'Safer to talk here than anywhere,' and led them to a table in the centre of the room.

The party at the next table had been to a matinée of *Oklahoma*, and were arguing among themselves as to whether it was better than *Annie Get Your Gun*. Kelleher studied the menu while Ben and Daphne studied each other – rather coolly, Alice liked to think. Kelleher said, 'You are our guests – it's the least we can do after all the trouble you have been put to.' He made it sound like a reward for some minor service rendered – smuggling tea through the customs or killing a goose. Alice thought there was something excited and almost celebratory in their manner, a certain recklessness, even. She did not know much about gambling, but fancied this was how people might sparkle who had broken the bank. This business of Angus's had been a great shock, of course, and they must be very relieved; but it seemed a little early for jubilation.

'Freshness,' said a man at the next table.

'So much more zip,' countered a woman.

When the main course was served, Daphne raised her glass. 'To castaways, perhaps?'

Peter said distastefully, 'Outcasts would be more appropriate, don't you think?'

Alice, who thought this altogether too obscure, decided the time for plain-speaking had come. 'Did he go by himself, or did you go with him?'

'We'd hardly be sitting here if we had gone with him.' Daphne was amused by the question.

Kelleher said politely, 'You were assuming – what?'

The conversation was not turning out as Alice had anticipated and she was reluctant to put her assumptions into words. Ben, who had taken an instant dislike to Kelleher, had no such inhibitions. 'That you handed him over.'

Daphne said, 'Yes, you could put it that way.'

There was an uncomfortable pause. The man at the next table said, 'That's as maybe, but it *wasn't* Ethel Merman.'

Kelleher addressed Ben and Alice in the manner of a good host, anxious that certain of his guests should not feel excluded by lack of knowledge from the conversation. 'You see, he hadn't bodged it completely. It was not one of those unconsidered actions. There was some kind of assignation arranged by his controller. We gave him the opportunity to keep it.'

Alice toyed with whalemeat before deciding she did not want to eat it. She lowered her voice, which was not necessary – a man was singing 'The Surrey with the fringe on top'. 'You didn't manage to persuade him to give himself up?'

'We didn't try,' Kelleher answered. 'He was much better out of the way.'

Ben said, 'And that was the only consideration?'

Kelleher looked faintly surprised by the suggestion that there might be another. Alice could see by the deliberate way Ben laid down his knife and fork that he was not going to eat another morsel until he had enlightened Kelleher. 'You were in the same sort of outfit at one time, I believe? What if Angus had given information that led to your being caught?'

'If you have any sense, you don't concern yourself with hypothetical situations.' Kelleher might have been a lecturer answering an obtuse questioner with patient courtesy. 'You just deal with the problems as and when they present themselves. I suppose you might say that imagination is not a desirable asset.'

'Ben isn't being imaginative,' Daphne told him. 'He is moralising.'

'*That* would bring about your downfall more certainly than any information Angus might give,' Kelleher told Ben.

A woman was standing up to sing badly what had come naturally to Ethel Merman. Daphne said to Ben, 'There *are* people who share your point of view, though. It was a friend of ours, Ivor Ritchie, who put them on to Angus – when he realised they weren't going to take any notice of Sergeant Fletcher.'

'Ivor apparently decided that someone fairly high up was shielding Angus and this seems to have annoyed him,' Kelleher said.

Daphne went on, 'He actually came to tell us what he had done! I think he found it more difficult to face us than to ditch Angus. If you can believe it, he was shaking all over, just like a little boy who is afraid he is going to wet himself with terror.' She spoke with contempt.

Alice said, 'Poor Ivor!'

'You are well rid of that little cripple!'

Alice was aware of Ben looking at her, but she was too angry to care what he made of this exchange. 'Didn't you have any doubts about what you should do?' she said to Daphne. 'You always hated communism so much. And you admired Mosley . . .'

'I still admire him, but I don't see what he has to do with this.'

Ben said, 'Alice is trying to say that Angus was a traitor and you have given him a helping hand.'

'He is my brother.' This was not a statement of love, but a declaration of a paramount interest which overrode all other considerations.

'He isn't *your* brother,' Alice said to Peter.

'Daphne is my wife.' Which, he made it clear, was a matter of possession rather than loyalty.

They both looked so inflexible, secure in the knowledge that they had been true to a code of behaviour which put them above the law, that Alice's anger dwindled into confusion.

Ben said caustically, 'And you think you did your best for Angus?'

'No.' Daphne was impervious to sarcasm. 'I don't think I owed him that. We gave him the chance to get out, that's all.' In another age, she would have handed him a pistol.

Ben said, 'Just supposing someone had followed him when he came to Alice last night? Would you rely on her when questioned – and she would be questioned – to conceal that note?'

Kelleher was massively patient. 'It doesn't arise, does it? They wanted him far too much to play games shadowing him around Holland Park. I don't think you need worry about his being followed.'

'You said that someone high up . . .'

'The Special Branch are involved now. *They* don't want him to get away.'

'Whatever happens, Alice isn't going to destroy that note. I hope that doesn't worry you?'

'Not at all. It could have been written any time over the last few years, and it only refers to "a package".'

It seemed that nothing could shake him. He was not interested in powers and principalities: he was his own country. Then Daphne intervened. Her cheeks were stingingly bright as she said, 'If you are thinking of that note as some kind of safeguard for Alice, let me tell you that if there was any chance of Alice getting into trouble, I should tell them what happened.' Kelleher regarded her in an amazement which dislocated his features. His jaw hung loose; his skin was very dry and beneath the overhang of his forehead, the nose was pushed slightly to one side and seemed to be flaking. Daphne leant across the table and said in a low, vehement voice, 'You don't understand about friendship. Alice is more important than Angus and *not* to be sacrificed.' He sat very upright, unseeing eyes staring across the crowded room, like a strange Polynesian statue which has weathered badly.

Alice said warmly, 'I wouldn't give them the note, Daphne, I wouldn't ever give you away. I should make up some story.'

Ben looked up and shook his head at the ceiling.

The man at the next table said, 'Yes, well, I prefer the scent of new mown hay. I'm sentimental, I suppose; but I actually want to believe that somewhere out there the corn is as high as an elephant's eye.'

Kelleher said austerely, 'Fortunately none of this is very much to the point.'

Later, as they walked along the Strand, Alice said to Ben, 'If she had done it because she *cared* about Angus I could have understood.'

Ben said, 'That is a very strange man she has married.'

It was a cold, clear evening, and standing on a traffic island, looking towards Trafalgar Square, they saw the full moon coming up over the Admiralty Arch, and Nelson lofted in glorious isolation on his column.

Alice said, 'I had a bit of a thing over Ivor Ritchie.'

Ben said, 'I had more than that with Daphne.'

'I thought you did.'

His arm tightened round her waist. They walked to the Embankment and sat on a bench near Cleopatra's Needle. Alice said, 'Angus told me he sat here – with a dog on his lap. Can you imagine it?'

People walked by without giving them a glance, yet somehow conveying that they knew they were there, just on the edge of vision. Alice had the feeling of having, without her knowing it, stepped outside some unmarked safety zone. This is another place where the boundary doesn't run, she thought; but it's not how I wanted it to be when I thought I glimpsed it up that track on the Downs. Perhaps there was something to be said for boundaries.

'The world is an upside-down sort of place at the moment,' she said to Ben. 'But we'll manage, won't we?'

He bent to kiss her, and, safe in the circle of his arms, she thought how blessed she was to have him here beside her. She could not have endured this sense of exile on her own, while with him, she felt there was nothing she could not face.

Ben said, 'I saw a film on the troopship. About a man who went – to France, I think – to bring back a flag. It wasn't convincing. I remember thinking it was an empty symbol – the flag – because on a battlefield you no longer raise the standard to rally troops. Symbols are only of real significance so long as the things they symbolise are relevant. It's just silliness, a man risking his life for a square of cotton.'

'Is this relevant to Angus?'

'It's relevant to where we are now. Old Father Thames and the Mother of Parliaments down yonder.'

'*Up* yonder.'

'Our traditions go back so far.'

'That's our strength, though, isn't it? Miss Blaize, of blessed memory, was very hot on tradition.'

'Is it strength, when they are misted with time and no longer really understood?'

'That's not true of *all* of them.'

'But which? Which do we jettison?'

'I don't like jettisoning things. Look what's happened to Claire.'

'Alice! You make everything so personal.'

'Life *is* personal. I can't live anyone else's life.'

They sat without speaking for a few minutes. The river was threaded with silver and on the far bank a few lights hung like jewels in the frosty air. Alice said, 'I wonder how Louise and Guy are getting on. Guy wants a house in the country, but Louise wants to live in Lewes. I think I agree with her, don't you?'

'Is that what you want?'

'A county town would have more to offer. Claire and I used to play a game about a big old house in the country where a large family lived whose roots went back and back into the past. I can see that *that* is something which has to be jettisoned.'

He said nothing, and after a few moments she shifted in order to look at his face. 'You don't want to move out of London. Is that it?'

'It's a question of keeping in touch with what is going on, of meeting people . . .'

'Lots of local government officers make a mad dash for the Surrey borders as soon as the office closes!'

'I wasn't thinking of local government.'

'Not this prisoners exercise?'

'It's more than an exercise. Quite a lot of field work is already being done, people have actually visited countries to observe, sometimes to give advice . . .'

'I hadn't realised you were quite so serious about it.'

'There's nothing else I'm serious about.'

Now she was the one to be silent. He said, 'Now look, I didn't mean . . .'

'No, no. I know what you meant. I just hadn't realised it was so important.'

'I could take a room in London, and we could have our home in the country.'

'Whatever we do, it won't be *that*.'

'We don't have to decide anything now. I don't know about you, but I'm getting cold.' He drew her closer. 'A closed circuit gives warmth.'

But even as his nearness began to warm her, she experienced again that chill of isolation. The stable life in the little county town had been lost almost before she had had time to contemplate it. How different her married life would be from that of her parents, with no place in this shifting world which would be home as they had known it. We shall live roofless as birds, she thought, bringing up our brood and sheltering them under our wings. She had grown up imagining that man is supposed to put down roots. Was *that* a mistake? Another belief to be left behind?

Louise and Guy returned with the children. It was not difficult to keep Angus out of the conversation because they were absorbed in their own affairs.

The next day Louise went shopping in Regent Street. In the late afternoon she lay beside Jacov listening to the throb of a cello and wishing they had put on something more sprightly. Usually this music carried her beyond herself; but today she was more conscious than ever of Jacov, so near yet separate. She propped herself on one elbow and looked down at his face, which was the part of him about which she knew the least. She tapped his forehead. 'I have no idea what goes on in there,' she said wonderingly.

He bit her finger. 'It's not an area you ever show much interest in exploring.'

'Don't be alarmed. I'm not going to start now. It just struck me as odd that I know so little about it, whereas I know what Guy is thinking without his telling me.'

'There are other ways of telling,' he said, and turned her to him. Yet Guy exposes himself to me more nakedly than ever you will, she thought.

Then thought ceased as power began to throb, spiralling throughout her body, touching hidden springs, insistent as the sun's warmth unfolding a tight knot of petals. How could she live were she to be denied this dark, secret flowering? Afterwards, the music seemed more potent than before: the notes of the piano trilled in the tips of her fingers and danced along the arteries; the violins sighed in her loins.

She said, 'I *shall* come back after we move. On shopping expeditions, like today. We shall carry on just as usual.'

He was silent for a time, listening to the music. What he felt about it she would never know, because they did not talk about it. This listening without the need for words was the thing she most valued in him.

'You will forget about me,' he said at last. 'You will find other men.'

She would forget about him for days, perhaps weeks; but he would always be a part of her, the foreign side of her own nature.

'You won't do so badly, either,' she said.

They made love again. They were not usually as agitated as this.

Catherine told Alice, 'We *are* going to move to Sussex. I'm not supposed to tell you.'

'Why not?'

' 'Cos Mummy says it's all very much in the air.'

'But why aren't you supposed to tell me?'

'Case you get upset.' Catherine observed Alice hopefully for signs of distress.

'Well, I'm not upset about *that*. And you can tell Mummy so.'

'I can't tell her. I'm not supposed to have told you.'

'That's your problem.'

'We're only doing it because of Daddy. *I* don't want to move. But no one cares about what I want.'

'Poor old sausage!'

'Will you and Uncle Ben live here? Mummy says you're going to marry him. Can I come and live with you?'

'No, but you can come and stay with us, provided you don't grizzle all the time.'

Alice told Ben about the conversation. The savouring of conversations so that she could later convey their flavour to him was one of the newly discovered joys of loving. During the two or three calm days before the police began asking questions, there were other bonuses. They went to a party given by a friend from Ben's old chambers where they separated and talked to different people. Occasionally, their eyes met across the room and each knew that no one else really existed. The party was a delightful charade put on by their host and hostess so that they might enjoy the indescribable pleasure of joining hands as they walked away down the drive when it was all over. And oh, with what relish they discussed the evening's encounters! Alice realised how incomplete all her social engagements had been hitherto. The long street stretched ahead, their feet sounded companionably on the paving stones, and they mimicked, reconstructed, expostulated, making something entirely their own of the event.

Daily, their love grew. She had waited so long for love, keeping a space within her, like a room, bare because the means to furnish it are lacking, fearing it would never be filled. Now, suddenly, she had riches at her disposal and every day added some small sign of occupancy.

They went to see *Tuppence Coloured* at the Lyric, Hammersmith, and were convulsed by Max Adrian as the blonde who did not remember Vienna, and as Emmett's mad signalman sending trains to Eastbourne by way of Beachy Head. On the way home, Ben entertained Alice with songs which he and Geoffrey had composed for camp concerts on the troopship. This was the first time he had laughed about his war experiences and she was surprised by his unexpected gift for the broadly comic.

The next evening the police called.

Ben, who had come to supper, insisted on being present while they interviewed Alice, and they raised no objection. She and Ben had already discussed what she would say in such an event. To questions about the Norfolk weekend, she replied briefly, but honestly. When asked if she had been surprised at the discovery of the equipment, she said she hadn't been sure what it was and had assumed that, in any case, the police would take whatever action was necessary. Her interrogator, who was not a senior officer, saw no point in pursuing this matter. It was apparent that this was a routine enquiry and that she was not regarded as an important witness. He asked her when she had last seen Angus and she said she could not remember, she did not know him very well. She would remember whether it was a matter of months or weeks, would she not? She said she thought it was weeks. She had seen him in the street. They had had a conversation about a dog. He had seemed to be in a hurry.

The policemen had other, more fruitful, lines of enquiry to follow up that evening. They said that it might be necessary for her to come to the police station to make a formal statement. If she remembered anything else that might be relevant, however insignificant, would she please contact Detective Inspector Frobisher; they gave her a number which she could ring, and departed.

'I lied to them,' she said mournfully to Ben.

'Would you have wanted to involve Daphne and Peter?' he asked gently.

'I needn't have involved them. I could just have said that while I was out trying to find you, Angus left.'

'They would have been very interested in *that* story. The questioning wouldn't have been left to those two. You might not have held out.'

'I can be quite obstinate when I choose.'

'Guilt undermines you, Alice. And you would still have been lying. I don't think you would have held out.'

He took her hand and gave it a little shake, seeing that she was not really attending to what he was saying. 'Alice, if you told them exactly what happened, they wouldn't believe you. You *must* understand that. They would assume that you and I were a party to whatever it is that Peter and Daphne did. It's a much more tidy story than this business of people playing Box and Cox with each other, and leaving notes about taking packages.'

'Whoever said it's always better to tell the truth just didn't know what they were talking about!' she said passionately.

'Luckily for us, it seems likely the police lost sight of Angus over ten days ago. Unless something unexpected crops up, there is no way they can link his disappearance with any of us. The way in which they are behaving doesn't suggest they have any grounds for suspecting that his friends or relatives were involved.'

'Yes, I can see we're lucky.' She was unconvinced.

He kissed her and said, 'Apply that Puritan conscience to being grateful for small mercies.'

But it was not her Puritan conscience which kept her awake at night. It was fear. She had been pushing something to the back of her mind. Now it claimed her. Louise heard her walking about the house at night and came down to her. 'Alice, you mustn't worry about this. Ben says there is nothing to worry about. After all, you hadn't seen Angus for weeks.'

Even to Louise she had lied.

She said, 'Do you think that was how it all began, with Katia? Two men coming at night, saying they had a few questions to ask?'

'You're not going to start up this obsession with Katia again!'

'She called my name. On the train. Claire told me.'

She told Louise what Claire had said, and Louise said, 'I could strangle Claire! And, anyway, whatever were you doing over at hers, fetching Ben out at that time of night?'

Alice burst into tears and Louise made her a cup of tea and forgot that her question had not been answered. Later, as she lay in bed, Alice realised that Ben had been right about one thing: she would never hold out under expert questioning. She had come very close to telling Louise. She clenched her hands and prayed for strength not to tell Louise. It was like having the plague and asking that she might not pass it on.

During the days that followed, Ben was a constant support and comfort, patiently going over and over the rights and wrongs of their course of action. But, troubled himself, sometimes he nearly foundered. When this happened, Alice's mind would clear, and just as if she had come out on top of the cloud level and was gazing down at him from a flawless sky, she would put forward arguments which he found convincing and soon imagined to be his own. It seemed hard that this should happen to them at a time when they should have been carefree and light-hearted in the early glow of love. Yet they found out a lot about each other, their relative strengths and weaknesses, the places which could stand tension and the points at which pressure must not be applied.

The one trouble Alice was unable to share with him, was her obsession with Katia. He had never known Katia well, and could no more understand the depth of Alice's feeling than she could share his lasting sadness at the loss of Geoffrey.

'No one knew about Katia . . . these dreadful things happened to her and no one knew.' Martyrs occupied centre-stage. The victims of massacre, however poor, had their moment in history – individual deaths might not be recorded, but people knew what went on; even in a place as remote as Glencoe, and more recently in Lidice, people knew. It was the silence which was so unbearable in Katia's case.

'She didn't *do* anything. It makes it seem that life is like a game of chess, and Katia just landed on the wrong square.'

'And was removed. It is still happening. Not on the scale of the concentration camps, but it *is* still happening.'

'Is *that* why you write letters to men who may never receive them?'

'Doing something is better than doing nothing.'

'*I* should have done something. I should have sat on a stool outside the German Embassy. The brother of a girl at the office had something wrong with his car and the makers wouldn't do anything about it, so he went and sat outside their London office, and in the end they were so embarrassed about it, they gave him the new parts for nothing. And he did that for a car!'

'It wouldn't have worked, Alice,' he said soberly, realising how disturbed she was. 'Not then. You've got to get a lot of support behind you before you can begin to be effective. It will take years. And in the Thirties, that support wasn't forthcoming. Most people didn't want to believe in the concentration camps, for one reason or another – because the idea was too monstrous, or they didn't like the Jews, or because it didn't suit their right-wing beliefs, or their pacifism.'

Katia continued to gnaw at Alice's mind. At night she made up stories in an effort to console herself, imagining that by re-writing events she might miraculously uncover the truth. She *willed* Katia to be free. Katia had been so rebellious; she wasn't an obvious victim and would not have allowed them to treat her like so much human cargo. She pictured Katia managing to get one of the doors of the train open. Katia never went to the camp; perhaps she was killed falling from the train, or perhaps she was alive now . . . One day, if she went on doing this, she would get the right answer, it would explode in her mind.

In the early evenings, on her way home from the office, she sometimes went into the church at Notting Hill. It was usually empty apart from people arranging or re-arranging flowers. One Friday, when she had taken the afternoon off to do Christmas shopping, she went to the church at the hour when people could make confession. This being the Church of England, few availed themselves of the opportunity, and on this particular afternoon none came. The vicar sat in the side aisle, quiet, unobtrusive, waiting. After a time, Alice approached him. 'It isn't a confession . . . at least . . .'

'Can you tell me about it?' He gestured to her to sit beside him.

She told him about Katia. He said nothing. It was difficult to think what comforting words he could have said, even St Paul might have found himself rather stretched; but she felt he should have tried. 'People say I should put it out of my mind,' she prompted. 'But I can't.'

'No,' he said. 'I don't suppose you can.' He was silent again, and this time she waited, pleased that at last someone seemed to be taking her predicament seriously. Late sun filtered through the narrow side window and Alice looked at the light reflected on a stone pillar, blue, yellow, gold, with an expectant lift of the heart. Eventually, he said, 'These things which will always be with us – and this *will* always be with you – we have to treat differently from our temporary afflictions. We have to make room for them – accept them as part of the landscape of our lives – bleaker, perhaps than we had imagined or hoped. Because, of course, it's not what happened to your friend that worries you after all these years, but the way in which it alters your perception of life. You see now that the skin of our civilization is very thin.' Alice listened with a sense of having had a sentence passed on her, of being told she was terminally ill. He went on, 'If you live on moorland, the elements won't go away. You may make a break of trees to give your home some relief from the full force of gale and snow; but you must always allow for them. Plan your garden accordingly. I know, because we lived for some time on the North Yorkshire moors. Forgive me, parsons are prone to this kind of Nature symbolism.'

Alice waited, for now that they were concerned with Yorkshire, he must surely mean to introduce hope in the form of rare fauna and flora. She would find this irritating, but she accepted his professional obligation to preach the Resurrection. Time went by rather slowly. The light from the window shifted, but did not pierce the dimness of the interior. In the distance, she could hear the erratic pulse of traffic. Here, there was nothing. Light flickered in the lamp in the Lady chapel. Behind the altar, the crucifix loomed, the spread arms casting dark shadows. She had come seeking hope and the restoration of joy, and now she felt stripped, all her little gifts taken from her; she was dry and there was a remote echo in her head as if she was slightly deaf. She understood at last that there was no way that Katia's death could be softened. There was no way round the crucifixion. She had tended to think of it as the prologue to Easter, and had not taken in the simple fact that Easter, with its triumphant abundance of flowers, was on the far side of death; and that the gate through which all must pass, and each alone, was Good Friday, that dark eternity when it all seemed to have gone wrong.

She said dully, 'So there is nothing I can do.'

'Do you pray for your friend?'

'I used to. As long as I could convince myself she might be alive, I prayed. But I've stopped lately.'

'But you should still pray for her.'

'If she's dead she doesn't need it, does she? I mean – one way or the other . . .'

'But *you* are still living. Your understanding of her – your friendship, is still developing. It will develop whether you do anything about it or not. Nothing stands still. Our way of thinking about people, our understanding of them and the things which happen to them, is always changing – for better or for worse.'

'Then I could pray for my father.'

'Indeed, you should pray for him, and for your friend. Pray in the hope that one day God will unite you in his perfect love.'

'I shall feel rather strange . . .'

'That doesn't matter. Our feelings are of no consequence when we pray, which is fortunate, since they are so mercurial we should scarcely utter a word if we waited for them to compose themselves. It is only the intention which matters.'

'I hope I'm well-intentioned.' Alice was doubtful.

'You must settle for the hope.'

There was a certain hardness about his utterances which she found unexpectedly calming. When she left the church she was not comforted so much as sobered. She accepted what she had known ever since Katia disappeared, that life would not be the same again. It was not going to be patched up and rendered back to her bright and shining in the dew of her illusions. The world was a much harsher, more dangerous place than her sheltered childhood had led her to believe, and she must learn to live in it or be broken by it. She did not ponder the fact that Katia had had no choice. The possibility that ultimately there is no choice was not an idea she was as yet ready to consider. She walked towards Holland Park, firm in the belief that she had at last come into possession of her world.

# 15

Ben had been right when he said that the police could not link Angus's disappearance with himself and Alice, or with Daphne and Peter. But there was one person who had been overlooked. Alice, in her confusion, had quite forgotten Angus's statement that he had called on Jacov who had turned him away. When, in late November, the story came out and Angus's picture was published in the paper, the stage doorkeeper, who had little to do to while away the dull hours other than remember faces, went to the police.

Rain was pouring down the window; Jacov saw the world beyond his flat as though distorted by glycerine, cracks channelled in chimneys, gables zig-zagging drunkenly against the grey sheen of tiles. The street name looked as if it had been painted on a greasy surface, only a U and a T were clearly outlined. He could not remember the name of the street. A car passed, its wheels sizzling like frying fat.

He tried to remember what had happened when the two men came to the theatre, but that scene was distorted also. They had come after the matinée, apologising for the intrusion but saying they had been unable to contact him at his flat. They had explained that they had come as a result of information given by the stage doorkeeper. Up to that, he could recall the scene only too clearly.

After that, the men tended to recede. He was afraid he had behaved as if they were members of the audience. One should never catch the eye of a member of the audience, it breaks the illusion. But the same rule probably did not apply to members of the police force. He had an idea he had talked rather a lot.

He had told them he had sent Angus away. *That* was the right thing to do, surely? But it couldn't have been entirely right, because one of them had asked whether he usually sent his friends away when they came to see him in his dressing-room. He had disclaimed friendship with Angus. An acquaintance, then? Something must have happened to make him shout at this acquaintance – the stage doorkeeper had heard him shouting.

He had protested about this. The stage doorkeeper's cubby hole was nowhere near his dressing-room. Apparently, the stage doorkeeper had had second thoughts as to whether he should have admitted Angus. Jacov recalled rising to that. 'If he was disreputable enough to get Sidney off his backside, how do you think *I* felt about him?' he had exclaimed, or words to that effect. 'He looked like a tramp. Something had gone wrong with him. A breakdown, perhaps.'

He hadn't felt he should help, fetch a doctor? Or at least advise Angus to go to a doctor, rather than ordering him out of the dressing-room?

This was the point at which he suspected he had taken off. 'If I felt anything, it was that I should make my entrance. They had already called beginners for Act Two.'

'*Were* you a beginner?'

'No, but I didn't have long enough to persuade someone who had had a breakdown to go to a doctor.'

'What did he want you to do?'

'I didn't *listen*. He said he was in trouble. But there wasn't time to listen. The second bell went just as he arrived and I knew the audience would be coming back. It shook me to see him like that. I could feel myself separating from the part. It is important that I am always *in* my part during the performance . . .'

This was arrant nonsense, but perhaps the police wouldn't know any better. After all, a lot of actors talked that way nowadays. In fact, he never thought of his part until he was waiting in the wings. He usually arrived late and made up very quickly, not giving himself time to think about the part. If he thought about it, it took the edge off his performance. He wasn't one of those actors who have to live each part – he was a performer, a bag of tricks. But he had had to listen endlessly to actors rumbling on about how they immersed themselves in their characters, so he had the language all there, ready to tongue. He used it. He worked himself up just as he did on a first night. And, just as on a first night, he was not sure afterwards whether he had gone right over the top.

He knew that at some time they had asked him if he was Russian.

Years ago, he had gone to the Foreign Office with Mr Fairley to make enquiries about Katia. He recalled Mr Fairley's dismay when told that Katia was not a British subject. Mr Fairley, his friend, was dead. But the man at the Foreign Office, whom he looked upon as his enemy, was probably still working there. He would remember. He would think that, after such a lesson, Jacov Vaseyelin should have made sure his own affairs were in better order. Now, of course, it was too late. Even if they did not arrest him for collusion, they would tell him he could not stay in the country. What would he do? Where would he go? He was a stateless person. He would be sent into exile in that Siberia of the West, Switzerland – a terrain hostile to all save skiers and mountaineers. In his panic, he had told them he was a Russian Jew. He never thought of himself as a Jew – his father was Russian, and his mother had been only half Jewish; but he had hoped it might help to prove his innocence, since the Russians were not well-disposed to the Jews. It seemed from what followed that they already knew he had Jewish blood.

'Your sister was in Buchenwald, I believe?' There had been more of accusation than sympathy in that statement.

'Yes.'

'Presumed dead?'

The man had studied him thoughtfully for signs of the instability one must expect in anyone unreliable enough to have a sister presumed dead in Buchenwald.

When he returned to his flat, Jacov looked through his drawers to see if there was anything among the few papers he had kept in connection with his family which might be regarded as incriminating. While he was doing this, he came across an envelope addressed to Claire and Terence Straker. He had promised to get complimentary tickets for the play and had forgotten about them. The Strakers wanted to treat their neighbours who had been very kind in baby-sitting with the twins. He stood looking down at the tickets, thinking of the Fairleys and all they had meant to him. He could not go to Louise. It would be too complicated, with Guy in attendance. In his distress he would be unable to separate the appeal to friends from the demands of the lover. But Terence might be instrumental in acquainting the Fairleys of his plight. Claire had once shown him an article which Terence had had published in a left-wing weekly, warning about the way in which liberty had been eroded during the war. While it had lacked Mr Fairley's moral rectitude, the article had shown an impressive mastery of invective. Jacov had reflected that this was a man he would not like to cross. So, perhaps a good man to have on one's side?

Terence had given him the telephone number of the school where he taught. The secretary, he had said, was a good sort and would take a message if there was a problem about the tickets. Jacov persuaded the secretary that he must speak to Terence. Fortunately, it was the break period. When Terence came to the telephone, Jacov explained that he had the tickets, but could not get over to Kew, so he wondered whether Terence could meet him in London? He did not like to say any more. He had already convinced himself that his every movement was watched, and it was but a short step to assuming that his telephone had been interfered with. Certainly something had happened to it recently – it roared like a distant heavy sea. He had put this down to his having dropped a lighted cigarette end into the mouthpiece, but now he was not so sure. Terence, from somewhere across the Bering Sea, sounded rather nonplussed, but, no doubt feeling himself under an obligation, agreed to meet Jacov for a drink. As Terence was at school during the day, and Jacov at the theatre in the evenings, it was difficult to arrange a suitable time. Eventually, they agreed to have morning coffee at the Cumberland on the next Saturday.

Claire was annoyed. She had looked forward to shopping in peace while Terence stayed with the twins. 'I have them all day,' she said.

'I have them multiplied by twenty all day,' he retorted.

'Secondary school children are old enough to know how to behave.'

'If you believe that, your motherhood is going to be a series of disillusions, culminating in . . .'

'And don't speak to me in that caustic tone, as if you were addressing your class.'

At this point, Terence, tired after a day in school, flew into one of his rare rages and said that everything he said and did was wrong and he was sick of it. When they had made their peace, they agreed there was plenty of time for Jacov to post the tickets. But although Terence telephoned Jacov's flat on several occasions, there was no reply.

So Terence met Jacov at the Cumberland on the Saturday morning. He had put on his one good suit in honour of the occasion. What with school during the day and domesticity in the evenings and weekends, every waking moment seemed to be ordered, and he was guiltily delighted to be travelling on the bus alone. His life was in danger of developing into one of those guided tours where you are never allowed a moment's respite. As Hyde Park came into sight, he found himself expanding his chest to draw in deep breaths of freedom. There was a place at the back of his lungs which had not had the air changed for a long time. Before he returned, he would take a bus to the Aldwych and walk up Fleet Street – just to remind himself that he was going to work there one day. In the meantime, he looked forward to having coffee in luxurious surroundings of which he would disapprove.

As soon as they met Jacov said, 'You don't want coffee, do

you? It's such a beautiful morning. I thought we would walk in the park.'

Terence expostulated, 'Well, I wouldn't mind . . .' and Jacov said, 'Yes, I knew you would prefer that,' and walked away.

Although Terence was a resolute hiker, he had difficulty in keeping up with Jacov who was considerably more nimble when it came to dodging fast-moving traffic in the vicinity of Marble Arch. Terence was relieved when they reached the park unscathed.

It was indeed a beautiful day, cold and crisp, with pale sun and fragile eggshell sky. Children romped on silvered grass and one toddler, slipping, let out a howl of frosted breath.

'Like a Christmas card,' Jacov said.

Terence said, 'Breughel, but it wouldn't be wise to skate on *that* ice.'

'No, no. Not Breughel. England!'

Terence peered myopically and said, 'I suppose so,' though he could not see what it was he had missed that was so particularly English.

Jacov gabbled, 'The trees aren't lopped. Flowers come up through the grass in spring. One isn't made aware of the pattern. There is a sense of space, freedom . . .' He clutched Terence's shoulder. 'I want to stay here. Oh God, God!'

Terence, startled, said hastily, 'Yes, all right. There's no reason why we shouldn't. I don't mind about coffee.'

'I want to stay in England!' Jacov sank down on a seat, head on knees, arms all-embracing. He did this neatly, in one movement, like an insect which folds itself up into a protective ball when touched.

Terence stood beside him, fists thrust in the pockets of his jacket, wishing he had worn an overcoat and wondering what to do. When, after a few moments Jacov had not moved, he said, 'Are you supposed to tour abroad? Is that the problem?'

Jacov spoke so softly that Terence had to bend down to catch his words. 'The police have been to see me.'

Terence said, 'I see!' and sat beside him, prepared to give his undivided attention; but Jacov sprang up like a jack-in-the-box and looked wildly round him.

Terence said, 'No one is taking any notice of us. But if you want to attract attention that *is* the way to do it.'

Jacov sat down again. In black sweater and tight trousers, he was no more suitably dressed for the cold than Terence and looked as if he might have come out for a breath of fresh air during a rehearsal of

*Hamlet*. There were purple pouches beneath eyes which seemed to burn holes in the pinched, white face. Terence felt anger beginning to warm him. He studied Jacov expectantly. A one-time refugee, probably not a nationalised British subject, Russian, and with Jewish blood. The classic victim. Well, he had found his defender. Terence produced cigarettes.

A small, feather-tailed black dog with fiendish red eyes and sharp teeth bounded up and sniffed appreciatively at Terence's trouser legs. Aware of the owners hovering lovingly near by, Terence nudged the animal which promptly bit his ankle. Its master came and hauled it away. Terence examined his ankle to see if the skin was broken. It wasn't.

He said to Jacov, 'Now, what's the trouble? Passport, identity card? Tell me all about it.' He sat back, the sun glinting on his pebbled glasses. Already he was preparing a searing indictment of the lack of humanity displayed by police and officials. 'Only a few years have passed since the horrors of Belsen, yet we have learnt no lessons . . .'

The dog attacked in the crotch this time. 'He's taken a fancy to you. I'll get my hubby. He's too strong for me.' The husband arrived and lugged the dog away; it careered across the grass, scattering children and ducks.

Jacov began to speak. Ten minutes later, the situation had lost much of its classic simplicity. Claire had said only the other day how relieved she was that the police had shown no further interest in Alice. Terence could see now the wistful smile that was uncertain as the sun after rain. His throat constricted. After a few moments, he was ashamed to hear himself substituting cravenly cautious advice for withering condemnation. 'You mustn't take this too personally. The police interviewed Alice. And Irene and her parents. I expect they have seen Daphne as well . . .' He stopped short of being jolly about Uncle Tom Cobley, and said, 'It was probably just a routine enquiry.'

'They felt I had been withholding evidence.'

'It doesn't matter what they feel so long as they can't prove it.' He was shrinking with every bland assurance.

Jacov said bleakly, 'They won't bother with proof when it comes to me,' and Terence uttered the ultimate in platitudes, 'This is England.' He made haste to temper this by adding, 'Whatever our shortcomings – of the which no one is more aware than I – we still believe in the liberty of the individual . . .'

'Liberty is always bad news for someone. In France they guillotined people in the name of liberty. In Salem, they burned witches.'

'But you are not a witch nor a French aristocrat.'

'My father is a Russian aristocrat and my grandfather was a German Jew.'

So now we have the answer to all this, Terence thought – the persecution mania of the Jews! And they had reason. Nevertheless . . . 'The Jewish connection is quite distant, isn't it? Not that there is anything wrong with being a Jew, of course; but in your case there seems no need to emphasise it. You don't want to make an emotive issue of it. Oh God, I'm sorry, I must have a pee.'

He was distressed at making such a cock-up of this test of his beliefs. Added to which, the cold had had its usual effect on his bladder.

Jacov seemed so much more relaxed as he sat looking towards the lake, his body uncoiled, legs stretched out across the path, that one might have supposed his conversation with Terence to have eased his mind. In fact, he had realised that there was nothing to be gained from this discussion. Their points of view were irreconcilable. Terence, for all his anger, saw injustice as an infection, a sucker sent up from a healthy plant, something to be cut out at the root; whereas Jacov saw it as a condition of life. Mercy, being more random, would have been easier for him to accept than the concept of justice.

Terence had gone behind a tree. The wretched dog, regarding this as a gamesome move, rushed up and began circling him, threatening further assault. Terence kicked out and caught the animal a glancing blow on its rump, whereupon it set up a hysterical yelping which brought its owners running to the rescue while Terence's flies were undone. The woman, as distraught as her dog, said she had never seen such a thing in her life; and Terence, with a nasty look at the husband, replied, 'My commiserations, madam.' They parted amid mutual threats of police action.

Terence polished his glasses while he composed himself, and wondered why he, who had such incisive dreams, should so often be a figure of fun. Jacov, he noted, when he returned to the seat, seemed to endow the part of the clown with a melancholy grace. He looked up, smiling at Terence, and said, 'Been importuning the dog, have you?' One must remember the man is an actor, Terence told himself; he is probably not as desperate as might be imagined from his talk. He couldn't recover so quickly otherwise.

As they walked across the park, Terence said, 'If they *do* take this any further, you must let us know. We'll stand behind you.' After a pause, he rephrased, 'We'll stand by you, never fear.'

Jacov accepted this with a face so bland it might have been moulded in plasticene. It was quite a surprise to see that the eyes were not of the same substance.

Terence did not take a bus to the Aldwych, but went instead to Holland Park. He was uneasy and felt the need to talk things over with another man. As he hurried towards the Imminghams' house, he met James who was taking the dog for a walk. 'They're all in,' James informed him. Which was not what Terence had hoped for. Louise had just returned from shopping and Catherine was playing the gramophone in her room. Guy was raking dead leaves in the back garden, and thin bluish smoke rose from a mound of dead branches and uprooted annuals. 'Is it important?' Louise asked. 'I've been on at him to do that for weeks.' Terence said it was important, so she made tea and they all went into the sitting-room, Guy blowing on his hands and making much of his labours. To Terence's relief, Louise was unexpectedly quiet while they talked.

'I think you were perfectly right,' Guy assured Terence. This was not a comfort, since Terence, viewing the performance objectively, could see that Guy's main concern was to ensure that the Fairleys should not be involved in this affair any more than was necessary. But he also, Terence noted, was not entirely at ease. 'Of course, if I really thought that this was *serious* . . .'

It was then that Louise joined in. 'Yes?' she said, in that deceptively quiet manner women adopt when they are ready to pounce. 'If it is serious, what then?'

'Then I should feel I had to do something.' Guy made a lame attempt at hauteur.

'And *what* would you do?'

Guy and Terence exchanged a look of wry, masculine fellow-feeling. Louise said more loudly, 'I want to know what you would do, both of you. What are we all going to do?'

'I said I would do something if it was serious,' Guy said coolly. 'But I am not convinced that it is. The police have interviewed Jacov, just as they interviewed other people who might have some knowledge of Angus.'

'Jacov isn't other people.'

He shrugged his shoulders. 'Nothing more is likely to happen.'

'It doesn't matter what happens! It's what he *fears* might happen that matters.' She turned her head away sharply, pressing her hand against her mouth in the manner of one fighting to contain sickness.

Terence was perplexed. Usually Louise had no qualms about expressing her feelings, and it was most unlike her to halt in mid-attack. She said, her voice muffled, 'He must be in a dreadful state, and he's all alone.'

Guy said spitefully, 'I doubt very much that Jacov is ever "all alone". Don't you agree? *Answer* me!' To Terence's intense embarrassment he flicked out a hand and buffeted her on the side of the head. Then he gave a nervous neigh of laughter and looked around, startled eyes daring anyone to suggest he had raised a hand in anger. It seemed an inappropriate moment for horse-play, Terence thought.

Her response, too, was strangely unfitting. She lowered her head, her face flushed, the features loosened in abandonment which invited a further attack. As Terence looked at her bowed shoulders, something stronger than embarrassment overcame him. He was torn by sadistic excitement at seing this woman, whose physical assurance he had always feared, at last broken and submissive; and a chivalrous longing to go to her and raise her up, not gently by the shoulders, but roughly taking hold of her hair and drawing her to him. He felt himself both wife-beater and rescuer. She shuddered, and the tremor went through him like an electric shock. Every nerve in his body jumped, and as he sat, hands clenched over his genitals, he was astonished that they took no notice of his condition.

Suddenly she recovered herself and, looking up, shook her hair back from her face in a characteristic gesture of assertion. 'And what is he going to do for Christmas?'

Terence, taking the challenge to himself, said hoarsely, 'I didn't think to ask. We had a lot of other things to talk about. It didn't come up.'

She said softly, 'He *can't* be alone at Christmas.' She reached out a hand to touch Guy on the knee. 'Not at Christmas. He must come with us.' She looked at Guy, appealing and intimate. He was unmoved, while Terence could hardly control his limbs.

Guy said sullenly, 'That is for your mother to say. The house will probably be full.'

'No, it won't. Mother had been expecting Ben and Alice, but they are going to Falmouth. And, anyway, if she says she can't have Jacov, then we must stay here.' She rubbed her cheek against his shoulder in animal abasement, appealing to something more than his compassion. 'We can't leave him alone at Christmas, now can we, love?'

Guy looked down at the carpet, resentment pulling at his face so that all the good nature was stretched out of it. Louise watched him pityingly, her face close to his, her breath warming his ear. She was so strong, so sure of her power, and yet so open that it seemed a man might do anything with her. No one spoke. Her hand moved on his thigh. Terence could bear this no longer. He jerked himself to his feet and croaked, 'If your mother won't . . . can't . . . put him up, he can come to us.'

Their gratitude was overwhelming.

As they stood at the door when he left them, Guy clamped an arm around Louise's waist in a gesture which had more in it of possession than tenderness.

Terence walked part of the way home. When he had gained some sort of discipline over his body, he fell to wondering how he was going to explain to Claire that he had more or less invited Jacov for Christmas. And also, come to think of it, that he had forgotten to take the tickets.

'I thought you were having coffee together, not lunch,' she greeted him ominously.

But when he had explained, she said, 'Of course he will have to come. It will only be one extra. As for the tickets, we'll have to pick them up at the box office on the night. I can't think why we didn't arrange to do that in the first place. There was no need to get yourself in such a lather.'

So, unable to relieve the tension within him by having a row with his wife, Terence went to bed with a bad migraine. When at last he had stopped being sick, he slept. And dreamt of a bland, ageless mask made of marzipan, with fluid eyes already dissolving the upper cheekbones. He wanted to staunch this process of decay, but a crowd of people surged out of a theatre and separated them. He ran through streets and down alleyways. From time to time, in unexpected places, the mask appeared briefly and then dissolved. He was never near enough to make contact. More and more people crowded the narrow streets, so many people one could not hope to single out a particular face. Yet there it was, swinging from an inn sign, hanging from a lamp-post. And, in the end, he found that he was no longer trying to reach it, but running away, hoping never to see it again.

# 16

Alice and Ben were going to Falmouth because Granny Tippet was ill. Judith, who had seen her a week earlier, had reported she was rallying, but by the time Alice and Ben arrived it was apparent she meant to die.

'She has set her mind to it,' her daughter, Grace, told them. 'The doctor says there is nothing wrong with her, except that she doesn't like old age.'

'Isn't there anything he can do for her?' Alice asked.

'He pretends to give her medicine. But when Charlie went to see him, he said, "If she feels this is her time, you should let her go."' Grace's face screwed up in misery. 'I don't want people saying we didn't look after her.'

'If you were to insist on her going into hospital and being messed about, people would say you should have let her go when her time came,' Ben said.

'I couldn't insist, anyway. My mother is as self-willed as ever. We wanted to move her into our house – we felt that was the least we could do. And Charlie and Prue offered to have her. But she says she wants to die in her own home. Which means we've all got to take turns in being down there with her, day and night. It's not that I begrudge the time. But we've got the house full for Christmas. The family always come to us because our house is so big. And they expect me to cope with that and Mother as well. I said to Prue the other day, "It will be me that will go, not her!"'

'Ben and I will do the night duty,' Alice said.

It was not onerous. Obstinate she might be, but when it came to her dying, Granny Tippet was content to go as quietly and unobtrusively as possible. Her children and grandchildren dutifully clustered round her bedside and, when she was conscious, she accorded them a weary courtesy, dragging herself reluctantly from the first of the Last Things to show an interest in the little affairs with which they sought to brighten her dwindling. But the effort was beyond her strength and she realised that at last it was no longer required of her. She watched the faces blur and become confused with a feeling very close to joy.

Once when he was with her, Ben said, 'I followed your advice. Do you remember? You gave me a cutting about a man in prison? I am doing something about him.'

She looked at him, wondering who he was, and said, 'Did I?'

'You're a wise woman.'

She gave a little smile at that, like a pleased child.

Alice sat holding her hand, not talking to her. Ellen, knowing she was kin, sometimes called her Judith, sometimes Elsie or Flora. 'She's very mixed up as to the generations!' Alice whispered to Ben. But to Ellen, life now seemed no more than the passage of a day: a morning of preparation for an afternoon's activity, followed by an evening for reflection.

The family insisted that Alice and Ben must get out as much as possible during the day. Alice was glad of the opportunity. This time together to which they had so looked forward was, in fact, proving difficult. Ben saw no reason why the marriage ceremony should be regarded as a watershed.

'I'm not saying it doesn't mean *anything* . . .'

'It's a sacrament – it means everything or nothing.'

He was taken aback by such intransigence on an issue on which he, not usually one for half-measures, was prepared for compromise.

Alice had grown up in the belief that she had something precious to bestow, a hidden treasure to be safeguarded. Ridicule had undermined this belief, but not fatally. The confusion of war had given rise to doubts and temptations to which she might have succumbed had the occasion presented itself with sufficient immediacy. But somehow the belief had held. Even if she was aware that she might have over-valued chastity, she could not subscribe to the view that it was of no significance. Now her attitude was strengthened by a measure of practicality. Fear of impending loss had given a sense of urgency to her relationships with Gordon and Ivor. She had wanted to pluck the flower in season before it withered. Marriage had not been a matter to which she had given serious thought because – in spite of Gordon's promises – she had not in either case considered it a reality. Ben was different. She saw her union with him not as a series of satisfactions, but as a relationship which could only be worked out over a long period of time and this early stage of preparation was necessary and precious.

'It's the way I am,' she said. 'If I had started from a different place, perhaps . . .'

'All right, all right!' he said crossly. 'Just so long as you don't think I shall respect you more for it.'

'Get right away from Falmouth,' Prue advised, seeing how tense they had become.

So three days before Christmas, they set out early one morning, Alice in borrowed oilskins and Ben wearing two of Joseph's old jerseys. They took the ferry to St Mawes and from there they hitch-hiked. Cousin Silas had offered the loan of his car, but they had preferred the freedom of travelling without knowing where they might end up.

They ended up at Kiberick Cove. It was a bright, windy day with a chaotic sky. Sturdy bands of strato-cumulus to the west were interspersed with dollops of fair-weather cumulus; while to the east, ribbed scales of altocumulus attempted to introduce some kind of pattern. As they walked up to Nare Head the wind was so strong that Alice had from time to time to stop and turn her back to it in order to gain control of her breathing. Ben breasted the gale with confidence.

On the far side of the Head, in sight of the cove, the wind was less violent. Alice said, 'We'll have you steaming along Offa's Dyke in the spring!'

'Yes, the last two months have made quite a difference.'

'Well, go on; I was hoping for a mention.'

He screwed up his eyes, appearing to give this consideration. 'You may well have made a small contribution.'

She turned to thump his shoulder and caught one foot on a stone. He tried to right her as she stumbled and lost his balance. They collapsed, panting on the grass. Arms wrapped around each other they thrashed about, not very effectively, Alice's oilskin making those squeaks which set the teeth on edge. He said disgustedly, 'It's like trying to make love to a Skipper's sardine!' He kissed her on the mouth and cheeks. 'Or Lot's wife. Did you know you were encrusted with salt? The fate of those who turn aside having once set out.'

She rolled over on to her stomach and looked out to sea. 'Isn't that the Gull Rock?' She pointed to the reef which had been the death of so many seamen. 'My Great Uncle Will went down on the *Hera*.'

'This coast seems to have accounted for quite a few Tippets if your grandmother is to be believed.' He began to take the wrapping paper from their packed lunch. 'Will you eat, or are you going to observe a period of mourning?'

They ate and then walked on towards Kiberick Cove. The sea heaved up moving mountain ridges, white-crested, with long creamy streaks in the troughs. Great cones of foam rose to mark the place of concealed rocks. The tide was not yet full and the sea was only now finding its way into the hollows beneath the boulders. It gurgled and gulped as if it was unstopping hidden soakaways. Seaweed swayed this way and that as waves broke into the still pools left from the last tide.

'I got carried away once when I was bathing,' Alice said. 'Fortunately, it was an incoming tide and it spewed me up on the shore.'

'A more friendly shore than this?'

'Yes, only sand.'

When they tired they lay down again, the wind shrieking above them. Below, the sea raced across the beach, its lofted turrets crashing just short of the base of the cliffs, breaking the images of sky and cloud into a myriad fragments and dancing them about in currents which ran hither and thither between the rocks.

They lay watching and making plans.

'Will you stay with the LCC?' Alice asked.

'For the present. But I hope this work I am doing on people imprisoned without trial may lead to something.'

'How could we possibly influence things which happen so far away?'

'*They* influence us. Why do you think your Education Committee is considering changing to oil-fired heating in its new schools?'

'That's commercial.'

'And so, you can bring in sanctions if you don't like the way your trading partner behaves.'

'Open all your prisons or we won't buy your pineapples?'

'Something like that.'

'We didn't get Hitler to release many people, did we?'

'We didn't try.'

'If it was there for the trying . . .'

'There *is* only the trying, Alice.'

She sat up and the wind tore through her brain. She could hear the boom of the sea on rocks and the grinding rattle like a thousand chains being dragged as the waves receded only to gather their forces for a renewed attack. The sea had its own awesome rhythm, but looking down at it boiling and bubbling in the rock hollows, there seemed more of madness than order of any kind.

Ben said, 'When the Council is planning something to which people have strong objections, the one thing which seems to give councillors pause for thought is when their mail bag is heavy with complaints. I've wondered whether that might work. Hundreds of thousands of letters from people all over the world, showing that they *do* know of the existence of a condemned man, and care what happens to him.'

'The letters to councillors are from potential voters, Ben. It makes a difference.'

'I'm not so sure.'

She did not see how anything could come of such an enterprise, but she liked the determination in him. Her father had spent much of his life hammering on closed doors.

'I'll do your typing,' she offered.

'You'll be typing your novels and helping to pay the mortgage.'

'No. I've decided I'm not a novelist. Once I start something big – and even a short novel seems big to me – I lose control of events and it begins to meander. I'm better with things small – the world in the palm of one's hand.'

'Is there a market for short stories?'

'Is there a fee paying audience for your prisoners anonymous?'

'This disregard for the morality of the market place is all very fine; but I don't know that we can afford so much nonconformity in one family. Think of our six children.'

'I daresay local government will keep our feet on the ground, to say nothing of our noses to the grindstone.'

The waves were breaking against the base of the cliffs now and the roar of the sea was continuous. Alice, secure in the knowledge that there was shelter, warmth and food not far away, experienced a thrill in witnessing a struggle which had gone on day in, day out, long before the first man set foot on this land.

'Do you think of your father when you look at this sea?' she asked.

'No.'

'I think of my Great Uncle Will.'

'He was a sailor. My father was a journalist who made the mistake of booking a passage on the *Lusitania*.'

'They were both shipwrecked.'

She contemplated shipwreck and how it might be contained within the formal structure of the short story. Yet by its very nature it confounded formality. To get the real feel of a shipwreck, one must allow the sea to tear one's work to shreds; just as it smashed the little toys men launched on it, reducing the work of all the craftsmen which had gone into their building to so much driftwood.

'How absurd we are, venturing on to that chaos in such hopelessly fragile craft!' she exclaimed. 'Why did the first people ever do it?'

'Perhaps because fear was an accepted part of their lives? Wild animals on land, and forests full of evil spirits. The sea was just another kind of risk.'

'But at least they knew where they were on land . . .'

'If you keep on asking yourself where you are, you'll never take a step, much less push out a boat.'

How unpredictable he was, with his plans for helping men who were beyond help, and yet so unprepared to risk his mind on even the smallest flight of the imagination! I shall find him maddening and abrasive, she thought. And I suppose I had better not dwell on *that*, or I shall never marry him.

'Are you going to risk *your* fragile craft down yonder?' he asked.

'Not now, not at high tide!'

'I meant at Portloe harbour where, with any luck, we might get tea.'

'You have no soul.'

'In an hour's time, if we stay here, you are going to be insisting you can't possibly set out for Falmouth until you have had tea. And by then it will be too late.'

'Do you know of a nice tea place at Portloe?'

'No, but I shall soon find one. Man *is* the hunter. You can count yourself lucky you're not walking behind me, bowed down with kindling.'

'I've done some kindling in my time.' She remembered walking along the Corniche at Alexandria with her first love, Gordon, and when Ben turned on her angrily, protesting, 'You're not very fair,' it was Gordon whom she echoed in her reply, 'There's nothing *fair* about it.'

He turned away, angrier than ever. She loved him for his impatience, as she would learn to love him for his eagerness, for taking the changes and chances of life hard and yet continuing to expose himself to them. While he, whom she imagined so unwilling to risk imaginative journeys, would find in her a wife as indispensable to his daily well-being as food and drink, and equally to be taken for granted; but also a symbol of that undiscovered country to which he would always be moving and yet would always be beyond him.

They walked down into the narrow sea-wracked streets of Portloe. When they were safe in a neat little tea parlour overlooking the harbour, tingling with excitement, lungs full of good strong sea air, Alice sighed, 'Oh, the sea, that wild sea!'

At night, when she was lying awake, thinking of Ellen in the next room, the sea roared in her ears. You could throw it a few hostages, but the next tide would bring more demands. This was a hunger which would never be satisfied.

She could see a pale light under her door, and knew that Ben was sitting with Ellen. In an hour, she would take his place. But Ben came to her door before the hour.

'Her breathing has changed.'

Alice put on her dressing-gown.

'Should I go down to Charlie and Prue?' she asked.

'There won't be time.'

They sat one on either side of the bed, Alice holding Ellen's hand. The breaths came at irregular intervals now, but there was no stress in the face; in fact, it grew calmer with each exhalation. Ben said hoarsely, 'She was very good to me.'

The breaths came more and more sporadically. The rhythm of life had already ceased. There was nothing for several seconds, then one final sigh. The face was composed beyond amendment. Ben got up and fetched the hand mirror, holding it to the slightly parted lips. There was no vapour. Alice cupped the dear face in her hands and kissed the lips which were still slightly warm. Then she found a napkin and, folding it under the jaw, tied it on top of the head. Ben had turned away and was standing with his back to her looking out of the window. The night was dark and there was no glimmer of light on the distant Carrick Roads.

She said, 'I'll go down to Grace now. She will want to lay her out.'

He did not answer and she did not disturb him further. He remained at the window, thinking of all that had been given him in this house, and the little he had rendered in return. Now, he was making a bad business of grief. Long after Alice had recovered, he would be unable to speak freely of Ellen.

He opened the window and listened. He heard Alice's footsteps hurrying down the street. Then there was silence. There were no rocks here for the sea to dash against, and at this distance he could not hear the waves lapping the harbour wall.

# 17

On Christmas Eve, when Jacov got back to his flat, the two policemen were waiting for him on the landing. This time they made no apology for the inconvenience; and he accepted them without surprise as characters long waiting in the wings.

'This is your flat?' one of them asked casually, glancing round when Jacov opened the door.

'No. It belongs to a friend who has been in America for several years.' He was not interested in the places which housed him; but he saw now that it was visually quite pleasing, spacious and comfortably furnished. He had never had any bad feelings on entering it. All that would be changed.

He put down parcels on the couch and, excusing himself, went into the kitchen. One of the policemen followed him – perhaps to ensure that he did not wash vital evidence down the sink, or slash his wrists? He poured water into a bucket and dunked Claire's carnations without unwrapping the tape from the stalks. His hands were not trembling, but he didn't trust his fingers to do anything intricate.

He hoped the men would not ask for whom the flowers were intended. He was afraid of bringing disaster on other people. This business of the ownership of the flat, for example: did his occupancy constitute a sub-let, and was his friend legally entitled to do this? Jacov paid the rent regularly and no questions were asked. Had the police already been to the landlord? This was the kind of thing one might expect to happen, of course. Once they were suspicious they would find ways of making life uncomfortable.

'Some of this furniture is yours, I expect?' the second policeman said when Jacov returned to the sitting-room.

'No. None of it.'

He was steeling himself to ask if they had a search warrant, when the first man said, 'We would like a few words with you, sir, arising from your statement about Mr Drummond's visit to the theatre.'

Jacov sat down and the two men also sat, so arranging themselves that they were positioned one on either side of him. This did not disturb him unduly, except that he did not like so many empty spaces in the audience. He had read that it is the hands which most frequently betray unease. Years on stage had taught him how to use – or not use – his hands. The simplest method of all, of course, was to find legitimate business for them. He offered cigarettes, which were refused rather primly, and then lit one for himself.

He had told the truth about that scene in the dressing-room – with a few elaborations, perhaps, but they would hardly have come to query his acting method. He must not elaborate this time. If he repeated what he had said before (and he hoped to God he could remember), he had Terence's assurance that there was nothing they could do about it. Eventually, they would have their way, but at least he might win himself a reprieve. His life had been a series of reprieves, some lasting rather longer than others. Looked at that way, he had been quite lucky.

The first policeman said, 'You stated that it was a long time since you had seen Mr Drummond.'

Jacov said, 'Yes.' He inspected the tip of his cigarette thoughtfully, which was one of his ploys when waiting for the prompt.

'What would be your definition of a long time, sir?'

The prompt wasn't coming through. He had the disorientated feeling that overcame him on such occasions of being in the wrong play, or even the wrong theatre. He flicked ash into a little silver dish and watched the smoke curl upwards.

'You don't recall meeting Mr Drummond early one morning at the Lyons near Westminster Bridge? About five months ago, that would be.'

God, it had happened! He *was* in the wrong play. He scrambled up a few lines to give himself time. 'I didn't meet him – at least, not intentionally.'

'But you do remember the occasion?'

Only too well he remembered that there had been a number of other people present – worthy little secretaries, men who were possibly journalists, or worse still, Members of Parliament, all no doubt eager for one reason or another to play their part in a cause célèbre. The police might lack proof of what passed in the dressing-room, but they had ample opportunity to find – or fabricate – what evidence they required in connection with the meeting at Lyons.

'Why didn't you tell us about this, sir?'

'It didn't seem important.'

'It would be better to let us be the judge of that.'

'We had breakfast, that's all. I don't remember much about it. I'm not at my best at that time in the morning.' To save them the trouble of asking why, in that case, he went to Lyons, he said, 'I had been to an all-night party. You know the kind of thing.' It was apparent the poor, dour creatures did not. 'A lot to drink and not enough food. So I went to Lyons.'

'You couldn't have had breakfast here?'

'I had some sort of disagreement with the lady in the next flat. I woke her up by playing music. So I went out.' At least *that* could be checked.

'So you had breakfast with Mr Drummond, who just happened to have gone to that particular Lyons.'

It was not such an extraordinary coincidence. He had first met Angus Drummond over fifteen years ago, and it was likely that at some time they would have a chance encounter. There did not seem any point in saying this since these men were not interested in chance encounters.

'Did anything happen to disturb you during this meeting?'

A clever question. If they had said they had evidence that he had been disturbed, he could challenge it – always supposing he had the nerve and thought it worth his while to antagonise them. Instead, they offered him the chance to make his own admission, or to lie. He tried to recall the scene in the café. Plenty of witnesses, but how many were near enough to hear what had passed? He could never be sure of himself; even when he was speaking quietly he had a tendency to match his voice to the size of the auditorium. He was, however, quite sure that Angus had spoken so quietly as to be inaudible to all save himself.

The policeman made his first mistake. He assumed that Jacov's silence was a refusal to answer. He said, 'If Mr Drummond tried to persuade you to become involved in – shall we say some enterprise of which you had doubts – you would be well-advised to tell us.'

Now, of course, would be the time to say, with a suitably wry, throw-away indifference, 'Well, if you consider giving a birthday present to his girl friend an "enterprise" – then the answer is yes.' But that would mean naming Irene. It did not even occur to him that it could do her little harm at this stage. Nor did he think of himself as shielding her. He only knew that the eleventh commandment was that you should not name names to the inquisitor.

The policeman said quietly, not without sympathy, 'Did he perhaps have a hold over you?'

'What hold *could* he have over me?'

'This is what we are trying to establish.'

'But I hadn't seen him for years.'

That would have gone down better if he had not concealed the meeting at Lyons. Why, oh why, when he had the opportunity had he not made something positive out of it – used it as his explanation for ordering Angus out of his dressing-room? 'I met him once by accident in Lyons. He was acting so strangely then I had to walk out on him. In this situation, *I* couldn't walk out. So I told him to go.' They might not have believed him, but it would have had a consistency. Whereas now everything was falling apart.

'What did you and Mr Drummond talk about?'

He had heard those girls discussing their summer holiday plans. Perhaps they had heard something of his conversation with Angus. In which case, it would be as well to make the best of it. 'There were two girls at a table near by talking about travel. So we got on to the subject. He asked me if I ever thought of going back to Russia.'

'And you said?'

'That I was only four when I left Russia.'

'Did he go on to ask you questions about Russia?'

'No, he didn't. He seemed to be more interested in the fact that I have settled down here. And then I think we talked about acting.'

'You seem to have remembered this conversation quite well. Did anything happen to make it stick in your mind?'

Someone will have told them I left hurriedly, with uneaten food on my plate. He said, 'He told me he was going abroad on a confidential matter. I got the impression he might not be coming back.'

'I wonder what gave you that impression, sir?'

'When we talked about my having settled down here, I had the feeling he was wondering if he could do the same – only somewhere else . . .'

'He didn't confide in you?'

Jacov took his chance. 'I think he wanted to. But I don't like confidences. That's why I left him.'

'You do realise how important this matter is, sir?'

Jacov looked at the man's blunt face and wondered if *he* realised the nature of the age-old charade in which he was taking part.

'We shall want to talk to you about this again. Will you be going away for Christmas?'

'I am going to friends in Kew tomorrow. I shall be at the theatre on Boxing Day.'

'May we have the address of your friends in Kew?'

It was the worst moment of all, but he gave the address because a moment's hesitation would have implicated them. When it was done he knew that there were now only a limited number of moves which he could make, all of which would lead to disaster not only for himself, but for the Strakers. He had already said too much to Terence. Now he was to spend Christmas Day with them. One day next week, policemen would call at their house in Kew. They would ask what had passed between them on Christmas Day. The police would have their own ideas of what had taken place and would no more be satisfied with an account of party games than they had been prepared to accept his preoccupation with making his entry when Angus came to his dressing-room. If he did not go to Kew tomorrow they would suspect that all three of them had a need to be careful.

He heard the men going down the stairs, and walking to the window watched them come out on to the pavement. Big, solid men, patient, persistent. They would never forget. They might not get him for this; but they would watch and wait and one day he would make some simple mistake. The law is a weapon as well as a safeguard: someone is always looking into the barrel of the gun.

Outside on the pavement, one of the men said to the other, 'Something wrong there! A man in his position isn't frightened by a visit from policemen making a routine check without good reason.'

'Not all that routine.'

'Whatever the other lot may get up to, *we're* never going to be able to pin anything on him, are we? He may be a naughty boy, not eating up his beans on toast, but it isn't a crime.'

They strode off purposefully in the direction of The Two Chairmen.

Jacov sat in the darkening room thinking about the Fairleys. When in 1929 they moved into the house next door in Pratts Farm Road, he had been curious about this different life which went on over the garden wall. He had made his first and only effort to penetrate the mystery of the English family. Slowly, cautiously, he had ingratiated himself into their lives. He had started by exchanging gardening tools with Mr Fairley. Then, after he and his sister and brothers had been invited to one of the Fairley parties, he had persuaded his mother to return the invitation. The Fairley children had come to that party, trusting and eager, and Louise had met Guy. Six years later, she and Guy had first made love in the basement. He had neither condoned nor prevented it. He had betrayed Mr Fairley's trust and helped to bring dishonour on the family. Yet still Mr Fairley had befriended them at the time of Katia's disappearance. And, one spring evening during the war, he had been killed, probably while answering some trivial call of Mrs Vaseyelin's. I should have withdrawn after that, Jacov thought. But he had persisted. He had become Louise's lover.

And now he was in a position to destroy the Fairleys. So convinced was he of his propensity to harm, that he hardly gave a thought to the role that Angus Drummond had played in this affair.

The Fairleys, who thought of themselves as active as opposed to Jacov who was passive, would have challenged this version of events. And although they did not like visits from the police, because this was not the kind of thing which happened to the Fairleys, they would not have regarded themselves as marked for the rest of their lives. They did not believe in guilt by association. The Fairleys were not, and had no intention of becoming, victims.

Only one person of their immediate circle might have had some understanding of Jacov's feelings at this time.

Irene Kimberley had learnt that innocence is not a defence. She had been relieved of her work in the Cabinet Office and had now been promised a post in the Ministry of Education. The senior civil servant who had handled her case had been very civilised. In fact, in a possibly well-meaning effort to spare her feelings, he had adopted an air which at times suggested a private amusement at the antics of the security agents which she was supposed to share. But she was far too shocked to be amused. One does not welcome the thought that the event which has blasted one's love life and jeopardised one's career is of little consequence. And it is no comfort to be assured that three years hence the matter will have dropped into oblivion. She would not so soon forget.

There was that which would remind her when thoughts of Angus himself had ceased to trouble her. On this Christmas Eve she hurried through Trafalgar Square in the direction of the Embankment. In a bright cherry red coat which had seen her through better times, she seemed to fit well enough into that group of last-minute shoppers bent on extracting the utmost cheer from the Christmas season. She was naturally lively in her movements and the need to thread her way quickly through the crowds gave her a semblance of sprightliness; while her face had a lightness of countenance which not even grief could dull. Her face had always been a true mirror of her intelligence but a less reliable guide to the state of her emotions. There was nothing to suggest as she bobbed in and out of the throng that she was on her way to visit her father in hospital. Even when she was standing in the rather dreary hall by the lifts, it seemed only impatience which made her turn away on sight of the waiting crowd and make for the stairs.

Her father's ward was on the third floor, the hospital having apparently decided that visitors to heart patients must put their own hearts at risk. For Irene, still sound of heart, the ascent of the stairs provided time to prepare herself. She had always imagined hospital visiting to have a routine sameness, an unvarying order imposed by the aspect and garb of the starched matron and her staff. Only now did she realise that every visit to the seriously ill is a different situation, requiring responses for which one is never adequately prepared. One day her father would seem better, alert and glad to see her and her mother; the next, they would go light-hearted in the expectation of further improvement only to find him absent among the white sheets, their presence a diversion to which he should not have been subjected.

Today a friend had taken her mother to see him in the afternoon and Irene was visiting on her own. She dreaded the moment of entering the ward and seeing yet another change in him. He played such tricks on them now, making up for all the years of courtesy and consideration.

She passed the doors to a ward where a carol party was singing 'Stilly night, holy night'. She could see holly and mistletoe, and one of the nurses looking pert as she talked to a young doctor. On the next floor, the door of a private room was open. The chaplain said, 'Sitting up now, are we?' to an autocratic old lady who would certainly not have been addressed in this fashion since she was in kindergarten. A spurt of rage shook Irene at the thought that he might talk to her father like that. Whom, she asked, pausing on the stairs to rid herself of a desire to rush in and do physical harm to the man, did he imagine he was protecting by this insensitivity? Did he think he could win some kind of dispensation for himself by being jocular with Death? Her hands clenched round the stem of the roses she was carrying, and a thorn reminded her of her indebtedness to the hospital staff. Whatever happened, she must not forget that she was now a dependent. Already, she noted a regrettable tendency to ingratiate herself with the ward sister. She told friends, 'The nurses are quite marvellous.' She was not in a sufficiently balanced state to make evaluations and would have said this even if they were not. Meekly, she took what crumbs of comfort were offered and was at pains to appear a model visitor for fear that otherwise they would withdraw co-operation, might refuse to answer the few questions she asked, even turn her away when her father was having a bad day. She had brought these roses for the ward sister at great expense.

As she reached the third floor, strains of 'We three Kings of Orient are' soared up the great well of the building, putting her in mind of carol services at school. She wished fervently one could be allowed a limited number of fresh starts at life. She would certainly use one of them now and hope to make a better job of the business of growing up. Something had been neglected and she would have liked the chance to identify it and make sure it didn't happen the second time around. But there were no fresh starts – life just went on powering away into the future. She entered the ward.

At first she thought he was dozing, but when she sat by the bed she saw that his eyes were open – they smiled and she thought how free of trouble they seemed. The anxiety which had brought on his illness had spent itself, leaving him not so much reconciled as disengaged. She was troubled by this disengagement. She looked away quickly, because it would be unforgivable to let him see her tears. He put his hand over hers, just as he might have done when she was a little girl and sick – their physical contacts had been few, but this gentle touch had been one of them. His hand rested on hers light as a feather, yet she sensed he was trying to steady her spirit. It had been one of their gifts that they could be quiet in each other's company, but now it was only with a great effort of will that she refrained from prattling. Her father, watching her, saw that she had grown into a woman without his having been aware of it. Her eyes were very bright. Tears on a young woman's face were like dew on a rose. Wasn't there something . . . there ought to be . . . His mind wandered, turning the pages of his scholarship. After a quarter of an hour Irene saw the ward sister hovering like a spectre beyond the foot of the bed. She kissed her father lightly on the forehead and whispered that she would be back tomorrow. His eyes traced the lines of her face.

She gave Sister the roses and was thanked graciously. In fact, too graciously. It wasn't the roses Sister was concerned about. She said, 'I think we should have a word,' and opened the door to the little cubicle at the end of the ward. There were two chairs and they both sat down. Sister said, 'You do realise how ill your father is?'

Irene said, pitching her voice higher than she had intended, 'Of course. He has had a heart attack.'

'You've seen him today.'

But not professionally. As soon as she entered the ward she began to add touches of her own to his countenance, bits and pieces from the past, to give substance to the picture. She took a deep breath, and said in that calm manner which always led people to imagine her to be more in possession of herself than she was, and which had earned her so much pain, 'Is there something I should know?'

'I'm afraid he hasn't much longer.'

'But the doctor said . . .' She looked at Sister. The doctor was young. Sister had seen much more of death.

'This will be a great shock to my mother.' She bowed her head, wondering how she was to break the news.

Sister said, 'Your mother knows.'

'You mean you told her this afternoon?'

'I didn't need to.'

Irene sat looking at the little glass panel in the door, a very slight frown drawing her brows together, her eyes narrowed. She might have been aware of an incipient headache, nothing more. Some people rock at the blows of life, others receive them less directly and it takes a long time for the bruise to show. She said in a matter-of-fact tone, 'Should we stay the night? Is that possible?'

'It's not as immediate as that. If I were you I would get what rest you can tonight.'

As Irene left, she said, 'He is not in pain, you know.' Irene did know.

She walked part of the way home to give herself time for recollection. She wanted to be composed when she greeted her mother. It is a myth that grief shared is a burden lightened: they had hardly spoken of it.

There was a carol party singing under a lamp on the Embankment. She put a shilling in a tin and they called out 'Merry Christmas!'

'I shouldn't have accepted it so easily,' she thought, guilty as if she had allowed him to slip away as a result of neglect on her part.

She stood looking at the inky water shot with light from Lambeth Bridge. She found it extraordinarily difficult to believe in the things which had happened to her over the past months. In spite of the war her expectations had not included tragedy. She had a good home, had been to a good school and had gained a good degree. That, she had imagined, and she was not alone in this, should be sufficient to launch her into a satisfying life. Not happiness, necessarily; she had never felt sure of that. But satisfying. And now this. Angus gone. Her father dying. And her mother? She was afraid her mother would not long survive her father. I shall be all alone, she thought, walking on past the bridge. She looked around her in amazement. How did it happen to me? How did it come about? It seemed important to trace the sequence of events, as though that in itself would make matters better, even rewrite the past. Some rewriting or reshaping was urgently necessary. People said she was self-sufficient, but she wasn't; she needed love as much as anyone else. When her parents died, there would be no one for whom she was the most important person in the world. Perhaps Angus would think of her sometimes, but that would be little comfort. And, in any case, now that she came to think of it, his view of her had been odd in the extreme. He had once told her she was like a Mozart sonata, crisp and sparkling, and complete in itself! She should have shattered that image. A Mozart sonata had a beginning, middle and an end. She was only just past her beginning.

When she came through the front door of her home she was greeted by the smell of roast chicken. 'I thought we would have Christmas dinner tonight,' her mother called from the kitchen.

Irene went into the kitchen. Her mother, who was not a good cook, was busying herself with various pots and pans over which she seemed to have established little control. Irene adjusted the heat of the oven. Her mother said, without rancour, 'Oh well, if you are going to take over . . .' She returned to the table where she had left a copy of *The Times*. 'Morgan Phillips says that communists are infiltrating the Trade Unions . . .'

Irene said, 'I don't think I'm going to be able to eat.'

Her mother said, speaking more sharply than usual, 'You must try.' She turned to the paper again and said, 'These people express themselves so badly.' She looked very fastidious, with her long thin nose and pursed mouth, the kind of person who might be more hurt by a split infinitive than an emotional disjunction. Yet Irene knew that her mother was not really reading the paper, only taking refuge in it. She does not want me to intrude on her grief, she thought. That is why she has prepared this meal, to give herself something to do which will also keep her at a distance from me. Irene clenched her hands. This oblique, glancing approach to life would not do! Some things must be met head on. Above all, *something* must be shared. She said, 'And so must you try!' Her mother looked at her, face pulled awry with wounded anger. She folded the paper and got to her feet.

Irene stamped her foot. 'I can't manage this alone, Mummy. Do you understand?'

Her mother went into the hall. My father and I would have managed much better on our own, Irene thought; but it is my mother, my amused, ambiguous, maddening mother, with whom I am to be left. She began to peel the potatoes, cutting deep and wastefully beneath the skin. I must hold on, she thought, and she called out, 'Don't imagine you can just fade away. Because I won't let you.' It was important to hold on to what you had got. It might not be what you had hoped for, but you must make something of it.

Her mother returned carrying the sherry decanter. 'Yes,' she said, as though continuing an interrupted conversation, 'That is why we are having dinner tonight.'

Jacov stood on the platform at Victoria District Line station, waiting for the train to Kew. He carried Claire's carnations which smelt rather sickly. He was feeling sick in any case. He had not slept all night and had had nothing to eat. He was convinced he had been followed here. The indicator announced the coming of an Ealing Broadway train and a Circle Line train in that order. No mention of a Richmond train.

He saw the people around him at the end of a long funnel, small and irrelevant, and in constant motion. While he was himself unmoving. It had been like this for a long time but he had managed not to notice it. During the war he had been drawn into activities of a communal nature, travelling abroad with shows to entertain the troops, meeting new people, seeing new places. This had kept him going and he had imagined himself more or less afloat on the stream of life. Only when hostilities had ceased did he realise that the war had passed him by without effecting any real change in his condition. It had been a travelling show which he had witnessed, a solitary bystander. Himself unmoving. But there had been the business of acting to keep him going. Now, as established as one could hope to be in a precarious profession, there were no incentives. Long-running plays might represent security for some, but they left him with too much time and too little activity to fill it. He had been appalled last night when he thought of the years stretching ahead, years during which he imagined himself imprisoned. He had been to church, but had been conscious only of the darkness surrounding the flickering candles. As the night wore on, he realised he was already in prison. And it was not the years ahead which concerned him, but the question of how he was to get through the next hour of his captivity. At daybreak he got up and moved about, making preparations slowly, methodically. Even so, the minutes were leaden. He had a moment of complete panic, standing by the sitting-room window staring at a spider's web, spun-gold in a shaft of sunlight. Although eventually he managed to turn to face the door, he was daunted by the prospect of the three-minute walk to the station. He clung to the front door while the world heaved like a ship in a storm. His neighbour, who had come to offer the season's greetings, said, 'Oh dear, and on Christmas morning!' and closed her door firmly. He launched himself at the stair rail, grasped it, and began to descend.

Each step demanded intense physical effort. Even could he have been assured that the end of his troubles lay a mile ahead, it would have been no comfort. His energy was running out fast and would soon be spent. But only a mile? One might as well ask why, when a rock pool is so close to the sea, it should remain dry. The question is irrelevant, since the pool *is* dry.

In the street, he had looked about for help. But if one looks intently at the human face, how often does one find one which seems to be completely trustworthy? To Jacov, usually the least censorious of men, the faces of people hurrying by bore the marks of the seven deadly sins; stiff with pride, jaundiced by gluttony, swollen with lust, pared to the bone by anger, they thrust their way past him.

He had reached the station faint with fatigue and lack of food. And now, looking towards the dark tunnel from which there was no rumble of an approaching train, he saw the track as a stretch of time along which he had been struggling for hours until he was so spent that he could not last another second. The station seemed to roll, and he rolled with it, pitched, and rolled into the darkness of that dry, rock-hidden pool.

He rolled, in fact, neatly and landed between the live wires, lying on his back looking quite composed with the flowers resting like a wreath on his breast, just as if he was in his coffin.

# 18

'Are you happy about this move?' Judith asked Louise when they were working in the kitchen on Christmas Eve.

'There's more than a move,' Louise said. 'I think I'm pregnant.' She sliced a cross in the base of a sprout and threw it on top of a rising mound. 'I *know* I'm pregnant. But I haven't said anything yet. I want the children to have a good Christmas.'

'Will they mind?'

'Whether they do or not, they have enough to think about at the moment.'

'How do you feel?'

'Angry.'

'With Guy?'

'We'd been careful and then something happened . . . Well, no matter. He got his way and I daresay I shall be pleased when the baby comes.'

'I was angry when Claire came.'

'Is that why you spoilt her, to make up for not wanting her?'

'Since you can see my mistakes so clearly, you won't make the same ones, will you?'

Louise continued with the sprouts. When she had finished them she laid the bowl in front of her mother. 'There! A labour of love if ever there was one!'

Through the window they could see Austin and Guy and a man to whom they referred as the Visiting Author coming along the lane, the children following some distance behind, indulging in mild horse-play. 'Where do you think they have been?' Louise asked.

'To see the old cottage Austin came across on that disastrous outing when Terence broke his ankle!'

'Oh no! I will *not* be buried in the country.'

'Austin had it in mind for the Visiting Author, who is looking for a rural retreat in which to write his masterpiece.'

Louise frowned, irritated because her mother sometimes adopted a different mode of speech now that she was married to Austin.

'Christmas pudding is by courtesy of America,' Judith said. 'A literary agent Austin knows over there sent us a food parcel! What do you imagine it will taste like?'

'Heavily spiced pumpkin pie.'

Austin's daughter and family arrived for lunch and, this being the start of the season of goodwill, most members of the party emerged with resolutions intact. 'You're so good for Daddy,' Judith's daughter-in-law told her in the brief time that they were alone together. 'And the house has really come to life again.' It was apparent she regarded Judith as a superior housekeeper who must be encouraged lest she give notice. 'I *am* sorry we couldn't stay for Christmas Day, but Derek's family would be *devastated* if we didn't go to them this year. Although I do dread the journey. Derek gets in *such* a paddy when the children are car sick.'

Judith, waving them on their way, thought of all the people setting out on journeys they would find exhausting to visit people who were bracing themselves for the disruption of their arrival; and wondered if a moratorium might not be declared every five years during which people would not be allowed to move out of their own homes at Christmas.

The author hoped that now things were momentarily quieter Austin would take the opportunity to discuss the draft of his new novel, which he had had for over a month.

Austin said, 'A drink is called for, I think.'

It was not until Christmas lunch that the subject of the country cottage was raised. The author thought it too large for one person, and the amount of work required daunting. He doubted if it was on main drainage.

'We aren't on main drainage,' Austin said. 'If it's main drainage you are after, you would be better to stay where you are.' He did not look forward to receiving a rural epic from a man who had been particularly successful in depicting the literary byways of Hampstead. Like all publishers, he viewed with alarm and despondency any tendency on the part of his authors to stray from their familiar pastures.

'It would make a splendid family house,' Guy said. 'And it has a paddock for a pony.'

'Supposing anyone wants a pony,' Catherine said.

James said to the author, 'We are going to live in Lewes. We're moving early next year.'

Guy looked at Louise. She raised her eyebrows and said to Catherine, 'Your father wants the bread sauce.'

Judith changed the subject. 'What about the Holland Park house?'

'We thought of giving Ben and Alice first refusal,' Louise said.
'You'll have to make some financial arrangement with Claire and Terence,' Judith told her. 'Your grandmother meant you all to have a share in it.'
'They could wait.' Louise was indifferent to financial claims.
'Oh no, they couldn't!' Austin exclaimed. 'Now is the time when they need money.'
They began to argue about this while the author made mental notes for a future novel about a minor inheritance which divides a family. He was disappointed when Guy said, 'We'll talk it over all together, so that Terence and Claire can have their say.'
Later, when he and Louise were doing the washing-up, Guy tried to revert to the subject of the country cottage. 'I wasn't all that struck with Lewes. Rather a grey little place, I thought.'
'I'm not all that struck with moving out of London.'
'You might at least look at this cottage.'
She laughed. 'I'll go and spit over the hedge, if you like.'
In the study Austin said to the author, 'It seems fine to me, except for this fellow Allenby. Rather a cold fish, I thought.'
The author, who regarded Allenby as a sensitive, profoundly feeling man, and moreover the pivot of the whole book, was filled with a sense of the futility of all artistic endeavour. It was while he was summoning his resources to meet this criticism, that the telephone rang. Austin went into the hall, delighted at having made his escape. Although a perceptive critic, and an excellent editor, he had little talent for buoying up the spirits of his authors, many of whom regarded *him* as a cold fish.
'Don't worry,' he said to Judith who had come out of the dining-room.
'I expect that is Alice, to say they are all thinking of us.'
'Then she can convey that happy thought to me,' he said firmly, and picked up the receiver. After a moment, he cradled the receiver beneath his chin and said, 'It is Claire, ringing from the house next door.' He listened briefly and then said jovially, 'You needn't have waited. We finished some time ago . . .' A further pause, and then, 'I see.'
'What has happened?' Judith asked sharply, unduly subject to misgivings since receiving the news of her mother's death.
He waved a hand at her irritably. 'Look, my dear, is Terence there? Well, let me speak to him.'
Louise joined her mother. 'What's going on?'
Austin stood, uncommunicative, gazing at the wall in front of him,

until there were noises at the other end of the wire. Then he said, 'When did this happen, Terence? And how?'

'At least *they* are both alive!' Judith said. Guy joined them, a nut held in the claw of a nut-cracker. It was apparent to all of them that, serious though the matter might be, it did not affect the twins. Austin's manner was too businesslike to suggest a tragedy of that dimension. Eventually, he said, 'Now, don't do *anything* at the moment . . . Yes, I can understand how you feel, but I don't think you should go on your own . . . Yes, I know Aunt May will be with the twins, but I still feel . . . Now, look, I will come up tomorrow – I think I can manage to get some petrol – and we will all go together.' After a little more discussion, he put down the receiver.

'It seems that, on his way to Claire and Terence this morning, Jacov Vaseyelin tried to commit suicide.'

Louise put her hands over her face and blundered into the kitchen. Guy looked down at the nut in his hand, and then slowly cracked it. Judith said, 'How?'

'He threw himself on to the District Line, but he fell between the live wires.'

She gave a little bark of laughter, and then shook her head. 'I'm sorry. But it is so like him.'

'You mean he made a practice of it?' Austin was angry with her.

She shrugged her shoulders. 'He's ineffective.'

Louise called from the kitchen, 'Is he badly hurt?'

Guy juggled the empty shell of the nut in his hands, wondering where to put it.

Austin said, 'He's unconscious. Concussion.'

Judith said, 'Then how . . . ?' and he cut her short, 'Do you think we might sit down to discuss this – that is, if you can spare the time?'

She turned away and went into the drawing-room. The author, who had been hovering in the doorway of the study, whispered to Guy, 'Is it bad news?'

'I'm afraid it is.'

The author said under his breath, 'Oh dear, *what* a nuisance!' Guy strolled across to the oak chest where there was a bowl of nuts. He could not decide whether to join Louise in the kitchen, or Judith and Austin in the drawing-room. He helped himself to a brazil nut. James appeared at the window, making signs to indicate that he and Catherine were going to walk the dog. Guy made signs indicating that he would join them.

In the drawing-room, Judith said to Austin, 'How did they find out he was going to Claire and Terence?'

'Apparently he had told the police where he was spending Christmas Day. It seems they had been to see him again about Angus Drummond's disappearance. He was very upset about it.'

'How pitiable!' There was more exasperation than compassion in the comment. She walked to the window and rapped her knuckles on the sill. 'But even allowing for that, how would the particular policeman who dealt with this attempted suicide have known? They can't have circulated his whereabouts to all the police stations in London, surely?'

'No.' Austin stood with his hands in his pockets, looking into the fire which needed attention. 'Unless he was followed. How damnable!'

She turned to him in surprise. 'You're just like Stanley! This is how he would have taken it.'

'Any liberally-minded person would!'

'You are reacting as though it was something you had read in the *Manchester Guardian*. In fact, that is how you react to most things.'

'While you?'

'Oh, I am one of those maddening women who are never objective, who always sees things personally. And in this case, it *is* personal.' She drummed her fist on the sill. 'These Vaseyelins! They have no right to ingratiate themselves into other people's lives.'

'They have so few rights. You can't deny them *that*.'

'I would deny them anything!'

He thought she had the look at this moment of one of those pioneer women defending the frontier – all that was needed was a rifle across her knees. While deploring her sentiments he found himself more than ever her admirer.

'There is something else that is worrying you?' he hazarded.

'How will the children feel about this?' She was looking out of the window where the day was already beginning to dwindle. A rime of frost was forming on the fallen leaves on the terrace, and the paving stones glinted as though sprinkled with icing sugar. She screwed up her eyes, trying to put herself in the minds of her children who, at this moment, were so much a part of her and yet as different as creatures inhabiting another world. 'They always had this feeling that something ought to be done about the Vaseyelins. Alice was for ever on at me to include Katia in all our family gatherings.'

'Has he no family – Jacov?'

'Brothers in Canada, and a father who lives in one room somewhere or other in London, and plays the violin in the streets.'

'Hmm . . .'

She said, without turning round, 'Where is Guy?'

'I think I heard him go out.'

'So long as he can't hear what we are saying.'

He came to her and put his arm round her waist. 'Tell me about it.'

'I have sometimes suspected that Louise and Jacov were lovers.'

He closed his eyes on the laughter which threatened them. Given Louise's strong sexuality, a lover was only too likely, but he could see that this was not something which Judith would take lightly. And if it was Jacov, then indeed there was no cause for lightness.

She sat on the window seat and rubbed her hand to and fro on the worn cushion. 'I know my daughter. She won't desert him. She will imagine that she can look after Jacov, *and* make this move to Lewes, *and* reconcile Guy to it, *and* keep the children's interests at heart – and all while she is carrying a child! I haven't had time to tell you *that*.'

'Guy's child?'

'Yes, thank goodness. She seemed sure of that – sure enough to be angry with him. But it would make no difference whose child it was; she would think that simply because she willed it, she could make it work, and she would wreck all their lives.'

Austin was not convinced that lives were wrecked so easily; on the other hand, he had to admit that he tended to judge complex situations rather in the manner of an editor – to be accepted if the author brought it off. Judith's might well be the surer judgement. He walked across to the fire and squatted, poker in hand, dubiously contemplating how best to bank it up.

Judith went on, 'And if it's not Louise, then it will be Alice and Ben, or Terence and Claire, that it will fall on. And they are young and still have a lot to learn about each other without taking on Jacov Vaseyelin.'

Austin was suddenly aware that his own involvement in this might be greater than he had imagined. He said bracingly, 'I think we are jumping rather far ahead. He will probably be quite all right after a week in hospital.'

She shook her head. 'No. He won't be.'

'How can you be so sure?'

'When we first came to Pratts Farm Road, I made up my mind I wasn't going to be involved with the Vaseyelins. But they just hung on.'

It was an irrational statement, yet it had an inner logic which was uncomfortably convincing. Austin squatted quietly, the poker between his knees.

She said, 'More than any of the others, I was the one who wanted to avoid involvement with the Vaseyelins.'

Austin ran his mind back over the words he had used not ten minutes ago, counting their cost. She turned to look at him. 'Could you bear it?' He looked up, refusing to find words for her. She could hardly bring herself to say it, but if she was going to do it, she must certainly say it. 'Could you bear to have him here?'

He said stubbornly, 'We'll see if it comes to that. It may not.'

'But could you bear it?'

He laid the poker down in the hearth. 'There may be a continuing police involvement. You would have to be prepared for that.'

She shrugged this aside. 'That would be the least of it. You still haven't answered my question.'

Austin, who had been verbally committed to liberalism for most of his life, could see no way out. He cheered himself with the recollection that once, a long time ago, he had agreed to have a man who had just come out of prison to stay. In the event, the chap had gone somewhere else. Jacov, no doubt, had plenty of theatrical friends who would come to the rescue – theatre people being so notably warmhearted.

'Of course,' he said.

'I'm not sure that *I* can.'

He realised then how daunted she was. He went to her and she put her hand in his. 'He frightens me. The whole family frightened me. *That* was why I didn't want to become involved with them.'

This is really going to happen, he thought. So far in their marriage they had found sufficient shared pleasures to satisfy them and where they had differed they had been able to go their separate ways without much resentment. There had been little to threaten their union, no pain and anxiety to deliver those hammer blows which can sever or weld together. Still scarcely able to credit it, he said, 'We shall manage.'

Late that night, while Austin was raking out the fires, Judith went into the garden. There was a hard frost now and the grass was silvered. The moon was up and she could see the dark swell of the Downs. The house was quiet, settled amid its orderly lawns and well-trimmed hedges. Beyond, other houses were dotted here and there as the centuries had discovered a need for them. It was all rather haphazard, because here things had happened slowly, giving people time to adapt themselves and their land to change. Some violence there had been – to the Cluniac priory in Lewes, the destruction of which Austin, not a Christian, had told her was a crime. But enough of the past remained to give a sense of continuity. She had accepted this scene as a pleasant backcloth to her new life, but now it seemed to have a greater value. This can't all pass away, she thought, looking towards the great yew trees which formed a sheltering wall around the old church.

She went slowly back to the house and moved from room to room, collecting crumpled napkins and nutshells, righting cards which had fallen, finding glasses put down in unlikely places, making minor adjustments to the fir cones and dried flowers with which she had decorated the dining-table. In the drawing-room, she paused in front of a photograph of Austin's son, taken, she judged, at that unreachable stage which some young people go through, his eyes looking beyond the photographer to a future which was not to be his. Yet, the expression told her that he knew better. At that age, of course, they always did.

She picked up the photograph, studying it for some objective truth. Austin had lost a wife and a son; Jacov Vaseyelin had lost a mother and a sister – well, two sisters, one of whom he scarcely remembered. Why all the fuss? What was the difference? Austin had probably cared more deeply for those whom he had lost. The difference, of course, she thought as she put the photograph back in its place, was this house, this village, this country; this unending tapestry into which each life was woven, grief and joy, love and rejection among its coloured threads.

Stanley would have been surprised that she should have such thoughts. She had never had his respect for the past in terms of tradition, but she had always had a strong awareness of the need for personal continuity. When during the war they had turned out the loft, she had been the one who had been disturbed to see the small family treasures cast on the scrap heap.

She thought of her own children. If she could take the burden of Jacov from her, Louise would manage. The changing moral climate would suit her, particularly as she thought she had invented it. She would grow – was already growing – into one of those rather too generous, pear-shaped women, always in season; yet maintaining her own idiosyncratic, but unyielding moral steadfastness. Alice would always make life more difficult than it need be, but she, too, had a certain buoyancy which would keep her afloat, like a minesweeper clearing a passage for herself through doubts and questioning. My poor Claire! she sighed. She will have the hardest path. She no longer believes in her country, and she has lost that far country to which, as a child, Stanley taught her to look. She and Terence must carry the world on their shoulders. And which of us can do that?

She went into the hall. The house creaked as the cold got into its joints. Austin had opened the trap door into the loft and put a paraffin stove beneath it in the hope that this would prevent the water freezing. The only result was to send a bitter draught along the passage and down the stairs. Judith crossed to the study – a room very much Austin's, but which Stanley would have loved could he have afforded it. So much patient scholarship which people like herself took lightly, or derided! She went to draw the curtains and saw that the glass was patterned with an intricate filigree of frost. She turned back to the room which looked comfortable in a musty way, the chairs hollowed, the arm-rests worn, the carpet pitted where the library steps had taken Austin's weight. Some things must change, of course, she thought. But others we shall hold on to. We, too, shall be wise in our generation. We must be.

That night she lay awake, wondering in which room she would put Jacov Vaseyelin.

At the beginning of January, Austin and Judith stayed for several days with Louise and Guy in Holland Park. The whole family, including Ben, gathered together on one occasion to discuss the future of the Holland Park house. After they had talked, they switched on the wireless to listen to Mr Attlee who, unnecessarily as far as they were concerned, warned of communist danger to democracy:

'A hundred years ago, the year 1848 saw Liberals and Socialists in revolt all over Europe against absolute governments which suppressed all opposition. It is ironical that today the absolutists who suppress opposition much more rigorously than the kings and emperors of the past masquerade under the name of upholders of democracy. It is a tragedy that a section of the movement that began in an endeavour to free the souls and bodies of men should have been perverted into an instrument for their enslavement . . .'

'I wonder if the Drummonds are listening to this,' Alice said.

'I met Cecily in Richmond the other day,' Claire said. 'She told me her parents never mention Angus. Her mother took everything that belonged to him out into the garden and burnt it. She said she didn't want a trace left of the son who had dishonoured his father. The police were furious!'

Louise switched off the radio. 'We don't want him maundering on at us, do we?'

'Ever since this wretched business, I've been aware of how often the subject of communist infiltration crops up,' Alice said. 'And it would be quite easy to imagine the remarks slanted in my direction. I can understand how people like Jacov develop a persecution complex.'

'There are probably a lot of other subjects that crop up regularly which you don't take to yourself,' Ben said.

'That's just what I'm *saying*. You don't listen before you . . .'

'It's the same with Freud. If you start from the assumption that all pointed objects . . .'

'Well, I *don't* start from that assumption . . .'

'The Jews have a ready-to-hand persecution complex,' Austin said.

While they were arguing, Jacov opened his eyes and looked at the night nurse who had just come on duty.

'Well now!' she said. 'It's nice to have *your* attention.'

He hastily closed his eyes. But it was too late. The first contact had been made. The next day when Austin and Judith went to see him, he was sitting up. 'He hasn't spoken yet,' the nurse told them. 'But he *is* with us.'

'You won't be able to stay here indefinitely,' Austin said to him. Jacov still showed no intention of conversing, but it seemed likely that not only could he hear but he could comprehend. In which case, it was time to give him something to meditate upon. Judith said, 'It will probably take you a little while to get over this, and Austin and I would like you to stay with us.'

Jacov turned his head away and studied the pattern of the cubicle curtains indifferently.

'So that settles that,' Austin said.

Over the last nine days, nurses had soothed, persuaded, cajoled. Louise had come and tried unsuccessfully to convince the ward sister that a cure might be effected if only they would play Mozart to him day and night. Visiting actors had wrought surprising variations on the theme of the sympathetic friend, much to the appreciation of the ward at large. The best performance of all had been given by Count Vaseyelin. The chair by the bedside was closer than he had ever been to any of his children and he had veered away from it, preferring to walk up and down the ward, tossing his leonine head so violently it seemed in danger of breaking free from the skeletal frame, and weeping for his dead wife and daughters, until the ward sister had asked him to leave. Jacov had remained impassive throughout. Now, disconcerted by the abrupt change of treatment, he spoke for the first time. 'I should be a nuisance.'

'When you become a nuisance, I shall tell you.'

Jacov said, 'It won't do.'

They talked of other things.

'You'll be back in the theatre before too long,' Austin assured him. 'There have been some notable theatrical breakdowns.'

Jacov gave the ghost of a smile at a card signed 'Noel'. Those who hadn't written had come personally to recount their own traumas.

No more mention was made during this visit of plans to move Jacov.

After they had gone, he said to the nurse, 'They won't take me out of here, will they?'

'You can't stay here for ever, can you?' she said with the good humour appropriate to a little display of unreason in the nursery.

As prisons go, it seemed to him not unsatisfactory. 'But I could go to another hospital. Somewhere for the mentally ill.'

'Now, you wouldn't really want that, would you?'

'I don't know what I want.' This was what they should be treating him for, instead of imagining that his normal state was one of knowing and trying to restore him to it.

Why was he here? Was it some secret want of his which had landed him here? This puzzled him. He puzzled about it for the rest of the evening, until they gave him his sleeping tablets. Even after that, half in and half out of sleep, he puzzled. Why was he lying here? Why had he not gone into the darkness? And why, oh why, with all his experience, had he looked that nurse in the eye? Was it that he wanted to live, or that he had not wanted to die enough? Must one pay as careful attention to the matter of one's dying as one's living? It had been a mistake to look to Death for a solution – it was, after all, only the first of the Last Things.

And now this offer of Judith Fairley's, what was he to make of that? It was one thing to be wistful about what went on over the garden wall, quite another to be asked to play a part in the mystery. And while it was permissible for him to be curious about the Fairleys, it was unthinkable that they should have questions to ask of him. But if the Fairleys (in his confused state he thought of Austin as another Fairley) took him in, might they not expect to get to know him better once he was on their side of the garden wall? And he had nothing to offer them. Over the years he had found no place for himself, even within himself. He felt more frightened of this barrenness than of anything else.

He thought about the place to which Judith would take him. Somewhere in Sussex. He had only been to Sussex once or twice. He remembered hills and empty green spaces. He was used to the theatre, to the crowded streets around Westminster in which it was possible to pass one's life without making connections. The country was different. Man, that upright tree that moved, was so conspicuous in the country. The hills and valleys offered no place in which to hide one's unrelatedness. He would always need somewhere to hide.

As he was thought to be improving, they supplied him with a newspaper so that he could read the theatre columns. He read that Mr Herbert Morrison had said, 'When the war ended, there was no prejudice in the democratic world against the Soviet Union. We were, on the contrary, full of admiration for the achievements of the Red Army, which we had assisted to the full extent of our power . . .' He went on to say how saddened he had been by the Soviet's unwillingness to 'reach accommodation, to give as well as take . . .'

The next time Judith and Austin came, Jacov said, 'I shall never be able to become a British subject now. The police will have my name chalked up. And they never wipe the slate clean.'

'In this country, it's the same law for everyone – even the police,' Judith said, patiently reminding herself that it was difficult for him to accept this with his background. The most difficult thing of all would have been for her to understand that the law is never impartial.

Austin said, 'You will have to make an effort.'

'How far will one effort get me?' he wondered wryly. It was the first time he had ever examined the possibility that he might have to search for a foothold on this shore on which he and his family had been washed up.

A week later, when they were discussing arrangements for his move, he said to Austin, 'Even if I try, I don't know that I'll succeed.' He had tried to walk that morning and had been unable to – and that was the least of his problems.

'Which of us can do more than try?' Austin himself was full of misgivings.

'There has been far more of failure in my life than anything else.' He said this, not in self-pity, but rather preparing his defence against the time when it should be needed.

'Let's assume failure, then,' Austin said. 'And try to make it comparative.'

Alice was to wear the wedding dress which Claire had worn, and which she, in turn, had borrowed from a college friend. The dress had had to be taken in for Claire and now it was being let out for Alice. Claire said, turning Alice so that she could see how the dress hung at the back, 'It's all very silly, but I know how you feel. I was just the same over my wedding.' She was insistent that Alice shared her views.

Alice said, 'I bet you didn't feel as constricted! I shall be too terrified to take a deep breath.'

'Will you stay long at the Holland Park house? I don't think we shall want to stay here.' She went on quickly before Alice could comment, 'I thought of our country mansion when Louise and Guy talked about house-hunting. I expect you did, too.'

'Yes, I did.'

'It was all very silly, wasn't it?' She sounded sad.

'It saw us through those first years in Shepherd's Bush.'

'It was all a dream, though. One can't live a dream. That's unhealthy. But I was surprised at how it all came rushing back to me when Guy talked about the old house we passed in that country lane.' She had been pinning the hem of the dress; now, for a moment, she stopped, crouched behind Alice. 'Do you know what I actually found myself thinking? Suppose we all took it over? That's how people lived at one time, several branches of a family in one house. It's very unnatural, the way we live now, don't you think? In little individual boxes. It would be much healthier, I'm sure, to have several people sharing their lives.' She began putting in pins again. 'You used to climb the tree in our garden in Pratts Farm Road to see that old house that was hidden away near us – Kashmir. Do you remember? You started telling me a story once about two children who climbed the wall that surrounded it. You never told me what they found there. You said it was the garden that mattered. You could sit on the lawn and pick the flowers and nothing was forbidden. I couldn't imagine a place where nothing was forbidden. It quite frightened me when I thought about it afterwards. Wasn't that silly?'

'It *was* frightening. That was why I couldn't finish the story. I didn't understand it. The fear seemed a part of the scene, the walled garden, the green lawn, the flowers, a boy and a girl . . . Every time I thought about it, I couldn't separate the fear from the enchantment.'

'Don't you wonder about it? Of course, all that dreaming we did wasn't very healthy. But you are a writer, so perhaps *you* ought to go on wondering. Besides, I should like to know the end of that story.'

'I don't think it has an end, Claire. But if ever I write any more about it, I'll tell you.'

Claire put the last pin in place and sat back on her haunches. 'Do you *want* to stay in London?'

'It's not what I expected, but it's the most sensible thing for us to do.' She turned to look at her sister. 'When the twins are a bit older, you'll be able to get out more.'

'I've joined a small group of singers – we do madrigals and that sort of thing. Not very exciting.'

'It's a start. And I expect there will be things we can do together. We're not all that far apart.'

That same day Judith and the daily help prepared the room which was to be Jacov's.

'I'd have given him that poky little attic,' Mrs Harman said, speaking of the room which had so pleased Alice. 'All those stairs to climb and a long walk to the lav. if he wants it at night. He'd not stay too long then.'

Judith was taken aback, not so much by this repudiation of the traditional idea of country hospitality, as by the fact that Mrs Harman should read her mind so unerringly.

'I don't believe you often have visitors you don't welcome,' she said. 'Your house has the reputation of an ever-open door.'

'That's Mr Harman. You turn anyone away from your door and it's the Lord Jesus. He was brought up that way and takes it very seriously.'

'Suppose it should be the Devil at the door?'

'He'd come with drink on his breath – or so Mr Harman believes. No good comes of arguing with him.'

'And you find you can manage?'

'Well, you might say I'm Martha and Mr Harman is Mary. When we've got someone with us I don't much take to, I keep to the kitchen.'

Judith had kept to the kitchen most of her life. When the children were young, the house had been full of people. But she had always been selective. Not only had she kept the Vaseyelins at a distance, she had not encouraged those children whom she considered to be bad company for her daughters, such as the dreadful Maisie of whom Claire had been so fond.

'Well, I can offer him good food and a cheerful countenance,' she said. 'We'll have to see how far that gets us.' Austin must do the rest.

He had surprised her by his willingness to come this far. She hoped they would continue to surprise each other.

Her domain had always been small, but it had been important to her that she was in command of it. This would no longer be so. She had started on something to which she could not set limits and there was no asssurance it would turn out well.

Even now, in the cold light of a late January afternoon, the room seemed to have changed in anticipation of its occupant. With its plain white walls and modest furnishings – there was only the bed, one upright chair and a small chest of drawers – it had seemed simple and uncluttered. The vase of gold and magenta chrysanthemums had contributed a homely gaiety. But now she saw that it had no distinctive feature and she was primarily conscious of the empty spaces between the pieces of furniture, already in shadow.

'I think we have an oil lamp downstairs,' she said to Mrs Harman. 'I'll see if I can find it. It will be useful if we have more power cuts.'

When she came back with the lamp, the sun had gone down but an eerie pink light lingered in the cold sky and in her absence it had crept into the room, falling on the wall behind the bed and touching the edge of the pillow.

# 19

On a warm spring day Alice and Irene met for lunch in Kensington High Street. Alice was to be married in three days, and they both knew that this was the end of a particular kind of friendship. Alice was confident that marriage could only deepen her relationship with Irene, while Irene was resolved that something should be salvaged.

Ben was decorating the house in Holland Park. Alice had visited this house frequently as a child and had lived there for the last three years; and until it became her property it had seemed to her perfect in every respect. Ownership had sharpened the eyes, and, making their first inspection, she and Ben had gone from room to room exclaiming, 'How could they have put up with *this* for so long?' and 'Whatever else had to be left, I should have insisted on *that* being done!' Just as Louise and Guy were exclaiming as they inspected their new home in Lewes.

'You must come and see what we are doing,' Alice said. She was about to add that Ben would always be glad to see Irene, when she remembered how dismal she had found such assurances which had seemed to emphasise the single woman's dependence on the goodwill of her friends' husbands. There would be other opportunities of eliciting from Irene a recognition – which had not yet been forthcoming – of Ben's warmth and generosity, indeed, of his possession of all the qualities most desirable in a husband.

Irene was saying, as if the relationship was comparable, 'And you and Ben must have supper with Mother and me. We are taking a home course in cookery, you will be glad to know.'

They talked about arrangements for the wedding, in which Irene evinced a sufficient, if not a lively, interest. When they were drinking their coffee, Irene told Alice that she was taking a job with a firm of brokers in the City. She talked eagerly about stocks and shares and risk-taking.

'I didn't think there were many women in that sort of job.'

'There aren't, that's what makes it so exciting.'

She had become animated. Alice was partially glad for her. It was good to see Irene recovering some of her sparkle after the blows which had befallen her, but sad that she might develop into a career woman.

'Is Daphne coming to the wedding?' Irene asked.

'Yes. They were going abroad, but she has delayed it. I don't think Peter is best pleased.'

'Do you think we shall keep up with her? Their way of life seems so strange.'

'We probably shan't see so much of one another, but we shall keep in touch.'

To lose touch with a friend was unthinkable. Daphne must be of the same mind, since she had been so insistent on attending the wedding. Irene was not so sure. Ideas were more important to her than to Alice and she could see that a time would come when she and Daphne had not an idea in common. She said, 'Peter and Daphne want the world to be a more dangerous place than it really is. When they get older and can't satisfy that particular craving, they will take to drink.'

Alice laughed, doubting this. 'Thus proving that the world *is* a dangerous place!'

'Whereas by that time Ben will be working ferociously hard on this enterprise of his which will have become worldwide. But the fact that he is part of an organisation won't make it any easier for him, because even though others may have put up signposts, he will always have to hack his own path through the forest.'

'And what shall I be doing?'

'Oh, I can see you quite clearly, writing short stories in the bedroom with a "do not disturb" notice pinned to the door on which someone has drawn a rude face; and then dashing down to prepare lunch and keep the peace among your six children who could do with more of their father's attention. You will never have much money; but you will keep your family well-fed and loved, while neglecting the housework. They will tease you by telling you how neat and tidy their friends' homes are.'

'It sounds as if *you* will have turned to writing short satirical novels!'

'I shall be Aunt Irene, always welcomed by the children because I take their ideas seriously, while tending to mock the pretensions of their parents.'

And I shall tell them, after you have gone, that your brightness was not always so brittle; in fact, there was a time when it seemed you might be the most profoundly sensitive of us all, able to strike notes quite outside our range.

'You have drifted away, Alice. Are you composing one of your short stories?'

'No, I was just waiting for you to put aside your crystal ball.'

'Don't you like looking into the future? Yours seems so assured.'

'The only assured thing is the present.' She was surprised to realise that she meant this. Until now she had always been wondering what was waiting for her round the next corner. This was perhaps the only time in her life that she would be content with the gifts of the day. Irene thought, when they parted, that if she looked half as happy on her wedding day, she would be a radiant bride.

Irene walked in the direction of Knightsbridge, stopping frequently to look in the windows of dress shops. Clothes were of particular interest to her. One's clothes made statements, and at the moment she wanted something to wear at the wedding which would enhance those qualities, seemingly irreconcilable, of liveliness and repose which had so attracted Angus, while holding him at bay. She sensed that in future she would always keep men at a distance, and it seemed more important than ever that – even if unfulfilled – the promise should not be dimmed. An air of amusement was essential; but the right clothes would help. Not that she intended to settle for superficiality. Far from it. She was convinced that comedy and tragedy were merely different ways of approaching life, and in her situation she found comedy the more congenial. And I do not propose, she vowed, studying a coolly feminine ballerina suit, to be observed smiling through my tears at this wedding.

Alice took a turning off the High Street and threaded her way confidently through the maze of little streets which surrounded Holland Park.

She came abruptly, at the turn of a road, to a row of bombed houses. Grass had come up between the bricks and someone, perhaps one of the neighbours opposite, had planted spring flowers where once a hearth would have been. A grey cat sat on a low, jagged wall, washing itself in the sun. And Alice remembered the elderly woman she had seen standing amid the smoking ruins of Coventry, her cat cradled in a shawl, indifferent to the chaos created by the German bombers and the attempts of the firefighters and soldiers to restore order. Spring flowers had not bloomed here: all around were heaps of smouldering brick, a city centre reduced to one great crumbling chimney belching ash; and this woman had stood, disdainful amid the ruins, her one concern to preserve the life of an old tabby. The memory brought a certain fierceness into this benign spring day, transforming vague longings into something of a quite different order: I hope because I am, there is no other possible condition.

Alice walked on to the park which, in early April, had the look of a tapestry largely unworked, a few colours pricking through the beige. It was a clear day, not a frown to wrinkle the pale blue sky. Over a near-by garden wall a lawnmower was at work. Ahead someone was lying, half-concealed, heels waving in air like giant flippers rising from a flower bed. She came eventually to the bench where Katia had sat twelve years ago, seeing how far she could spit cherry stones, exhilarated after an encounter with Angus Drummond which had further darkened his mind. Alice watched a schoolgirl ambling slowly past, wide-hipped, lethargic, hair the colour of dark treacle toned with amber. She felt life stirring around her and was aware, as Katia had been, of a change in her own body, a sense of at last being in command. She, too, was happy. There had been other happy moments, and they came to her now, clear and distinct, untarnished by the past or shadowed by the future. For time is only the area in which we have to live, the space into which we are fitted, the distance we have to run. Nothing is erased. Hope does not cancel out despair, nor despair invalidate hope. Each note once struck has its place in the whole composition. It belongs, now, and as long as the music lasts.

Alice raised her face to the sun and for a few minutes, perhaps only a second, she had that feeling, usually associated with the edge of sleep, when the mind relaxes its hold and the spirit floats free of its prison. The sun is warm, the world is greening, it is now. It is always *now*.

A small child on some purposeful mission stumped between the shrubs and a white Sealyham bobbed up and down with a rocking motion like a sailing boat making its way across the grass. A blackbird fluted. In one of the houses fronting the park a typewriter was in use behind an open window. Alice took her notebook from her handbag.

'I've been sitting in Holland Park and something of tremendous importance came over me,' she called out to Ben when she entered the house.

'And what was that?'

'It went, as soon as I tried to write it down.'

'Perhaps it will come back if you set your mind to some mundane task – like cleaning the paint brushes.'